THE SEDUCTION
OF
PARADISE

THE SEDUCTION OF PARADISE

Kevin J. Ward

KEVIN J. WARD

The Seduction of Paradise
Copyright © 2015 by Kevin J. Ward. All rights reserved.

No part of this publication may be reproduced, stored in a retrieval system or transmitted in any way by any means, electronic, mechanical, photocopy, recording or otherwise without the prior permission of the author except as provided by USA copyright law.

This novel is a work of fiction. Names, descriptions, entities, and incidents included in the story are products of the author's imagination. Any resemblance to actual persons, events, and entities is entirely coincidental.

The opinions expressed by the author are not necessarily those of Tate Publishing, LLC.

Published by Tate Publishing & Enterprises, LLC
127 E. Trade Center Terrace | Mustang, Oklahoma 73064 USA
1.888.361.9473 | www.tatepublishing.com

Tate Publishing is committed to excellence in the publishing industry. The company reflects the philosophy established by the founders, based on Psalm 68:11,
"The Lord gave the word and great was the company of those who published it."

Book design copyright © 2015 by Tate Publishing, LLC. All rights reserved.
Cover design by Junriel Boquecosa
Interior design by Gram Telen

Published in the United States of America
ISBN: 978-1-63418-807-4
1. Fiction / Thrillers / Suspense
2. Fiction / Family Life
14.12.01

Acknowledgments

This book is dedicated to my family: my children, Erin, Ryan, Megan; my son-in-law, Brett; my grandchildren, Kinsley and Kaden; and, of course, my wonderful wife, Julie—all of whom helped inspire me through this effort and were extremely patient with me over the months I spent creating this. I love you all!

Special thanks to Carolyn Kosidowski for your invaluable editing skills. This book would not have been the same without you!

Ancient One, you have great wisdom. Please tell me, when may I rest from all my efforts and know that I have given enough?

Young lad, you say that I have wisdom, but I cannot answer your question, for no one can ever know when one has truly given enough. But can you tell me, when will no one benefit from your continued efforts?

Prologue

The tropical sun shone brightly on the white-sand beach at the base of the huge monolith rising several hundred feet into the western sky. The rock face of the cliff was sheer and ominous, preventing any access to the land beyond for miles in each direction. It was nature in its most raw and rugged form. The crashing waves could scarcely be heard by the two men sitting on the veranda atop the cliff, virtually undetectable from any vantage point other than an aircraft directly overhead. The veranda was just a small part of a magnificent estate, appearing out of context in the otherwise unspoiled jungle surroundings.

The older man, wearing a spotless white suit, appeared passively content as a steady stream of fragrant smoke circled up from his fine Montecristo. His skin was a deep olive, and his white hair and beard were neatly trimmed. The younger man wore a pair of dungarees and a loose-fitting cotton shirt with enough buttons open to expose a muscular chest and a heavy but somewhat gaudy gold chain. He was black, but he was not African. He may have been Jamaican or Haitian, or possibly even Cuban. His teeth sparkled like polished ivory when he smiled. They both spoke English, but each had a very strong yet uniquely different accent. They could have been on an island in the Caribbean or possibly on the coast somewhere in Central America, or even in one of the remote areas of South America. But where they were was not important. The only point of significance was the subject of their conversation.

"So, my friend, you do not approve of my plan," the white-suited man with a commanding air stated.

"It is not that I do not approve, sir, it is just that this operation is being handled so differently than ever before. Are you sure of all the risks involved?"

"One is never totally sure, that is why it is called risk. But we are moving into a new area where people are different. A good businessman first develops an understanding of the people he wishes to deal with, and then plans his strategy accordingly. I fear that the old 'strong arm' methods will not be effective in this new location, and there is far too much potential business at stake to risk losing it all on hasty action. I believe this new approach will be much more appropriate. Much planning has been done, preparations have been underway for months, key personnel are already in place. Everything will be ready soon. I feel that the risks have been adequately controlled."

"I am sure you are right, sir. You have always been right in the past. But I must admit I am very surprised you were able to get the support you needed from the people in…what is the name of the town?"

"Paradise, my friend. And what a wonderful name for the focal point of our new business venture. As far as soliciting support, there is a lesson that you should learn from this: everyone has his price. Honesty and morality in a person simply means he has a higher price than others, but everyone has a limit at which their standards dissolve into the insignificant façade that they really are. A smart businessman will determine that limit for the people he requires services of, and he will use it to his advantage."

He stopped for a moment, a small but arrogant smile on his face. "It is surprising how low that limit is for people in a small town, like Paradise. You will learn, my young friend, that loyalty is only as strong as the dollars attached to it. Why do you think that I pay you so handsomely?"

He laughed deeply and heartily, slapping the younger man on the back. "You are aggressive, you are strong and determined, you like to move quickly and forcibly. I like that. Those are the qualities that make you useful to me. But this time, it is patience that is required, patience and planning. Do not worry, my young friend, nothing can go wrong. And if something should happen, we will always be safe here."

Book One

The Seduction

We humans, of superior intellect to all God's creatures, pride ourselves on our ability to distinguish good from evil, to choose right from wrong. We hold honor and integrity as the greatest virtues attributable to an individual. But one constant throughout all history is the relentless threat to these virtues by the overpowering temptation of material wealth. Money, in whatever form, brings to the surface the dark side that lurks within us all. The desire for material wealth can eat away at the qualities we all hold so dear, and as the value of the monetary temptation increases, the value of our soul is diminished, until even the strongest of people can find themselves compromising every standard—victims of their own greed, living out their lives as empty, broken shells of what they might have been.

Chapter 1

Joseph McGowen made one final review of the documents on his desk before leaving work for the evening. It was his habit to make sure everything of importance was either completed before he went home or at least properly organized for an efficient start in the morning. As the director of a large research and development department, he usually did not have the luxury of taking time in the morning to prepare for the day.

He walked out into the warm spring air. It was a beautiful afternoon, the kind that a person looks forward to during the long cold months of a Minnesota winter. The late afternoon sun cast a red glow on the Minneapolis skyline. He paused for a moment before stepping into his Durango to reflect on the beauty of the city and the surrounding landscape. He loved Minnesota. He had always loved it, and the fact that he had been gone for so long made days like this all the more gratifying.

Leaving downtown Minneapolis, Joe headed northwest on I-94, then exited north onto Highway 169, toward the small suburb of Paradise. The town got its name, as legend had it, because its founding fathers believed it to be the only place on earth that was comparable to heaven. The current populace of Paradise, though not quite so pretentious as their forefathers, still felt that the town was a wonderful place to live and raise a family. Joe and his wife, Sheri, agreed, although Joe recognized that part of his feelings may be due to nostalgia, for Paradise was the town where he and his younger brother, Ryan, were born and raised. But through his extensive travels throughout the world, Joe was familiar with many places and cultures, and he knew it was more than just memories that made him love this place; it was a good town with good honest people, the kind of town that a person was proud to claim as his home.

Most suburbs of Minneapolis and St. Paul—or any large city, for that matter—tended to be nothing more than sprawling housing developments for people who worked in the city. Paradise was different. It was a small town, about fifteen thousand in population, located twenty minutes northwest of downtown Minneapolis. By definition, it was a suburb, but unlike a typical suburb, Paradise did not develop as an overflow from the big city. In fact, it was actually older than Minneapolis by a few years. It was originally a trading settlement at the junction of the Mississippi and Whiskey Rivers. Due to a number of reasons involving business and politics, Paradise never grew for many years while Minneapolis mushroomed with prosperity. The people of Paradise amusingly referred to Minneapolis as their southern suburb. Yes, Paradise was a nice little town, but to Joe and Sheri, the best part of Paradise was the people themselves. It was a community that truly felt like a family.

Joe crossed the Mississippi River, which formed the southern border of Paradise. To his right, about four hundred yards away, ran the Whiskey River, which actually bisected the town before it emptied into the Mississippi. For the first mile or so, the Whiskey was completely concealed from view by thick clusters of pines, oaks, and elms. Joe passed this wooded area and turned left onto the residential road of Bryant Street, drove about a mile, turned right onto Port Avenue, and, one block later, turned left onto Cottonwood Drive. The McGowens lived in a nice but modest home a half mile down on Cottonwood on the left side, just one block north of the Mississippi. This was a fairly new section of town with a considerable amount of undeveloped land. The area between Port Avenue and their house was densely wooded with large oaks and pines (no cottonwoods, strangely enough). This area not only provided privacy for their family but also served as a wonderful playground for their three children.

Immediately after turning onto Cottonwood, Joe knew something was very wrong. Up ahead were three police cars and an ambulance, all with their lights flashing. At first, it appeared to Joe that the vehicles were parked in his driveway.

My God, Joe thought. *Something has happened to one of my kids!*

He felt his heart racing as he quickly covered the half mile to his house. As he approached, he felt a tremendous sense of relief when he realized that the activity was not at his home but at his next-door neighbor's, Harry and Fran Rosten. They were a couple in their midsixties who had lived in Paradise most of their lives. Joe knew of them when he was a boy, and they had become close friends during the past year as neighbors. Almost instantly, after feeling his relief, a new sense of dread set in as he realized that something must be seriously wrong with his friends.

Joe pulled into his driveway and saw Sheri standing by the edge of the yard, observing the activity but keeping out of the way. A number of their neighbors were doing the same. He could not see Harry or Fran anywhere. Hearing the car, Sheri looked up to see Joe and instantly ran to meet him. Her eyes were red, and her cheeks glistened from recent tears.

Joe jumped out as Sheri nearly fell into his arms, burying her face into his shoulder. As she tried to speak, she lost the composure that she had been maintaining and, for a few moments, could manage little more than uncontrolled babbling.

"Take it easy, Sheri," Joe said, holding her tight and stroking her hair. "Just be patient. It will come." He was having difficulty fighting his own anxious anticipation, but he knew he could not press her. Finally she was able to force out a few words.

"It's Harry," she stammered. "He's...he's dead!"

"What?" Joe blurted. "He can't be! What the hell happened?"

Sheri again lost her composure. Then, with a great amount of effort, she nearly screamed, "He killed himself! He hung himself in his garage!"

Joe was horrified. *No*, he thought. *I know Harry. He wouldn't do this. Not to himself. Not to Fran. Oh my God, what about Fran?*

"Sheri, where is Fran?"

"In her house. She found Harry herself no more than half an hour ago. I heard her screaming and came out to see what was wrong. Oh, Joe, it was so terrible! She was convulsing. I thought she was going to collapse right here in our driveway. I think they have her sedated now. I heard a doctor or paramedic or whoever those people are say that she will be all right."

"Poor Fran," was all that Joe could think of to say. And then, "What about the kids?"

"They're all inside. They don't know what's happened, but they obviously know something is wrong."

"Sheri, let's go in. We're just in the way out here. We need to explain this to the kids."

Chapter 2

Seventeen years ago, in 1988, Joe McGowen had left Minnesota to attend the United States Naval Academy. His deep love for his country, along with his strong interest in history, seemed to suggest the academy was a perfect fit for him. However, as is often the case, reality did not match expectations. The high ideals that are associated with the academy seemed to be more myth than truth, something to create an image for the public more than standards to live by. Not that the academy was a bad place; Joe felt it was an excellent school. But as far as having high standards of morals or ethics, he felt it was no different than most schools, and maybe a notch below some. After two years of frustrating disillusionment, he decided the academy was just not the place for him.

While the decision to leave was difficult, it turned out to be a blessing in disguise. He entered the University of Minnesota and graduated two years later as a structural engineer. This was the first of a number of incidents in his life that convinced him any problem could be converted to an advantage with the proper attitude and effort. It was during his two years at the university that he first realized how much he had grown to love Minnesota.

Within two weeks after graduation, he married Sheri Murphy, an attractive girl who was as sweet as she was pretty, and her being of Irish descent was a definite plus. He never consciously looked for an Irish girl, but his heritage was important to him, so he could not deny the possibility that he had a subconscious voice influencing him in that direction.

Joe and Sheri lived for four years in a manner many people would consider "typical Midwestern." They bought a house, had a baby girl name Maureen, owned two cars, and did most of their social activity as a family. After Maureen was born, Sheri quit her job as an elementary school teacher to become a full-time mother. They were the perfect *Leave It to Beaver* family. In 1996, Joe was dealt a painful blow that would subsequently prove to be another blessing, the second such experience of his life: the company he worked at ran into serious financial issues, and he, along with many of his colleagues, was laid off. While such an event can damage or even destroy a marriage, it only strengthened Joe and Sheri's commitment to each other and to their family. After a number of months of job hunting, Joe was finally forced to accept a position at General Dynamics in San Diego. It was an excellent job, but it obviously meant relocation out of Minnesota. They both deeply dreaded the idea of moving, but with their savings nearly exhausted, there was simply no choice.

Eight years in California proved to be exciting and prosperous. A son, Brandon, was added to the family soon after they began their lives there. Joe found his job to be personally as well as financially rewarding, and all in all, the McGowens adjusted very well to life in California. But seven and a half years after their move, a somewhat unexpected daughter, whom they christened Katelin, arrived. Somehow this third child caused them to reevaluate their lives and the goals they had for their children. The strong calling to return to Minnesota was rekindled.

With a much more impressive résumé and a strong economy, Joe had many more options opened to him, and finding a good position in Minneapolis was not difficult. He had been hired as the director of research and development for Defense Tech Systems, the largest defense contractor in Minnesota. Upon their return, they marveled at how fast the years had passed. It almost seemed that they had never left.

Now, in April of 2005, Joe knew in his heart he would never leave again. He and his family were content. Life was good.

On Sunday morning, two days after the traumatic experience of Harry Rosten's suicide, Joe was up early reading the newspaper, but his mind was still on Harry. He just could not believe Harry had done this. He had always heard that people contemplating suicide could appear normal and even happy to others who were not trained to see the symptoms, but that was not good enough for Joe. He knew Harry. His business was going well. He loved his wife and his home. He was the oldest member of the Paradise city council and was personally responsible for many of the improvements made to the town over the years. He was always making things better for people.

What Joe enjoyed most about Harry were their impromptu backyard visits when they were mowing, raking, tree trimming, or doing any of a number of other tasks necessary to keep a house looking nice. Joe found these jobs to be somewhat monotonous, but Harry loved them. He thoroughly enjoyed working outside to keep his home beautiful. They would routinely take a break from their work to discuss different ideas of yard grooming, and Harry's enthusiasm always inspired Joe and lifted his spirits. Harry was always so upbeat, so positive. And now, out of the blue, he kills himself. Joe just could not accept that, but then, when it came right down to it, he really had no choice.

Fran had been taken to the hospital for a couple of days. There was nothing wrong with her physically; she just needed time to adjust. She would be coming home today, and Joe and Sheri knew that they would have to be very strong for her. It would take her a long time to get over this, and a part of Joe doubted that she would ever truly get over it.

Late that afternoon, the phone rang. Sheri answered it, and immediately, her eyes began to glisten with tears. Joe knew instantly who was on the other end.

"Oh, Fran," Sheri said, in almost a whisper. "We're so very sorry." A short pause and then, "Of course we will. We'll be right over." She replaced the phone and turned to Joe.

"Fran needs our help in getting something down from her attic. She's not able to climb up there by herself. I think maybe she's just looking for some company."

Maureen and Brandon stayed at home, content to have time to themselves in which they could do things, like pick their own TV show, without interference from parents. Sheri thought it best to take eighteen-month-old Katelin with them. The three of them made the short walk over to Fran's house, knowing she needed companionship and support but not being confident that they were strong enough to provide it. They were not totally sure of what they were expecting from Fran, but it certainly was nothing like what they encountered. She met them at the door and was all smiles.

"Hi, kids," she called out as they were coming up her walk. "Come on in. It's good to see friendly faces again after being in that depressing old hospital."

"Hello, Fran," they each said, surprise clearly showing on their faces.

"Joe, I hate to trouble you, but Harry put a box of old photos up in our attic about two years ago. They weren't anything special. In fact, at the time, I wanted to throw them away. Just some silly pictures of me and Harry and some of our friends around the house. I got to thinking that this might be a good time to take them down, but be damned if I am strong enough to climb up there at my age."

"No problem, Fran," Joe said. "I'm glad to do it. I might even like looking at those pictures myself."

Fran led them down to the end of a hallway. In the ceiling was a recessed piece of finished oak, obviously the entrance to the attic. She had a stepladder standing ready. Joe climbed the ladder, lifted the door up into the dark cavity, and raised his head and shoulders up through the opening. It was very dark, but he did not have to see far. Just inches from the frame of the door was an old box flowing over with pictures, a few of which had slid off the top and fallen to the floor. A fairly thick and even layer of dust covered everything. Almost everything, that is.

He was not sure why it caught his eye, except possibly because it was the only thing that had no dust cover whatsoever. It was a simple manila envelope, the size that would hold a standard piece of writing paper. It was very light, containing only a few sheets of paper. He almost ignored it but finally could not control his curiosity.

"Fran," he said, "I assume you know there is a small package up here. By the looks of it, it couldn't have been here more than a few days. It's the only thing that has virtually no dust on it."

"I have no idea what you're talking about," she responded. "But bring it down. I'm anxious to see what treasures Harry has buried around here."

Joe climbed down the ladder, holding the box of pictures in his hands with the package tucked under his arm. It was clear that everyone was eager to see what was inside. He set the box down and held up the package. Written by hand across the front with a large black marker was the word COUNCIL.

"Oh, that's where that thing went," Fran remarked. "Harry gets those packages every month from the city council. Each council member is supposed to review the information before their monthly meetings. Then they send them back to city hall by way of a police squad car. I always used to tease Harry that they protect those things as if they contained top-secret material.

On the few occasions that I saw any of the information, it generally involved things such as proposed ordinances or plans for repaving roads. Certainly nothing that most of us would consider interesting."

"It sounds like you have been looking for it for a while," Sheri stated.

"No, not really. But Spencer Thurman came to the hospital and asked me if I knew where it was."

"You're kidding!" Joe cried. "He actually confronted you in the hospital? Couldn't he wait a few days!"

"It did kind of upset me. In fact, if you don't mind me saying so, it really pissed me off! But you know Spencer."

They did know Spencer. He was the forty-six-year-old chairman of the city council. While he was basically a nice person, he was very excitable and had an overly inflated ego. He was consumed with self-importance and struggled with the knowledge that not everyone shared his views. But this seemed extreme, even for him.

"I wonder why Harry put it up there," Joe asked, more thinking out loud than asking a question.

"It sure beats me," Fran answered. "He was so absentminded he probably never knew he left it there. I'm not sure what he was doing in the attic at all. The only thing we have up there are these pictures. And from what you say, Joe, it sounds like they weren't disturbed at all."

"Well, it's probably nothing," Joe remarked. "It's still sealed, so I suppose we shouldn't open it. If you want, Fran, I'll notify the police and have them come and get it."

"I would appreciate that, Joe. Thank you."

The next half hour was spent looking over the many photographs from the old box. Fran acted very pleased with them, but both Joe and Sheri noticed that she seemed distant, almost cold. After all, Harry wasn't even buried yet!

Finally, Sheri felt it was time to go. Fran thanked them and walked them to the door. As they were about to leave, Sheri felt that something needed to be said.

"Fran, you seem so strong. Are you sure you're all right?"

Fran's eyes immediately began to get moist. She had trouble blurting out her words. "I don't know how to act or what to say. All I know is that if I don't try to be myself, I'll come completely apart."

She bowed her head and covered her face with her hands. Brief light sobbing could be heard. "How could Harry have done this to me? Why? I thought he was happy. I don't understand what went wrong. Don't mistake this charade for strength. I've always been a coward at heart."

Sheri could not hold back her own tears. She reached out and embraced Fran.

Joe put his hand on Fran's shoulder. "We're always here for you, Fran," he said quietly.

"I know you are," Fran replied, regaining her composure. "Do you think I would have come home if I didn't know that?"

"If there's anything you need, please don't hesitate to ask," Sheri said, almost in a whisper.

"Well, there is just one thing."

"Name it," Joe responded.

"I'll need help with the funeral."

Joe looked at Sheri, knowing she would be the one to help Fran the most. Sheri swallowed hard, then smiled. "Of course, Fran, of course. We'll talk tomorrow."

They went out the front door and walked slowly home, Sheri clinging tightly to Katelin, Joe loosely holding the manila package.

That night, after the kids were in bed, Joe sat looking at the package. Strange, he thought. Nothing in the attic was disturbed. He did not know what Harry was doing up there, but it was clear he did not accidentally forget the package. His only purpose for going to the attic must have been to put it there. But why? To hide it? If so, from whom? Fran? It didn't seem to make sense. But then, can you really make sense of the actions of a man only hours before he kills himself?

A distant thought roamed through Joe's subconscious. Harry was not a complex or mysterious man. Now here were two incidents, his suicide and hiding this simple package, that occurred closely together. There couldn't be a connection, could there?

Joe thought it best to just let it go. Who knows, if Harry was here, he would probably have a rational explanation for the whole mess. It might not even seem so strange if it were not for the fact that Harry's suicide was so shocking. The one thing Joe did know was that he should inform the police immediately that he had the package. He picked up the phone and dialed the Paradise Police Department.

"Paradise police," a man barked into the phone. "Officer Williams speaking."

It was Bob Williams. Joe was familiar with him but did not know him well. He was not originally from Paradise. He was a young man in his midtwenties who had more enthusiasm than sense. He was often the butt of the generally tasteless pranks that police officers tend to play on one another. By and large, he was considered harmless.

"Bob, this is Joe McGowen. I just came from Fran Rosten's. She found a package that must have been Harry's. It's a sealed manila envelope marked COUNCIL. I assume it belongs to the city council. Fran said a squad car usually picks these things up, and I was wondering if you could send someone over."

"Well, Joe, we're pretty busy down here. I'm not sure if anyone is free. Besides, the council information is normally sent out at the end of the month. The next one isn't due out for two weeks."

Joe was irritated. "Look, Bob, I don't care if you want this thing or not. I'll keep it until tomorrow, and then I'm going to toss it. I just wanted somebody to know it was here, in case it was important."

He slammed down the phone then immediately started feeling guilty. It had been a long couple of days, but there was no sense in taking it out on poor Bob. Maybe he would drop it off tomorrow after work. He needed to sleep now.

Twenty minutes later, just as Joe and Sheri were crawling into bed, a car screeched to a stop in front of their house.

"What in the hell is that!" Joe cried.

Sheri quickly put on her robe and ran to the front window. She pulled back the curtain and peered out. "It's the police," she said with surprise. "I think it's Bob Williams."

No sooner had she spoken than they were startled by a loud rapid pounding on the front door. Joe opened it up to find Bob dancing impatiently, looking like a little boy who needed to go to the bathroom.

"What on earth is wrong with you, Bob?" Joe bellowed out angrily.

"Do you have the Rosten package, Joe?" Bob shot back. "I decided I would take it tonight."

"Of course I have it. I told you that twenty minutes ago. What the hell made you so interested?"

"Just doing my job, Joe. Are you sure it hasn't been opened?"

"Does it matter?"

"Just answer my fucking question, Joe! Has the package been opened?"

Joe glanced at Sheri. She caught Joe's gaze with her eyes and gave just the slightest shake of her head. Joe knew this meant that he should not get into it with Bob. He took a deep breath and slowly let it out. "No it hasn't. See for yourself."

He handed the package to Bob, who quickly examined the seal, first visually and then by clawing at it with his fingernails. Finally satisfied, a slight smile came to his face.

"Thanks, Joe." And he was gone.

"This whole town's gone nuts," Joe said.

"Come to bed, Joe," Sheri said quietly. "Let's just worry about ourselves tonight."

Officer Williams sat across a large mahogany desk from an elderly man with distinguished white hair. The plush carpet was a deep red; the walls were paneled in dark oak. Behind the desk was a large fireplace, and above it hung the head of a huge moose, looking fierce in his death. It was the kind of room that you instantly knew belonged to a powerful man.

The coldness of the man behind the desk was not a result of being angry or upset; it was simply a void of emotion altogether. Not that he couldn't create the façade of emotion when the situation required it, but in the privacy of his own world, his empty, almost lifeless character revealed itself. It was the look of pure evil. He sat slowly swirling a glass of brandy, staring at the amber liquid as if contemplating some profound thought. On his pinkie finger he wore an exquisite ruby ring. He spoke softly, calmly, "Has anyone seen the contents of this package, Bob?"

"No, sir," Bob replied, somewhat nervously. "No one at all."

"It is very important that you are absolutely sure."

"I'm positive, sir. I'm as sure as I can be. I got it directly from Joe McGowen, the guy who found it at Rosten's place. It was still sealed when he gave it to me."

"Joe McGowen," the man muttered to himself, as if making a mental note for later recall. Then he looked back at Williams. "So then I can assume you are the only person besides myself who has seen this information."

"That's the truth, sir." Bob could not resist a small smile. He was beginning to feel important.

"That's good, Bob. That's very good." He slowly leaned forward in his plush leather chair and rested his elbows on the top of his large desk. Looking up, he smiled warmly at Bob, but the coldness in his eyes only intensified. Then calmly, but with a swiftness that left no time to react, he produced a .9 mm Beretta from inside his coat, aimed, and fired. Bob Williams's face disappeared into a mass of blood and brains.

Chapter 3

With the beginning of the new week, things seemed to get back to normal, at least as close to normal as one could expect under such tragic circumstances. Sometimes the routine of day-to-day life can be therapeutic after dealing with highly stressful circumstances. Joe was unexpectedly called out of town on business, although none of his trips were ever totally unexpected. As a defense contractor, he had become accustomed to last-minute "emergencies" on the part of the government. Defense Tech Systems had contracts with all of the military services, but the majority was with the department of the army for tank ammunition. Every time the government did not understand something relating to a new design, they would call an "emergency meeting." Rarely were these issues what most people would classify as an emergency, but they were the customer, and as everyone knows, the customer is always right. His travels took him all around the country and to numerous international locations, but when he met with the army program office—mostly civilians employed by the government to manage army contracts—it was nearly always at their offices at Picatinny Arsenal near Dover, New Jersey, about an hour's drive from New York City. Under normal circumstances, these meetings irritated him since he felt most of the issues could be handled over the telephone, but this time, he was somewhat relieved to be able to get away for a couple of days. His work allowed him to focus on issues other than his friend's suicide or the mysterious package that the weirdo Bob Williams took from him. However, this trip caused him to miss Harry's funeral, and even though he had no choice but to go, he could not escape the feeling of guilt.

Sheri also attempted to get back into a normal routine, but for her, it was nearly impossible. She never particularly liked the idea that Joe had to travel as much as he did, but she understood and had become well adept at taking care of things while he was gone. But this week of all weeks. Couldn't Joe have found an excuse this one time? Surely people would have understood. She suspected—and, in fact, she was quite certain—that Joe may have been looking for a reason to get away. Even though she felt he was being a bit selfish, she knew she would relish the opportunity to get away herself, and if she were in Joe's shoes, she would be on a plane at this very moment. But this was not about her, it was about Fran, and Fran needed her help.

They decided to have a small funeral and keep things as quiet as they could. Fran was just not up to facing a town full of sympathetic eyes, each feeling a genuine sense of pity but also asking the unspoken question: "Why did your husband kill himself?"

By Thursday, it was all over, and the nearly unbearable sorrow started to be slowly replaced by an exhausted form of relief. After the death of a loved one, even the strongest of people cannot think seriously about moving on with their lives until the funeral is over and the body has been laid to rest. For Fran, it would take a long time to adjust to her new life, but for Sheri and Joe, this ugly mess was over. Joe would be home on Friday, and their lives would continue on as normal.

Joe woke up to the early Saturday morning sunlight and stretched his arms and legs. For some reason, being on the road always seemed to make him stiff. He looked over at Sheri and saw she was still sleeping soundly. He glanced at the bedside clock: six o'clock. He could smell the aroma of freshly brewed coffee wafting in from the kitchen. Programmable coffeemakers were wonderful! He quietly rolled out of bed, put on his robe, and walked to the front door to get the morning paper.

Every day, the *Minneapolis Star Tribune* was delivered, but on Saturdays, they also received the local *Paradise Union*. This typically contained information from local events such as city politics, high school sports, or general human-interest stories. It was very similar to virtually every small town paper in America. Joe usually spent about fifteen minutes perusing through it before turning to the serious news in the *Star Tribune.*

On the front page of the *Union,* there was a small article about the death of Harry Rosten. Joe was not surprised, since Harry was a longtime leader in their community. The article treated Harry very respectfully, with no mention of suicide, although everybody in town knew that was how he died. It briefly related some personal facts about Harry and highlighted his many years of service to the town. Joe thought that it was a very well-written piece.

"You're up early," he heard from behind him. Sheri sat down next to him and brushed a few strands of tangled hair from her eyes.

"I just felt like reading the paper while we still had some peace and quiet. Once the kids get up, I never have time to read anything. By the way, there's an article in the *Union* about Harry." He passed the paper over to Sheri.

"That's nice," she said after quickly reading the article. "I think Fran will like that."

Just then they heard a faint half-cry, half-groan sound from Katelin's room.

"It sounds like our baby is ready for her breakfast," Sheri said with a tired smile. She left the room and return moments later, holding a smiling Katelin. "Babies are always so happy in the morning," she said in her best baby talk voice.

"Well, they should be," Joe said amusingly. "They have someone to come and get them, feed them when they're hungry, and then clean up after them."

"So do you," Sheri responded with a playful grin.

"And I'm happy." Joe grinned back.

"What's for breakfast?" came a little cry from across the room.

Joe and Sheri looked over and saw their two other children, in pajamas, walking into the kitchen.

"Six thirty," Joe mumbled, shaking his head. "So much for peace and quiet."

"Oh, this is good quality time," Sheri said. She got up and gave Joe a quick kiss on the top of his head. Then she turned to Maureen and Brandon. "You two play with Katelin, and I'll get some bacon and eggs started."

Joe returned to his paper, briefly scanning the pages for anything of interest. He was almost ready to put it down when he spied a small headline on page 3 that caught his eye.

Whereabouts of Officer Unknown

Police Chief Byron Winfield reported this week that they have been unable to locate Officer Robert Williams, a twenty-seven-year-old patrolman who has been with the Paradise Police Department for the past three years. Officer Williams was last seen on April 14 by Melissa Jurgenson, the night dispatcher. She stated that he rushed out of the office with no instructions or messages except that he expected to return within the hour.

While he was not seen after that time, he did return to the police station later that evening, for the following morning, his patrol car was found in the parking lot and his personal car had been removed. Williams has no family in the area, and he lived alone in an apartment just outside of Paradise.

Chief Winfield commented that while they will do everything possible to locate Officer Williams, we should be aware that Williams has a history of irresponsible actions, and at this point, he does not believe there is need for alarm.

"You won't believe this," Joe called out to Sheri. "That goofy Bob Williams took off some place. I always knew he was kind of flaky, but I didn't think he was totally nuts."

"I believe it," Sheri replied. "By the way he acted the other night, I think he's crazy. What I can't believe is that we have someone like him on our police force."

"April fourteenth," Joe mused. He began rubbing his chin with his right hand, as was his habit when he was thinking. "That was last Sunday, the day he came for Harry's package. They say here that he left in a rush without saying where he was. You don't think that was when he came here, do you?"

"It must have been," Sheri replied, "unless he returned and then hurried off somewhere else. Could he have been on two emergencies in one night?"

"I don't suppose so," Joe said, still thinking, still rubbing his chin. "I'd better notify the chief that Bob was here that night."

Ten-year-old Maureen was interested in this new piece of information. She was a very bright child and often joined in family discussions, even though she did not always comprehend everything that was being said.

"I'll bet that cop left because he was afraid of what happened to Mr. Rosten," she remarked.

"He's a policeman, not a cop," Sheri corrected, knowing it probably didn't register with her daughter at all. "And why do you think he would be afraid? Policemen handle those kinds of things all the time. And besides, he wasn't really involved. Other officers came to help Harry and Fran." Sheri wasn't sure how much Maureen understood, but she always believed that when

The Seduction of Paradise

children ask questions or wish to take part in a conversation, parents should show sincere interest and not stifle them.

"All I know is that he was okay until he got Mr. Rosten's package from Dad."

"How about if we just don't worry about this right now?" Joe cut in firmly. "This package just isn't that important. I'll talk to Chief Winfield tomorrow and let him worry about it."

The conversation was over, but Joe continued to rub his chin. *It's interesting*, he thought. Sometimes adults refuse to see the obvious, whereas a child only sees the facts without making any biased assumptions. There couldn't possibly be a connection between that simple little package and Bob's disappearance, could there? But things did seem so strange: Harry apparently hiding it in the attic without even telling Fran, and then Bob's total apathy toward the package, followed by his near obsession to get it. Joe wondered if there could have been something valuable in it, something important enough to Bob for him to steal it and run away.

Joe closed his eyes in deep concentration. The more he thought about it, the more plausible it seemed. That would explain everything, he thought. All the weirdness would start to make sense. That must be it! But what could there be in a city council package that would be worth so much? And if it were something other than a council package, why was it marked that way, and why did Harry have it? Then Joe opened his eyes, leaned back in his chair and began to silently laugh at himself. *I can't believe I'm getting this carried away*, he thought. *Harry's suicide has affected me more than I thought. I need to relax.*

"Soup's on!" Sheri called as she set a plate of bacon and fried eggs before Joe. "Get 'em while they're hot."

"Thanks," Joe said. "This looks great. Nothing like a hot breakfast to start the day." He was not going to worry about Bob or the package or any of this mess anymore. Tomorrow he would call Chief Winfield just to report what he knew, and then he would be done with it. Just out of curiosity, though, he would like to know if Bob ever turned the package in. He would ask at least that much.

He briefly entertained the idea of asking his friend Andy Hoffman, who was also a member of the city council, about it. He would know if the package was important or if it had been returned. But after a moment's consideration, he decided to hold off. He did not want to make a mountain out of the proverbial molehill, and besides, he could end up looking pretty foolish.

No more was said about Bob Williams or the package as the family ate their breakfast. But as they were finishing, Maureen looked at Joe and cautiously asked, "Daddy?"

"Yes?" Joe responded. He sensed her hesitation, then smiled and ruffled her hair. "If you have something to say, don't hold back."

"I was just wondering, if the package isn't very important, why wouldn't Mr. Thurman wait until Mrs. Rosten was home from the hospital to ask about it?"

Again Joe smiled. "I think that Mommy and Daddy should be a bit more careful when we discuss things around here. To answer your question, who knows? People do strange things when they're under stress."

But as Maureen wiped her mouth and left the room, Joe began rubbing his chin again. First, he thought little Maureen was an amazing kid. Secondly, he had a sudden change of mind; he decided he would talk to Andy Hoffman.

Chapter 4

Andrew Hoffman had been a friend of Joe and Ryan McGowen for as long as they could remember. He was thirty-five, the same age as Joe, and had been in his class in high school. He had been an excellent athlete in his younger years and still continued to keep himself in good condition. He never married and never really got out of Paradise, except for the four years that he attended Hamline University in St. Paul. Now he worked as an accountant for a local electrical supply company and was proud of being the newest member on the Paradise city council.

The council consisted of six members, four men and two women. Spencer Thurman was the chairman; Andrew Hoffman, Leonard Malekowski, Kathleen Bently, and Elizabeth Wence made up the rest of the team, which, until a short time ago, included Harry Rosten. They were all fairly experienced except for Andy, who was in the second year of his first three-year term. But on a city council for a town the size of Paradise, experience was not necessarily required. Most of their decisions concerned issues such as what roads should be repaved or if a stoplight should be added to an intersection. Rarely did they deal with anything that someone might consider exciting. But they did control the town, and in Paradise, that meant they were in a position that received much respect.

In addition to the city council, Paradise naturally had a mayor. Sharon Carlson was the first woman to ever be elected mayor in this town, and that was twenty years ago. Now, at age sixty-eight, she was still at the helm. When she was last elected two years ago, she made a public statement that this would be her last term, but most people in Paradise remembered that she made the same statement after the previous election, so no one took her seriously. Yet everyone who knew her, which was almost everyone, could see that she just did not have the energy and enthusiasm that at one time had been her greatest attributes. Not that she had become apathetic, for she deeply loved Paradise and its people. She was simply getting old. But no one in town was more respected, and as far as the people were concerned, the job of mayor was hers for as long as she wanted it.

This group of seven ran the town of Paradise. Now it was only six, and no mention was made as to getting a replacement for Harry, and no one seemed to be in a rush to discuss it. In time, this matter would be taken care of. For now, Paradise could manage with one less councilman.

"Well, Joe, what's on your mind?" Andy asked as he was perusing his menu.

"Why do you think something is on my mind? I just felt like taking a break from the routine at work. And it's not like we haven't had lunch together before."

This was true. Andy worked in Paradise and Joe in Minneapolis, and occasionally, they would meet for lunch at a small restaurant called the Burger Salon, which was roughly halfway between their two offices. It was only slightly fancier than a greasy spoon type of joint, but it had great burgers, and most importantly, it was relaxing. Joe frequently entertained business associates by taking them to lunch at some of the more exclusive establishments in the area, but when he was on his own time, he found that the Burger Salon provided a kind of haven from the fast-paced rat race of business. He enjoyed the casual atmosphere even though he looked somewhat out of place in his suit. Shortly after his return from California, Joe and Andy began occasionally meeting here for lunch, and without consciously planning it, they evolved into a routine of meeting about once a month. It was good therapy to periodically meet with an old friend and discuss issues other than business.

"Why do I always read this menu?" Andy asked of himself. "I always get the Burger Deluxe. I don't even think about anything except the Burger Deluxe. But I always read the other selections." He set the menu down as the waitress approached with her pad of tickets.

"The Burger Deluxe, medium, and an iced tea," Andy ordered before she had the chance to ask.

"Make that two," Joe added.

"You got it," she said, and headed for the kitchen.

Andy finally responded to Joe's earlier comments. "Before, you only wanted to meet when you felt like taking a break. But when you called me this morning, I sensed a definite note of urgency in your voice."

"Maybe having friends that know you so well isn't always an advantage." Joe laughed. "But you're right. I want to ask you about something, but I don't want to give you the wrong impression. I'm not really concerned, just curious."

"I'm not only curious, I'm completely confused. What's your question, Joe?"

"After Harry Rosten died, I was helping Fran with some things, and I found a sealed package marked COUNCIL. Fran said the police always picked up similar packages, so I called the station. Bob Williams answered and acted like he couldn't care less."

"That's understandable." Andy chuckled. "The police don't particularly like carrying those packages around. A lot of people think that the police pick the packages up to ensure their protection, but in truth, they are just being used as a delivery service. Since they are funded by the city, the city expects a few services like that. But the police are not fond of doing jobs that they feel are wasting their time. Bob's reaction was not that unusual. In fact, it could probably be considered typical."

"But then he showed up about twenty minutes later, so excited that I thought he would piss his pants. So I gave him the package, and he rushed out like he was going to a fire."

"Seems odd," Andy admitted. "But then, Bob is odd. I don't see it as a big deal."

"I didn't either, but then Bob disappeared, and it turned out that it was shortly after he left my house."

"Joe, you're making this sound like a great mystery, but so far, it is nothing more than a set of somewhat odd circumstances. They seem strange to you, but do you realize how many strange things happen every day that go unnoticed? Harry's death was so tragic that it's got you overly suspicious. If you're concerned, call the police."

"I did. Yesterday. I talked personally to Chief Winfield. He said Bob had returned from my house with some kind of large envelope. It had to have been the package I gave him. He went into his office, made a quick call, came out, and left. The only one who saw him was Melissa Jurgenson. She couldn't remember for sure, but she thought he had the package with him. Winfield isn't concerned that Bob's gone. He said Bob was always doing strange things."

"Well," Andy said, "I'm not supposed to let this out, but if you can keep a secret, I guess I can make an exception."

"You know you can trust me."

"I'm sure you're aware that any hiring or firing of police officers has to be approved by the council. Well, Chief Winfield has been trying to get rid of Bob for several months now. But the documentation that is needed to fire a cop is horrendous.

Winfield sent us a preliminary report, and his biggest complaint was that Bob would occasionally take off, sometimes for days at a time. He was disciplined on a few occasions, but nothing seemed to prevent him from doing it again. That's why Winfield isn't concerned. In fact, he's probably happy. It gives him more ammunition to use against Bob. So you see, Bob may be weird, but he's just Bob. Nothing overly mysterious is happening."

"If Bob has been missing before, why wasn't more made out of it then? Why did it get splashed all over the papers this time?"

Andy burst into loud laughter and shook his head. "I can't believe you, Joe. What do you mean, 'splashed all over the papers'? It was a short article buried deep inside a small town paper. And I can't say for sure, but I'll bet anything that if you checked, there were similar articles for the other occasions. You either didn't see them or didn't care enough to read them. You probably wouldn't have read this one if Bob had been anywhere but at your house that night."

Joe sat back and let out a deep sigh. "How about that. You're probably right. I told you up front that I was only curious, not concerned."

Their conversation shifted to other lighter topics as they ate their lunch. They were both looking forward to the upcoming fishing season, and Andy was contemplating the purchase of a new fishing boat. When they were nearly finished, Joe again took on a more serious air. He leaned forward, looked hesitantly at Andy for a moment, and then finally asked, "Andy, Bob Williams mentioned that the packages were not due for two weeks, so why would Harry have an official package before everyone else on the council?"

Andy rolled his eyes, feeling something between amusement and disgust. "How the hell should I know, Joe? It obviously was not the standard package that we all get. Maybe it was something of his that he wanted to present to the council. Maybe it was information from a previous meeting that he forgot to return.

That happens sometimes, you know. For all I know, Joe, it may not have even been for the council. Maybe he just used an old council envelope to store something personal. Anything is possible. Personally, I don't give a shit about that damn package."

"You don't give a shit, Andy, but Spencer Thurman does. He was pestering Fran about it when she was still in the hospital. Why would he do that?"

"That one's easy, and you know the answer as well as I do. Spencer's an asshole, big time! I imagine he just wanted to make sure all loose ends were taken care of after Harry's death. You know how impatient he is. Now, are you through?"

"Almost. Maybe Spencer is an asshole, but even so, it still shows that the package had some kind of value to people besides Harry. He certainly was not using it to store some personal things. As long as we've gone this far, I'm going to ask one more question. Has the package been turned over to the city? By your comments, I would guess not."

"I honestly don't know, and I won't know until our next meeting, which just happens to be Monday."

"Well, I suppose I should just drop this whole thing, but just for the hell of it, I would appreciate it if you would check on it for me."

"If an appropriate opportunity comes up, I'll ask some questions. Is that good enough?"

"Good enough. Let's get back to work. Next time, let's keep the conversation light, okay?"

"You bet. I don't want to ruin another good burger with your bizarre anxieties," Andy said humorously.

They each laughed and left the restaurant. Joe felt better as he drove back to work. He knew Andy must be right. Still, why had Harry hidden the package? He decided not to worry about it any longer. If Harry were here, he would explain it all rationally. For now, the matter was closed.

The white-haired man with the ruby ring got up from his leather chair and walked over to a bookcase covering one entire wall of his impressive office. He gazed over the rows of books as if he were contemplating which one to select, but finding a book was the furthest thing from his mind. This was just his way of creating an air of superiority, an act of intimidation for the man who sat facing his desk. Without looking back, he remarked, "Our little project is getting off to a slow start, isn't it?"

The other man in the room made an attempt at displaying confidence, but his nervousness was all too apparent. There were no signs remaining that the chair in which he sat was the same chair where Officer Robert Williams breathed his last horrifying breath. "We're a little behind schedule, but it's coming along."

The white-haired man turned sharply, his eyes ablaze with fury. "We cannot afford to lose any time at all. That should have been clear from the beginning!"

"It was, but who anticipated this mix-up with the information outlining our plans? You're the one who insisted on disguising it as a city council package. I told you it could get confused. And you're the one who wanted to hold off on getting started until we had the package back, not to mention the fact that you drove poor Harry to suicide with your intimidation, and you still didn't get the package. We're damn lucky McGowen found it. We could have been searching for months for that thing. Or, worse yet, McGowen could have kept it!"

"Don't you dare point any fingers at me. It was your job to safeguard that information, and you fucked up. You're the one responsible for Harry, not me. As far as the package is concerned, that's why I wanted to see you tonight. Are you aware there is still one document missing?"

The man in the chair froze. "That's impossible! It was sealed when Bob got it from McGowen, and it was still sealed when he gave it to you. You told me so yourself."

The man in charge laughed. "So it was sealed. It's not like it was in a vault. How hard do you think it would have been to open it and reseal it later? Anyone could have done it. You, Bob, Harry. Even Joe McGowen. He had it for a couple of days."

"I think we can be sure it wasn't Bob. He didn't have the time. I guarantee that it wasn't me. McGowen would have no reason to. And if he did see what was in it, he certainly would have made a bigger issue out of it than he did. So that leaves Harry."

"Has anyone else been involved that you know of?"

"Not really, except I did get a call from Andy Hoffman last night. He asked if a package had been received for the city. He actually sounded a little embarrassed about asking. He said he heard about it from a friend who just wanted some reassurance that the package reached the appropriate people. I told him I wasn't aware of a package, but I don't think he totally believed me. But I came up with a story that will cool him off soon. I'll explain things at our council meeting on Monday. There won't be a problem."

"His friend." The man in charge smiled. "This town isn't that big. You have known Andy for years. Who do you suppose his friend is?"

"Andy is a popular man in town, but his closest friend has always been Joe McGowen. But I just don't believe Joe opened it. And if he did, why would he be asking about it?"

"Possibly to check on people's reactions. He may be worried that he is in trouble."

"I'm sure it wasn't Joe. I would bet anything that it was Harry."

The white-haired man returned to his desk and poured a glass of brandy. "I'll tell you one thing: that document had better be recovered, and I mean now. It obviously had to have been taken by someone who had the package in their possession. I agree that the odds are in favor of Rosten, but I don't totally rule out McGowen. I think we should keep an eye on him."

He stood up again, taking his brandy with him. "There is another point of business we need to discuss. Our customers have asked that you pay them a visit. They would like to have a meeting with the man who is running this operation."

Beads of perspiration began forming on the forehead of the man in the chair. "Aren't you the one who's running the show?"

"Oh no, I am merely a liaison between you and them. Don't worry, it's just a routine visit. They would like you to fly out in about three weeks, on May 22."

The man in the chair began rubbing his moist palms together. "How will I explain my absence to everyone else?"

"That's not my problem. You're smart, in your own way. Think of something."

"Sure," the man in the chair said. "I'll just think of something."

The white-haired man with the ruby ring turned back to the bookcase, letting the other man know that their conversation was over. "That's all for tonight. I believe you can find your own way out."

The man in the chair quickly left the room. He walked down the hall and out the front door into the cool night air. His mind ran wild with paranoid thoughts. *Shit! This is too much of a coincidence, wanting me out there right after they found out about the missing document. I have to get things straightened out before that trip. Why did I ever get involved with this in the first place? I had a feeling I might be getting in over my head, but who could turn down that much money? The damned money!*

He got into his car and started for home. Spencer Thurman would not sleep well this night.

Chapter 5

Andrew Hoffman pulled into the parking lot of the Paradise city hall. While only three stories high, it was still the largest building in town, stretching out for nearly two blocks atop a low hill running along the east bank of the Whiskey River. The southern end of the building faced Main Street, which crossed the river on a quaint Old World–looking bridge. It was a very impressive setting, especially for a small town like Paradise.

Finding an open parking spot at seven thirty in the evening was not difficult. The early May air felt pleasantly warm to Andy as he walked through the front door and down the steps to the lower level where the council chamber was located. He opened the heavy oak double doors and entered the auditorium-like room. Along the front of the room was a long curved table with seven chairs sitting in a single row behind it. On the table in front of each chair was a nameplate—one for the mayor and one for each of the six council members. The mayor's chair was in the middle with the council chairman, Spencer Thurman, to her right. The remaining positions were randomly placed with no particular significance. The name Andrew Hoffman was on the mayor's far left at the end of the table. The rest of the room was filled with chairs facing the table for the people of the town who attended council meetings. There was room for about two hundred people, but on a typical night, no more than fifteen or twenty would sit in.

The council would routinely assemble for a formal public meeting once each month. The day-to-day city business was handled by the mayor, the council chairman, and a staff of administrators. Two weeks prior to the meetings, a package of issues to be discussed was put together by the chairman and sent out to the other council members. They would review the material, make any appropriate comments or suggestions, and return the package to city hall by way of a police squad car. As Andy had explained to Joe, the police were used as a convenient courier service more than as a means of safeguarding the packages.

The members of the council found it convenient to occasionally meet in private, which generally happened every fourth month. During these sessions, no city expenditures could be approved or policies adopted, and in fact, no official decisions could be made at all. The private meetings were usually spent prioritizing agendas for upcoming meetings or for informal discussions regarding city events, allowing members to bring up concerns or ideas for more or less brainstorming without having to risk attacks from the public. The meeting this evening was such a session.

It had become a practice to keep these private meetings informal and comfortable, so it was no surprise to Andy to see the mayor and the council members in casual dress and seated in a circle in the open chairs rather than taking their positions at the table. He was surprised, however, to see two men who were not a part of the council present.

"Nice of you to make it, Andy," Mayor Carlson said, looking at her watch with just a hint of a smile. "We can begin now. First of all, I would like to introduce the two gentlemen here and explain their presence. This is Ronald Capsner from the New York Historical Society." She gestured to a tall distinguished elderly man seated next to her. He was the only one present wearing a suit, and one did not need to be an expert in fashion to realize it was a very expensive suit, something not common in Paradise.

"We've been discussing for several months now about restoring the old Brewster mansion. I think we all feel it is very much a part of this town's identity, and it should not be allowed to go to ruin. A restoration effort had been started, but the cost was much greater than we expected. We were only able to finish a couple of rooms before the work had to be put on hold. As we discussed last month, without more funding, we would have to terminate the entire effort. With that, I'll let Mr. Capsner explain why he is here and what he can do for us."

"Thank you, Madam Mayor," Capsner said, and stood up to address the small group of people. "As Mayor Carlson said, I represent the New York Historical Society. We are a small group of individuals who have a strong interest in the history of this country. We are unique in that we feel we lose so much of the true history because we tend to focus on only the major events such as wars, explorations, political events, and the like. Obviously these things are important, but what about the many less visible, less publicized events that helped shape this country? Many of these are more meaningful to people than those that make the headlines. We have made it our charter to focus on these kinds of issues."

Ronald Capsner clasped his hands behind his back and began pacing as he continued. "Each year, we select one project that we feel is worth funding, usually in a small town such as Paradise, where finances tend to be limited. In fact, the major factor in selecting a project—beyond the historical significance, of course—is that no other funding can be available. We do not make it our business to put money into something that will happen regardless of our presence. It is our sole purpose to provide funding for projects that would otherwise die. In effect, we are saving portions of a community's history from extinction. If a project meets the criteria of our charter, we approach the people involved and see if they are interested in receiving any aid." He stopped and looked at the group, a broad, friendly smile covering his face. "Amazingly, no one has turned us down yet."

The council broke into laughter, and the mayor nodded, acknowledging the fact that people usually do not refuse to accept money for any reason.

"There are a number of ways we search for the projects we select," Capsner said. "One of the simplest, but probably the most effective, is to read newspapers from smaller communities. All of us at the society travel extensively throughout the country, and just by chance, I was in Minneapolis a couple of months ago, and I read a small article in your *Paradise Union* stating that the restoration of Brewster mansion may have to be terminated. I spent the next three weeks doing some research involving both the actual history of the place as well as the feelings of the people in Paradise towards the mansion. We would never waste our time with something that the local people did not feel strongly about. I discovered what you obviously already know: this was the residence of what would be considered the first business tycoon in the entire area. Henry Brewster was not only responsible for Paradise, but he contributed significantly to the growth of Minneapolis.

"But what we at the society found most interesting was the role that the mansion played after Brewster's death, mainly its conversion to an army barracks during the early Indian conflicts and later to a hospital. In addition, it appears that the people of Paradise truly feel that this mansion is a reflection of them as a community, something that they are very proud of. To cut to the chase, we think that the restoration of Brewster mansion is just the kind of project that we like to support. I am here to offer financial aid to complete the restoration effort."

Everyone was still, totally surprised by the more-than-generous offer.

Beth Wence spoke first. "Do you mind me asking where your finances come from?"

"Of course not," Capsner answered. "In fact, that is always the first question. I never know how to explain it without sounding pretentious, so let me be blunt. There are five of us that make up the society, all retired and, quite frankly, very wealthy. It has been a dream of ours for years to be able to do this kind of work. Few people have the resources to do the things they truly love. We do, and since none of us are young, we thought why not go for it while we are still able to enjoy it. This will only be our fifth year of operation."

"So this is your personal money?" Leonard Malekowski cut in. "You realize that we're talking about something near a million dollars?"

Again Capsner smiled. "It would be a million dollars to carry out your original plan, but that would be limited to the mansion itself. We propose to restore the grounds and the old servant's house as well. I think the final amount would come to nearly 1.8 million."

"Very impressive," Spencer Thurman said. "And there's no catch, no strings attached?"

"Absolutely none, except that we would like to oversee the project ourselves. You would obviously have considerable input since it is your property and your history. But we are very meticulous about certain details, and we reserve the right of approval for all work. In fact, I personally will stay in town until the project is completed, which we estimate to take about one year, or eighteen months at the most."

It was Andy's turn to speak up. "Not to sound skeptical, but this is a tremendous offer. Why haven't your previous projects received more publicity? We've never even heard of your organization."

"That's a good question. As I said, we do this mainly for self-gratification and to do our part for the preservation of our country's history. We will only continue as long as we have the freedom to seek out and choose our own projects. Can you imagine if this became public knowledge? We would be overwhelmed with requests and proposals. It would destroy everything that we are attempting to achieve. Which brings up the only other condition: no one can acknowledge the source of this funding. For the sake of the public, you can make a single statement that finances were obtained through donations from interested private businesses. It is not unusual for someone making a significant contribution to any charity to request anonymity. It happens all the time, since a person or business may wish to support something without suffering any attacks from people or media with differing views. In fact, we won't even identify what other projects we have been involved with. I hope this request does not seem unreasonable."

"I don't believe that would present a problem for us," the mayor remarked. "Does anyone have any questions, concerns, or comments in general?"

Spencer Thurman spoke up. "I would just like to say that I think this is absolutely fabulous, and I certainly want to thank Mr. Capsner for his extreme generosity. And while I appreciate the society's desire for anonymity, I do feel it would be prudent to have at least one meeting with all of your people. Do you think I could be permitted a visit to the society prior to making any formal agreements?"

"We tend to discourage that, but I believe a type of kick-off meeting could be arranged. In order to get things moving, we should try and make it happen soon."

"How about in a couple of weeks?" Thurman suggested. "May 22 would fit nicely into my schedule. I have some free time about then."

"That would be fine," Capsner said. "I'll set it up. Any other questions?"

There were none.

Mayor Carlson again spoke. "Before we totally get off this subject, let me just say a few words about our other guest. He, of course, needs no introduction. Sherman Salinger has been the curator of our little city museum for the last fifteen years."

"Seventeen," the second man seated by the mayor interjected, a man who looked older than his fifty years.

"Seventeen," Mayor Carlson corrected herself. "Mr. Capsner requested that Sherman be our official interface with the historical society as far as the actual restoration is concerned since he has more knowledge of the historical details than anyone else. I felt Sherman was a very appropriate choice, but I thought you should all have a chance for inputs."

Andy had known Sherman Salinger for years. He was all the things that a museum curator is thought to be: serious, soft spoken, very elegant, and well mannered to the point of having a perpetual air of formality. He was, for the most part, a likeable person yet not the type to loosen up and shoot the bull over a couple of beers. In fact, most considered him to be a bit stuffy. Those who knew him well even thought him to have an arrogant side. But by and large, he got along with everyone.

The museum of which Sherman was the curator was small, but it contained a disproportionate amount of artifacts for a town the size of Paradise, mainly due to the age of the town and the role it played in the history of the area. And being that the people in the town felt very strongly about their heritage, the museum was held in high regard. Sherman took his position as curator very seriously, and it did seem only natural that he should be involved with this new project.

The mayor's suggestion was met with unanimous approval. Sherman Salinger acknowledged their decision with a quick statement of thanks and assured everyone that he would be very committed to making this project something that the town would be proud of.

The rest of the meeting was typical, with the hottest topic of discussion being the suggestion that a stoplight be installed at an intersection that was becoming more and more busy. By ten o'clock at night, everyone was tired and the meeting was ready to adjourn. Andy thought this might be a good time to bring up Joe's concerns about the missing package. He hesitated, not wanting to sound foolish, but finally decided that it was now or never.

"There are two points which I would like to mention before we break up," Andy blurted out. "We don't need to resolve these issues tonight, but I feel we should at least be thinking about them."

Everyone turned to Andy, attempting to look interested but their impatience being all too obvious.

"First, what about Harry's replacement?"

Mayor Carlson cut in quickly. "I don't believe we need to concern ourselves with that for a while. This thing is so tragic, let's just let it rest and give Fran a chance to adjust. We can discuss it at our next meeting. In fact, let's make sure it's added to our agenda. You should all be thinking of potential candidates to fill in for Harry on an interim basis until the next election. As mayor, I can appoint a replacement as long as it's considered temporary."

"That's good enough for me," Andy said. "Secondly, is anyone aware of a council package Harry had that was returned a week or so ago? Spencer and I briefly discussed this a couple of nights ago, but he wasn't aware of it, and—"

"That's not exactly true," Thurman interrupted. "I apologize for the white lie I told you before, but I didn't feel at liberty to discuss the contents of that package before this meeting. I guess I overreacted. The package you are concerned with contained Mr. Capsner's proposal to us for the restoration project. Harry got it by mistake and would have returned it, but well, obviously he couldn't." He turned and addressed the mayor specifically. "I didn't even mention it to you, Sharon, because I was embarrassed about misplacing it. The package was returned to me by Officer Williams. I'm sorry for lying earlier, Andy. I probably should have told you the truth, but I didn't want word to get out about the historical society's proposal until we were all here together."

Andy smiled, somewhat red faced. "Don't worry about it, Spencer. I should have just let it drop."

"Just out of curiosity," Thurman asked, "who is it that was concerned about the package?"

"Joe McGowen," Andy responded. "He wasn't really concerned or worried, but since he was the one who turned it in, it's only natural that he would ask about it, especially since Bob Williams disappeared shortly after Joe gave it to him. I think he would be irresponsible if he didn't follow up on it."

"Of course," Thurman said. "Well, you can assure him it's in good hands."

"And now we are adjourned," the mayor stated. "See you all next month. Have a good trip to New York, Spencer."

Chapter 6

Joe finished pumping air into the tires of his old ten-speed bicycle. He squeezed both tires a few times to assure himself that the pressure was sufficient, not believing that a gauge was necessary.

"Come on, Dad!" Brandon yelled, racing around in circles in their driveway.

"I'm all set," Joe called back. He hopped on his bike and peddled out onto Cottonwood Drive. Brandon was close behind, followed by Maureen. Sheri brought up the rear, with Katelin in a baby seat over her rear wheel. Family bike rides were one of their primary sources of exercise, and they were particularly enjoyable on beautiful Saturday afternoons like this. The May air was feeling more like summer every day.

Joe slowed up and waited for Sheri. "Do you want to ride anywhere in particular?" he asked.

"No, I just like the exercise. How about you?"

"How about if we ride past the old Brewster mansion? The restoration project Andy told me about will be starting soon. I must have driven past that old place a million times in my life, but I have never really been up close to it. It might be fun to take a look."

"That's fine by me, but if we run into anyone, remember what Andy said: no one is supposed to know about this project."

Joe laughed out loud. "Sheri, how do you suppose they will restore the entire mansion and the grounds around it without anyone knowing? What Andy said was that no one was supposed to know that this Capsner guy represents something called the New York Historical Society. Don't worry about me, I'm sworn to secrecy."

Even though the council members had promised not to divulge information about Ronald Capsner and his organization, Andy had let it slip to Joe. The mansion was a historic backdrop to Paradise; it was truly a landmark in town. Ironically, it was one of those places that people appreciated but never really got up close to. It was much like a rare library book: always there to see and talk about but not something that a person would actually use.

When they were kids, Andy and Joe would walk by the old mansion and make up stories about it being haunted. When the city council agreed to begin restorations last year, he and Joe were ecstatic, only to be disappointed when the effort was terminated after only finishing a couple of rooms. After hearing Capsner's pitch, Andy could not help but mention it to Joe. He initially intended only to talk about the project itself and not discuss the source of the funding, but he and Joe were so close, and he was so excited that everything just poured out.

The McGowens turned right on Port Avenue and then left onto Bryant Street, which took them to Highway 169, the primary road connecting Paradise to Minneapolis. Directly across the highway was a large wooded area that extended nearly three quarters of a mile back to the Whiskey River. This small forest was dense with trees and brush, and over the three-quarter-of-a-mile expanse behind the mansion, the terrain dropped over one hundred feet to the edge of the river. It was a part of town left completely in its natural state, partly for its scenic value but mostly because the terrain made it nearly impossible to develop.

They crossed Highway 169 and turned left. After a short distance, they came to a stone wall that stood about three feet high. The wall marked the start of the property belonging to the Brewster mansion, now owned by the city. The wall had, for some time, been in need of repair, with a few sections having almost completely crumbled. It was approximately three hundred yards long and was divided roughly into thirds. At each division point, two stone columns rose up about twenty feet and were capped off by a concrete pyramid. The two sets of columns served as an entrance and exit to the property, with a long horseshoe-shaped driveway extending between them and stretching back to the mansion.

The mansion itself sat up on a small hill, looking very distinguished from the road. It sat at a nearly forty-five-degree angle to the highway, with the left side facing the general direction of the river, the back bordering the heavily wooded area, and the front facing a large sprawling lawn and the long driveway. The building was a three-story structure with four large pillars across the front, which were not unlike those of pre–Civil War mansions in the South. Off to the right was a smaller building that originally served as the servant's quarters but had long since been left to ruin. Both buildings were totally white, and since they sat about one hundred yards back from the highway, the cracked and peeling paint could not easily be seen.

While the forested area stopped abruptly at the back edge of the mansion's property, there were numerous trees that dotted the entire expanse of the yard. The majority of the property was fairly flat except for the low rolling hill on which the mansion sat, but over the years, the river had eroded the bank along the edge opposite the highway, leaving a sheer one-hundred-foot embankment overlooking the river. This embankment was nearly as densely wooded as the area behind the mansion, with several of the larger trees having fallen under their own weight from growing out the side of the steep slope. The remains of an old stairway zigzagged up from the river, barely detectable due to the over grown brush from many nears of neglect. A deserted, dilapidated boat house still stood on the water's edge at the base of the steps.

At the first set of stone columns, Joe turned into the horseshoe drive. Sheri hesitated by the wall. "Joe, are you sure we can go up there?"

"Of course, this is public property."

"It seems kind of spooky."

"You're thinking too much about those stories the kids tell. Trust me, this place is not haunted."

The children sensed Sheri's uneasiness.

"Daddy, I don't want to go up there," Brandon whimpered.

"Me either," Maureen chimed in.

"I guess I'm outnumbered." Joe sighed. "I've always wanted to walk through that place. I thought this might be my chance."

"I'm sorry," Sheri said. "We'll come back when it's open, okay?"

Joe hung his head and put on his most convincing little-boy-pout face.

Sheri rolled her eyes and shook her head. "My God, do you have to act like one of the children?"

Joe shrugged, still hanging his head.

"All right, all right," Sheri said. "If you want to go up there, fine. But don't take too long. I'll wait here with the kids."

Joe broke into a victorious grin. "It always works!" he said. "I'll be back in just a few minutes."

He rode up to the front of the mansion and parked his bike. He climbed the four steps to the large veranda that ran the length of the house and walked between the two center pillars to the large double doors of the front entrance. Not surprisingly, they were locked. He walked along the veranda to his left and peered through the first of several narrow windows that ran up two of the three stories. The thick dust on the inside of the glass pane made it difficult to see through, but he was able to make out what appeared to be a large room that had probably been a ballroom. It was empty now, but he could see that it filled most of this end of the mansion and was two stories high. Three pillars ran down the center of the room, which were probably as much for aesthetics as for structural support. The walls were severely cracked, and the remains of one-time-impressive chandeliers hung from the ceiling.

He turned and went back across the veranda to the right side of the front entrance. This end of the house was divided into two rooms, at least in the front. Presumably there were another two rooms behind them in the back of the house. The room just to the right of the door was a type of sitting room that people of wealth used to have next to the entryway. It was similarly run-down like the ballroom. The second room, on the far right end of the house, was a surprise. The glass windowpane was clean, and with the aid of the brightly shining sun, he could easily see inside. It looked to be a game room, but what set this room apart from the others was that it looked like new. The walls were covered with a blue and ivory paper, and the floor was a highly polished natural wood. A billiard table sat in the center of the room with a rack of cues and balls hanging on the far wall. In one corner, two chairs sat on either side of a small square table on which stood rows of chess pieces like two armies ready to do battle. This was obviously one of the rooms that the city had restored.

Looking into this old house sent a tingle of excitement through Joe. He could tell this had one day been a grand home for some important people. He walked back to his bike, thought for a moment, then called out to Sheri, "I'm just going to run around back for a minute." He could see Sheri wave him on, so he quickly darted in the direction of the river to circle to the back of the mansion.

Along the left end of the house was a screened-in porch, which extended out to the edge of the embankment dropping to the river. During the winter, the view of the river was impressive, but during the spring and summer, all vision was blocked beyond just a few yards by the dense greenery on the slope. Joe stood at the corner of the porch where it met the drop-off. A few feet away was the start of the old stairway down to the river. The breeze felt cold as it came across the river and up the steep wall of trees and bush. He could see that at this point, it would be very difficult and dangerous to try and slip by between the porch and the embankment to the back side of the house. He quickly retraced his steps to the front entrance and then ran around the right side. This was the first time that he had ever been behind the mansion. He had always been curious about this place, but now that he was finally seeing it up close, he was fascinated. He tried to imagine the things that went on here in years past, and what it would be like when the restoration was complete.

Once in back, he went to the river end of the house next to the porch and behind the ballroom. Straining to see through the window, he was able to make out an old stove, a small table, and a row of small doors, which appeared to be cupboards. He was looking into the kitchen, one that was obviously for cooking but not for eating, as was commonly the case in the days that this mansion was constructed. The kitchen had the same dark, dirty, battered look of the other unfinished rooms. He moved to the next room, also dark and battered. It was fairly long and totally empty, but he could see there was a door on the end providing passage into the kitchen. Joe knew this must be the dining room. Further on down, moving toward the highway side of the house, he peered into another dark room. This was possibly a guest room, or maybe a storage room, or any one of a number of other kinds of rooms. But it was dark and empty, like the others.

When he reached the last room, the one that was behind the restored game room, he saw that the windows were clean and were covered with drapes that completely concealed the room from view. Joe knew that this must be the second restored room. His curiosity was overwhelming as he felt an almost desperate need to see inside. He stood back and studied the window then noticed a gap or seam down the center of the drapes, where they had not been completely closed. It was not much, but it was enough to allow him at least a peek into the room beyond.

He pressed his face to the glass and closed one eye, as if peering through a telescope. His field of view was very narrow, but he was able to make out a few distinguishing features. The room appeared to be a study or library, with a deep-red carpet and dark oak paneling. He could see just the corner of what must have been a large desk, probably mahogany. Along the far wall was a large bookcase filled with books. It appeared to be the kind of room that belonged to a powerful man.

Chapter 7

Two weeks after his bike ride to Brewster mansion, Joe found himself on another trip to Picatinny Arsenal in New Jersey, which was the facility the US Army used to manage many of their weapons contracts. His business turned out to be straightforward and uneventful, allowing him to finish his work several hours earlier than expected. Driving east on Highway 80 toward Newark airport, he decided this would be a good opportunity to go to New York City. He had always loved New York, at least in small doses. He did not feel that he could ever live there, but he enjoyed his occasional luncheon engagements downtown or on afternoons like this, when he had time to just walk around and experience downtown Manhattan. What he liked most was when he and Sheri would spend a long weekend there, which they did about once a year. New York had a sense of excitement about it, whether it was attending a play on Broadway, shopping on Fifth Avenue, or just simply walking along the streets or through Central Park and watching all the activity. New York was truly a unique city.

Joe's philosophy on lunching out held true for New York as well as for Minneapolis. When on business or with his wife, he would typically go to a "nice" place—anything from a trendy bistro to a high-end restaurant. But when alone, he kept it much more simple. He generally ate at a place called Paul's Pizza, the most incredible pizza in the world, including Chicago, or at one of the corner hot dog stands, which were almost everywhere. Today he chose the latter.

He parked his car in a ramp just off Fifth Avenue and began walking southwest along the ever-crowded sidewalk in the main shopping area of Manhattan. The mass of people was so steady and constant that they almost seemed to be part of the structure of the city itself; there were buildings, roads, monuments, and people, and none of them ever significantly changed. The number of people was so great that it was almost as if they were not there at all, allowing a person to feel very isolated and alone among the thousands of bodies roaming the pavement.

He passed the front entrance of Sacks and paused for a moment. When he had time, he usually liked to pick up something for Sheri—something romantic, like perfume or body oil, preferably kinds that could not be obtained in Minneapolis. It was not so much for the sake of the gift itself, but he knew Sheri often felt lonely when he was gone, and it pleased her to know that he was thinking about her. But today, time was tight, so he passed by and went on to the corner, where he bought two hot dogs and a Coke. It was amazing how good a hot dog tasted when consumed on a New York corner on a sunny spring day.

Joe believed that it was good to occasionally spend some time alone. It was easy to get caught up in the day-to-day activity of his job or work around his house or personal problems. A little time alone allowed him to sort things out and put all these external factors into their proper perspective. Not that he was into any kind of soul-searching meditation, but taking some time to clear the cobwebs was important for him. When in New York, his favorite place for this kind of introspective thinking was on the observation deck of the Empire State Building.

Joe crossed over Fifth Avenue and continued southwest for a number of blocks. When he arrived at the historic skyscraper, he went inside, bought a ticket, and hopped on the first available elevator, thankful that there was no wait of any significance.

Somewhere on the way up, he was never quite sure what floor, they had to get out and change elevators. Finally, he arrived at the observation deck.

Stepping out onto the deck always created the same effect in him. It was truly an amazing experience. As far as he was aware, this was the only building of any notable height having a public observation deck that was not enclosed. Most tall buildings had an area with large floor-to-ceiling windows offering a beautiful view, but the feeling in these buildings was never the same as being outside in the open air, leaning over the edge, hearing the sounds of the city, and feeling the ever-present gusting wind blowing through your hair, occasionally having the sensation that it was strong enough to blow you right over the edge if you were not holding on to the surrounding railing.

Joe stood on the deck, facing the Upper Bay where the Hudson and East Rivers met. In the distance, he could see the Statue of Liberty, proudly holding her torch above the passing boats in the bay. He had been up in the statue a few times, and the view from the crown created a feeling of being on top of the world. But from here, he could barely make out where the statue stood in the bay far below.

The past several weeks had been an emotional roller coaster for him, but now things seemed to be back to normal. He missed Harry, but Fran was doing surprisingly well. Bob Williams never returned, but no one seemed to care a great deal. The project at the Brewster mansion was scheduled to start the following week, and everyone in town was excited about it. The suspicions he had had about Harry's package had diminished to nothing more than a lingering curiosity of what Harry had been thinking, and even those thoughts rarely crossed his mind anymore.

Joe walked around to the opposite side of the deck and looked down on what was essentially downtown Manhattan. The massive crowds looked so insignificant from up here, but the view of the city was breathtaking. The screeching and laughter of a group of teenage girls echoed everywhere each time a gust of wind would blow. It seemed there was always a group of high school students from somewhere on a field trip out on the deck. The high-pitched shrieks were so commonplace that they were almost like a permanent part of the deck atmosphere. At another time and place, he would consider this irritating, but here he thought it was amusing and actually found himself enjoying it.

His thoughts again turned to the Brewster mansion restoration project. Andy had told him very little about the New York Historical Society, except that they were adamant about anonymity. He supposed there would be little chance of their being listed in the phone book, but purely out of curiosity, he decided to check. He went inside the closed-in area of the deck, where a public telephone was located, with books of phone listings from all of the five boroughs of New York. He started with Manhattan. There was nothing. He proceeded through Brooklyn, the Bronx, Queens, and Staten Island. Still nothing. Then he thought his chances would be better of finding a personal listing for Ronald Capsner. He knew he would not call the number if he found it, but again, he was curious.

He again started with Manhattan and then laughed to himself when he turned to the page where "Capsner" would be found. While not as common a name as Johnson or Smith, it was common enough to have a page full of listings, many with an *R* initial and a few that actually listed "Ronald." He didn't bother to check the other books.

He was not completely surprised that the society was not listed, but he knew that even if they want to maintain a low profile, people must, on occasion, need to get a hold of them. He tried calling information, knowing that there was little hope of getting a number that was not published. The nasal operator confirmed his suspicions; there was no number for a New York Historical Society. He walked back out onto the deck to enjoy his last few minutes before heading back to the airport.

Sheri was rushing about the house trying to get both herself and Katelin ready to go out for the day. Fran would be there any minute, and Sheri did not want to keep her waiting. Fran had called a half an hour earlier and asked if Sheri would mind taking her to the mall to do some shopping, and Sheri thought it would be good for both of them to get out for a while. Fran was adjusting to Harry's death fairly well, but it was important for her to start getting out into the world and interact with other people. As for herself, Sheri always enjoyed doing things with friends on days when Joe was out of town. He was in New Jersey meeting with the army people and would be home tomorrow. Since Maureen and Brandon were in school, she and Fran would have as much time as they wanted.

Sheri never particularly cared for the times Joe was gone from home. She had gotten used to it for the most part, but there were times when she felt lonely, or needed help with things around the house or with the kids, and she would find herself wishing that Joe would never have to travel. She knew Joe did not like the traveling any more than she did. He frequently expressed his dislike of being away, especially if he had to miss something that one of the kids was involved with. On many of his trips, he would bring her a small present to show her that he missed her. Actually, compared to many people today, he really was not gone all that often, and generally it was for only one night. But with three kids and a house to run, even one night could be very demanding on her. Whenever she found herself getting too down or depressed, she would remind herself of how fortunate they really were. Joe made good money, which allowed her to stay home and be a full-time mother for their children. There were many people in the country who were not nearly as lucky, and she remembered all too well the months when Joe was unemployed before they went to California. She knew she should count her blessings. The little bit of traveling that Joe did was a small price to pay for the good life that they had.

Sheri finished dressing Katelin then walked to the full-length mirror to give herself a quick inspection. Even though she was a housewife and a mother, she was still fussy about her appearance. She resented the idea that housewives are typically frumpy. True, she liked to dress comfortably, usually in jeans or light cotton pants, but she could still look attractive and well groomed. Today she wore a denim skirt and a white turtleneck, which flattered her long shapely legs and attractive figure. Her shoulder-length brown hair was straight but curled under at the ends. She was not vain, but she could not help but think that she survived thirty-four years and three births pretty well. She picked up Katelin and grabbed her purse just as she heard a light rapping on the door.

On the way to the mall, Sheri could tell that Fran was upset.

"Are you feeling all right, Fran?" she asked.

"Oh, I'm okay. I just get so irritated over that Spencer Thurman. Why can't he leave me alone?"

"Spencer Thurman? Has he been bothering you?"

"I guess it wasn't really a bother. He stopped by this morning and asked if he could look for some documents that were part of that stupid package that Harry had."

"Documents?" Sheri asked, surprised. "He told Andy Hoffman that the package had been delivered to him."

"It was, but apparently, part of it was missing. I let him look, but he didn't find anything. That's why I called this morning. I was feeling upset and just wanted to get out. I hope you don't mind."

"Not at all. I wanted to get out myself. But something should be done about Spencer. I think he is getting just a little out of hand. If he bothers you again, let me know. Joe has friends on the council, and they can have a talk with him."

The sky in the northwest began to look black on the horizon. A very low rumbling could barely be heard in the distance.

"You know, Sheri, I really don't have much shopping to do," Fran said. "I just felt like getting out and talking with a friend. It appears a storm is moving in, so what if we skip the mall. Let's just have lunch someplace and visit."

The rest of the afternoon was spent in leisurely conversation over a light helping of salad and soup. Fran seemed to be more relaxed than she had been in weeks and appeared to be having a genuinely good time. Finally, Sheri said that school would be over soon, so she must be getting home to meet Maureen and Brandon. They left the restaurant and were home within just a few minutes. As Sheri pulled into her driveway, drops of rain from the slow-moving storm began to sprinkle the windshield.

"Looks like we made it just in time," Sheri said.

"It sure does," Fran agreed. "Sheri, thanks so much for today. I feel so much better."

"Anytime at all, Fran. I mean that. But you had better get home before the storm starts getting wild."

The storm continued to move in slowly. The thunder became louder, and occasional flashes of lightning lit up the sky. The full intensity of the storm did not hit until later that night, shortly after Sheri had put the kids to bed. She sat in the living room, watching the fierce wind bend the tall trees in the yard to the point where she thought they would break. The rain was falling in torrents, and the lightning was almost continuous. She sat alone, thinking of Fran. Without wanting them to, her thoughts turned to Spencer Thurman and his obsession with the conspicuous package. She cared nothing about the information in the package, but she realized that if something were missing, it disappeared either with Harry or after Joe gave it to Bob Williams. She obviously could not check with Harry, but there was a chance she could find out something about what happened after Bob took it. She knew Melissa Jurgenson, the night dispatcher at the police station who had seen Bob with the package the night Joe had given it to him. She and Melissa were not really friends, but they were close enough so that she felt comfortable asking her if she knew anything. Melissa would be working this evening.

Part of Sheri felt like the whole thing was ridiculous, but part of her thought that sooner or later, questions must be answered. She picked up the phone and called the Paradise Police Department and asked for Melissa Jurgenson.

"Melissa, this is Sheri McGowen. I don't want to bother you, but I wonder if I could ask you a question?"

"Sure, that's what I'm here for."

"Thanks. This won't take long. Remember the night Bob Williams came and got a large envelope from Joe?"

"How could I forget? That was the night he disappeared."

"That's right. I wonder if you know whether Bob opened the envelope and took anything out?"

"Wow, you too?" Melissa remarked.

"What do you mean by that?"

"Yesterday, Spencer Thurman asked me the same thing. Earlier tonight, another guy called and asked about it. Somebody I don't know, and he didn't leave a name. And now you!"

"What did you tell them?"

"The same thing I'll tell you. I barely remember the package at all, but I believe it was sealed when Bob left with it. He was here for such a short time that I don't think he could have opened it and removed anything. But I have no idea what he did after he left. Why are you so interested?"

Sheri explained the situation with Spencer pestering Fran.

"I wouldn't worry about Spencer," Melissa said. "He gets in everybody's craw once in a while, but then he settles down."

"I suppose so," Sheri said. "Well, thank you for the information."

Sheri hung up and went back to the living room. She was not surprised that Spencer had asked about the package, but who was the other man? The package! Why did it keep coming up? She wanted to believe it was nothing, but it just did not seem to want to go away.

Just then thunder cracked loud enough to shake the house. Lightning continued to flash as rain pounded on the windows in the driving wind. Sheri pulled her knees to her chest and wrapped her arms around her legs. As she sat nervously watching the wildness outside, she could think of nothing except that she wished Joe were home.

Chapter 8

Joe returned home the day after the storm. As he drove down Bryant Street toward Port Avenue, he could see the damage left in the storm's aftermath. Broken branches and debris were everywhere. There were even a couple of large trees completely uprooted. He was relieved when he finally reached his house and saw that all was well. He had talked with Sheri briefly this morning, so he knew there was no serious damage, but it still felt good to be home to see things for himself. It was nearing twilight when he pulled into his driveway.

Joe was used to the routine of coming home after a trip: he would come into the house and get a kiss from Sheri and hugs from the kids. He knew the actions of his family were sincere, yet somehow, they became mechanical the way things get when they are repeated over and over. He was surprised on this occasion when Sheri rushed to him and hugged him tight, holding him for several seconds without saying anything. Moments later, Maureen and Brandon came in, followed by a toddling Katelin.

"Dad, you should have been here!" Brandon exclaimed. "It was the most awesome storm ever. Trees and cars and houses were all blowing away!"

"Oh, Brandon, no cars or houses blew away," Maureen corrected. "You always exaggerate."

"I don't *xagrate*," Brandon said. "The storm was scary. We could hardly sleep!"

Sheri continued to hold Joe through all of this.

"It looks like the storm really spooked you," Joe said to her with a smile. "You've been through thunderstorms before. Was this one that bad?"

Sheri finally released her embrace and stepped back. "Joe, you know I don't like storms. And this was one of the worst we've had in a long while."

Joe sensed that there was something more. "You guys should be getting ready for bed," he said to the kids. "Why don't you get cleaned up? I'll be up in a few minutes and tell you about my trip before lights out, okay?"

The two older children scampered up the stairs. Katelin continued to stand by Joe's feet. He smiled and picked her up and gave her a big hug. "I guess you can hang out with us." He kissed her lightly on her forehead. She giggled and snuggled down in Joe's arms. Joe put one arm around Sheri. "Is there something else? You seem to be concerned about more than the storm."

Sheri shook her head and sighed. "It's silly. I can't believe I'm even worried about it."

"Come on," Joe said. "You know you want to talk about it. Might as well get it out."

"It's Harry or Spencer or that stupid package. Oh, I don't know, it's the whole thing. I can't even get my thoughts straight. Yesterday, Spencer came to Fran's and wanted to search her house. Apparently, a document was missing from that package you found. He thought it was still at Fran's house. He didn't find it, of course."

"Why did he tell Andy and the rest of the council that everything was all right?"

"I don't know. Are you sure he did?"

"Come on, Sheri. Do you think Andy would lie?"

"No, of course not. Not really. Oh, I don't know. But there's more. Last night, I called Melissa at the police station, and she said Spencer had called there, looking for it. I guess that isn't surprising, but she said a stranger, a man, also called and asked about the package. He wanted to know whether or not Bob Williams had opened it. She didn't know for sure but thought that he had not. How many strangers are in this town, and who would know enough to ask if the package had been opened? Most people don't even know it existed. I know Andy assured you that nothing strange was occurring, but I just don't feel comfortable about this. I'm worried about Fran."

Joe set Katelin down and began pacing the floor. "I've had it with this crap!" He scowled. "I'm going to Spencer myself. I found that package, and I turned it in. If something is wrong, he can deal with me. I'm going to put a stop to this once and for all!"

Sheri hugged Joe again. "I think you're right. The storm did have me spooked, and maybe still does a little. We're not in any trouble, are we?"

"Of course not. We'll get this whole mess straightened out soon. But I think I'll talk to Andy first, just in case there are any recent developments I should be aware of. Let's have him over tomorrow and discuss an appropriate way to deal with this."

Sheri held Joe tight. He stroked her hair with one hand and caressed her back with the other. They each felt safe, but each had an inexplicable feeling deep in the pit of their stomachs that maybe things were not quite as they appeared. But the important thing now was that here, in each other's arms, they did feel safe.

The following evening, Joe and Andy were sitting on the deck in the back of the McGowen house. Through the patio door, they could see Sheri and Maureen in the kitchen, getting things ready for dinner. Katelin sat in her high chair, watching. Brandon was in the back yard, playing football against an imaginary defense.

Andy picked up his bottle of beer and took a quick drink. "Don't you have glasses for your guests?" he asked Joe.

"Sure we do, for the important ones," Joe shot back. They each laughed.

"You've really got it made, Joe," Andy said, watching Brandon dive for a touchdown. "I sometimes think I've missed out on a lot by not getting married."

"Well, it's like anything else. There's a lot of good times and a lot of difficult times. It seems like nowadays most marriages have more of the latter."

"That's true, but you've got so much to grow old with. Someday you'll be an old grandpa with grandchildren all over visiting you at holidays and being part of your life. I'll just be a lonely old man who may as well be dead."

"You're talking as if it's too late. You're not that old, you know."

"I know, but I just don't see me as a good family man. How about if I just become an honorary part of your family?"

"Oh, sure," Joe said. "Now that Katelin's almost potty trained." Again they laughed together as the patio door opened.

"Who's grilling the hot dogs and brats?" Sheri asked.

"Our new family member," Joe answered.

Sheri looked at him, an expression of bewilderment clearly showing. "I don't even want to ask what that means," she said. "Just cook the meat. Everything else is ready to go."

Throughout dinner, Sheri waited for Joe to bring up the subject of Spencer Thurman and his obsession of the mysterious package, but the conversation remained light, focusing mainly on how well the Minnesota Twins were doing this year. She assumed Joe was waiting for what he thought was the right moment. But when dinner was over and there still had been no mention of the subject, Sheri thought she had better take the lead. As Andy began to say that he should be going, Sheri walked out onto the deck carrying three more beers.

"Why don't you stay for one more?" she said. "This is my first chance to relax this whole night."

"I don't think so," Andy said.

Sheri popped the top of a beer and set it in front of Andy. "Sit!" she commanded.

He immediately obeyed. Joe laughed and said, "I was trying to find a way to tactfully bring up a subject. I guess the direct approach is more effective."

"We need to talk to you about something," Sheri began.

"Why do I feel like I've been through this before?" Andy asked, only partially joking.

"This is different, Andy," Sheri continued. "And it's serious, at least serious to me."

Andy could see in her eyes that it was indeed serious. He sat back and took a sip from his beer. "All right, what is it?"

Sheri glanced at Joe, wondering if he would want to take over.

"Go ahead," Joe said. "You're doing fine so far."

"To begin with," Sheri started, "are you aware that Spencer Thurman is continuing to pester Fran Rosten about that package Joe turned in?"

"We talked about that before," Andy said. "Spencer explained why he was looking for it, and now he's got it. It's a dead issue."

"That's what we thought," Sheri said. "But just the other day, Spencer actually had the nerve to ask Fran if he could search her house. Apparently, a document was missing from the package."

"I can't believe that!" Andy exclaimed. "He assured me everything was fine."

"That's what troubled us," Joe cut in. "He should have known at your meeting if something was missing. And even if he didn't, he should have told you when he discovered it. Normally it wouldn't be a big deal, but Fran is getting very upset. I guess we feel that, under the circumstances, we need to look out for her. So this becomes our concern too."

It was Sheri's turn to speak again. "Think about it, Andy. Harry gets this package by mistake. That's very believable. He must have opened it, and if he did, he would have known about the New York Historical Society. That would be interesting information, but not something that would send him into a panic. He would almost certainly have notified the council, or at least the mayor. But instead, he tells no one, not even Fran. He reseals the package to make it look like he never opened it, yet he kept out an important document. Then he hides the package in the attic and apparently hides the document somewhere else. Then, after all these precautions, he kills himself."

Andy started getting flustered. "Look, when he read the information in the package, he would have known that he got it by mistake. Maybe he just wanted to do Spencer a favor by trying to keep things quiet. He may have even hidden it so Fran wouldn't see it. Once information gets out in a small town like this, everyone else knows within days. The fact that he kept a document out might have been purely an accident. I'd bet anything he accidentally threw it away. As for his suicide, it was tragic, but things like that happen."

"But then I give it to Bob Williams, and he disappears," Joe said.

"I believe we have adequately covered that before," Andy responded.

"Yes, and before, it fit a pattern," Joe said. "But this time, he never returned. Then you mention the package to Spencer, and he either lies or doesn't give you all the information."

"Maybe he plans to," Andy said. "We haven't had another council meeting yet. Maybe he will fill us in then."

"Andy, I talked to Melissa Jurgenson at the police station," Sheri said. "Spencer was looking for the missing document there too."

"Makes sense to me," Andy said. "Bob could have been the one who lost it."

"She said another man called and asked about it," Sheri went on. "A stranger that not only knew of the package but also of the missing document."

"It could have been anybody," Andy said.

"This whole thing ties into the New York Historical Society," Joe said. "I was in New York last week. There is no phone listing for anything by that name."

"Boy, you are paranoid," Andy said. "After what I explained about their method of operation, you couldn't have been surprised."

Sheri finished her beer and leaned forward in her chair, the intensity showing clearly in her eyes. "I guess the real point is this: each of these events may have an explanation if taken as a separate incident. But nothing overly alarming has happened in this town for years, and now suddenly, all of this comes together at once. And it all ties into that package."

Andy thought for a moment, realizing that what Sheri said was true. "So what's your point?" he finally asked.

"There is no specific point," Joe answered, "except that we believe something is very wrong. Something that may be quite serious. And something that most probably involves the city council. Our biggest concern is for Fran. She can't handle this alone. Whatever else is going on is someone else's worry. I'm going to Spencer myself, Andy. I'm going to get this resolved once and for all."

"No," Andy quickly said. "Let me do it. I brought it up to him before, so I'll follow up on it. Besides, he owes me an explanation about this supposedly missing document."

Joe thought for a moment then looked at Sheri. She gave a slight shrug of her shoulders, essentially saying that it didn't matter to her.

"All right," Joe said. "But do it soon. I don't want to have to wait for another council meeting."

"I'll set up a meeting right away," Andy said. "I think I'll ask Capsner to be there too. This involves his organization. In fact,

I may as well get everyone involved who could have any input, which would include Mayor Carlson and Sherman Salinger."

"That sounds like a good idea to me," Joe said. "What do you think, Sheri?"

"That's fine," she answered. "Whatever finally gets this resolved. But make sure they understand we're not going to let this drop until we're satisfied."

"I must be out of my mind," Andy mumbled, rubbing his eyes with his thumb and forefinger. "This is Paradise, not Detroit or Chicago. Big things don't happen here." He paused then looked up at Sheri. "May I leave now?"

"Yes, you may," Sheri answered, speaking in the tone that an elementary teacher uses to grant permission for a child to go to the bathroom. They all laughed as Andy walked down the steps of the deck and disappeared into the darkness.

The mood was somber as the group sat in Andrew Hoffman's living room. It was a rainy Sunday night, not like the storm of two weeks ago but a cool light drizzle that was typical during a Minnesota June. Sharon Carlson sat in a rocking chair by the fireplace, watching the flickering flames dance on a single log. Ronald Capsner sat across the room on a couch, in muffled conversation with Sherman Salinger. At the end of the room, Spencer Thurman sat in one of two recliners, fidgeting about nervously. Andy Hoffman entered the room from the doorway next to Spencer. He was carrying a tray with a coffee pot, creamer, sugar bowl, and five empty cups. He set the tray on the TV table in front of the couch. "If anyone cares for coffee, help yourself. I'm afraid all I have is the regular caffeinated kind. I don't drink decaf at home."

Everyone took a cup except Spencer.

Andy had given this meeting considerable thought. After a sleepless night of thinking about all that Joe and Sheri had said, he agreed that the coincidence of all these things happening at once was too great. Yet he was not convinced that anything was seriously wrong. It would be good to get everyone together to discuss the situation, but it must be done tactfully. If he was not careful, he could greatly offend someone or even sound like he was accusing people of something unethical or possibly even illegal. The problem was that he really didn't know how to be tactful with what he had to say.

"I'm glad you could all make it tonight," he began. "There is something which I am sure is not a problem, but yet I still feel needs to be discussed before it gets totally blown out of proportion."

"Well, you certainly have our curiosity piqued," Sharon Carlson said. "What's on your mind, Andy?"

"At our last council meeting, we briefly discussed a package that Joe McGowen found at Fran Rosten's house after Harry died," Andy said. "Spencer explained what it was and cleared up the mystery about it, but apparently, there is still a problem: a portion of the package seems to be missing, and Spencer has been trying to locate it. Spencer, I apologize for putting you on the spot, and I wish I could think of a better way to do this, but Fran has been getting very upset, and I believe she, as well as the rest of us, need to know what's going on."

"I definitely agree," Mayor Carlson said. "Fran and I have been friends for years. If there is something involving her that needs our attention, I would like to know. In fact, if someone from the council needs to deal with her, it would be more appropriate if I handled it."

Spencer looked flustered, something between angry and frightened. "What I told you at the last meeting was the truth. But when I got the package back, I didn't look through every page, just the first couple to make sure it was the right material.

Subsequent to our meeting, I was reviewing the material and discovered that a portion of it was missing. It was the part that actually described Mr. Capsner's organization. I talked to Ron about it, and we decided that if we could locate it quickly, it wasn't worth mentioning to anyone else."

Eyes turned to Capsner, who gave a slight nod of confirmation.

"Maybe that wasn't the best decision," Spencer continued, "but I really don't believe a meeting like this was necessary."

"As I said, I apologize for making such an issue out of this," Andy said. "But I thought I really didn't have a choice. With Fran getting so upset, Joe and Sheri McGowen were getting pretty serious. They feel very protective of Fran, and they were ready to start causing a scene. I thought it best to nip this thing in the bud now, once and for all."

"I think you did the right thing, Andy," Mayor Carlson said. "Were you able to find the missing information, Spencer?"

Spencer sat for a moment then replied simply and quietly, "No."

"Does anyone know who else might be looking for the package?" Andy asked. "Apparently, a stranger also inquired about it at the police station."

Spencer's face went white as he shot a look at Ronald Capsner. Capsner was also taken aback but maintained an outward appearance of calm control.

"I'm afraid that I must own up to that," Capsner confessed. "I thought I would help Spencer out, so I went to the station to see if Bob had possibly opened the package. I didn't know Spencer would be checking there too."

"Of course," Andy said. "I should have known it was you."

"Just out of curiosity, how did you find out about that?" Sherman Salinger asked.

"Sheri McGowen called Melissa Jurgenson to see if she knew anything about the package or the missing document. Melissa told her about the stranger making the same inquiry."

"How important is it that this document be recovered?" the mayor asked.

Spencer started to answer, but he was cut off by Capsner. "I don't believe it's anything to be alarmed about. We thought that if we could get it, why not do it? But we never intended it to get this kind of attention. I guess my personal feeling is that it inadvertently was discarded somewhere and now lies in a heap of garbage at the city landfill."

"Fine," the mayor said. "Then from this point on, no more talk about the package, and no more bothering Fran Rosten. Is that clear?"

Everyone acknowledged that they understood, and the subject was laid to rest. But Andy wasn't quite finished. "Before we conclude, there is one other thing I would like to ask you all about. Does anyone think that there has been a rather odd set of circumstances occurring in this town lately? I mean, with the package, and Harry and Bob Williams and the New York Historical Society—all of this. Does it strike anyone as odd that all this is happening at once?"

"Not really," Sherman Salinger responded. "I'll admit it sounds strange when you put it all together, but think of it this way: if the historical society hadn't become involved, there would be no package and, therefore, no tie into Harry Rosten or Bob Williams. So, what appears to be a string of strange circumstances is all a result of one event: the historical society's offer to help. I don't believe it's anything to be concerned about."

"Well, when you put it like that, I tend to agree. After listening to Joe and Sheri McGowen, it sounded like an evil conspiracy existed here in Paradise. By the way, Ron, is it true that your historical society is not listed in the phone book?"

For the first time, Ronald Capsner appeared to be flustered. "Well…uh…why do you ask?"

"Joe McGowen mentioned that he tried to find the number last week when he was in New York. He couldn't find it, so he naturally assumed it wasn't listed."

"Joe McGowen!" Spencer exclaimed. "Why doesn't he keep his nose where it belongs!"

Capsner regained his composure and said, "No, it isn't listed. For the reasons I stated at the last council meeting, we don't believe it is prudent to have a number available to the public. But I have a question for you, if you don't mind. Why was Mr. McGowen looking for our number? Isn't our identity supposed to be kept in confidence?"

Andy's face turned red as he realized his error. "I guess I owe you all an apology. Especially you, Ron. Joe and I go back such a long way, and the Brewster mansion has always been so intriguing to us. I guess I let it slip about your offer to restore it. I'm sorry, but I can promise you that Joe won't tell anyone else. I guarantee it."

"Don't worry about it, Andy. We expect a few leaks. I was just curious as to how Joe found out about us. However, I can't help but wonder about him. He seems to be the focal point for all of these concerns. If he has a problem, why doesn't he bring it to our attention?"

"In a way, that is exactly what he's doing," Andy responded. "Only I suggested that he go through me. As far as his involvement in this business, remember that he was close to Harry Rosten, which is how he happened to find the package. His concern for Fran is all that is keeping him involved now."

"Hopefully he will be satisfied now," Spencer remarked sarcastically. He was clearly agitated. "Maybe now he will start minding his own business."

"Well, this has been enlightening," the mayor remarked. "I suggest we adjourn while we're all still speaking. But first, if you all can spare a few more minutes, maybe Spencer could fill us in on his trip to the society. We really haven't had the chance to talk since you returned, Spencer. How did it go?"

Spencer showed signs of calming. "It went very well. I'm preparing a detailed report that I will submit at the next meeting. But essentially, we just discussed all the things Ron mentioned when we last got together. They seem like a fine group of gentlemen. It appears that everything is ready to proceed."

"Great," the mayor said. "We'll have to plan the entire project and get bids on the effort soon. We can discuss the details at our next meeting."

"Sharon, might I make a quick suggestion?" Sherman asked.

"Of course, what is it?"

"At the last meeting, we discussed a replacement for Harry," Sherman said. "You told us to be thinking of potential candidates. I realize this maybe isn't the time or place to discuss it, but I have a recommendation."

"We won't select anyone tonight, but I'll certainly take a recommendation," Sharon said.

"How about Joe McGowen? He's from this town originally and seems to care a lot about it. And for whatever reason, he seems to be getting involved in much of our activity anyway. He seems to be the likely candidate. And if he doesn't work out, there isn't much risk since the position is only temporary."

It was decided to bring it up formally at the next council meeting, but everyone was very supportive of the idea. Then, finally, Mayor Carlson said, "If there are no other questions or comments, let's all go home."

After a short pause, everyone got up and funneled through the front door into the cool, drizzly night.

"How much does McGowen know?" the white-haired man standing behind the large mahogany desk demanded.

"I don't think he really knows anything," Spencer Thurman responded.

"I don't believe that! He's asking far too many questions. He's going to become a problem."

"He's just curious about a few things. People in small towns are like that. It will all blow over soon, and everything will be all right."

"All right? Nothing is right! That document is still missing. If someone gets their hands on it, it could blow our whole operation. And the project is coming along very slow. We're supposed to be ready to start receiving merchandise by the end of July. That's only six weeks away, and we have barely gotten started. Now McGowen keeps sticking his nose in. And what about Andy Hoffman? I think he's becoming as much of a problem as McGowen."

"We're lucky Andy's involved," Spencer said. "If it was not for him, Joe might be making more trouble than he is. I'm not concerned about Andy, and I'm not really concerned about Joe. But who was the stranger who went to the police asking about the missing document?"

"Oh, don't be a fool. Who do you think it was? It was your friend from out of state coming to check on you. You still don't realize who we're dealing with, do you? Do you know what will happen to you if things don't get straightened out soon? Didn't they make that clear to you on your last trip?"

"They said to do whatever we could to make things work, that's all. They would not dare come here and make trouble."

The white-haired man laughed a deep, humorless, almost-sinister laugh. "You don't think so? Look what they did to Rosten."

Spencer stared at the man in disbelief. "What are you talking about? Harry committed suicide!"

"You are a fool! Harry got your package and wouldn't listen to reason. There was no choice. He had to be dealt with. Unfortunately, he managed to hide the package first."

"Harry was my friend! What's going on here? This was never part of the plan. You knew he was going to be killed, didn't you? You son of a bitch, you let it happen! What's happened to you? I thought he was your friend too."

"I didn't know anything until it was over. Don't you get it? That's the way these people operate. They're so nice and generous up front, so understanding and helpful. But once you're involved, you do things right, or you're history, and you never see it coming. So you just do your job and make sure no more problems come up—problems like Joe McGowen asking questions."

"I can't believe it," Spencer said. "Harry was murdered. This has gone too far. No amount of money is worth it. I'm getting out."

The white-haired man walked over to his desk and sat in his leather chair. He was beginning to calm down, and the air of arrogance that was his nature returned to him. "Getting out?" he said, more of a statement than a question. "There is no getting out, and don't pretend you didn't know that. You will do what you have been contracted to do, and if you're lucky, you will get it done in enough time to keep them happy. Right now, I believe they are upset with your lack of progress."

"Can't you explain things to them, pacify them?"

"Oh no, I'm through explaining things. You will have to explain this yourself, and you're going to get an opportunity soon. They want to see you again. Friday."

Spencer felt a pang of fear deep in his gut, like the blade of a knife. "Friday? That's too soon." It was odd that they would want to see him on such short notice. "I don't feel good about this. If there is a problem, I want to know."

The white-haired man chuckled. "Oh, there is a problem, all right. And if the problem isn't resolved soon, they will think it is my problem. I cannot have that. No, this is your problem, and you had better handle it. Soon! You don't want them to have to teach you a lesson."

"Teach me a lesson? You little weaselly chickenshit! You are as responsible for this mess as I am, maybe more. And if they don't know that, I'll tell them."

"Tell them whatever you like. But remember who it was that assured them it could work in this town. I simply said I would help coordinate the activity, be their point of contact. You're the one who promised to make their plan a reality. You always wanted too much, Spencer. You were too greedy. Go ahead, tell them it's not you're fault. But remember, they're not the kind of people to listen to excuses."

Spencer slumped into a chair, looking defeated. "You little prick," he mumbled.

Again the white-haired man chuckled.

Chapter 9

The telephone rang as the McGowans were just finishing their dinner on Wednesday night. "Let the answering machine get it," Sheri said. "I hate when people call at dinnertime."

"We're almost done," Joe said as he got up and snatched the receiver from its place on the wall. "Hello?"

"Joe, this is Andy. Got a few minutes?"

"Sure, what's up?"

"I thought I should fill you in on the meeting we had the other night. Without boring you with the details, I think I can safely say that all problems have been worked out and all questions answered. Everyone agreed that the lost document Spencer was looking for was not important enough to cause problems for people. It was decided to just let it stay lost."

"That's good to know," Joe said. "Fran was our main concern, so at least we can be thankful about getting that issue resolved. Did you have a chance to discuss any of the other odd occurrences?"

"To some degree, but I should tell you that people are starting to get a little irritated with you."

"With me! Can't a guy ask a few questions without everyone getting upset?"

"It's mainly Spencer, but that's nothing new. I was able to find out who the stranger was that contacted the police about the missing document. It was Capsner."

"That makes sense," Joe said. "I should have thought of him before."

"It was strange, though. I don't want to make an issue out of something trivial, especially with the way you like to blow things out of proportion, but didn't you say that the stranger called the police station?"

"Yes, that's what Melissa told Sheri."

"Capsner said he went to the station personally. It's not a big deal, but it sure doesn't seem like the kind of mistake someone would typically make."

"Unless it really wasn't him," Joe suggested.

"The thought crossed my mind," Andy admitted. "But there would be no reason to cover for someone else, and who would that someone else be? By the way, Capsner also confirmed that the society is not listed in the phone directory."

"Of course." Joe sighed. "So what do you think, are the mysteries clearing up or getting more cloudy?"

"Clearing up, Joe, definitely clearing up. Don't try and find a way to make things look worse than they are."

"All right, all right. Anything else?"

"Well, one interesting development did occur that you should be aware of. You were recommended to be Harry's replacement on the council."

"What!" Joe exclaimed. "Who recommended me?"

"Sherman made that actual recommendation, but everyone else agreed that it was a good idea. Do you think you would be interested?"

"No!" Joe answered firmly. "Not in the least."

"Well, it's not official yet, anyway. It will be discussed at our next council meeting, but I'm sure everyone will approve. I thought you would jump at the chance."

"Why on earth would you think that? You know how busy my travel schedule is, and you know how I detest politics, even on a small scale."

"That may be true, but it would give you the opportunity to be involved in all these mysterious activities that you seem to be interested in. You could stop using me as a go-between."

Joe thought for a moment. He suspected Andy was only joking, but nevertheless, there was some merit to the idea. "I'll think about it, Andy. That's all I'll say for now. By the way, how is work progressing on the restoration project?"

"Getting bids from contractors took longer than we expected. We got a pretty slow start, but things are really beginning to roll now. Spencer's going to New York tomorrow night for a meeting with the society on Friday."

"Another meeting?" Joe questioned. "I thought the society was only going to allow one."

"That's what I thought too, but this meeting was actually their idea. Apparently, they called last night and asked him to come out."

"They asked him out right after the meeting you had," Joe said, more thinking out loud than talking. He brought his right hand to his chin, pondering the situation and debating in his mind whether or not this was truly a coincidence. He decided not to mention his suspicions to Andy. "Okay, Andy. Thanks for the update, and thanks for helping us out. Fran will be pleased to hear that she's off the hook. I'll talk to you later." He hung up the phone and briefly related the information to Sheri.

"So everything is back to normal," Sheri said, more of a question than a statement.

"That's what Andy says. At least Fran should be left alone, and that was what we were really trying to accomplish. But I still have an uneasy feeling about this whole situation."

"How do you mean?" Sheri asked, somewhat cautiously. She was having doubts herself but had been willing to dismiss them. But if Joe was having similar doubts, perhaps they were justified.

"First off," Joe said, "nothing explains the odd set of circumstances involving Harry and Bob Williams. But even if we ignore that, there's Capsner's statement about going to the police station. He either made a very unlikely mistake, or he's covering up for someone. If that's true, that brings up two fairly serious questions. First, why would he feel a need to cover up anything? People don't cover up things unless something is wrong. Secondly, who is this other person? He is obviously a stranger, and since Capsner is protecting him, it only stands to reason that he's associated with the historical society. Tie that in with this whole mess about the package, which contained information about the society, and things start to look pretty suspicious.

"The other point that doesn't sit well with me is Spencer's trip to New York," Joe continued. "He was just out there a short time ago, and apparently, the members of the society weren't thrilled about that. Now, with almost no notice, they're asking him back. And it just coincidentally happened after he was confronted about some of these issues. I know I can let my imagination get carried away at times, but this is too much."

Sheri slowly nodded her head in agreement. "I must admit, Joe, I feel the same way you do, but I was hoping it was just me. Something just doesn't feel right about this whole situation. How about your recommendation to serve on the council? Are you even considering it?"

"Oh, I don't know. I never really liked politics, but it's only for a few months. Andy pointed out that I could keep an eye on things easier. I think he was only joking, but it's true. I could get a lot closer to some of these problems, especially concerning the New York Historical Society."

"You could keep a better eye on them, but then again, they could keep a better eye on you."

Joe laughed then suddenly realized that it might not be such a humorous idea. In fact, it almost sounded like a real possibility.

Sheri suddenly became very quiet. She slowly walked into the dining room and sat down next to the window, aimlessly gazing into the backyard. Joe watched as her stare became fixed on nothing in particular. She sat very rigid, and her eyes could not conceal the fear that was rapidly building within her. "Joe," she said quietly, with a calm that belied her emotions, "Harry did commit suicide, didn't he?"

The words shot through Joe with a jolt. Hearing them spoken only made him more aware of the same feelings he had been trying to suppress.

"Of course," he assured her. "Let's not get too carried away with this thing. There is no doubt in my mind that he died by his own hand."

"That's good," Sheri said, still gazing out the window. "I believe you are right."

But deep inside, they each knew the other was lying.

Joe sat quietly for a moment, rubbing his chin with his right hand. "You know, Sheri, all the mystery, all the unexplainable events all revolve around the New York Historical Society. Spencer has dealt with them more than anyone else, and he's the one who is creating problems here. If something is wrong, it has to do with Spencer's relationship to the society. There is a way we could find out what's going on."

"What is that?" Sheri asked.

"I have some vacation time, and I have several free airline tickets saved up from my frequent-flyer program. It's possible that I could follow Spencer to New York and check up on exactly what this society is really all about."

"That's ridiculous!" Sheri exclaimed. "You're not a private investigator. Let's just call the police."

"What would we tell them? Nothing illegal has happened that we know of. And Spencer, for all his quirks, is a fairly respected man in town."

"I don't care. If we can't tell the police, then we'll just forget about it." Sheri got up and left the room.

Joe continued to sit deep in thought. It did seem a little crazy, following someone to New York just because of a few suspicions.

But he felt there were questions that needed to be answered. Silently evaluating the whole confusing situation in his mind, his thoughts began to wander, and he found himself being irresistibly curious as to what flight Spencer would taking to New York. He was sure it would be Thursday evening, and from his own travels, he was also fairly sure it would be a Northwest flight to Newark. Getting to Newark was much more convenient than Kennedy or LaGuardia, and it was just as close to downtown Manhattan. And with Northwest's hub being in the Twin Cities, it was the most likely airline to take anywhere.

He picked up the phone and called Northwest reservations. He knew the airlines were not allowed to give out passenger information, but he also knew from his own experiences how easy it would be to find out what he needed to know.

"Northwest reservations," a young female answered.

"Hi. My name is Spencer Thurman, and I've got a flight booked for Newark tomorrow night. My secretary booked the flight, and I just realized that she never gave me the itinerary. I was wondering if you could tell me the flight number and the time of departure?"

"Sure, Mr. Thurman. Let me pull your name up on the computer." Joe could hear the clicking of a keyboard. After what seemed like an unreasonably long time, the voice came back. "I'm sorry, Mr. Thurman, but there must be some mistake."

"I don't have a flight booked?" Joe asked.

"Yes, sir, you do, but it's not to New York, it's to Miami. Flight number 1020 leaving at 1:05 in the afternoon."

Joe paused for a moment, stunned by this new piece of information.

"Mr. Thurman?" the voice asked.

"Oh, of course." Joe laughed. "I've been traveling so much lately, I forget where I'm going from one day to the next."

"No problem, Mr. Thurman. Is there anything else?"

"No. You've been very helpful. Thank you."

He hung up the phone, not believing what he had just heard.

Sheri came back into the dining room. "Who were you talking to?" she asked.

"I was just curious about Spencer, so I called Northwest and checked on his flight."

"Joe, I don't want you getting involved with this!"

"Sheri, I found out he's not going to New York, he's going to Miami."

Sheri stood motionless. She felt puzzled, frustrated, afraid. "That doesn't make sense. Why would he go there? What does this mean, Joe?"

"I don't think I can find out sitting here. I could ask Andy."

"No. If Andy knew, he would have told you. At least he would have if he wanted to."

"What are you implying? Do you think Andy's been holding back something?"

"I don't know. It just seems like every time he gets involved, he says he has cleared up everything, and then we find out later it is even more confusing."

"Then what do we do?" Joe asked.

A blank, emotionless expression crossed Sheri's face. She swallowed hard, wishing she could suppress the words that were about to cross her lips. "Follow him," she whispered. "But be careful, Joe. Be very careful."

Chapter 10

Ronald Capsner sat in a large comfortable chair next to a fireplace in the living room of his apartment, trying to understand how all the latest events were unfolding. The situation was not totally out of control, but it certainly was not without its problems. A number of things had gone wrong, things that probably should have been anticipated. First, the city council took far too long to put a bid package together to send out to the contractors for the restoration project. That was Spencer Thurman's fault. Then when a contractor finally was selected, they took much more time than expected to actually start work, which really is not all that unusual for these kinds of projects. They should have expected this and planned accordingly.

It did not help that the officials from Paradise had very little experience managing a project of this size. He, as well as his associates, had overestimated the abilities of Spencer. Everyone knew up front it was imperative that the restoration project be fully underway by the end of July. Beyond that, the schedule was no longer important. It was only necessary that the effort be started so as to provide a cover for the real work to be done.

Now it looked like they may have to delay their actual purpose about two weeks. There were dangerous people who were very upset over this delay, but he doubted whether any serious action would be taken if there was a guarantee that the delay would be limited to two weeks. But if it were to stretch longer, the whole operation would be in jeopardy. Months of planning and research would have been for nothing, and a rare opportunity would have been lost, probably forever. Then, of course, there would be the other, more immediate consequences: everyone involved would undoubtedly be eliminated.

The situation could definitely be better, but it was not beyond hope. He felt all the obstacles had now been overcome, and they could come close to meeting the scheduled milestone dates, at least close enough to save the operation and their lives. But one very bad mistake had been made: a package outlining the operation had accidentally been given to Harry Rosten. Even this would not have been a problem in itself. In fact, it was this accident that provided him and his people the opportunity that they now had. The problem was that the information could not be retrieved. No one had been able to find it until this man named Joe McGowen stumbled across it.

At first, it seemed innocent enough, and Capsner was greatly relieved that the package had been returned. Everything could then have started progressing as planned, and any suspicions that had arisen would have just blown over. But for some reason, McGowen would just not let things be. What did he really know? He had never met McGowen, but by his actions, it was obvious he was a very smart man. Even more disturbing, he was dedicated to Paradise and its people. Experience had taught him that smart people with a cause should never be taken lightly. Hopefully, he would take the position on the council, where he could be watched closer.

Normally, it would be wise to take him out now, but too much had already happened. The advantage of operating in a small, sleepy town is that people are not overly suspicious, even if unusual occurrences take place right before their eyes. People in towns like this have a way of rationalizing things or explaining away odd happenings simply because they cannot comprehend or accept that something terrible could be developing within their own community. But with the suicide of a prominent figure and the disappearance of a police officer, even the most naive person would start to take notice. Another person disappearing would be too much. No, he could not afford to take McGowen out now. And if the time ever came when he would have to take him, he knew that he would have to take his entire family also. There could be no other way. But for now, he would just keep an eye on him.

Spencer Thurman was leaving for his Miami meeting the next afternoon. Hopefully, he could pacify the people running this operation and convince them that there would be no further delays. But Capsner was skeptical. He had talked to them himself just this evening, and there was no question that they were upset with the current developments, especially concerning the lost document. They insisted on seeing Spencer personally. That was a bad sign because it meant the problems went beyond Spencer and indicated that he himself was losing control. He had to be very careful. It was important that Spencer's trip went well.

Capsner picked up the phone and dialed a long-distance number.

"Yes," came the answer from the other end.

"Thurman will arrive in Miami at five twenty-five on Northwest flight 1020. The meeting place will be the same as before, the beach house, at eleven o'clock. Are you ready for him?"

"We're ready," the voice replied. "There should not be any problems."

"I hope not. I want to hear immediately about the outcome. I don't want to wait until Thurman returns."

"Understood."

Capsner replaced the phone. There was nothing more he could do now. Of all the difficult parts of his job, having patience was undoubtedly the hardest to endure. His thoughts again turned to his more immediate problem, that of Joe McGowen. This was probably a good time to meet him, talk to him about the restoration project and the historical society's involvement, assure him that nothing was out of the ordinary. McGowen was a potential problem, one that no longer could be ignored. If McGowen could not be handled with force, Capsner decided he would have to win him over with diplomacy: become friends with him, make him feel part of the restoration effort. But whatever it took, McGowen would definitely have to be handled.

Northwest flight 1020 arrived promptly at 5:25 p.m. at the Miami International Airport. A large crowd of people waited outside the Jetway to greet the new arrivals, predominantly tourists looking for a few days of Florida sun and sea. In the back of the crowd stood a lone man dressed in white cotton trousers and a brightly flowered shirt and wearing a pair of dark glasses. In Minnesota, he would have stood out like a flashing neon light, but here he could barely be noticed among the droves of tourists roaming the concourse in similar apparel.

Joe McGowen had taken Northwest flight 571 earlier that day. He arrived at 12:30 p.m., rented a car, and began his vigil of waiting to spot Spencer Thurman coming out of the jet way. While sitting in one of the many airport restaurants, he noticed that the majority of the people wandering about were dressed in this stereotyped tropical outfit. He decided that the best way to avoid being spotted would be to look like a typical tourist, so he purchased the trousers and shirt from a clothing/souvenir shop and changed in a nearby restroom. Then he continued to wait and wait and wait. It was amazing how long five hours seemed to take when there was nothing to do to occupy his time. Finally, the announcement had been made that flight 1020 had landed.

Joe did not have long to wait. He assumed someone as arrogant as Thurman would use city money to fly first-class, and his assumption proved to be correct. Spencer was the third person out of the gate. Joe had no experience of following someone inconspicuously, but it proved to be a remarkably simple task. He surmised that since Spencer was inexperienced at this game himself, and since he undoubtedly had a lot on his mind, he would not be looking for anyone, especially someone from Paradise.

The first challenge Joe faced as a shadow came almost immediately as Spencer stepped out into the street. If he were to hail a taxi, Joe would have to quickly jump into another cab and have the driver follow him. The timing would have to be just right, and there was the strong possibility that Spencer would get away. Joe thought it was much more likely that Spencer would rent a car, and soon saw with great relief that this was the case.

When Spencer stepped onto an Avis commuter bus to go to the car rental area, Joe quickly rushed to his car and drove to the Avis lot, parking just a few yards down the road but close enough to see Spencer in the glass-walled rental office filling out the necessary paperwork. After a few minutes, Spencer emerged from the office, stepped into a nearby car, and pulled up to the exit gate. The road around the rental agencies was a one-way, so Joe did not have to worry about him turning in the opposite direction of which he was parked.

Spencer turned right and headed for the airport exit, and Joe cautiously followed at a few car lengths' distance. They went only a few miles when Spencer turned into the parking lot of a Hilton Hotel. Joe parked a short distance away from Spencer and wondered what he should do next. He was sure Spencer would only check in to get his room and then leave again in a few minutes. It was already six o'clock in the evening, so if he had a meeting tonight, it could not be too much later. He should probably just wait here in the car for him. But just as Spencer entered the hotel through the large glass doors, Joe decided it would be better to follow him. Moments later, he passed through the front doors of the hotel and quickly scanned the area for a convenient position to stand guard. Past the entryway was a large lobby, with the registration desk off to the right. A small lounge was on the left with a row of elevators straight ahead. Joe sat at a table in the lounge that offered a view of the lobby yet allowed him to remain adequately concealed. He could see Spencer take his room key, walk over to the elevator, and disappear inside.

"Can I help you, sir?"

Joe looked up, startled to have his concentration abruptly broken, and saw a pretty young waitress waiting for a response. "Just coffee, thanks," he ordered, then immediately turned his attention back to the elevator doors. He sat and waited, sure he would not get a chance to finish his coffee before Spencer returned. When he was on his second cup, he decided Spencer probably needed to freshen up, maybe even had taken a shower and changed clothes. The anxious anticipation he had been feeling all day kept him going, but at the same time, it was beginning to wear him down. It had been a long day, most of it spent waiting. A part of him was very nervous about this whole adventure. What was he doing here, in Miami, following a member of his city council? But a larger part of him was still curious, knowing the situation in Paradise was not what it appeared to be, and the key was definitely Spencer Thurman. He had to admit that there was another part of him that was very excited. Sitting here among the palm trees near the ocean, with gorgeous girls in bright-colored skirts everywhere, following a man on a mysterious adventure, he felt like a cross between James Bond and Sherlock Holmes. He also had to admit that there was a part of him, although a very small part, that was afraid. What was he getting into? But deep inside, he was convinced there was no real danger. The worst thing that could happen would be getting discovered by Spencer, and while that may be very embarrassing, it certainly would not be dangerous. Consciously he believed that, but a small part of his subconscious would not let the fear go completely away. But for now, the immediate problem was to wait. He could not allow himself to relax, for it would take Spencer only seconds to cross the lobby and go out the front door. He had to have complete concentration, never daring to take his eyes off those elevator doors for a moment.

By seven o'clock he was exhausted, but more than that, he was afraid something had gone wrong. Suddenly a thought occurred to him: could the meeting be taking place in Spencer's room? Damn, why hadn't he thought of that! His inexperience as a sleuth was beginning to show. This thought jolted him out of the almost trancelike condition he had fallen into, and he realized that in his effort to follow Spencer, he had overlooked a number of things. Was there another exit? Of course there was. As much time as he spent in hotels, he should have thought of that right away. Could there be another lounge or restaurant where Spencer could go for his meeting without having to come back through the main lobby? In a hotel like the Hilton, that was also probably true. He felt a deep aching pain in the pit of his stomach as he realized he had probably blown it. When would he ever get this opportunity again? He silently cursed himself. He was smarter than this. Why didn't he think?

On the verge of panic, he got up and rushed out the door to the parking lot, feeling sure that Spencer's car would be gone. But it was right where Spencer had left it, meaning that either he was still inside or someone else had picked him up at another exit. He had to know for sure, so he decided to call his room. If Spencer answered, he would pretend it was a wrong number; if not, he would have to assume he had lost Spencer for good.

He walked up to the registration desk and tried to appear calm. "Could I please have the room number for a Spencer Thurman?"

"I'm sorry, sir," responded the young man behind the desk. "But we are not allowed to give out room numbers. I could call his room for you and let you speak to him."

"That would be fine, thanks."

The man behind the desk punched numerous keys on the computer in front of him. Joe was always amazed at how many keys had to be hit to locate someone at a hotel. Finally, the man shook his head and said, "I'm sorry, sir, but we do not have a person by that name staying with us."

Of course, thought Joe. *He used an alias.* "I must have the wrong hotel. Thanks, anyway." He turned away, frustrated, disappointed, angry. He had planned this so well, how could he have let this happen? He walked back toward the lounge, trying to decide what to do. Just then the elevator doors opened, and a group of people walked off. Among them was Spencer Thurman.

Joe froze for just a second then quickly turned his back to hide his face. His heart was racing as he was nearly overwhelmed by the combined emotions of elation from having found Spencer and of anxious excitement from trying to remain inconspicuous while he continued his pursuit. He breathed a quiet sigh of relief, realizing his incredible good fortune. He had played this portion of the game all wrong, yet he was still right where he wanted to be. From here on, he would not rely on luck. He must be careful, and he must be smart.

Spencer left the parking lot and, after a short series of turns, entered onto US Highway 1 south. Traffic was fairly heavy, but it was not difficult for Joe to follow him. They continued on US 1 for about twenty-five miles then exited west onto the smaller State Highway 20. They drove for nearly an hour, passing through Everglades National Park and continuing all the way to the southernmost tip of Florida to a town called Flamingo. Joe had never seen the Everglades before, and he was amazed at how desolate this part of Florida was. The area around him appeared to be as wild and potentially dangerous as he had imagined the Everglades would be.

In Flamingo, they exited onto a quiet side road. Joe was concentrating so intently on following Spencer that he was not able to identify the names of the roads. Fatigue was beginning to set in. It was now just past nine o'clock in the evening, and he was even more exhausted than before. Physically he had done very little today, most of his time being spent sitting on planes or in hotels or in automobiles, but mentally he had very little time to relax since he first awoke at five thirty that morning.

From Flamingo, they headed west along the coast to East Cape. Here Spencer pulled over to the side of the road, got out of his car, and walked up to a public phone standing on a corner. Joe parked a block away and watched Spencer fidget with his coins, apparently having difficulty inserting them into the slot. He was noticeably nervous, periodically looking up and down the road, constantly shifting his feet around. Joe knew that from here on, he would have to be especially careful. There was very little traffic, and Spencer was obviously watching to see if he was being followed.

Spencer danced impatiently, holding the phone to his ear. Finally he said a few words and hung up, then got back into his car and drove off.

They continued to follow the coastline as it curved north through Middle Cape and then North West Cape. As tired and anxious as Joe was, he could not help but be impressed with the beauty of the area. The landscape was dense with palm trees and tropical foliage. The white caps of the waves could be seen as they broke on the beach. The sun had set, but the western sky was still a brilliant red. It was truly beautiful.

A few miles north of North West Cape, the area appeared to be totally desolate. There was no one on the road but Joe and Spencer, and since it was now dark enough for headlights, Joe knew he could be easily spotted and was concerned that Spencer would suspect something. He waited until Spencer's taillights disappeared around a curve, knowing that at that point, Spencer would not be able to see his headlights. Joe quickly turned them off, hoping he would have enough light to see the road. It was difficult, but he was just able to find his way. He increased his speed until he could again see Spencer's taillights then continued to follow him at a safe distance. Finally he saw the taillights turn left and come to a stop a short distance off the road then go out. Joe drove about a quarter mile past the turnoff, turned his car around, and pulled as far to the side of the road as he could. He actually drove partially into the roadside foliage, and with the tall palms nearby shadowing the moonlight, his car was completely undetectable from a distance of more than just a few yards.

He quietly opened the door and checked his watch under the dome light. It was ten twenty. He stepped out of the car and carefully closed the door, then briefly surveyed the area and attempted to get his bearings with his surroundings. It was dark, but the moon was bright, and with the help of the countless stars, there was enough light to see. He could hear waves breaking and knew that the ocean was not far away, but it was blocked from his view by a wall of bushes and trees. He decided it would be safer to follow the beach under the cover of the foliage back to where Spencer turned in rather than walk back along the road.

Joe looked for a path or entrance into the quasiforest, but nothing visible appeared suitable. Believing that the foliage was the thickest along the edge, he forced his way through a mass of tall tropical bushes and began meandering in the direction of the sound of the waves, hoping that it would thin out soon. He quickly discovered that the foliage was very dense all the way through, making passage extremely difficult. The trees and bushes blocked most of the light, limiting his vision to just a few inches. He crept forward inch by inch, feeling his way along with his hands more than seeing with his eyes. The soil beneath his feet was damp, and it became softer as he progressed.

He suddenly became aware of the sounds that filled the darkness, sounds of living creatures all around him. He was not sure what produced these sounds, but he was reminded of the large bullfrogs and crickets he frequently heard back home. He was quite familiar with the sounds of the wild in the northern forests, but the things he heard here, while somewhat similar, had their own distinct quality. He felt himself being overcome by an eeriness that was nearly overwhelming. He tried to move faster but only became entangled in some unseen plants, grabbing him and holding him like a monster from a horror movie.

For the first time, he realized he was in an environment that was totally foreign to him. Visions of dangerous beasts flashed through his mind: crocodiles at his feet with jaws opened, snakes hanging from trees, ready to drop. The more he tried to fight his way forward, the more he was overtaken by panic. Cold sweat poured down his face as his heart pounded fiercely in his ears. Finally, with no regard to what was before him or to how much noise he would make, he lowered his shoulder and lunged straight ahead. Thrashing his arms and legs wildly, he fought through a last set of bushes and fell facedown in the soft beach sand.

Joe lay motionless for several minutes, breathing deeply and allowing the panic to subside. When he had fully regained his composure, he stood up and brushed the fine sand off his clothes and body. The ocean was visible about one hundred yards away, with the waves gently breaking and rolling up the beach. Joe cursed himself for his lack of control. He had been caught off guard by this new environment and panicked like a little boy who was afraid of the bogeyman. He could not let that happen again.

The dense foliage that had seemed to go on forever was actually no more than forty yards wide. It appeared to stretch the full length of the beach, the end of which he could not see as it seemed to disappear into the night. The first ten or twenty yards of the sandy area bordering the foliage was filled with a series of small dunes, which also appeared to run the full length of the beach.

Joe looked to his left in the direction he expected to find Spencer Thurman. He could see a large two-story building that was completely dark except for one dim light a short distance away, in the direction of the water. He slowly started walking

The Seduction of Paradise

toward the building, staying close to the shadows of the foliage and behind the dunes. He wished he had changed out of his white pants, but with the shadows and the dunes, it would not be difficult to remain hidden. After covering most of the distance on foot, he got down on his hands and knees to conceal himself behind the dunes and crawled to within thirty yards of the building.

From this point, he could see that it was an impressive beach house with a large deck facing the ocean. Spencer Thurman was alone on the deck, nervously pacing back and forth in the faint light, which was mounted on a post a few feet away. Joe laid flat on his stomach and tried to mentally prepare himself for whatever might happen next. His senses tingled with excitement, knowing that there could be trouble if he was caught, but still not sensing any real danger. He tried to relax, but the anxious anticipation within him prevented it. He lay quiet, watching Spencer pace, appearing to become more nervous as each minute passed. It was the third time in this very long day that his patience was tested. The warm breeze blowing in from the ocean felt fresh and soothing across his face as he watched the restless man on the deck. After what seemed like hours, he checked his watch: 11:05 p.m.

Suddenly, a shadowy figure emerged from a clump of trees on the opposite side of the deck from where Joe was lying. Then another and another until finally there was a group of six, or possibly seven, figures approaching the beach house. Spencer looked up and, for an instant, froze. As the figures moved close enough to be recognized, Spencer appeared to relax.

"Shit, Rodriguez, you scared the hell out of me!" Spencer exclaimed.

The man in front, obviously the leader, responded coldly, "We wanted to make sure you came alone. We don't take chances in our business."

His English was good, but he spoke with a distinct accent. Joe was not sure exactly where the accent was from, but it sounded Cuban or Puerto Rican, or maybe Jamaican. He had never really heard those accents before except on television, but he was pretty sure it was from that general area.

As the group of men—and they were all men—stepped up onto the deck and into the faint light, Joe was immediately struck by two points. The first was that they were all black, very black. The second, and by far the more alarming, was that they all carried guns. He knew very little about guns other than from the training he had received when he was in the navy. He had qualified as an expert with both the .45 caliber pistol and the M16 automatic riffle. But beyond that, he had virtually no experience with guns whatsoever. It appeared that all the men—except the leader, Rodriguez—carried AR-15s, the semiautomatic version of the M16 typically used by police SWAT teams. However, Joe strongly suspected that these guns had been modified to be able to operate in a fully automatic mode. He knew it was very easy to make such a modification, and it was also illegal, but the group before him did not look like the type to be concerned about legalities. Rodriguez had a type of gun Joe had not seen before, but from descriptions Joe had read in various books, it reminded him of what an Uzi would look like.

"You didn't really need to bring an arsenal, did you?" Spencer asked.

"Look, Thurman, in our business we are always prepared for anything. You should know that."

As Joe watched them swarm around Spencer with their weapons ready, the tingle of excitement he felt earlier rapidly transitioned to fear. His mind was flooded with all the questions and second thoughts one gets through hindsight: why did he have to follow Spencer? There must have been a better way to handle this. He was too much of an amateur to be spying on these kinds of people. If he were caught, would he be killed? The cold sweats returned as he was convinced the answer to the last question was a definite yes.

"What did you need to see me about?" Spencer asked. "It's difficult for me to get away like this. It's starting to look suspicious."

"I'm tired of fucking around with you, Thurman. I'll get right to it. We came to you with a deal. Part of the deal was that we had to start moving in merchandise by August. All the other details were secondary, but it was imperative that we meet that schedule. Otherwise, we wouldn't have even needed you or your little friends up there. You were supposed to expedite things—pave the way, so to speak. And you were paid a lot of money. Now I hear we may be delayed."

"You know the situation. We talked about it already. Some things happened that we couldn't foresee."

"I don't want to hear that bullshit, Thurman! We had a deal, and you're not performing. Mr. Salvo is not at all pleased. He wants me to take more aggressive action. I may have to be paying you a visit up there."

Spencer looked terrified, a kind of terrified that Joe had never seen. He had seen people afraid, and he had seen countless movies of people portraying fear, but nothing could match the expression he was now seeing on Spencer's face. When Spencer spoke again, it was more of a stammering babble. "Look, all the obstacles have been overcome. Things are moving along now. If there is a delay, it will only be a few days. If we're lucky, there won't be any delay at all. You don't need to be coming up yourself. People will get suspicious. Besides, you have Capsner there. Don't you trust him?"

Rodriguez relaxed for a moment. "Mr. Salvo trusts Capsner, but I don't. Besides, his job is to build public relations, not to take care of the technical problems. And as far as me showing up, do not be overly concerned. I've been there several times already. When you have problems, I like to help out." He chuckled in a kind of arrogant, menacing manner and began stroking his Uzi.

Suddenly, a thought struck Spencer. "You're the man who went to the police to ask about the missing package."

"Oh no, I couldn't do that, not even by phone. A Jamaican going to the police in a town like Paradise? Those hicks would probably make a front-page story out of it. But I knew you couldn't handle it, so I got a guy off the street in Minneapolis to call for me, someone who sounds like all the rest of you." He laughed again. "And it only cost me ten bucks—and a bottle of wine, of course. Street people always work cheap. By the way, when you see Capsner, be sure to thank him for covering for me."

Spencer was feeling a little more comfortable. "You can tell Mr. Salvo that since the missing package has been resolved, nothing will get in our way. We can—"

"Resolved!" Rodriguez shouted. "You call that resolved? The most important part is still missing!"

"We're convinced it has been destroyed, and—"

"It had better be! Can you imagine how Mr. Salvo feels with truckloads of cocaine being prepared to ship and a document is missing, which describes the whole operation?"

"It doesn't really say anything about the cocaine or where it will be stored. It just refers to 'merchandise.'"

"Don't act like a bigger fool than I already think you are. Anyone who reads that will know exactly what it means. Misplacing that package was your biggest blunder. If we didn't need a connection to the council, I would have handled that problem more decisively."

"So what is it you want me to do?" Spencer asked, an expression of fear returning to his face.

"Fulfill your part of the deal, that's all. The first shipment of cocaine will arrive on August fifth, and if you're not ready to receive it, well, you may get to visit your friend Harry."

Spencer's eyes widened, projecting a combination of fear and anger, or something even more than that: terror and loathing. His eyes took on the look of a crazed man, and even Rodriguez was momentarily taken aback.

"Settle down, Thurman. Just do your job, and there won't be any trouble."

Spencer said nothing but continued to glare at Rodriguez. From Joe's vantage point, he could see that Spencer was trembling, but he could not be sure whether it was due to his fear or his anger. This was clearly not the Spencer Thurman whom he knew in Paradise. This was a man who had been pushed one step too far, a man who was approaching his emotional breaking point. Spencer took a step forward, and it was obvious even to Joe that his anger was winning out over his fear.

"You killed Harry?" Spencer asked in a low controlled voice. His teeth were clenched so tightly that veins were visible in his neck and forehead.

Rodriguez collected himself, then burst into his typical arrogant laughter. "You truly amaze me, Thurman. Who else would have done it? Or did you believe it was really suicide? You never did understand what this was all about, did you?" Rodriguez laughed again, but in his eyes there was no humor, only the cold hate of a man who enjoyed the opportunity to destroy human life.

"Besides," he added, "I didn't kill him, you did. You gave him the package and that put the rope around his neck. So don't blame me, you pathetic little man. Blame yourself!"

Spencer's face reddened. He took another step forward. "You talk about our 'deal.' What about your promise that there would be no killing? You promised! Harry was my friend. His wife is my friend."

"We're done here, Thurman. Get out and go back to your miserable friends. Who knows, if you're careful, maybe you can keep from killing more of them."

That was it. It was the proverbial straw that broke the camel's back. It turned all of Spencer's emotions into bitter hate, leaving the fear behind, where it could no longer protect him. He lunged at Rodriguez like a crazed bull, his eyes fiery red with uncontrolled rage. Rodriguez struck him along side of his head with the butt of his Uzi, but it had little effect. Spencer gripped the throat of the surprised Rodriguez and squeezed with all his strength. Had they been alone, Spencer may have been the victor, but as Rodriguez had said, they were prepared for anything. Immediately two men grabbed Spencer and, with a great, struggling effort, pulled the raving wild man free from Rodriguez.

"You are crazy, man!" Rodriguez shrieked. "No one does that to me!" He lashed out with a vicious kick that caught Spencer square in the face. Blood and teeth shot into the air as Spencer's head snapped violently backward from the blow of Rodriguez's foot. This did nothing to slow Spencer down. His anger increased until he could think of nothing but destroying the monster standing before him. With strength he never knew he had, he broke free from the two guards, and with a wild scream of hateful rage, he again lunged for Rodriguez. This time Rodriguez was not surprised, and the excuse he had been looking for was handed to him by Spencer's violent assault. He raised his Uzi and released a long burst into the attacking body of Spencer Thurman.

Joe lay behind the sand dune in stunned horror. It had all happened so fast. One moment it appeared that Spencer was ready to leave, then suddenly, the air was filled with the terrifying echoing of gunfire as Spencer's body violently twitched and flopped, his chest exploding into a gush of red that looked more like fruit juice than blood. Two thoughts raced through Joe's mind: he must get out of there immediately and, if he were caught, his fate would be the same as Spencer's.

Chapter 11

Joe was sure this would be his only opportunity to escape unnoticed. The men on the deck were in a state of confusion: Rodriguez cursing the two men for not controlling Spencer, the men cursing Rodriguez for overreacting, all of them cursing Spencer for being such a fool. Occasional shots were fired, not at anything in particular but just as a reaction of violent men to a stimulating situation. Joe quickly crawled back in the direction from which he had come, not even daring to rise to his knees. When he reached a point where he felt safely out of sight, he rose to a crouching position and began to run along the edge of the foliage, hoping to get back to his car undetected.

He had only taken a few steps when suddenly, out of nowhere, he felt a sharp, crashing blow to the side of his head, sending him sprawling into the sand alongside a nearby dune. He painfully rolled to his back and looked up to see a man standing above him aiming an AR15 at his head. His thoughts were blurred, but he knew what must have happened. This was a guard, a sentry patrolling the perimeter. He was probably just lucky to not have encountered him earlier. He should have suspected there would be guards. This time, his amateurism had cost him dearly.

"I found a spy over here," the sentry yelled to the group on the deck. "What should I do with him?"

"Kill him!" came the answer.

Joe saw the rifle of the sentry being leveled at his head. There was nowhere to go, nothing he could do. His thoughts turned instinctively to his family: Sheri, Maureen, Brandon, Katelin. He was such a fool! Why was he here? He closed his eyes, wondering if he would feel the lead tearing through his skull.

My poor children, he thought. *My poor wife!*

A shot rang out, not as loudly as he expected. He felt—nothing! He opened his eyes and saw the headless corpse of the sentry collapse beside him.

"He's got a gun!" he heard someone shout. "Get him!"

Joe did not have time to try and figure out what had happened. Most likely a stray shot from one of the wild gunmen struck his would-be assassin. His immediate concern was survival. He jumped up to his feet and saw the group from the deck racing toward him. He knew running would be in vain, so he snatched up the AR15, pointed in the general direction of the oncoming attackers, and pulled the trigger. His earlier suspicions were correct: the rifle was modified for automatic fire.

The men scattered and dove for cover, returning fire in a haphazard manner. Joe knew they could not see him clearly enough to take an accurate shot. He started moving toward his car, firing short, sporadic bursts. All he needed to do was fire enough rounds to make his pursuers cautious, keeping them more concerned about protecting themselves than about catching him. He did not need to be accurate; the noise of the gunfire and the muzzle flash would be enough to keep his attackers at bay. He knew he would expend all his ammunition in only one or two seconds if he fired continuously, and if he ran out of rounds, he would be dead.

He reached the point where he had passed through the dense foliage. This time, his motivation was far greater than before, and he pounded his way through the quasiforest with amazing ease. He exited just a few feet in front of his car, and without hesitation, he jumped behind the wheel, started the engine, and sped off, thankful that he had pointed the car in the direction of his retreat. For several hundred yards, he expected to see the muzzle flash of rifles from the side of the road, but amazingly, all was quiet. His pursuers had undoubtedly been caught up in the trees and underbrush, probably not realizing themselves the difficulty of passing through these obstacles at night. It also may have helped that he left his lights off until he was convinced he had made his escape. Under the veil of darkness, it would be nearly impossible to get an accurate shot at his car from more than a few yards' distance.

His heart continued to pound as he made his way back through Everglades National Park and all the way to Miami International Airport. He had the presence of mind to discard the AR15 along the roadside in the Everglades; he did not want to have to explain having a hot automatic weapon in his possession.

When he reached the rental car return at the airport, he opened the car door and sat for a few minutes, breathing in the fresh air. He was safe, he had made it out, but he had no idea what had happened. An innocent, exciting adventure had unexpectedly turned wild and violent. He needed to calm down, get his thoughts in order. Finally, it all caught up with him, and his stomach began retching violently. He leaned out away from the car and expelled everything he had eaten that day, throwing up again and again.

Then he fell back in his seat and rested. He could not return to Minnesota until tomorrow, but he would not leave the airport. He was not sure that he was safe here, but he certainly was not safe anywhere else. He would spend the night in the terminal, thanking God every minute for his life, wondering how such a terrible thing could have happened to him and the good people of Paradise.

After a sleepless, agonizingly miserable night, Joe was able to catch an early flight back to Minneapolis. He had not slept for over twenty-four hours, and his appearance reflected his condition. He was oblivious to everything and everyone around him. All he could think of was getting home to Sheri and his kids. Finally, after a long flight and an hour's drive, he pulled into his driveway, still fearful of what almost happened and what possibly could happen. He sprang out of his car and bolted into the house. Sheri met him at the door, and like a lost little child who had just found his mother, he threw his arms around her, desperately clinging to the woman who had become part of himself.

"Sheri, oh my God, Sheri. I love you, I love you so very much."

"Joe, what happened? You're trembling, and you look terrible! Are you all right?"

"How are the kids?" he asked in almost a demanding tone of voice.

"They're fine, Joe. Katelin's sleeping, and the others are in school. Please calm down. Everything is okay. We heard about Spencer. But I'm afraid I have some disturbing news." Sheri stepped back and looked at her husband. She had never seen him so emotionally drained. "Joe, what has happened to you?"

"You heard about Spencer? I didn't think anyone would know yet. Maybe there is still something we can do."

Sheri smiled, but very cautiously. "It's not that important, Joe. But the news I have is. You had better sit down."

"Not that important!" Joe blurted out. "What—"

"Joe, listen to me," Sheri cut in. "Something terrible has happened. They found Bob Williams, at least what's left of him. His body was pulled out of a lake a few miles north of here. Joe, he was murdered!"

Joe heard the words, and for a moment, he stood motionless. Then he walked over to a chair and slowly sat down. "So they got both of them," he whispered, more to himself than to Sheri.

"Both of whom?" Sheri asked, obviously confused.

"Who do you think? Spencer and Bob."

"Spencer! He wasn't murdered. He just left town suddenly."

"Left town? Sheri, what are you talking about?"

"Mayor Carlson announced just this morning that Spencer had decided to move away. An opportunity came up for him that he didn't think he could afford to miss, but it meant leaving immediately. I thought that was probably why he changed his flight to Miami, but I assumed you would have figured that out. He wanted to convey his apologies and his appreciation to everyone in Para—"

"Sheri, it's all a lie! Spencer isn't moving anywhere. He's dead! He's lying on a beach in Florida with a body full of lead!"

"Joe, it can't be."

"Don't tell me it can't be, damn it! I was there, I saw it happen. Then they tried to kill me! It's a miracle I'm still alive!"

Sheri sat down, confused, afraid, trying to absorb what had happened and what it all meant.

"Sheri, listen. I don't know any details, but apparently, Paradise was being set up as a kind of holding base for large quantities of cocaine being shipped into this area. Spencer, and who knows who else, was being paid a lot of money to make it all happen. They had something going on that would serve as a front, something that would allow them to bring the cocaine in unnoticed. That's what the package was, Sheri, the package I found in Fran's attic. It described the operation. I don't know how Harry got it or what he did with it, but apparently, part of it is still missing. Harry didn't commit suicide, Sheri. He was murdered!"

"Oh my God, Joe, what is happening? This is Paradise, not New York or Los Angeles. Things like this don't happen here."

"Maybe that's why they chose Paradise. It's quiet and out of the way. I just don't know what to think, but we have to do something."

"We must be in terrible danger, Joe. We have to get out of here, now!" Sheri jumped up, wanting to run somewhere, some place friendly and safe but without clearly thinking of what they should do. Joe grabbed hold of her shoulders and held her firmly in an attempt to calm her.

"Calm down, Sheri. I don't believe we are in danger. No one in Florida saw me, at least no one still alive." He winced as he remembered the horror of seeing the sentry standing above him with his automatic weapon, believing he would be killed within seconds then seeing the sentry collapse in a lifeless pile of blood and flesh. "But I am concerned about the questions we were bringing up before, when we had Andy ask the council about the package, and when I called Chief Winfield about it. People know we have been poking our noses around. I don't believe anyone suspects us of anything yet, or I'm sure we would be aware of it. These people don't screw around if they think someone could be trouble for them. But it is very important not to say any more about the package, the missing document, Bob Williams, or any of those things, especially about Spencer. From now on, we will be just another family in this town."

"What are you saying, Joe? That we can't trust anyone? These people are our friends, they're not criminals. We must at least call the police."

"No!" Joe shouted. "Most of these people may be our friends, but there is someone out there working for whoever is behind this whole ugly mess, and we don't know who it is. Why did Mayor Carlson announce that Spencer had moved away? Did she really believe he could have left so suddenly without word to anyone? How about Chief Winfield? He assured me there was no problem concerning Bob Williams's disappearance. Could he really have been fooled that badly? Who knows, Sheri, this might involve the whole city council, the police department—hell, maybe the entire town. Until we know for sure, we can say nothing."

"Joe, if it involves the council, then—"

"Yeah, I know, then it involves Andy. I just cannot believe he would be mixed up in this."

"How could this happen, Joe? This is such a nice town with such good people."

Joe hung his head, looking defeated. "It's a simple matter of being seduced. I never believed that everyone had a price, but apparently, it's true. What a person wouldn't do for a thousand dollars he might do for ten thousand, or a hundred thousand, or a million. If the price keeps going up, I suppose there is a point where everyone will eventually give in."

"I don't believe that, Joe. I refuse to believe it. I know you don't believe it either."

Joe collapsed in a chair, exhausted. "I don't know, Sheri. I just don't know."

Sheri had been on the verge of total panic, but the realization struck her that now, more than ever, they both must be strong, and that meant remaining calm and in control. It was important for them to develop a plan of action on how to handle this terrible predicament. She sat next to Joe and began going over in her mind all that had happened.

"Joe," she started, "you said there was something going on that would serve as a front for drug shipments. That, of course, is the key, but what could it be?"

"I have no idea," Joe responded. "It almost has to be connected to the Brewster mansion restoration, at least to some degree. It's the only large project that has been started recently, and most importantly, it involves all the key players, namely Spencer and Capsner. All kinds of trucks will be coming and going for months. No one would ever question what was in them. If every so often one was loaded with cocaine, who would know? But there are too many things that just don't fit. First, the council checked out the New York Historical Society, so if it's true they are a phony outfit, then it must also be true that the entire council is involved. Even with what we have learned, I just cannot believe that.

"But the biggest missing piece to this puzzle is the lack of any sizeable storage area. Where would they keep all the cocaine? The mansion will eventually be open for tourism, which will include virtually every room of the house as well as the old servants' house nearby. And even if they did find a place to keep it, once the project is completed, it would be impossible to move large quantities of drugs in and out without being noticed.

"What you're saying is true, but the mansion still must be the key," Sheri said. "The coincidence is just too great."

Joe thought for a moment, his right hand on his chin. "You know, maybe the whole council wouldn't have to be in on it. When they decided to check out the society, Spencer was the only one who went out there. No doubt he actually went to Miami. It's possible no one else knew anything about what he was up to."

"That's right," Sheri said, her eyes starting to gleam with enthusiasm. "Maybe he is the only bad apple."

"I don't know if I would go that far," Joe said. "I really don't think the entire council is involved, but there must be someone besides Spencer, someone in a position to ensure the shipments won't be checked, or even suspected."

"Mayor Carlson?" Sheri asked quietly.

"My God, I hope not," Joe replied. "But unfortunately, she seems to be a leading candidate. As far as the storage area is concerned, I still don't see where they could possibly put their merchandise. Maybe out in the woods somewhere, but that seems awfully risky. It might be worth checking out, though."

"Not by us, Joe. This is way over our heads. You said it yourself: from now on, we're just another family in this town."

Joe closed his eyes and relived the scene on the beach: Spencer Thurman being riddled with bullets, a man ready to kill him, the miraculous accident that killed his assassin and saved his life, his narrow and frightful escape.

"You're right," he said. "But we can't trust the police. The Paradise police force probably isn't capable of handling something like this, anyway. I should have thought of this before, but I was so confused I couldn't think straight. I'm going to call the FBI."

They each felt a simultaneous sense of relief at the realization there were people out there who could help and protect them.

Joe did not bother to check if there was a local field office. He called long-distance information to get the number of the FBI in Washington then dialed the number given to him by the operator.

"Federal Bureau of Investigation," came a woman's professional, almost mechanical voice.

"Hello," Joe said, suddenly aware that he was not at all sure of how to begin. "My name is Joseph McGowen, and I'm calling from Paradise, Minnesota."

"Yes, Mr. McGowen, how may I help you?"

"I have something very serious to report, and I guess I don't know exactly how to begin."

"Can you contact your local authorities?" the voice asked.

"No, no, I can't. I need to speak to someone out there."

"What is the nature of your concern, Mr. McGowen?"

"It's very serious. I witnessed a murder, but it's related to drug-trafficking activity."

"Thank you, Mr. McGowen. That will help me to direct your call to the appropriate personnel."

Joe heard a series of clicks as his call was transferred. After a moment, a man's voice broke in, "Special Agent Kowalski, may I help you?"

Joe started again, telling his story in slightly more detail. Again he was cut short and transferred, this time to a Special Agent Mack. Mack seemed to be interested and listened to a bit more of his story, then said that the person who could help him was Special Agent Thompson. Again he was transferred, and a few moments later, he heard a woman's voice, "Special Agent Thompson, may I help you?"

"I sure as hell hope so!" Joe bellowed, intentionally letting his frustration be known. His patience had run out. "I'm Joe McGowen, I live in Paradise, Minnesota, and I have information that I hope somebody out there is at least a little bit interested in."

"Calm down, Mr. McGowen. I believe I can help you. Please tell me what is on your mind."

Joe went through the entire story of his Miami trip and included how he thought it related to Paradise. Frequently Thompson stopped him and questioned a specific point, as if testing him to see if his story was true. He continued for nearly twenty minutes, and when he had finished, he waited anxiously for some kind of response or instruction. After a pause that lasted long enough to renew Joe's frustration, Special Agent Thompson again spoke.

"Mr. McGowen, let me start by telling you that the reason you were transferred to me is I am responsible for all narcotics investigations in the southeast region of the US. As you might imagine, we have numerous field agents in and around Miami specifically to monitor drug-related activity, especially the trafficking of any type of narcotic in or out of the area. Our network of information is very complete; virtually nothing of any significance could take place without us knowing about it either when it happened or shortly afterward. Unfortunately, we are not always able to prevent such things as what you have just related, but we are at least there to pick up the pieces. I feel I must be frank with you, Mr. McGowen. We have no knowledge whatsoever of the events which you have described, and I can assure you we would know. I also feel obligated to inform you that even though the entire country suffers from the sale of illegal drugs, the Minnesota area does not even approach the proportions to which you are alluding."

"What the hell does that all mean?" Joe demanded. "Are you suggesting that I'm lying to you?"

"I'm not suggesting anything. But for every call we get that is legitimate, we get twenty more that are frauds. Generally, we can tell if a story has a ring of truth to it, but in all honesty, what you have told me sounds far-fetched, to say the least. I'm not saying we won't check it out to some degree, but we're far too busy to make a serious investigation based on the information you have given me. Can you provide any kind of proof that what you say is true? Are there any other witnesses or anyone else in your town that will support you?"

Joe was furious, yet he knew how all of this must look to the FBI agent. "No," he replied emotionlessly, "I have nothing else to offer."

"Mr. McGowen, you must understand that if we launched a full-scale investigation every time someone called with a problem, the FBI would need ten times as many agents. We will go ahead and make a few inquiries, but unless you can provide us with some kind of proof or evidence that your story is true, I'm afraid there is nothing else we can do."

"Thanks," Joe said, maintaining his monotone voice. He knew further comments were futile, but his frustration would not allow him to let it go that easily. Not caring whether it seemed fair or not, he added, "I know this isn't going to faze you, but just for the record, I think you're a worthless bitch."

"I'm sorry, Mr. McGowen."

Joe hung up the phone and sat down. Sheri had not been able to hear all the details, but she heard enough to know that they could not expect any help. "What is wrong with them?" she asked Joe, becoming more frightened than angry.

Joe was beyond anger, beyond frustration. He sat staring straight ahead, a blank expression on his face. "I guess it does sound kind of preposterous, when you think about it."

Sheri sat next to him and leaned on his shoulder. Joe put his arm around her, loosely at first then a bit more firmly, then finally pulled her tight and held her with both arms. There was no need for words. They each knew what they were facing; they were completely alone amid a terrifying set of events that threatened their lives and their entire town, like a tiny island lying in the path of an oncoming hurricane, powerless against the mighty storm. But they had strength, a strength that neither of them could summon alone but one that swelled within them as a couple. They had felt it before during times of adversity, and never did they need it more than they did at this moment. But having this strength did not mean they were without fear.

Sheri buried her head in Joe's shoulder, not wanting him to see her tears that were beginning to fall. Joe continued to hold her, stroking her soft hair, thankful that she could not see the tears forming in his own eyes.

Special Agent Thompson leaned back in her chair and considered the phone call she had just received. Finally, she picked up the phone again and dialed a long-distance number.

"Hello, this is Thompson," she said to the person who answered. "I have some startling news. McGowen was the guy on the beach last night. He heard everything."

She paused while she listened to the other person's response.

"He told me so himself. He called looking for help. I don't believe he knows any of the specific details, but he certainly knows enough to make me nervous."

Pause.

"No, leave him alone for now. Far too much has happened up there already. The disappearance of any more people would be questioned by even an idiot. He doesn't have any proof or evidence whatsoever, so he can't create too much trouble. But it is very important to keep a close watch on him. If anything else goes wrong or even looks suspicious, we'll need to take him out immediately. Naturally, that would have to include his whole family."

Pause.

"This is really getting messy. We may have to pull the plug on the whole operation, but let's go with it for a little while longer. This is too important to not give it every possible chance."

Special Agent Thompson hung up the phone and again leaned back in her chair. Everything had been planned so carefully and thoroughly. How could things be falling apart like this? Who the hell was this Joe McGowen? He should never have gotten involved, but somehow he did, and now he had become a real threat. If he was smart, he would just let everything drop, but one way or the other, Special Agent Thompson knew that sooner or later, Joe McGowen would have to be dealt with.

Chapter 12

Elizabeth Wence poured herself a cup of coffee and sat down to her breakfast of toast and a half of grapefruit. She was still amazed by the news of Spencer Thurman leaving town. Sharon Carlson had called all the council members personally the previous night and suggested they have a meeting soon to discuss how they would handle this situation. Then Sharon made a public announcement over the local radio station to inform the rest of the town. Now two council members needed to be replaced, and the chairman slot was a full-time position that needed to be filled immediately. Sharon said she could handle the responsibilities for a while, but she would like a replacement within a couple of weeks.

It was nice of her to share her concern, Beth thought sarcastically. She had heard about the meeting that took place at Andy Hoffman's house a short time ago. She and the other council members who were not invited could not help but feel a bit resentful. Even if the meeting did not concern them directly, they would at least like to have been informed about it.

Beth was not by her nature a suspicious person, but things were happening that could not be ignored. Harry Rosten's suicide was a terrible tragedy but not necessarily anything overly strange. Even in Paradise, there were usually two or three suicides every year. But then came these questions about the package from Andy, although it was clear that they originated from Joe McGowen.

The Seduction of Paradise

She knew Joe very well and, in fact, had dated his younger brother, Ryan, for five years during high school and college. They had been very close, and two days after graduating from Augsburg College in Minneapolis, Ryan had asked her to marry him. She had refused, feeling she was not ready for marriage, even though deep inside she knew that she loved him. Shortly after that, Ryan was offered a basketball coaching job at a high school in California, an offer he could not refuse. They kept in contact for a while, but effectively, that was the end of their relationship.

One year later, Beth met Stephen Wence, then the editor of the *Paradise Union*. They fell in love, and this time, she would not take a chance by waiting. They were married six months after they met, and for the next few years, they were happy together. She began working at the *Union*, writing short human-interest stories, but later moved into covering sports for the local high school and junior college teams. She found sportswriting to be far more exciting and satisfying than she ever could have imagined. She was very happy, but she could not help but wonder from time to time what it would be like covering a game coached by Ryan McGowen.

Five years after they were married, Stephen was killed in an automobile accident on an icy road during a cold January storm. That was over three years ago, and she had adjusted well to being alone; too well, she sometimes thought. She literally never dated and rarely went out with friends. She took her work very seriously and spent most of her time at the *Union* office or at one game or another. She was now on the Paradise city council, and at age thirty-two, she was the youngest member.

Now, as she sat sipping her coffee, she was troubled by the way events were coming together—or not coming together would be more appropriate. The questions Joe asked, through Andy, she had found somewhat offensive, apparently suggesting some kind of cover-up. It was offensive, but it was also a little amusing, even the idea of a cover-up in Paradise.

But then Bob Williams disappeared. Sure, he had done that before, but only for a couple of days. Then the private meeting where some of the council members were excluded, but Ronald Capsner and Sherman Salinger were invited. It was explained why it happened that way, and it was even believable. But now, with Bob Williams found murdered and Spencer Thurman—a man whose life was dedicated to this town—suddenly leaving with no farewell to anyone, things just did not seem to fit.

The question Beth was struggling with was what to do about it. She could wait for the meeting Sharon was setting up and express her concerns, but for some reason, she did not feel comfortable doing that. Was she afraid? No, of course not, but—she was just not comfortable. She was aware that Joe McGowen had been proposed as Harry's interim replacement, and she hoped he would accept. She knew she could trust him. Perhaps she would discuss this situation with him. That would be good, she thought. At least it would be a starting point.

Also, so much of this seemed to revolve around Ronald Capsner and the New York Historical Society. The man acting as the historical interface with Capsner was Sherman Salinger. He may not know anything, but he is definitely close to the whole situation, so he may have some insight. She would talk to Sherman also. Yes, she decided, she would ask both Joe and Sherman over to her house to discuss all of this very soon.

The news of Spencer Thurman's sudden decision to move was disturbing to Andy Hoffman. He was not sure in his own mind if he would have felt this way had Joe not created so many suspicions. But whatever the source of his doubts, the fact of the matter was he could not accept what had happened without further explanation. Aside from the fact that it was not Spencer's nature to do something so drastic without even the slightest word to anyone, it also came during his visit to the historical society.

Andy had questioned Mayor Carlson about this situation, but either she honestly did not know anything or she was holding something back. He could not imagine any reason why she would, so he had to conclude that she was in the dark as much as he was.

Possibly Spencer's decision to move was related to his meeting with the society. Maybe they offered him a position which he found irresistible. But still, he would have come back and discussed it with the council, or at least with his friends. Unless, of course, he was forbidden. There was no apparent reason why this would be so, but the society did seem to like to keep things secret. Andy was not sure what was going on, but he strongly sensed that everything was somehow connected to Ronald Capsner and his organization. He started to realize how very little they knew of him. In fact, they knew virtually nothing. It was time to have a meeting between the council and Mr. Capsner.

Andy walked into his kitchen and took a bottle of Molsen out of the refrigerator. *I have to be careful*, he thought as he sipped his beer. *I really have no idea what is happening, and there is not even the slightest amount of evidence that a problem exists at all. To call a formal meeting and question Capsner may appear to be an interrogation of sorts. True, he is somewhat mysterious, but it might not be prudent to run the risk of offending him. After all, he is providing a tremendous service to Paradise.*

No, it might be more appropriate to pay him a visit alone, a quiet social visit where they could talk as friends rather than as business associates.

Sharon Carlson sat in her office, reading a copy of her release stating that Spencer Thurman had suddenly and unexpectedly left town. Things were happening at an awfully rapid rate, much too fast for a town the size of Paradise. She was not comfortable with the way things were developing, but she was not sure what her options were. She found herself not fully trusting Ronald Capsner. In hindsight, she believed that she probably never fully trusted him, but her suspicions had previously been held in her subconscious. Now she felt it was time to do something, to confront him directly, but how could she approach him? She was in charge here, but she sensed Capsner had powerful connections. She would need to be very careful. She wished she had an ally whom she could take into her confidence. In the past, she shared nearly all her concerns with Spencer, but with him gone, who else could she trust? But even without an ally, it was time to confront Capsner.

Chief Byron Winfield paced in circles around his desk, smoking one cigarette after another in anxious nervousness. He had not counted on the fact that Spencer Thurman would disappear so abruptly. He had been making plans, preparing strategies, developing different possible scenarios of how to proceed. Everything was different now with Spencer gone, but as much as that bothered him, he was not sure that things had changed for the worse. Maybe Spencer's departure presented him with a unique opportunity which he could use to his advantage. But then again, maybe it was worse. Maybe he lost the one element that tied everything together. Chief Winfield was just not sure, and he did not know what to do next. He needed time to think. He continued to pace and to smoke, oblivious to all other concerns and issues.

Sherman Salinger sat relaxed in the restored study of Brewster mansion, leaning back in the soft leather chair and resting his feet on top of the polished mahogany desk. He had been spending much more time at the mansion lately, preparing for the full-scale restoration effort, which was scheduled to begin soon. This was a very exciting time for him, something he had dreamed of for years. He had always been content with his position at the museum, but he knew he had so much more to offer than he could possibly contribute there. Working for the city of Paradise was far too limiting, far too confining. Funds were never available to do the things he felt were important, and the members of the city council, whom he honestly believed were well intentioned, rarely agreed with his plans of growth and expansion not only for the museum but also for his responsibilities as curator. To report to a group of people with virtually no experience in his line of work was somewhat degrading. He had suppressed such feelings for a long time, but now, with the new opportunities he had, he began to realize how much he needed a change, how important it was that he make the best of this new situation. He had been aggressive in trying to become part of this project, and it had paid off.

The situation with Spencer initially alarmed him. Spencer had been the mover and shaker of the project, and his departure could potentially have thrown a monkey wrench into the whole operation. But after evaluating things further, he recognized an even greater opportunity for himself. In typical fashion, Spencer had not been nearly as much of a mover and shaker as was needed, and things had gotten off to a very slow start. But now, Sherman could become the person responsible for the project. He could make things happen. He might even have a future beyond Paradise, if all went well. Yes, Spencer's departure was not a problem for him. In fact, it actually pleased him.

Capsner was another story. When this whole business started, it was his understanding that Capsner's role would be one more of appearance and image rather than one of responsibility. But lately, Capsner had become more forceful, to the point of being pushy. Sherman did not like that, and he resented Capsner for it. He no longer trusted Capsner's motives and was not comfortable working with him.

Capsner's new attitude even surfaced in issues such as this study, the first restored room of Brewster mansion. Sherman believed it should become the office of the curator, his office. Capsner considered it to be his, and in fact, he made a request to Mayor Carlson that it be made officially his until his business was complete here and he was ready to leave for good. Mayor Carlson had not yet made a decision since at this time the study was periodically used by officials in town. That had been part of an agreement with the business people in town prior to the initial restoration effort, before funds became available from the New York Historical Society.

Over the past year, the study had been used by a number of people but, by far, the most frequently by Police Chief Winfield. Winfield's own office had undergone renovations in the spring, and he was given nearly exclusive use of the Brewster study for several weeks. Although he could not easily conduct routine business here since it was at such a distance from police headquarters, it was an ideal place for small meetings where privacy and quietness were desired.

Once construction for the restoration was underway, it would not be feasible for anyone else to use this study or any of the facilities at the mansion, for that matter. Sherman was sure that at that time, Mayor Carlson would turn the office over exclusively to Capsner. Capsner was definitely getting in his way, yet he felt a bit intimidated about challenging him outright. Too much could be lost. He would carefully consider what alternatives he had before acting on any of them. For now, he would be patient.

Sherman heard the main door of the mansion open and close. He knew it must be Capsner. He quickly jumped out of the chair behind the desk and pretended to be dusting the woodwork.

The breeze blowing across the veranda was stronger than usual. A dark cloud bank could be seen coming in from over the ocean. The older man with the neatly trimmed hair and moustache stood on the edge of the veranda, facing into the wind, the characteristic cigar and white suit an ever-present part of his being.

"A storm is approaching, Antonio," he said calmly.

"Yes, Mr. Salvo," Antonio Rodriguez replied.

"Storms are good. They make things fresh. They make you appreciate the times when the weather is not so violent. Don't you agree, Antonio?"

"Yes, Mr. Salvo," Rodriguez replied, not bothering to decide whether he agreed or not. He knew the answer must be yes.

"Storms are good," Mr. Salvo said again. "But they can be dangerous. One must be sure he is prepared to deal with a storm. If he is, he will be protected until the storm passes, then he can carry on his business. If he is not, he can be destroyed by the storm."

"Mr. Salvo, I—"

"I am giving you a lesson about storms, Antonio. It is rude to interrupt." Salvo's tone was patronizing and degrading. "Tell me, Antonio, are we expecting a storm from our Paradise project?"

"No, sir. There was some trouble, but it is over."

"Look around you, Antonio. Do you know why all of this is mine and you are only a guest? Because I am smart. I understand people and situations. I see things, good opportunities as well as danger signals. I see storms, Antonio. I see one now. You, on the other hand, see nothing. You do what you are told, and that makes you valuable. When you stop doing what you are told, you are no longer valuable."

Rodriguez said nothing, but his anger began to show.

"So, I make you angry. Possibly you find me humiliating. But you see, it is you who makes me angry. Very angry, Antonio. Who stands to lose from your blunders. You? Ha! You lose nothing. But I lose millions. Many millions. I have networks all around the world. I have business dealing with virtually every nationality on this earth. True, you Jamaicans are my biggest source of revenue. You have done excellent work in the past, and I believe you have been well rewarded. But I made it clear that this time, the approach was to be different. You are not to think, Antonio, you are to do what I say. Bodies disappearing from Miami are a regular occurrence. Bodies disappearing from Paradise are not. You have been careless. You are losing control."

"Mr. Salvo, the Rosten man had to be killed. There was no choice."

"Agreed, and you did an excellent job. But what about the cop?"

"I didn't kill him. I think Capsner did."

"He assures me he did not."

"Believe him if you like, but I don't trust him. But I assure you, it was not I that killed Williams."

"And now our friend Thurman. A very unfortunate blunder not easily forgivable."

"He had it coming. He is the cause of many of our problems."

"Maybe. I thought Thurman would work out. Maybe I was wrong. But even so, what now? What will the people in Paradise think?"

"I have passed a story along to our contact—"

"Capsner?" Salvo questioned.

"No. As I said, I don't trust him. I mean our direct link to Paradise. Everyone's curiosity will be satisfied."

Salvo chuckled humorlessly. "Please, Antonio, try not to think. Let me do that. I tell you, some people's curiosity will not be satisfied. We must watch everyone closely from now on."

There was silence for a moment as Salvo considered all of the new developments. "What of the man on the beach?" he finally asked.

"He is of no concern. He was executed immediately."

"Another blunder, Antonio. Who was he? Why was he there? Who else knows what he knows? You found out nothing."

"He was firing at us. He killed one of my men. We had no choice."

"You are getting sloppy, Antonio, and I cannot tolerate that. One more mishap, and this operation will be terminated, and it will cost me more than you know. And I have never liked being the only one who suffers a loss. Do you understand me, Antonio?"

"Yes, Mr. Salvo. I'll take care of everything."

"What is to happen in Paradise?" Salvo continued to question. "How will suspicions be controlled? How will new contacts be developed?"

"Sir, I believe—"

"No, Antonio, I will tell you. No new contacts. We have already risked too much. You have Capsner, and you have one remaining contact from the town itself. When I planned this operation, I accounted for the fact that we may need more than one ally. Use these two, but no one else. As far as the unfortunate Mr. Thurman, he will not totally disappear. He will occasionally keep in contact through letters to the council. It will not be long before everyone forgets how abruptly he left."

"Yes, sir. As far as Capsner, he is smart, but I do not feel comfortable with him having so much responsibility."

"There is no more discussion of this matter. You have your orders. But there is one very important point left. What of the missing document?"

"We had thought that the man who found the package kept it, the McGowen man. But he has taken no obvious action which would indicate that that is true. I now believe Rosten has it hidden. We searched his house, but it could be anywhere. It is probably hidden well enough so no one will find it, making it as good as being destroyed."

"That may be true," Salvo said, "but it is the only loose end left. I will never feel comfortable until it is in our hands. Do what you can to find it."

"Yes, sir. I will continue our search."

"When we meet again, Antonio, I will expect to hear much better news."

"Of course, Mr. Salvo. You have my word that all will be well."

Drops began falling from the clouds as the wind increased in intensity. Salvo looked to the sky, unshaken by the rain. "Some storms are good, Antonio. Some are not. If the storm you have allowed to develop cannot be controlled, you will experience one of my storms. And, Antonio, my storms are never good."

Chapter 13

"There is one thing we must do," Sheri stated. "We must tell Fran about Harry. We cannot allow her to go on believing he committed suicide."

"I suppose you're right," Joe agreed. "But that means we must tell her everything. There is no way we can let her know about Harry without explaining how we found out. She will have to promise to remain quiet."

"Poor Harry," Sheri murmured, staring idly ahead. "Somehow he inadvertently got that damn package, and now he's dead. He was just an innocent victim."

"That package has sure caused its share of trouble," Joe said. "First Harry, then Bob, now Spencer."

"The police don't think that what happened to Bob was related at all to Harry or the package. They believe he probably came across a crime in progress and was killed trying to stop it. Either that, or a crazy man killed him just for the pleasure."

"I guess that would be logical to assume if you had no knowledge of everything going on, but we know better. Who knows, maybe the police know better too. I can't help but wonder about Chief Winfield. He seems to be taking all of this pretty lightly."

"When you think of it," Sheri said, "it's the package that is the source of all the trouble. That must mean the missing document would provide proof of what is happening around here."

"I believe you're right," Joe said thoughtfully. "If we could find it, we could take it to the FBI. They would believe us then. But apparently, people have been searching for it pretty diligently. Why should our luck be any better than theirs? Where would we even start to look?"

Sheri thought for a moment. "Well," she started, "we know it was given to Harry as part of the package."

"That's true," Joe said. "And it wasn't with the package when we found it. So that can only mean Harry hid it someplace. And as far as we know, Spencer and his cronies didn't find anything during their search. Sheri, I think we need to go to Fran's and search her house from top to bottom."

"That's already been done, and nothing was found."

"True, but before when it was searched, it had to be done without raising suspicion. The search probably wasn't thorough enough. I'm talking about checking everything: attic, garage, everything. Hell, even loose floorboards or under carpeting, if we can."

It was Saturday afternoon in late June. They knew Fran would be home. Maureen and Brandon had gone to a neighbor's house to play and were not going to be home until that evening. Joe picked up Katelin, and the three of them headed over to Fran's house.

Fran invited them in and started brewing a pot of coffee. After a few minutes of exchanging idle chitchat, she could tell Joe and Sheri were very anxious about something. "All right," she said. "What is going on? No beating around the bush here. What's on your minds?"

Sheri spoke first. "Fran, we have something very important to tell you, something that seems almost unbelievable. It's something you need to know, but we must have your word that you will not mention it to anyone else."

"Well, if you don't mind, I would prefer hearing this 'unbelievable' news before I give my word about anything."

"Fair enough," Joe said. "Let's sit down first."

Fran poured them a cup of coffee, and they all sat in the living room. Sheri and Joe took turns telling Fran the entire story. Her expressions continued to change from surprise to anger to concern to fear, but never was there a sign of disbelief. When they had finished, she sat quietly for several minutes, obviously considering the impact of all that she had heard. Finally, with a small tear beginning to form in her eyes, she stood and walked over to an end table with a picture of Harry on it. She picked it up and looked at it, gently fondling it with her fingers. There appeared to be a strange sense of peace in her eyes. No longer able to hold back the tears, a light trickle began to fall from each eye.

"So, my Harry did not commit suicide. You don't know what a relief that is." A small but obviously proud smile touched her lips as she added, "From what you say, my dear sweet Harry was even a bit of a hero."

"I believe that's right," Joe said. "He probably could have given in and been allowed to live. But he would not be intimidated. He would not be seduced like the others."

"You see, Joe," Sheri said, remembering their earlier conversation, "there still are people who do not have a price, people who will do what's right regardless of the cost."

"And I think there are three more such people in this room," Fran said.

They all looked at each other, afraid and lonely yet feeling a sense of pride and teamwork developing within themselves. They did not know what they could do, but they started believing they could make a difference.

"If we had only opened that package," Joe said. "We could have stopped this thing before it got started."

"But we didn't know," Sheri said. "We did what was right at the time."

"Poor Harry," Fran said. "I know why he hid the package."

"Of course," Sheri said. "He didn't want them to find it, whoever they are."

"Yes, but it was more than that. He didn't want me to find it so I wouldn't be in danger. Oh, Harry," she said, looking at the picture, tears now streaming down her face. "You protected me to the end." She began a light sobbing, but it was not due to sadness. There was an element of sadness, but it was more the result of relief and love; she thought she had lost Harry emotionally as well as physically, but she now had him back. All her fond memories of this proud and caring man were restored. She could now be at peace with her loss. But with the peace, there was a new sense of anger. Harry had been murdered, and those who were responsible were still out there.

"Joe, if it's the last thing we do, we must catch those dirty bastards."

"I agree, Fran, but we must be careful. We don't know who we can trust, so we cannot say anything to anybody. Do you understand?"

"Of course, but what can we do?"

"If we can find that missing document, we will be able to go back to the FBI. We think it must be here someplace."

"Let's have at it," Fran said. "If it's here, we will find it."

The three of them spent the next four hours searching everywhere. They looked through drawers, closets, under beds, behind furniture, even under a piece of linoleum that had come loose in the bathroom. Joe crawled through the entire attic and the rafters in the garage. Finally, they had to admit that the document was not in the house.

"I wonder why Harry hid it separately from the rest of the package," Fran said.

"Maybe he thought it needed special protection," Joe responded.

"I suppose it's not totally out of the question that Bob Williams could have taken it," Sheri remarked.

"Highly unlikely," Joe said. "If he had, I'm sure Rodriguez or one of his sweet friends would have gotten it back. It could be possible Harry hid it at his office, or even somewhere in city hall, or anywhere else, for that matter. It is even possible that he destroyed it."

"So what's the next step?" Fran asked. "I agree we can't be talking about this openly, but we can't let those bastards get away."

"I agree," Joe said. "But we must let things blow over for a while. In the meantime, we need to learn anything we can. I will notify Mayor Carlson that I'm accepting the temporary position on the council. That will at least keep me close to things."

"It could be dangerous, Joe," Sheri said.

"We have no choice. And we must remember that they are also most likely continuing their hunt for the document. They probably haven't given up on searching this house. It might be a good idea if you stayed with us for a while, Fran."

"I couldn't put you out like that. Besides, wouldn't it look suspicious?"

"I don't think so," Joe said. "Everyone knows we've been spending a lot of time together. We could just let it out that you're having trouble coping with Harry's suicide, and you need more constant help. I hate to make you look weak, Fran, but I think people would accept a story like that."

"Well, if you're sure you don't mind, I do think I would feel a little safer. And I don't mind telling you that it would be nice to have some company. It gets awfully lonely at night."

"We insist," Sheri said. "Actually, I think it will be fun. We can move your things over tonight."

The move did not take long. Fran only had to bring a few items of clothing and some personal bathroom supplies. Being right next door, it would be easy to come back for anything else she needed.

Maureen and Brandon were elated at the idea of Fran spending some time at their house. They had always considered her to be like a grandmother. Sheri's parents had both died a number of years ago, and Joe's had spent the last eighteen months in Ireland. When his father retired, they went to visit relatives there and fell so much in love with the country that they decided to stay indefinitely. Fran became a kind of surrogate grandma and was more than happy to accept the role, having no grandchildren of her own.

After a late and informal dinner of hamburgers, french fries, and baked beans, Katelin was put to bed, and Maureen and Brandon were given the exciting task of preparing the guest bedroom for Fran.

"I get to carry the pillows," Brandon called as he raced up the stairs to the linen closet.

"I get to put the sheets on," Maureen added, close at his heels.

Joe laughed and shook his head. "Look at them go. Why do you suppose they fuss and moan so much about making their own beds?"

"That's true for a lot of people other than kids," Sheri said with an accusing tone.

"What?" Joe objected, catching the implication. "I make our bed once in a while."

"You don't even know how to make a bed," Sheri said. "At least the kids try when they're told to."

"Oooo," Joe said quietly. "The old 'Joe doesn't ever do anything around here' syndrome. It strikes every five or six weeks."

"You see what I have to put up with?" Sheri asked Fran with a glint of humor in her eye.

"It is so nice to be around a family again," Fran replied. "You two better be careful. I may decide to stay permanently."

Joe smiled warmly at her. "You're welcome to stay as long as you like," he said. "And I mean that."

Fran's eyes began to glisten. "I know you do, Joe. And you can't imagine how good that makes me feel. But for now, let's just concentrate on our immediate problem. What is our first step?"

Joe thought for a moment, his right hand absentmindedly rubbing his chin. "I suppose the first thing to do is to call Sharon Carlson and formally accept the council position. I think I should also talk to Mr. Capsner fairly soon. I don't know exactly what to ask him, but I think I need to get to know him, feel him out a little. I can use the excuse that I want to thank him for supporting me as a council member."

"Joe," Sheri said gently, "if Capsner is wrapped up in all of this, he must be very dangerous. Do you really think it's safe to meet with him privately?"

Joe looked into her beautiful round eyes. The humor from moments ago was replaced with sadness, and maybe even a little fear. "I don't believe Capsner would do anything to me unless he felt seriously threatened. But I also think we need to make up our minds that we are in a very dangerous predicament. There is an element of risk, but we have no choice but to take that risk."

"I wish we had more people on our side," Sheri said quietly, as if thinking out loud. She sat down next to Joe on the sofa and laid her head on his shoulder. Joe put his arm around her and gave her a gentle but firm squeeze.

"I think it's important to remember that most of the people in this town probably are on our side. But until we know who is and who isn't, we can't discuss this with anyone. I'm sure that within time, we will be able to determine who our true friends are. But like we all agreed before, we must be patient."

"What about Andy?" Fran asked. "You don't really suspect him, do you?"

Joe looked at Sheri and squeezed her again. Then he slowly shook his head as words came out of his mouth that he wished were spoken by someone else. "I don't know. I want to trust him. I almost feel morally obligated to trust him. But he's resisted all this from the beginning. He's on the council, so he knows more than we do. And he met with Spencer and Capsner right before Spencer's trip to Florida. Can all that really be coincidence?"

"What you said before was right," Fran said. "We don't know who to trust yet. Andy's probably okay. Let's just be patient. We'll get these bastards. I look at you two, and I feel the strength you generate. We'll get them, there's no doubt in my mind."

Sheri smiled and winked at Fran, then gave Joe a quick kiss on the cheek. "What a team we are. Can we really take on these guys?"

Joe began to feel the inspiration from people close to him, people he shared a special bond with. He looked at Fran and saw the confidence in her eyes. He ruffled Sheri's hair as he let out a light chuckle. "You know what, Fran? I believe you're right. We will get these bastards."

Just then Brandon ran into the room. "Mrs. Rosten, come and see! Your room is ready!"

Fran smiled with genuine affection. "Thank you very much, young man. I think I will come and take a look."

An hour later, with Fran and the kids in bed, Sheri began her "get ready for bed" ritual as Joe sat watching the ten o'clock news in the family room, which was on the lower level of their split-entry house. The front door was on the ground level and opened into a fairly spacious entryway. From the entryway, a half flight of stairs went up to the living room, dining room, kitchen, bathroom and two bedrooms, and another half flight went down to the family room, laundry room, playroom, study, bathroom, and two additional bedrooms. A beautiful stone fireplace covered an entire wall of the family room, which served as the primary room for games, television or for entertaining friends. The lower level was only partially underground, which allowed for large windows in virtually every room.

Joe and Sheri had decided that while the children were young, it was more convenient to put their own bedroom in the lower level since the family room, laundry room, and study were there. That allowed them to be up at night working or entertaining friends without disturbing the kids. Katelin had been put in the extra room in the lower level next to their own, but there were plans to move her in with Maureen when she was a bit older. The study, being equipped with a sturdy sleeper sofa, also served as a guest bedroom, which, beginning tonight, would become Fran's room. There were two side doors entering into an attached garage: one through the dining room on the upper level and the other through the laundry room on the lower level. The floor of the garage was on ground level, halfway between the two doors. On the back wall of the dining room was a large sliding glass patio door opening out onto a fourteen-foot-square deck. It was a nice house. Some would even say it was better than nice, but it was certainly not anything overly special.

As Joe sat watching the news, his mind began to wander. *It's odd*, he thought, *that so much could be going on here in our little town that the rest of the world is completely unaware of.* He had been struggling for hours with ideas for some kind of plan of action, something they could do to at least get enough information to go back to the FBI. It was abundantly clear to him that they were no match for people like Rodriguez and his organization. Without help from the FBI or some other authority, they really did not have any kind of chance whatsoever. But what kind of evidence could they get, and how could they go about getting it?

He had called Mayor Carlson earlier that night to inform her he would accept the temporary position on the council. She had expressed her gratitude, saying that with Spencer gone, it was now more important than ever to fill this position with someone dedicated and competent. The appointment would not be official until the next meeting, but that would be merely a formality. The meeting was scheduled for the following Monday evening, and it was open to the public. She would look forward to seeing him there. Maybe, thought Joe, through his involvement with the council, there would be an opportunity to obtain the kind of evidence that they needed.

His thoughts turned to his good friend Andy. How he wished he could be sure about him. For the most part, he still trusted Andy, but there was too much at stake to not be cautious.

From the recesses of his mind, Joe suddenly became aware of the telephone ringing. He quickly snapped out of his almost-trancelike concentration and picked up the receiver. "Hello."

"Joe, how are you? This is Beth Wence."

"Beth, how are you doing? I haven't heard from you in a long while. What's up?"

"Oh, nothing much. I guess I was curious about your decision to fill Harry's spot on the council. Have you made up your mind yet?"

"Before I answer, can I ask which way you are hoping I go with this? I suppose you don't want me any part of the council."

Beth laughed, knowing that he was joking. "Same old Joe, never a serious answer to any question. You know we would all love to have you."

Joe realized she was sincere, so he took on a more serious air himself. "I really appreciate that, Beth. As a matter of fact, I talked to Sharon just this evening. I told her I would accept."

"That's wonderful, Joe. We need people like you."

Joe thought he detected something odd in her voice. Was it a sense of alarm or concern? He could not be sure. "Is anything else on your mind, Beth? You sound a little worried."

"Oh, you know me, Joe. I get upset over the littlest things. There has been so much going on I guess I get a bit flustered. If you don't mind, I have a small favor to ask."

"Sure, ask away."

"With all the events recently, I just feel a need to talk with someone, an old friend that I feel comfortable with. Would you have time to come over for an hour or so tomorrow night, around seven o'clock?"

"I wouldn't mind at all, Beth. I've been a little disturbed myself lately. I think you're right, it would be good to talk to an old friend."

"That's great, Joe. It will help me out a lot. By the way, I've also asked Sherman Salinger to stop by, if that's okay with you."

"Of course. It's your house. I'll see you tomorrow at seven."

Joe hung up the phone, contemplating what he had just heard. This was not the same Beth Wence that he knew from before, when she had been so close to Ryan.

"Who was on the phone?" Sheri asked as she walked into the room, wearing her bathrobe over her nightgown.

"Beth Wence. She wants me to stop over tomorrow night to talk. She's feeling a little upset over all that has occurred and wants to talk to an old friend."

"If this has her upset, it's a good thing she doesn't know what's really going on," Sheri remarked. "What time does she want us?"

Joe sat looking straight ahead, slowly rubbing his chin with his right hand. "She only invited me," he said.

"Only you! That doesn't seem right," Sheri complained. "I don't know if I like the idea of another woman inviting my husband over without me." She smiled as she said it, but her eyes did not contain any humor.

Joe continued to sit and stare, rubbing his chin in deep concentration. Finally he spoke. "Something is troubling me. Beth said she was really flustered over all the recent events. I suppose that is possible, but Beth has always been a very strong woman. And like you said, she doesn't know half of what is really happening."

"I suppose living alone for a few years could change a person," Sheri considered. "She may still be strong, but everyone needs someone to talk to once in a while."

"That may be true, but then why not invite us both over?"

"Well, I must admit that I feel slightly offended, but you have known her much longer than I have. Maybe it's just due to nostalgia."

"Maybe," Joe said. "But she also invited Sherman Salinger. I don't think she knows him well at all, at least not on a personal level. I imagine they work together on city business issues. But would her nostalgia cause her to invite him too?"

Sheri watched Joe and could see his mind working. She knew he suspected something and was trying to sort the different pieces of the puzzle out in his head. "What is it, Joe? Keep me in the loop here."

"Beth and I haven't talked seriously for a long time, and she hasn't called me in years. Suddenly she calls and invites me over. She is more than just flustered. She must be deeply concerned about something. It just happens that she is also on the city council. Besides me, she invites only one other person, who just happens to be the town's contact with Capsner's historical society. Doesn't that suggest anything to you?"

"You think maybe she knows something," Sheri stated more than asked, feeling that tingle of excitement that so closely resembles fear.

"She either knows something or is at least becoming suspicious."

"There is one other possibility," Sheri whispered. "Maybe she knows everything. Maybe she's part of it. Maybe she is setting you up, Joe."

"I don't believe this is any kind of setup. It would be so easy to get to me almost anytime. She wouldn't have to bring me to her home. But she might be trying to feel me out, to see how much I know. Maybe they're starting to suspect me. I think I had better initially play dumb, make her show her hand first."

"I don't think you should go at all, Joe."

"I have to, Sheri. This could be the break we've been looking for. This could be the first step in getting some evidence for the FBI. I have no choice."

Chapter 14

The sun was still bright on this late June evening as Joe arrived at Elizabeth Wence's house promptly at seven o'clock. From the car in the driveway, he assumed Sherman was already there. It was a hot and muggy day, the kind that drained all energy and ambition out of a person. In general, Joe had come to like the four seasons of Minnesota, but since his return from California, he found that the hot and humid days of summer were his least favorite, especially once the mosquitoes came out in full force. With its more than ten thousand lakes, Minnesota was a natural breeding ground for those irritating, ghoulish little pests.

Joe parked in the street and walked up the double driveway to the elegant large brick house. Beth's husband had done very well for himself, and between the two of them, they managed to afford this impressive home that some would consider a mansion. After her husband died, her first reaction was to get rid of it, but a few weeks later, she decided that this was her home and she was not about to leave. With the insurance money she received, there was no problem with being able to afford it. Her husband had planned well.

It was obvious even before entering the house that it kept Beth busy; the grass and all of the shrubbery were neatly trimmed, and the concrete driveway was swept cleaner than most people's kitchen floors. It was truly an impressive house but somehow lacking in character. No flowers, no toys in the yard, no birdbaths or bird feeders. Essentially, there was no sign of a lived-in appearance at all.

Joe could not help but feel sorry for Beth. It seemed like such a short time ago that he thought she would become his sister-in-law. Now, he rarely saw her, and he was not sure if he really knew her anymore. He hoped fervently that she was not caught up in this mess with Rodriguez and the drugs.

Beth answered the door with a smile and gave Joe a quick little hug. She was wearing a snug pair of blue jeans and a bright-red tank top. Her looks had always been simple and plain yet attractive. "Glad you could make it, Joe. Sherman arrived just a few minutes ago. Come on in."

Joe stepped into the large entryway and followed Beth through a door to his left into a spacious, luxurious living room with a high vaulted ceiling. The wall at the front of the house contained a beautiful arrangement of bay windows extending from nearly floor to ceiling, providing a splendid view of the yard and most of the neighborhood. Sitting in a plush chair on the far side of the windows was the quiet figure of Sherman Salinger. Joe seated himself in a matching chair opposite Sherman, on the near side of the windows.

"Can I get you a drink?" Beth asked. "Some wine or a beer, maybe?"

"No thanks, I'm fine," Joe answered. He noticed Sherman was not drinking anything either. "How are you doing, Sherman? I haven't seen you for a while."

"I am doing very well, Joe. Awfully busy, though, with the Brewster project, you know."

"I'm sure you are. I can't wait until it's done."

Beth sat on a sofa across the large room from the two men. She was clearly feeling uneasy then finally got up, darted into the next room, and returned with a wooden chair from her dining set. She placed the chair closer to the men, forming a triangle with Joe and Sherman. "No sense having to shout at each other," she said with a chuckle. "Someday I'll probably get rid of this big old house and get something more suited for a single person."

"It's a mighty fine house," Joe commented quietly, knowing that her attachment to it was more emotional than anything else.

"It certainly is," Sherman agreed.

There was an obvious tension in the air as Joe and Sherman waited to discover why they had been summoned.

"I suppose you guys think this is a bit odd that I've asked you here tonight," Beth began. "I don't quite know how to put into words what I've been feeling, but…" She paused for a moment, thinking.

"I think I understand," Joe said soothingly. "Some big changes have occurred recently, first with Harry dying, and now Spencer leaving. It can be alarming. And with you living alone—"

"Oh, that's bullshit, Joe!" Beth cut in sharply. "Don't be so damned patronizing. I haven't been a little girl for a long time."

It was enough to finally break the ice, at least between Joe and Beth. Looking at her, Joe now saw the strong and feisty woman who had won his brother's heart. Suddenly, they both burst into spontaneous laughter. Sherman smiled uneasily, sensing that something had been communicated but having no idea as to what it was.

"Sorry, Sherman," Beth said, regaining control of herself. "It's been a long day."

"That's quite all right, Beth. I take no offense."

"Let me jump right to the point," Beth continued. "Something is very wrong around here. I don't know why no one else has noticed it, but it seems obvious to me. Every town has its share of strange occurrences, but I just cannot buy some of the explanations I've heard for what has happened."

"What specifically are you referring to?" Sherman asked.

"First of all, I knew Harry Rosten very well. We all did. Joe, you probably knew him best of all. I just cannot accept the fact that he committed suicide."

Joe was becoming very intrigued. Being here with Beth brought back old feelings. He felt he should trust her. Deep inside, he desperately wanted to trust her, and it was so refreshing to hear someone else have the same suspicions and concerns he had. From what she was saying, it seemed as if he had found an ally. It was difficult to keep himself from agreeing with her, from opening up and telling her what he knew. But then he remembered the beach and Spencer's bullet-ridden body. He must be careful and remain on his guard until he was absolutely sure this was not just a clever ploy to get him to divulge his information.

"Beth, everybody is always surprised after a suicide," Joe said. "No one believes someone they know could do such a thing."

"I'm sorry, Joe, but I don't buy that. Not with Harry."

Joe looked over at Sherman. Sherman was visibly bothered by what he was hearing. Did he have suspicions too? Did he know something more? Or could it be possible that he was involved and Beth was getting close enough to the truth to make him feel uncomfortable?

"Beyond that," Beth went on, "Spencer's departure was so out of character. In fact, that's what bothers me about both incidents. Not so much that they happened, but both were so very much out of character. And what about Bob Williams? His murder in itself wouldn't be overly suspicious, except for the timing of it. It happened right after Harry's death, and not too long before Spencer's departure."

"What are you leading up to, Beth?" Sherman asked nervously.

"I'm not leading up to anything. I'm only pointing out that something is wrong, and I don't feel good about what's happening."

"So why tell this to us?" Joe asked.

Beth suddenly became very somber. "I initially intended to go to the police, but I was afraid I would sound like a lunatic. Then I started thinking that this could possibly be dangerous." She looked straight into Joe's eyes. "You may think I'm being paranoid, but I'm afraid to say anything publicly. I don't know who I can trust."

Joe was amazed, almost to the point of being stunned. With only a fraction of the information that he had, she was able to comprehend at least the concept that something very serious was taking place, even the idea that there may be some kind of conspiracy in town. Maybe she knew too much. Maybe she had pieced the puzzle together too easily. This may have been some kind of a test, but Joe did not think so. Beth's eyes were filled with such passion, her face so sincere. If this was an act, trying to lure Joe or Sherman into her confidence, it was very convincing. But Joe continued to act ignorant.

"You can trust me," he said, then reached over and lightly squeezed her hand.

"Me also, certainly," Sherman added.

"I know that," Beth said quietly, beginning to calm down again. "That's why I asked you here, that and the fact that you each are involved with this in some way."

"How so?" Joe asked.

"You, Joe, because you have been questioning things for a while now, even before Spencer left. Andy brought up a number of your concerns with the council. He even had a special meeting at his place. I wasn't invited, of course, but I heard about it." The sarcasm in her voice was obvious. "I believe you were there, Sherman."

"Yes, I was asked to attend. It was really quite uneventful."

"Nevertheless, it happened. I can't help but think that you have doubts or suspicions yourself, Joe."

Here it was, the pressure point. Up until now, it had only been Beth talking and Joe and Sherman adding comments or opinions. But this was a direct question, attempting to get him to commit. How bad he wanted to level with her, but the risk was too great. He still felt it was too early to acknowledge what he knew, but on the chance she was telling the truth, he did not want to discourage her. They may need each other soon, and possibly Sherman too.

"My concerns were purely related to protecting Fran Rosten. Beyond that, I had not thought anything seemed odd or out of place. But you make a pretty convincing argument that something is. Maybe we should dig into this a little bit."

"What about me?" Sherman asked somewhat tentatively.

"There is one other strange coincidence," Beth responded. "All of this happened in the same time frame that the New York Historical Society has been involved here. Spencer was the main contact to the society, but you are the interface with Capsner directly. Spencer's last official duty was a trip to visit the members of the society. Sherman, is there anything you know that could shed some light on this?"

Sherman quietly cleared his throat to begin to speak. "Well, first of all, let me say that I believe our imaginations are getting just a bit carried away. However, that is not to say I have not suspected that problems exist. I have had a great deal of trouble working with Mr. Capsner lately. He seems to be completely taking over. He is much more arrogant than was originally apparent. I am currently attempting to pick up some of Spencer's responsibilities with regards to the Brewster project, but Capsner seems to want to run the show himself. I was going to talk to Mayor Carlson about this soon. But as far as any illegal or dangerous activity, I certainly have not been aware of such things and have no reason to suspect anything. It has always struck me as odd, though, that…well…oh, it's nothing."

"What!" Beth almost screamed.

"It really is nothing, but I have always been puzzled by the fact that we could never contact the New York Historical Society directly. I understand the reasons Mr. Capsner explained about wanting anonymity, but those of us involved knew about the society. Why could we not then discuss business matters with them?"

"You have a very good point," Joe commented. "I suppose that's why they finally did allow at least one person to contact them." He was intentionally trying to make a connection between Spencer and the bogus historical society. From the comment that followed, it was apparent that his tactic had worked.

"That one person was Spencer, and now he's gone," Beth said. She sat quietly for a moment, thinking. Then finally she let out a deep sigh and said, "What do you say, should we take this to the authorities?"

Joe froze for a moment. One of two situations was developing. It was still possible that this was a trap or some kind of test to see how he or Sherman would respond. He was reasonably confident that Beth was being truthful, but there was still a small element of doubt. At this point, being too eager to go to the police may imply he knew more than he was letting on. On the other hand, if Beth was telling the truth, she had no idea of the real danger involved. Going to the police, or even to Mayor Carlson, could potentially be suicide. In either case, going to the authorities was a mistake.

"As you said up front, Beth, based on the lack of any real evidence, we would look like lunatics. Let's just be patient and see how things develop."

"I agree with Joe," Sherman added. "There is no need to jump the gun on this. I agree a few peculiar incidents have occurred, but I cannot believe we are in danger. Let's do as Joe suggests and be patient."

"All right," Beth agreed, somewhat grudgingly. "We will wait for now. But I would like to discuss this again soon to see if anything new has developed. Let's all keep our eyes and ears open. In the meantime, is it too much to ask to keep this quiet?"

"Not at all," Joe assured her.

"Of course not," Sherman agreed. "I must say, I believe I am beginning find all of this kind of exciting. We historians do not get too much action, you know."

Joe and Beth both laughed heartily. It was a good laugh, one that neither of them experienced in awhile. They all stood up, and Beth walked them to the door to say good-bye. Sherman thanked her quickly and properly and left. Joe stopped for a moment and lightly grabbed her hand.

"It was wonderful to see you again, Beth," he said softly.

"You too, Joe. By the way, how is Ryan?"

"He's fine, as always. Still coaching, still looking for that first championship season."

"He'll get it someday, I'm sure of that. And I'd be willing to bet it won't take him too long."

"Thanks again, Beth," Joe said. He gave her a small peck on the cheek and walked out the door. He could not believe she would be involved in anything like drug trafficking or murder. He had promised himself he would not reveal what he knew, and he stayed true to that promise, but he was sure that the next time they met, he would tell her everything. And Sherman too, most likely. Slowly but surely, a team was beginning to evolve. Hopefully, Andy would be on this team soon. Joe had more hope now than ever before that everything would work out.

Walking down the driveway, he was completely unaware of the small black automobile parked a short distance away around the corner. He stepped into his own car, started the engine, and drove off toward his home, oblivious to the small black vehicle that was now cruising at his same speed a safe distance behind him.

<hr>

The following week, Joe attended his first official city council meeting. It was a public meeting, but as was typical, only a handful of residents sat in. The mood was unusually somber, obviously a result of Spencer Thurman's absence. As people began taking their places, there was very little of the customary chitchat that preceded normal meetings. It was almost too somber, as if people were aware that the situation was far more serious than anyone publicly acknowledged. Of course, there were people at the meeting who knew just how serious it was. Capsner, for one, and probably at least one member of the council, if not a number of them.

Ronald Capsner and Sherman Salinger, now regular attendees of council meetings, were seated in the front row of the public section. Chief Winfield also sat in the front row but across the center aisle from Capsner. Chief Winfield typically did not attend these meetings, but Mayor Carlson had requested that he be present for at least the next three or four months. She had not given him a specific reason as to why, only that it might be a good idea to have the police force properly represented.

The meeting started off with Mayor Carlson's announcement that she had formally appointed Joseph McGowen as the temporary replacement for Harry Rosten. She herself would be taking Spencer Thurman's responsibilities for the time being. His position as council chairman was more difficult to fill, and she did not intend to rush into any decisions.

The agenda was fairly routine, and Joe actually found himself becoming quite bored. He remembered now one of his primary reasons why he avoided this kind of involvement: it took a lot of time to accomplish very little. Finally, Mayor Carlson officially closed the meeting but quickly added that she would like the council members—along with Chief Winfield, Ronald Capsner, and Sherman Salinger—to remain for a few moments. Within minutes, the city chamber was deserted except for this select group.

Mayor Carlson was brief and to the point. "There are two brief points I wish to make," she began. "First, Mr. Capsner will be leaving Thursday for New York to meet with his colleagues at the historical society. If anyone needs to get ahold of him, he will be back on Saturday."

For a brief moment, Joe considered the idea of another spy trip, this time following Capsner, but the next announcement jolted him out of any other thoughts.

"Secondly, I thought you might be interested in a letter I received today. Actually, it was addressed to the Paradise city council, so it's really your letter as much as it is mine. It's from our good friend Spencer Thurman."

Joe could feel his face flush. How could this be? This was obviously some kind of scam to quiet people's concerns about Spencer's sudden departure. He glanced about quickly to check the reactions of the others. Was it only his perception, or was everyone a bit uncomfortable? Maybe Beth was not the only one who was suspicious.

Mayor Carlson continued, "It's only a couple of paragraphs, so let me just read it to you."

> Dear Sharon and friends,
>
> First let me apologize for the way in which I left you so suddenly. I know it must have been a tremendous shock to most of you, but I really felt that I had no choice. Actually, it was not a sudden move at all; I had been planning a new venture for the past couple of months, but until I was sure that things would work out, I thought it best to keep it a secret. Without going into elaborate detail, let me just say that I have accepted a position as vice president of a small consulting firm near New York City that I felt I could not refuse.
>
> I realize that the way this was handled may appear somewhat deceitful, but I assure you that is not the case. On my last trip to New York, I received the formal offer of employment, but due to a sudden personnel problem at the firm, I was requested to start immediately. In retrospect, I feel somewhat embarrassed by the way everything developed, but in the long run, I'm sure it will not inconvenience any of you too terribly much. I do wish to say that I have thoroughly enjoyed working with all

of you, and I will always be proud to say that I am from Paradise, Minnesota. I will hopefully have time to come back and visit soon.

Your friend,
Spencer Thurman

"Well, that explains a few things," Mayor Carlson concluded. "Any comments?"

There was a strange silence that filled the room. Joe again glanced from person to person around the room, checking for any suggestive reactions. Someone, at least one person, knew this was a lie. For sure Capsner knew, but there must be someone else. The "contact" he had heard mentioned when he was on the beach in Florida. It was almost certain that whoever this person was, he or she, or possibly they, were present in this group of city officials. Would their expression give them away?

First he turned his eyes to Beth Wence. She already had her gaze fixed on him, staring at him firmly, confidently, as if telling him she did not believe a word of this. Next he turned to Sherman, who, in typical fashion, kept his head down, not wishing to make eye contact with anyone. Sherman sensed Joe's stare and briefly looked up then gave an almost undetectable shrug, letting Joe know that he did not know what to make of this letter.

Joe quickly turned to Mayor Carlson. She was oblivious to his eyes, her own eyes directed toward Chief Winfield. Winfield was returning her stare but with more of a quizzical look, as if trying to interpret the silent message the mayor was sending him. Leonard Malekowski and Kathleen Bently each were fairly expressionless, as if nothing of any consequence had occurred. They either believed the letter totally or were well-enough prepared to conceal any telltale expressions. Joe was almost afraid to check the last council member, but he finally turned to Andy Hoffman. Andy kept his head down, but his face was flushed, and he was obviously quite disturbed. Was it a result of concern or confusion, or could it be a sense of guilt? Joe sensed an unseen stare and looked over to see Beth Wence watching him, then turn her eyes to Andy, then back to him. What was she implying? Did she suspect Andy?

Finally, Joe turned his eyes to Capsner. He must know about Spencer. From the things that were said on the beach, it was unimaginable that he did not know. Capsner returned his stare firmly and coldly, as if he were sizing up Joe at the same time that Joe was analyzing him. Joe's eyes darted away quickly, and he immediately cursed himself for allowing himself to be intimidated by this evil man.

The tension in the room was thick, so thick it was nearly suffocating. It was not obvious to Joe that anyone knew anything for sure, but it was certainly clear that the letter made an impact on the entire group.

Sharon Carlson finally broke the uncomfortable silence. "Well, I certainly did not intend to put you all in a trance. I think it was good of Spencer to write, even if he did leave us in a bit of a lurch. He is still our friend."

A thought suddenly struck Joe. "Did he leave a return address?" he asked the mayor.

"No, unfortunately he did not. I'm sure he will write again when he is more settled and let us know how to get ahold of him."

The group again became silent.

"If there is nothing else, we all may as well go home," Mayor Carlson said.

No one hesitated as they all said their good-byes and left the chambers. On the way out the door, Joe noticed that Andy was still looking upset.

"Hey, are you okay?" Joe asked quietly.

Andy paused for a moment and looked at Joe, but his mind was miles away. "Yeah, sure, I'm all right," he mumbled. "I don't have time to talk, Joe. I'll see you later." He rushed up the steps and out the door.

Joe felt that he should do something to help his friend, maybe just sit down and talk about things over a beer, but now was obviously not a good time. He decided to call Andy in a day or two to see if he felt like talking. It seemed like ages since they were last together on his deck for a barbecue.

Joe was the last person to leave city hall. The parking lot was nearly deserted when he stepped out into the night air. It was warm, but not nearly as muggy as the previous week. Only two vehicles besides his own remained in the lot, and two silhouetted figures stood next to his Oldsmobile Firenza. For a quick instant, fear jolted through his body like a lightning bolt. His palms turned moist as he slowly approached his car, mentally preparing himself to either fight or flee, whatever seemed the more sensible response. He felt a wave of relief when he finally recognized the figures.

"What did you think of that letter?" Beth Wence snapped.

"Well, good evening to you too," Joe said a bit sarcastically. "Thanks for nearly scaring the hell out of me."

"Let's cut through the crap, Joe. That letter was a lot of bullshit. Sherman thinks so too."

Sherman looked slightly embarrassed. "Now, wait a minute, Beth. I simply said I had a difficult time understanding why Spencer would have handled the situation like that. Why not just call, and why wait for so long?"

"That's just your way of saying it's bullshit," Beth shot back.

Joe smiled at Sherman, letting him know he understood that the strong-willed Beth was putting some unwanted words in his mouth. He was convinced now more than ever that Beth was on his side, and probably Sherman too, although the feeling was not quite so strong with him. He could not see Sherman as being crooked, but he also did not believe he could be relied upon to be strong and supportive of their efforts to stop this madness in their peaceful town. He decided he would confront Beth, but not here, not in front of Sherman. He needed allies he could count on.

"What is it that you think we should do?" Joe asked Beth.

"First, we should talk to Andy. Did you see his face? Something was really bothering him. You would be the best one for that, Joe, since you two are such close friends."

"I've already decided to do that," Joe replied. "But I thought he needed some time to cool off. He did look pretty upset."

"That's fine," Beth said. "But more importantly, we need to get ahold of Spencer and find out what the hell is going on. I don't care if he didn't leave an address, he can't be that hard to find."

Joe suddenly became concerned that Beth would do something to get herself into real trouble since she had no idea of the magnitude of what was happening.

"Beth, just settle down. I'll tell you what, why not stop over at my place and relax for a few minutes. Sheri would like to see you again, anyway."

"I can't. I have a deadline tomorrow on a story I'm writing for the *Union*. I haven't even gotten started on it yet."

Sherman had wandered a few steps away, appearing somewhat bored with the whole situation. It was clear he was only here as a result of Beth's prodding. Joe grabbed Beth's shoulders, and looking her squarely in the eyes, he whispered in a barely audible voice, "There is something extremely important that I must tell you. You must not do anything about all of this until we talk."

Beth realized Joe was not willing to say any more until they were alone. "When?" she whispered.

Joe did not want to delay any longer than necessary, but he would be out of town for the next couple of days on a business trip, and he also wanted a chance to talk to Andy alone first. "Saturday morning," he answered.

"I'll be there," Beth said.

"I really see no need to be out here like this," Sherman suddenly cut in. "Could we possibly go somewhere and sit down if there is more to be discussed?"

"No, let's just go home," Beth replied. "It's getting late." She reached out and squeezed Joe's hand, then turned and walked off toward her car.

Chapter 15

The phone continued to ring with no answer. Unable to control his frustration, Andy slammed the receiver back into its cradle. He had decided that he should speak with Ronald Capsner before he left for New York, and he spent the better part of the day trying to get hold of him. He was becoming more and more disturbed with the development of events, and the letter from Spencer did nothing to pacify him. He could not put his finger on it, but it just seemed very wrong. He had known Spencer for years, and somehow, he could not picture him writing that letter. He thought he should talk to Joe again, but he did not want to encourage his overactive imagination. First, he would talk to Capsner. Then, regardless of the outcome, he would talk to Joe.

Earlier that day, Andy had tried from work to reach Capsner at the office of the Brewster mansion, but either no one was around or no one was answering the phone. Next he tried city hall, where he was informed that Capsner should be at the mansion. He waited for a couple of hours and tried the mansion again, still with no answer. After returning home from work, he tried Capsner's home phone but was met with a recording saying Capsner was not available. Finally, Andy had tried the mansion one last time but still was unable to make a connection.

He checked the clock on the living room wall. Eight o'clock. Where the hell could Capsner be? Andy remembered him saying that there was a lot to be done during the next few days and that he would probably be working late all week. It was possible that Capsner was so busy he was not answering the phone. The mansion was only about a ten-minute drive from his house, so Andy decided maybe it would be best if he took his chances and drove over. If Capsner was there, he would be easy to find.

Andy pulled into the long horseshoe driveway at eight fifteen. Capsner's car was parked in front of the mansion, but there was no sign of Capsner himself, or of any activity. Andy stepped out of his car and walked up to the large double doors of the front entrance. The sun was just over the tops of the trees, providing plenty of light but beginning to cast long shadows. It would be dark within an hour.

He turned the knob on the door, but it was locked. Capsner had to be inside, so Andy rapped firmly on the door and waited for a response. Nothing. As his frustration grew into anger, he raised his powerful arm and pounded on the door with his fist, sending booming echoes throughout the grounds of the estate. The echoes faded, and the silence returned. The mansion appeared deserted.

Andy decided to look in back to see if a light was on in the office. It was dark enough so that a light would be needed inside if work was to be done. He was bound and determined not to let Capsner ignore him. He walked around the right side, remembering from Joe that the left side was nearly impassable due to the steep embankment. Andy, like Joe, had never been around back of the main building. His anger began blending with curiosity, and even a little excitement, as he rounded the corner and strolled into the backyard.

As was typical with such architecture as this, the back side was very simple in design as compared to the front since it was not intended to be seen by guests. It struck Andy almost immediately how private and isolated it was here. A short distance off was the edge of the wooded area, and the house itself totally cut off any view of the highway. It was as if he had left civilization altogether.

Andy was relieved to see that the light in the office was indeed on, but the drapes were pulled to prevent him from seeing inside. Since Capsner had not answered the door, either he was not accepting visitors or he was not in the office. But where else could he be? Andy began feeling a deep resentment toward Capsner and his arrogant manner.

He's probably sitting inside refusing to see anyone, he thought. Part of him wanted to run up and pound on the window, but that was probably not the way a member of the city council should behave with an "important" guest, even an arrogant ass like Capsner. Andy resigned himself to the fact that he would not meet with Capsner tonight, but his fascination with the mansion would not let him depart without a more detailed scrutiny.

He walked over near the edge of the trees to take in the full perspective of the mansion and the grounds, at least what was visible from the back side. The shadows were rapidly growing in length as the sun continued to fall below the horizon. Near the trees there was almost no light remaining at all, making it difficult to see even a few yards into the woods.

Andy suddenly became aware of a very faint sound somewhere in the distance behind him, coming from deep within the woods. At first he thought he had imagined it, but then there it was again. He stood perfectly still, attempting to identify both the location and the source of the sound. He heard it distinctly now, and it sounded familiar. As he listened, he became more and more confident of the source. It was a very faint whirring sound, and he was certain that it was from some sort of distant machinery or heavy equipment. But deep in the woods? It did not seem possible.

Andy's curiosity got the better of him, and he briskly moved along the edge of the trees, looking for some convenient entrance into the forest. In the fading twilight, he observed what appeared to be a dark spot along the tree line. He knew from experience that this was undoubtedly an opening, which he quickly confirmed to be true. A closer inspection revealed that this opening was actually the entrance to a narrow path. It was difficult to tell in the limited light, but it appeared that the path had seen some recent and probably frequent use. There was very little overgrowth, and touching the ground, he felt mainly dirt. He knew that in a wooded area like this, weeds would quickly overtake a clearing if not in constant use.

This was a strange set of circumstances. A frequently used path leading into an area where he thought nothing but forest existed, originating from behind the mansion where few people had access, and the sound of heavy equipment at night. What was going on? Could Capsner be out there somewhere? The adventure was too exciting to resist. Andy began moving slowly down the path into the woods and into the darkness.

He had only gone a few steps before he realized that traversing the path in the dark would be a difficult task. It was well worn, but it was very narrow, causing him to be cautious of each step. A number of times, he stumbled over a root or a large rock that did not wear evenly with the rest of the path, but as he mentally adjusted to the terrain and his eyes became acclimated to the darkness, he was able to move with a bit more ease. He could feel himself gradually descending as he proceeded, most likely moving closer to the river. The dense trees obliterated nearly all of the light from above, now predominantly from the stars and a crescent moon. He could tell the wind had picked up considerably by the swishing sound of the leaves atop the large elms, oaks, and maples, but he was so sheltered by their canopy that he was not able to feel even the slightest breeze.

The path seemed to wind on forever. Andy considered turning back after about fifteen minutes, but the whirring sound of the equipment had become increasingly louder, and by now, his curiosity was too much to control. He began to feel that distinctive tingle in the pit of his stomach brought on by adventure and excitement; at least he consciously told himself that that was the source. He did not allow himself the possibility that there may also be an element of fear, like a father who boldly walks into a dark room without turning on the light to prove to his little boy that there is no reason to be afraid, yet his heart rate quickens and his palms become moist, and he stays in the room no longer than necessary to prove his point. Andy, like so many young men who value strength and courage, forgot that fear was a reaction of the mind, which provided a warning to the body of imminent danger. To ignore the fear was to ignore the danger and, thereby, making it more threatening.

He continued along the meandering path, surprised at how far he was going. He could now hear the trickle of the Whiskey River as it splashed over rocks along the shoreline. It was difficult to guess how far he had walked, but he mentally estimated that he had gone about three quarters of a mile. How that equated to a straight line distance from the mansion to his present position was almost impossible to tell, but he had to think it was at least half a mile. Where could this be leading him? It was as if he were in some new place completely foreign to him rather than in the town he grew up in.

Suddenly, it struck him from out of nowhere. Of course! He was headed for the old wastewater treatment center. Years ago, Paradise had built its own plant for sewage treatment, located at the junction of the Whiskey and Mississippi Rivers. As the town grew, and as neighboring communities developed, the facility was not capable of handling the amount of sewage being generated, so Paradise and the other communities changed over to a larger and more modern system of sewage treatment provided by the county. The old plant, which consisted of essentially one large concrete building, had been shut down and completely closed up. That was over thirty years ago, and it was now so overgrown by the surrounding woodlands that it was completely obscured from view from virtually anywhere. It was still owned by the city of Paradise, but most people in town who were in their midthirties or younger either never knew it existed or had totally forgotten about it. Andy had never seen it himself, but he remembered hearing some mention of it at a few council meetings.

He could tell that the path had leveled out, which could only mean he had reached the bottom of the bluff. The Whiskey River was very nearby, possibly within feet. The whirring noise had now become the loud growling and grinding that was unmistakably a sound of heavy equipment, like a bulldozer or a crane, or possibly something smaller like a bobcat. He was now close enough to hear voices—several voices, all of which sounded to be male.

Finally he could see lights flickering between the trees, and a few steps later, he emerged into a small clearing providing an open view to all the activity. About two hundred yards ahead stood the dark and somewhat foreboding structure of what was once the wastewater treatment center. Two large spotlights atop ten-foot poles provided light for the working party, which appeared to consist of seven or eight men—one operating a bulldozer, two or three digging with shovels nearby, and the rest moving in and out of the concrete structure carrying items that appeared to be building materials. He was not sure whether or not it was an illusion created by the poor light, but it looked as if most or all of the men were black.

Andy was totally bewildered as to what the purpose of all this was. What were they doing to this old abandoned building? Even more confusing, why were they doing it at night? Whatever was happening here, he was sure Capsner was involved. Andy could no longer deny the feeling of fear that had been growing within him, but he was determined not to let himself give into it. If he were here in the daylight, he thought, he would just walk up there and ask what was going on. There was no reason to let the darkness cause him to behave differently.

He walked out into the clearing and took a few bold steps in the direction of the treatment center, but then he caught sight of something that immediately changed his thinking: not more than twenty yards away, a silhouetted figure glided by to his left, presumably walking along the shore of the river. Andy could not make out many details, but there was enough light from the moon and stars for him to see that this person was carrying a rifle!

What the hell is this? Andy thought. *A sentry?*

Instinctively, he ducked back into the bushes as quietly as he could. Had it not been for the noise of the bulldozer, he was sure the sentry would have heard him.

He had no idea who these people were or what they were doing, but it was obvious that this was something he should not, or even could not, handle by himself. He knew he must get to a phone immediately and call the police. He knelt quietly, trying to determine the exact position of the guard who had disappeared into a dense cluster of trees. Finally, Andy felt it was safe, so he slowly began moving back toward the entrance of the path.

Suddenly, the noise of the bulldozer stopped. Andy had never remembered a quietness so intense. Even the whistling of the wind through the trees seemed to die down. He froze for a moment, listening for any nearby sounds. Not far off, he heard the rustling of leaves, apparently from the sentry. Then voices—two sets, heavily accented. They sounded close, very close, in the direction of the river. From the sound of the rippling water that was now so audible, he was aware that he was only a few steps away from its bank.

"How long are we to stand guard here?" came one voice.

"Late," the other replied. "From what I hear, we are much behind schedule. That's why we must work at night. We may be here until the sun comes up."

"I hate this walking back and forth for hours. You wouldn't happen to have anything to perk me up, would you?"

"You mean crack? Don't be a fool. You know what would happen to you if you were caught using while on duty?"

"Yeah, man, I know. But this is driving me crazy. Besides, why should anyone care? Isn't that what this is all about? In another month, there will be more crack here than anywhere in the whole Midwest. At least that's what I've heard."

"That doesn't mean you can get stoned on duty. Keep up with your patrol. I'll see you here again in thirty minutes." More rustling of leaves as the sentries parted, then the sounds of walking faded away.

Crack! Here in Paradise! Andy could not believe it. And those accents, where had he heard them before? Television, probably. He could not pinpoint exactly where they were from, but it reminded him of a Latin American type of accent that he had heard a number of times in the movies. But not exactly that, either.

His thoughts turned briefly to his friend Joe. Joe had been right. Something was very wrong in this town. But while Joe had been perceptive enough to recognize it, Andy himself had refused to accept the fact that something this wild could happen in this quaint little community. And Spencer Thurman was undoubtedly involved. For all he knew, Spencer was with those men this very minute in the old treatment center. That dirty bastard! Andy never did particularly like Spencer, but he never guessed Spencer would be involved in something like drug trafficking. But it did not matter. What was important now was to get out of here and get help.

He took a few steps up the path then halted as he heard twigs and leaves snapping under his feet. On his trek down the path, these sounds had been drowned out by the noise of the bulldozer. Now he had a real problem: how could he get out of here without being heard? It would probably be best to wait until the bulldozer started again, but that could be a long time, and there was no guarantee that it would start at all again tonight.

He tried to remain calm and patient. After several minutes, he noticed that the wind had begun gusting in powerful spurts high through the trees. Possibly, thought Andy, there was now enough noise to conceal the sound of his steps. And since he could not hear either of the sentries, it seemed logical that they could not hear him. He started forward, moving as quickly and as quietly as he could.

The journey back seemed to take forever, this time going predominantly uphill. About halfway back, he came to what in the dim light appeared to be a fork in the path. Traveling in the opposite direction, the direction from which he had come, this fork could be easily overlooked since it gradually blended in with the main path headed to the treatment center. But moving in this direction, the main path actually split, making the fork more noticeable, although just barely so in the darkness of night. He was not positive which branch he should take but surmised that the right branch must lead down to the river, leaving the left branch as the route to take him back to the mansion. He chose this course and soon realized with a sense of relief that he had chosen correctly, feeling the path wind steeper up the hill and knowing that the mansion would be at the top.

Somewhere off in the distance, he heard the low rumbling of thunder. Feeling safer now, he became more conscious of the strong winds that were beginning to penetrate into the depths of the forest. He was moving with much more ease than before, having adjusted to the darkness although clouds now covered the moon and stars, increasing the blackness of the night. Finally, he felt a fresh breeze across his face, and he knew he was nearing an opening in the trees. After just a few more steps, he exited the woods and stood in the large backyard of the mansion. The light in the study was still on, and except for the few raindrops that were beginning to fall, it was as if he had never left this spot on his surprising and alarming journey. Andy now relaxed, feeling safe.

He was not aware of the presence of anyone. He only felt the crushing blow to his head that dropped him to the ground. He lay still for a moment, aware of the blood streaming down his neck, then slowly rolled over to see a large black man standing above him with a rifle pointed at his head.

"Going somewhere, man?" the man asked cynically.

Andy's head throbbed. "I'm on the city council. I was looking for Mr. Capsner. Who the hell are you?"

"You want Capsner, man? Well, you're in luck, 'cause that's who I'm taking you to see. Get up."

With great effort, Andy forced himself to his feet, staggering slightly from the dizziness caused by the blow to his head. The black man relaxed when he saw Andy having trouble standing. He lowered the riffle and pushed Andy back toward the path.

"Get going, man. I'm sure you know the way by now."

Andy knew that once he got back to the treatment center, he would have virtually no chance of escape. If he was going to make an attempt, this would be his best opportunity. He paused for just a moment to let his head clear and to regain as much strength as the short time would allow.

"I said move!" the sentry barked, and stepped forward to give Andy another push.

This was his chance. Andy quickly lunged at his captor, seizing the riffe in both hands and trying to wrench it free. Normally, Andy's strength would have been equal to the black man's, but in his weakened condition, he was easily thrown aside. Again the man brought the butt of his riffle down hard on Andy's skull. Blood splattered out through a second gash in the back of his head. Andy lay facedown in the mud at the entrance to the path. This time he did not get up.

Chapter 16

The sun was typically brilliant over the desert sand, causing invisible heat waves to rise off the pavement of Highway 8 heading east out of Yuma, Arizona. Both sides of the highway were lined with rich green vegetation, giving an uncharacteristic splash of color against the otherwise barren landscape. Joe had often thought it odd that such a place as Yuma was known for its agriculture. In almost every field, rows of people, predominantly Mexican, moved steadily in a line followed by a large wagon with empty crates and water bottles. These were the pickers, people who quickly and efficiently picked the crop of cabbages, radishes, and onions and loaded them into the crates for very little pay. An old dilapidated bus waited on the roadside to take the pickers to wherever they came from at the end of the day.

A few miles farther on, the farms disappeared, leaving only the barren and rugged desert landscape. Joe never particularly cared for the desert, but it did have an almost foreboding sense of beauty. He knew enough desert people to know that they loved all the things he disliked, the main point being the solitude. The average desert person was thrilled that most people in the country did not want to live there.

Joe was on his way to the Yuma Proving Ground, a large weapons-systems test facility run by the government. There had been a test two days before on a tank ammunition program that Minnesota Defense Systems had supplied rounds for. The test had not gone very well, and Joe was now on his way to a posttest evaluation to review the problem with the test crew and various government personnel. He had wanted to send one of his engineers, but the government insisted that he personally attend. The timing was not good, with all that was happening in Paradise, but it would only be a one-day trip, and he would be home again tomorrow.

Twenty-three miles east of Yuma, Joe turned right onto Aberdeen Road, seemingly leading to nowhere. He was briefly checked by a uniformed guard at a small security shack nearly invisible among the hills and ravines, and was quickly cleared through to Test Range 17A, where his meeting was to take place.

Sheri and Fran sat in the living room, sipping coffee and watching the clouds roll in from the west. Maureen and Brandon were getting ready for bed, and Katelin was already asleep in her crib.

"Looks like another storm," Fran said idly.

"It seems like it always storms when Joe's gone," Sheri said, somewhat absentmindedly.

"You're not afraid of a little thunder and lightning, are you?" Fran chided her.

"Not usually, but sometimes, if it's bad enough and I'm alone, it gets me a little nervous. I've been that way since I was a kid."

"Well, I don't think this will be too bad, and you're definitely not alone."

"You're right, Fran." Sheri smiled and relaxed back into her chair. "You see, staying here isn't a burden on us at all. It's best for all of us."

"Thank you," Fran replied, her tone quiet and sincere. "Which reminds me, I need to get a few things from my house. With the clouds moving in, I had better hustle over there before it starts raining. I'll be back in a few minutes."

Fran hurried out the front door and crossed through the side yard to her own house. The wind had picked up considerably, and the increasing cloud cover seemed to bring on the night at an accelerated rate. She climbed the step to the front door, unlocked it, and quickly stepped in to get out of the wind. She pulled the door closed firmly to ensure it was secure, and as she turned to face her living room, she froze in horror at the scene that met her eyes.

Never had she seen anything like it: every chair was overturned, every piece of stuffed furniture was slashed, and broken dishes were scattered everywhere. The side door leading into the garage was completely broken off from its hinges. Fran could see through the opening that the back door exiting from the garage was also broken down. Anger and terror simultaneously grew within her. She started to feel faint and looked for a place to sit down. She started to reach for a nearby chair that had been torn and overturned but then stepped back and took a long, deep calming breath. This was no time to lose control. She decided that whatever she had come over for was no longer important. She would return to the McGowans with a proud, confident strut. Some bastard may be out there watching, and if he was, he would know that Fran Rosten does not scare easily.

Just before she left, a thought crossed her mind. She weaved her way through the debris to the kitchen, opened a small cupboard above the refrigerator, and smiled to herself, relieved to see at least one item had survived. She reached up and grabbed hold of the bottle of Christian Brothers brandy then left through the front door and slowly walked back to Sheri's house, making sure to send the message to any unseen onlookers that she had not been shaken.

"You were right, that didn't take long," Sheri remarked as Fran entered the house and closed the door. "What was it that you needed?" She looked up and saw Fran holding the brandy and could not resist a large playful grin. "Well, it looks like we're going to party down tonight! But you didn't have to go home for that. I'm sure we could dig up something around here if you feel like a drink."

"Oh, for Pete's sake, Sheri, I didn't go to get the booze, I went to get a clean nightgown. But I changed my mind after seeing what my poor house looks like."

"Your house! What is wrong with your house?"

"Someone got inside, apparently through the garage. They were looking for something, undoubtedly that missing document. My poor house has been totally ransacked. Everything in it has been destroyed!"

"Oh, Fran, no." Sheri rushed to Fran and embraced her, then helped ease her into a chair. "At least you weren't there. You may have been killed."

"I doubt it. They probably broke in because I wasn't there, otherwise they would have done it long ago."

"I'm sure not everything is destroyed. We'll call the police and go through it in detail tomorrow. I'll bet most of your things can be salvaged."

"I know of one thing that can for sure," Fran said with a hint of humor in her voice, the type of slap happy humor that results from frustration and exhaustion. She held up the bottle. "Harry's favorite drink. I haven't touched it since his death, but I believe I will have just a slight nip now."

"I normally don't drink, except for an occasional glass of wine or a beer with dinner," Sheri said. "But maybe I'll join you this time. Let me see if I can find something to mix it with."

"Ice is all I need," Fran shot back.

"Ice it is. I believe I will put a splash of water in mine."

Sheri's nerves were suddenly jolted as she heard a high-pitched shrieking from Maureen's room.

"Mommy, Mommy, I see the bad man! Come and help me!"

Sheri dropped her glass, oblivious to its shattering on the floor. She bolted into Maureen's room and found her sitting on the floor below the window that looked out the side of the house into the wooded area. The room was dark except for the light flooding in from the hallway. Fran joined Sheri in the doorway as Maureen rushed into Sheri's arms.

"Whatever are you talking about, honey?" Sheri whispered reassuringly.

Maureen was trembling, on the verge of sobbing. "The b-b-bad man's out th-th-there," she finally stammered out.

Long ago, with all the problems of child kidnappings in the country, Joe and Sheri attempted to teach their children to avoid strangers. Since they were too young to fully appreciate or understand the seriousness of the threat of kidnapping, they told the children that the "bad man" roamed around looking for small boys and girls to take away with him. Any stranger could potentially be the bad man. Sheri knew this is what Maureen was referring to, but she also knew Maureen would not get this frightened simply by her own imagination. She must have seen something.

"What did you see, Maureen?" Sheri asked soothingly. "You were supposed to be in bed."

"I was, but I wanted to see the lightning. I was watching though the window, and when the lightning flashed, I saw a man standing by a tree, looking at our house."

"Oh, sweetheart, you probably just saw a shadow. Lightning can make things look pretty spooky. Why would a man be out there in weather like this?"

"I don't know," Maureen whimpered. "But I was scared."

"There's nothing to be afraid of. Let's look through the window and see."

They closed the door to make the room as dark as possible. The three of them—Sheri, Maureen, and Fran—all peered out the window at the woods. After several lightning flashes, all were convinced that there was no one there.

"You see," Sheri said, "no bad man. It was just a shadow."

"I suppose so," Maureen grudgingly agreed. "But it was scary."

Sheri put Maureen back to bed, tucking Maureen firmly under her covers so she would feel safe and secure. Both Sheri and Fran kissed Maureen good night and went back out to the living room.

"Do you think all of our talk has spooked the children?" Fran asked. "I certainly hope my presence here isn't causing them a problem."

"Don't worry about that, Fran. I know my kids, and they haven't been spooked at all. They have been enjoying this."

"Then what do you make of this?"

Sheri turned her back to Fran and hung her head, trying to maintain a calm appearance. "Well," she finally was able to force out, "I believe that…well—"

"Sheri," Fran cut in, "you believe that Maureen saw someone, don't you?"

Sheri looked up, the fright clearly showing on her face. "Yes, I do. I believe there is someone out there right now watching us. My god, we're prisoners in our own home."

"Stop it, Sheri!" Fran barked. "We are not prisoners. If anyone wanted to harm us, they have had plenty of chances. If there is someone out there—and after what happened at my place, I believe there is—then he is only monitoring us. He won't do anything to harm us."

"But the fact that he's there at all is so frightening. We've been assuming all along that no one suspects us, but that's not true. Someone must suspect us of something."

"He's probably just keeping an eye on us to get a lead on that document. I'm sure he doesn't suspect anything else."

"Fran, aren't you scared at all?" Sheri's voice quivered.

"Being scared is a luxury," Fran replied. "When you have a choice, fear is an emotion that helps you make the right choice, a way of protecting you. We have no choice, so being afraid isn't an option. We will do what we must do."

"You almost make that sound logical," Sheri said with a smile, feeling a bit more relaxed. "But just between you and me, I'm still scared."

"Just between you and me," Fran responded, "I'm terrified."

Chief Winfield sat at his desk, feeling somewhat perplexed. For the past few weeks, he had been feeling frustrated, unsure of exactly what course of action to take. Then out of the blue, Sharon Carlson asked him to start attending the city council meetings "just in case he was needed." What the hell did that mean? Now he had a message from her, asking him to meet her tonight. The part he found strange was that she wanted to meet at her home instead of at either of their offices. He had known Sharon for years, and he never knew her to be a secretive woman. In fact, what he had always admired about her most was her openness to people, both professionally as well as personally. Something must be going on with her, he thought. Did she know something he did not? Or was she suspicious that he knew something she did not? In either case, it would have to wait. He had been laying the groundwork for a plan for some time, and tonight, he intended to set it into action. He would be meeting Capsner at the Brewster mansion, but he did not want to wait too long since a storm was forecasted for later that evening. He would meet with Sharon at another time, but when he did, he would need to be very cautious; when a normally open person becomes secretive, trouble is usually not far away.

The telephone in the FBI office rang with two quick bursts, followed by a pause. Special Agent Thompson knew that meant it was an outside call. She snatched up the receiver and rattled off her usual answering spiel. "Special Agent Thompson, may I help you?"

"Are you tracking McGowen?" the voice on the other end asked.

"Of course. We picked him up in Phoenix, where he had a layover before going on to Yuma. He's out at the test site now. It appears to be a legitimate business trip. What about his family?"

"They're still under surveillance. Nothing seems suspicious. Maybe we'll get lucky, and they won't cause any trouble."

"Maybe," Thompson responded. "But I'll feel a lot better in a couple of months. How is your little project going up there?"

"We're finally making some real progress. It's actually better for us now that Thurman is gone. He created more obstacles than he resolved."

Somewhere in the background, some distance from the voice she was hearing, Thompson became aware of other voices—loud, shouting voices. "What's going on up there?" she snapped. "What the hell is happening?"

"I don't know," came the nervous reply. "Apparently they found a prowler in the woods."

"Shit!" Thompson exclaimed. "You take care of whatever is going on and get that situation under control, do you hear me?"

"I have to go," the voice said. "I'll take care of this. But just for the record, I am to keep you informed, but I don't work for you, so don't get too damned bitchy, you got that?"

The next sound Special Agent Thompson heard was a loud click from the slamming of the phone.

Chapter 17

It had only been a dream; it had to have been a dream. This was impossible to be happening here in Paradise. He would wake up and see that nothing had changed. As his mind cleared a little more and he slowly regained consciousness, he became aware of the intense throbbing in his head. The pain was not a dream. The pain was very real. He blinked his eyes, unable to focus clearly on his surroundings, but he was able to determine that he was in a dark and musty building, lying on a cool, hard floor. The wastewater treatment center! He must be inside of it. It had not been a dream after all.

Andy was lying facedown on a damp concrete floor in a room with very little light. He struggled to sit up, but with every move, the pain in his head intensified. He finally rolled over on his back and more carefully surveyed the room. It was very large, with a maze of water pipes going every which way. There were no windows, and the only access he could see was a heavy steel door in a nearby corner. This was not built to be a prison, but it certainly served the purpose well. He slowly dragged himself to the cement block wall a few feet away and managed to raise himself to a sitting position, leaning his back and head against the wall.

Touching his hand to the wound on his head, he realized it was still bleeding freely. He knew his injury needed attention, but he did not expect that he would receive any medical treatment in this dungeon. With a supreme effort, he was able to stand to his feet, using the wall as a support. After a few minutes, his dizziness began to clear, but his head continued to throb. He had no idea what was in store for him, but he felt he must be prepared to react whenever someone came for him. He was convinced that his life was in serious peril, and the longer he remained captive, the more difficult it would be to escape. His wait turned out to be only a few minutes as the screeching of metal on concrete announced the opening of the door. Two black men with rifles walked into the room, followed by a third unarmed black man, followed by Ronald Capsner.

"You were right," the unarmed man said, directing his comment to Capsner. "He is very strong. I thought he would never get up."

Capsner rushed over to Andy, a genuine look of concern on his face. "Andy, are you all right?" he asked.

"You dirty son of a bitch!" Andy roared. "What are you doing here?"

Capsner backed off, his expression of concern being replaced by a cold and distant look. "It's unfortunate that you stumbled across our operation. There was never an intention of hurting anyone."

"Just what is your operation?" Andy inquired, his anger giving him the strength to move about.

"To make money," the unarmed man said with a broad, beaming smile. "There's nothing wrong with that, is there?"

"Shut up, Rodriguez," Capsner snapped. "I'll take care of this. Why don't you go back and get your crew started? There's still plenty of time before dawn."

Rodriguez glared at Capsner with disgust. "Okay, man, but I want to know what you plan on doing with your friend here."

"I don't know yet. He's no threat to us now, so we do not have to make any hasty decisions."

"Hey, we need to dump this guy. Tonight!"

There was no doubt in Andy's mind what was meant by this. They were actually talking about killing him. *My God*, he thought. *This couldn't be happening.*

"I said I'll take care of this," Capsner said. "You just have to worry about getting the loading dock built. Mr. Salvo will be more concerned about another schedule slip than about dumping another person."

"Fine, but I think there's trouble if we keep him around." Rodriguez gave Capsner one final glare and stomped out through the door.

Andy recalled the earlier conversation of the sentries by the river, referring to shipments of crack. "You're building a loading dock to receive drugs?" he said, more of a statement than a question.

"That, and making a few other modifications to this old place," Capsner said.

Even with the pain in his head, things started to make sense. "So this whole story about the New York Historical Society is all garbage. You're only here to smuggle drugs."

"It technically isn't smuggling, but I think you have the idea."

"And Harry Rosten and Bob Williams, and who knows, maybe even Spencer Thurman, they stumbled across something too?"

"You know, Andy, I really would rather you had not gotten involved. I was beginning to think of you as a friend. Believe me, it is better for you that you don't know too much. However, suffice it to say, Spencer and Bob were greedy people who expected too much too fast. Harry…well…Harry was an innocent victim of Spencer's bungling. Spencer had the idea of keeping documentation of our project in envelopes similar to those used by the city council. That way, he could carry them in and out of his office without arousing suspicion. But as was typical with Spencer, he screwed up and accidentally mixed up the packages, sending out the wrong one. It could have gone to anyone, but it just happened to end up with Rosten. Harry had the chance to become part of this and make quite a handsome profit, but you know Harry. Unfortunately for him, he was one of the few people in this world who could not be bought."

"Are you telling me Spencer was working with you? I never particularly cared for him, but I never suspected that he would have gone for something like this. I suppose he's not really working for a consulting firm in New York."

"Wasn't that a nice letter he wrote?" Capsner asked with an arrogant smile. "I spent a lot of time on that letter. I had to say just enough, but not too much. As far as Spencer is concerned, let me just say I wouldn't waste any time looking for him."

A stream of blood flowed from the wound in Andy's head into his right eye. He reached up and wiped it away with his hand, and was startled to see the quantity of blood covering his palm and fingers. "I need to see a doctor," he stated firmly. "That is, unless you decide to let your charming friend have his way."

"I intend to see that you are taken care of," Capsner assured with believable conviction. "My role in all of this is not as an assassin. But we need to discuss something first. Obviously, an operation like this requires the support of someone working for the city, someone to allow us access and provide a cover for us from the more honest members of the council. Spencer had been that person. We have another contact that is now filling the role, although I don't feel it prudent to mention names just yet. But this contact is having trouble working alone, for reasons I can make clear at a more appropriate time. If you were willing to step in and help, we could have you fixed up in no time, and of course, you would be handsomely rewarded financially. How does two hundred thousand dollars sound?"

"Two hundred thousand! To be involved in drugs and murder? To betray my friends? You've got to be joking!"

"I suspected your standards would be higher than the others. But remember, the offer also includes your life. But let's not emphasize the negative. It makes for bad business relationships. You tell me, what is your price?"

At first, Andy was taken aback. How callous these people were, reducing everything to a mere dollar figure. The lives that were lost meant absolutely nothing to them. But after a few moments, a thought struck him: this could be his one chance for survival. No amount of money in the world would get him to cooperate with these evil men, but apparently, Capsner did not know him well enough to understand that. However, he knew if his price was not high enough, he would not sound convincing.

"One million dollars," Andy said as coolly as his fear and pain would allow him.

Capsner roared with laughter. "A million dollars! That's more than I get, and a fair amount more."

"Apparently, I'm worth more. It seems this project might not be able to be completed without me, but I bet it can without you."

"Salvo was right." Capsner sighed. "Everyone has his price. But he will never go for this. No one is that important to him."

Andy sensed that this Salvo was calling all the shots, and he apparently was a man to be feared. "I suggest you find out before you make any rash decisions."

Capsner snarled in disgust. "You're mighty cocky for a man who may be dead in a few minutes."

"If I am to be killed, this dispute over money becomes rather academic. If not, my price is a serious issue."

"How do I know you won't run to the police as soon as you get the chance?"

"That should be obvious. First, that is one of the reasons I'm worth a million dollars. I wouldn't want to lose all that cash. But even more than that, I'm smart enough to know that sooner or later, either you or one of your cronies would find me, and my life is too important to me to waste on some useless sense of nobility."

Capsner studied him, obviously unsure of how to proceed. A number of times, he glanced at the guards, giving Andy the impression that he was not comfortable with them present. Finally, he spoke, "I'll ask Salvo, but I would not count on him being very accommodating."

With a great effort, Andy was able to conceal his tremendous sense of relief. He had succeeded in buying valuable time, but he still needed to get out of his prison. This Salvo was likely to say no to his demand, and then his life would be worth nothing to Capsner and his murderous crew. He must be in a position to at least have a chance for escape.

"One other thing." Andy winced, only partially acting. "I need a doctor, and soon."

Capsner again paused and studied him, again glancing almost nervously at the guards. Finally he turned to them and barked out an order, "Take him to the mansion. Try to make him comfortable and let him rest. Don't call a doctor yet, though. I need to talk to Salvo first. We may not need a doctor."

One of the guards pulled open the heavy steel door, and Andy was able to see the periodic flashing of lightning and hear the distant rumbling of thunder. The storm outside had grown to be fairly severe. When he reached the doorway, he saw the rain pouring down in sheets.

"I don't think I can make it without help," he lied. He was weak, but there was no doubt in his mind that his life was on the line. He knew he could summon the strength to run for freedom when he saw the opportunity, but he also knew he could not sustain the physical exertion for long. It would be smart to get help now and save his energy for when he needed it. But his act did not fool Capsner.

"If you cannot make it, that will save me a call to Salvo."

Andy glared at Capsner with as much disdain as he could muster and walked out into the rain. The construction work had temporarily ceased, and the men were all crowded under a clump of trees for shelter. Andy and the two armed guards had almost reached the entrance to the path when he was surprised by a sudden command from behind.

"Stop! You two men, where are you taking this prisoner? Answer me, now!"

Andy turned to see Rodriguez running up to them, anger and hatred flashing from his eyes.

"Capsner said to take him up to the mansion," one guard answered, obvious traces of nervousness in his voice.

"No!" Rodriguez barked. "He is to remain locked up. Take him back. Now!"

Capsner had heard the shouting and sprinted from the concrete building to intercept Rodriguez. It was abundantly clear that these two men despised each other.

"Get out of the way, Rodriguez!" Capsner bellowed through the wind and rain. "You are here only to oversee the building project. I am in charge of this operation, including what to do with this man. We may need him later to help maintain our cover with the townspeople. I've had it with your interference. Get back to your men, or I'll inform Mr. Salvo of your insubordination."

Rodriguez laughed, his brilliantly white teeth gleaming through the night. "Go ahead, motherfucker. I'm also tired of you and your weak, spineless way of running things. Maybe this is the time for you and me to get into it. I'll go with you when you call Salvo, and he will be on my side, you can count on that."

Andy suddenly realized that the guards were much more interested in this potential showdown then they were in watching him. This was the opportunity he had been hoping for. He would not have time to get much of a lead, but between the denseness of the woods, the darkness, and the storm, a few yards might just be sufficient for him to stay out of sight and prevent them from getting a clear shot at him. The problem would be at the top of the hill when he exited the path; he would have to reach the highway and hope a passerby would stop and take him to safety before the guards could catch up with him or shoot him. Even at this hour, there was usually some traffic. It was a long shot, but it appeared Rodriguez was winning their dispute, so this would most likely be his last chance.

With the guards being distracted by the shouting men, Andy quickly ducked into the entrance of the path. It was several seconds before he heard the infuriated Rodriguez bellow with rage, "Where is the prisoner? You miserable scum, you let him get away. Find him, or you die!"

Immediately, the night erupted with the terrifying sound of automatic gunfire. Even with the storm, Andy could hear the ripping of a wall of lead through the trees and brush. He bent low as he ran, but he did not dare take the time to stop and flatten out on the ground. To remain on his feet was a risk, but the gunfire bought him valuable seconds as it delayed the guards in their pursuit, and seconds could be the difference of his living or dying. Finally, the echoing subsided, and Andy knew that the race for his life had now commenced. He tried not to think of the pain in his head but only that he must push himself harder than ever before. The running was difficult on the narrow path, but he fought his way along with sheer will and determination.

As he made his way farther into the woods, the dense trees provided shelter from the storm, causing the wind and rain to seemingly subside and easing the difficulty of navigating the narrow meandering trail. He was aware of voices behind him in the distance, but he sensed that his lead was enough to give him a reasonable chance when he reached the top.

Suddenly his foot caught under the root of a large tree near the edge of the path. Andy fell to his face in the mud, feeling an excruciating pain in his ankle. *No*, he thought. *No, not now.* He lay still for a brief moment, the feeling of utter disappointment and fear becoming overwhelming, raising his already high level of anxiety to that of a panic. Then from somewhere in the recesses of his mind emerged the image of his old high school football coach.

"Anyone can play for three quarters," the coach would always preach to them. "But the measure of a champion is the ability to maintain a hundred percent effort all the way through the fourth quarter. During a battle of strength, endurance and perseverance always win out."

It was now the fourth quarter, and Andy had to perform like a champion. Without hesitation, he rose to his feet, took one step, and again fell to the ground. *My God*, he prayed. *Give me strength.* He rose again and began hobbling forward. He pushed on with a determination reserved only for those who are grasping at life.

Andy froze in horror as he suddenly broke into a clearing. Before him flowed the Whiskey River, and a newly built boathouse sat on the bank alongside the recently repaired dock. To his left was a long flight of steps zigzagging up the steep bluff.

"What the hell is this!" Andy screamed out loud. With an overwhelming sense of defeat, he collapsed to the ground, realizing with total frustration what had happened. It was the fork in the path he had seen on his previous trek up to the mansion. This time, he had taken the wrong fork. His efforts to overcome his pain and fatigue prevented him from realizing he had been running downhill, back down to the river. He closed his eyes, ready to accept his fate, when he became aware of what should have been obvious: there was no one behind him! His pursuers had obviously followed the path to the mansion, thinking they were still on his trail. Maybe he had a chance after all, but he must move fast. As soon as Rodriguez and his men reached the backyard of the mansion, they would be sure to realize what had happened and be back after him in minutes.

From here he had two choices: swim down the river and hope he was not spotted by a sentry, or climb the long flight of steps up to the mansion. With his energy all but exasperated, Andy felt that the steps might be more than he could handle, leaving the river as his only alternative. He grunted and groaned as he dragged himself to the water's edge, but just before he plunged in, he heard voices from out on the water.

"Shine that light in those bushes. He could be hiding anywhere along there. Don't worry, he's not armed."

Andy looked downstream and saw the dark silhouetted figure of a small rowboat about a hundred yards off coming in his direction. A light beam was projecting out from the boat and panning along the riverbank. In a few minutes, they would reach his position. With the swiftness of the current, he knew that swimming upstream was not feasible in his condition. The patrol boat effectively eliminated the river as a possible escape route. He turned to face choice number two and, for the first time, began doubting that he had the strength to continue. But with no other choice available, he rose to his feet and limped toward the towering flight of steps.

Suddenly, the door to the boathouse flung open, and in the darkness, he saw a man emerge out onto the adjoining dock. The darkness prevented Andy from seeing details of the man's features, but from the way his body turned rigid, it was obvious he had spotted Andy and was even more startled than he was. Then the man relaxed and let out a deep, sinister laugh, calling out to Andy in a strong, accented voice, "So you found your way down here. And I thought I was going to miss all the fun." He was a black man, like the rest, and obviously a Latin American. He cautiously approached Andy then slowly reached behind his back and produced a hideous knife with a terrifying ten-inch blade. The man moved closer, oblivious to the rain, taunting Andy as he quickly passed the knife back and forth from one hand to the other. The man was like a shark who had tasted blood and was now moving in for the kill.

There was little chance of overpowering the man, so Andy knew that he must somehow surprise him and catch him off guard. He waited until the man had moved within ten feet then let out a deep, painful-sounding sigh and collapsed on his back, as if he had lost his last ounce of strength and could no longer defend himself. Watching his assailant closely, he could see that he now relaxed, his former cautiousness slipping away and being replaced by an unguarded sense of confidence. He came and stood above Andy, now close enough for Andy to clearly make out each distinguishing, disgusting feature of his evil face. There was no mercy in the man's eyes, no pity for the defenseless person before him.

"Good-bye, fool," the man uttered as he lifted the knife in preparation to strike.

In sheer desperation, Andy thrust his foot hard to the man's groin. He hit his target perfectly, causing the man to scream in both pain and astonishment. His eyes bulged wide as he fell to his knees, bringing his hands down to his groin but not relinquishing his grip on the knife. With a quickness that Andy had thought was beyond him, he rolled to his side and up to his knees then, with all his might, he smashed his fist into the man's face. The man went down to his back, somehow still maintaining his grip on the handle of his weapon. Even in his weakened state, Andy was able to pounce on top of the man and grab hold of the hand holding the knife. Timing was critical; he could not allow his enemy time to recover. He tried to wrestle the knife free but to no avail. The man struggled to force the blade into Andy's chest, but being on top, Andy could use his weight to his advantage. It was a fight of desperation on both their parts, a battle not so much of physical strength as of will. Both men knew there would be only one survivor.

Slowly, agonizingly, Andy was able to turn the blade toward his would-be killer, and drawing on a reserve of energy he never knew existed, he let out a wild primeval scream and rammed the blade into the man's throat, killing him instantly. Andy, like most good people, had never killed another human being. Looking down at the bloody corpse beneath him, he was surprised at how little it affected him. But then, he hardly felt that what he had killed could be considered human.

"There is some screaming over by the dock!" Andy heard from the direction of the boat. It was now only about twenty yards away, but moving very slowly in the dark and the rain. He again rose to his feet and painfully began climbing the seemingly endless flight of stairs. His head throbbed, his ankle could barely support his weight, his energy was nearly exhausted from fatigue and loss of blood. But his only chance was to somehow reach the top and make it to the highway.

Step after step, with agonizing determination, he slowly climbed upward. In the far recesses of his mind, he was aware that the men from the boat were now in pursuit up the stairs below him. Finally, unbelievably, he was nearly at the top, but as he looked up and prepared to climb the final flight of steps, the sight that met his eyes caused his heart to sink, lower than he ever could have imagined. On the platform at the staircase summit stood Rodriguez, glaring at him with a smile of pure evil, a .38-caliber pistol held firmly in his hand.

Andy was barely conscious of the sound of the shots, and vaguely aware of the muzzle flashes, as two pieces of hot lead ripped through his chest, propelling his body out from the staircase and plummeting into the dark waters of the Whiskey River.

Chapter 18

There were few indications that a storm had passed through the previous night as Joe McGowen turned into his driveway on this bright Wednesday morning. It had not been a storm like the last time he had gone out of town; no trees had been uprooted, and very little debris lay scattered about. It was essentially a typical Minnesota thunderstorm. Nevertheless, he could not help but smile to himself at the sheer coincidence of bad weather coinciding with his travel. According to Sheri, it always stormed when he was gone, which, of course, was not true. Lately, though, that did seem to be the case. At least this time, Sheri had Fran to keep her company.

He turned the knob on the front door and was surprised to find it locked. It was ten thirty, and Sheri usually did not keep the door locked during the day. Rather than ring the bell, he let himself in with his key and was equally surprised to find the house quiet. The only sound was the faint voices coming from the television in the family room. He quickly went to investigate and found Maureen and Brandon watching *The Price Is Right,* their favorite game show. Maureen was holding Katelin, who appeared to be more than content.

"What's going on around here?" Joe asked as cheerfully as he could, not wanting to let on he was a bit concerned.

"Hi. Daddy," Maureen and Brandon said in unison, not taking their eyes off the screen.

"Boy, some welcome for me. It's like I wasn't even gone."

"Oh, Daddy, you were only gone one night." Maureen sighed.

"I must be traveling too much if nobody misses me after just one night." Joe's voice was jovial, but inside he felt this must be true. "Where are Mommy and Fran?"

"Sick" was Brandon's typically short reply. "Both of them."

Maureen filled in the details. "Mommy got up a few hours ago and said both her and Mrs. Rosten were sick. She asked us to be very quiet, so we've been watching TV."

Joe was initially struck more by the odd coincidence of both women getting sick at the same time than he was by any real concern for their well-being. Maybe they ate something bad for supper. He thought about checking on Sheri but then decided to wait. If it were serious, she would have said something to the kids. What she probably needed most was rest. There was no sense in disturbing her now.

He went upstairs to fix a pot of coffee, but when he entered the kitchen, he encountered a sight that filled him with a combination of amusement and anger. Sitting on the counter was a three-quarter empty bottle of brandy, undoubtedly the cause of the women's mysterious illness. After a moment's hesitation, anger won out, and he raced back down the stairs to the family room.

"It's a beautiful day out, guys. Why don't you go out and enjoy the sun?"

"Daddy!" Maureen complained. "We love this show."

"Daytime TV is for rainy days. Come on now, you'll have more fun outside."

After a few token objections, Maureen switched off the television, took Katelin's hand, and the three of them went out to discover what adventures could be had. When the front door closed, Joe went to the bedroom, flipped on the light, and bellowed out angrily, "Rise and shine! Everybody, up!"

Sheri pulled her pillow over her head, moaning her objection to Joe's attack. "Please keep your voice down. Didn't the kids tell you I was sick?"

"Sick people get to stay in bed. Hungover people have to get up."

"Joe, give me a break. I feel terrible."

Joe's anger began to mount. "Sheri, I mean it. This is inexcusable. Even under normal conditions, this is totally irresponsible, but with all that is happening, I just cannot believe you would do this."

Sheri sat up, anger showing in her bloodshot eyes. "Don't you lecture me. Do you have any idea what it's like around here when you're gone? You can just waltz off anytime you please, but I'm left here with the kids and this damn problem you got us into. Last night—"

"Who is doing all the screaming?" a haggard Fran called as she shuffled into the room. "Aren't there enough problems around here without you two fighting?"

"I've got a bone to pick with you too," Joe countered.

"Settle down, Joe," Sheri cut in. "We don't have to listen to this garbage."

"Everybody, quiet!" Fran almost shrieked. "First off, Joe's right. I'm ashamed of what we did, and I think you are too, Sheri. Secondly, Sheri's right. It doesn't help to start badgering two poor, misguided ladies. What say we all calm down and have a little chat?"

Joe took a deep breath and began to relax. "Fair enough. Why don't you two shower up? I'll put on some coffee. Then we will talk."

Forty-five minutes later, Joe and the two semirecovered women sat in the living room, sipping hot coffee. With everyone's tempers having cooled to a rational level, Fran and Sheri began to fill Joe in on the previous evening's events. Fran related the portion concerning the ransacking of her home, and Sheri picked up with the strange man Maureen thought she had seen.

"You see," Sheri concluded, "we didn't intend to drink anything, but with all of this, and then the storm, I guess we lost control. It just felt so good to laugh again. But I'm not making excuses. You were right, what we did was inexcusable. I promise it won't happen again."

"I know it won't," Joe replied soothingly. He leaned over and kissed her on the forehead. "I'm sorry for flying off the handle like that."

"Now that's the way I like it." Fran smiled. "Save the fighting for the bad guys."

Joe sat back in his chair and began to rub his chin. After a few moments, he looked up and began to reveal his thoughts. "It looks like we have two serious issues to deal with. First, we must report the break-in of Fran's house to the police. Then, we need to think about this stranger watching our house. Is someone really out there? Is he watching everyone, or just one of us, and if just one, which one? Then, of course, the obvious question: why?"

Sheri was the first to attempt an answer. "I firmly believe someone is there. Fran thinks he might be watching her, trying to locate the missing document. That may be true, but we don't know for sure. If he is watching anyone else, it can only mean someone has found out we know something, or at least suspects we do."

"I think that is a fair statement," Joe agreed. "But I think we can devise a plan to answer the first question. We should be able to determine who is being watched."

"How so?" Fran inquired.

"It does not seem likely that someone would spend time just watching the house. If we are right about him watching a specific person, it would seem natural that he would follow that person when he or she went somewhere."

"That sounds reasonable," Sheri agreed. "So what do we do?"

"Test the theory," Joe continued. "First, Fran will take the car and go someplace, anyplace ordinary that wouldn't arouse suspicion, like the grocery store. When she leaves, I'll be in position to spot anyone that might be following her. That will also have to appear ordinary. I could be jogging along the road, or something. If no one follows Fran, then we repeat the test with me, after an appropriate wait so it doesn't seem unusual. If we still don't spot anyone, we try again with Sheri."

"That could work," Fran mused. "It certainly doesn't hurt anything to try."

"It is very important to understand what's happening here," Joe finished. "Fran, I suggest we try this right away and call the police about your house later. What do you think?"

"That's fine with me," Fran said. "What happened to my house is done. This thing with the spy out there has me a little worried. Let's go do it."

Half an hour later, Fran walked out to the driveway where she could be easily seen from the wooded area. She got into Joe's car and headed down Cottonwood to Port Avenue. As she reached the corner, Joe was just coming out of the house in his running clothes and started out on his normal route, which took him to the corner of Cottonwood and Port, right on Port and down the hill bordering the wooded area.

Fran turned left on Port and headed toward the small strip mall a few blocks away. She was completely out of sight while Joe was still in position to spot anyone attempting to follow her. It was clear that at least this time she was left alone.

By the time Joe finished his run, Fran had already returned with a token package of bread and milk. "I guess now it's your turn," she said to Joe. "But I was wondering if we shouldn't be just a little bit more subtle. With one of us standing out in the middle of the road, maybe he wouldn't dare attempt to follow anyone."

"Good point," Joe said. "We'll wait for a couple of hours, then I'll run over to the hardware store. It seems I go there every few days, anyway. Fran, you'll leave about a half an hour before me and position yourself to observe me when I go."

Both Sheri and Fran looked puzzled. Sheri finally spoke for both of them. "I don't understand. You had better explain that in a bit more detail."

"I intend to. Now listen."

One minute before two o'clock in the afternoon, Joe idly backed out of the driveway and headed to the corner of Cottonwood and Port. Timing was extremely critical. He had to be at the stop sign at precisely two o'clock; too soon and Fran would not be ready, too late and she would be gone. As he approached the corner, he tried to maintain a calm appearance, but his heart was racing in anticipation. He came to a full stop then slowly turned left down Port in the direction of the hardware store, which was located in the same strip mall as the grocery store that Fran had gone to. As he turned, he nonchalantly glanced to his right, to the intersection of Brent and Port at the bottom of the hill. Fran was just coming to a stop at the corner. Joe could not contain a broad smile as he briefly reflected on the admiration he was developing for Fran. She was definitely the kind of person who could truly be relied upon in a crisis. There was no doubt in his mind that she was going to be a tremendous ally in the battle that lay ahead of them.

Fran parked along the side of Brent Street three blocks from the intersection with Port Avenue. It would be almost impossible to time her stop at Port accurately if she continued to drive around, so she decided to park and wait, being only seconds from the corner. She was not concerned about arousing suspicion, for if someone was watching the McGowen house, they would never see her here.

Fifteen seconds before two o'clock, she shifted into drive and eased forward. As she slowed to a stop at the corner, she just caught a glimpse of Joe at the top of the hill to her right, turning and driving off down Port Avenue. She paused for just a moment and then slowly eased through the intersection. Suddenly, from about halfway up the hill, a small black four-door automobile emerged from the heavy brush bordering the wooded area and quickly sped off in the direction Joe had gone.

Fran's first instinct was to pursue the vehicle, but she would undoubtedly be spotted and reveal that they discovered Joe was being followed. That would cost them a tremendous advantage and could potentially put them all in severe danger. Besides, the car would only follow Joe to the hardware store and back. There would be no real benefit in observing that.

Struck by sudden inspiration, she decided there was something of value she could do. Quickly she turned her car around and headed back to the intersection she had just crossed. She turned up Port and parked alongside the road in the area that she had seen the car emerge. Stepping out into the street, she immediately noticed a narrow clearing in the brush with distinct signs of tire tracks embedded into the short weeds covering the earth. Although it was obvious a vehicle had recently passed there, she would not have given it a second thought had she not been looking specifically for it.

The tire tracks led a short distance behind a row of dense bushes about five yards off the road. They did not appear to be very large when compared to the tall trees beyond, but their five or six feet of height would be ample to completely conceal the car she had seen. There were no definite signs of anyone venturing farther into the woods, at least none that her untrained eye could detect. However, after carefully surveying the surrounding area, Fran determined that the natural terrain of the trees and undergrowth presented only one feasible avenue of passage. She slowly followed this path, reminding herself that she only had fifteen to twenty minutes before Joe and his shadow returned.

Passage proved to be fairly easy as the undergrowth became much more sparse the farther she progressed into the woods. This was not a large wood, not like along the banks of the Whiskey River, but it was enough to provide more than adequate shelter for someone wishing to remain hidden. Fran was gripped by a sudden sense of surprise when she finally caught site of the McGowen house. It was startling because of how far she had come—or had not come, to be more accurate. She estimated that she was only about a quarter of the way through the woods, but due to the orientation of the trees, a clear channel of visibility was open through the remaining distance. That makes sense, she thought. It would give an observer time to get to his car and be ready when he saw Joe depart. If he had to go through the entire expanse of the woods to see the house, he would never be able to return to his car in time to follow Joe.

Fran briefly studied the area around her. No signs of human presence at all. The unknown observer knew what he was doing. He was obviously a professional. There was clearly nothing she could do here, so without risking being discovered, she quickly returned to her car, intending to drive back to the McGowens. But as she pulled out into the street, another thought struck her: it might be of value to be able to identify the shadow. She turned and headed back down the hill and positioned her car at the intersection of Brent and Port, in the same place that she had been to initially spot the shadow. When Joe returned, she would pull out and head up the hill, knowing that the shadow would be only a short distance behind.

Her plan worked perfectly. As she turned up the hill on Port, she could see the black car at a safe distance behind Joe. She continued on Port through the Cottonwood intersection, and as she passed the black car, she glanced over at the person behind the wheel. She was only able to get a quick glimpse, but she saw that he was a big man with short black hair, probably in his early thirties. He wore a loose-fitting sweatshirt, which would be practical for spending several hours or even days in the woods. She wished she could have gotten a better look, but she was fairly sure that she would be able to identify him if she ever saw him again. She drove around for a few minutes longer then returned to the McGowens.

"Where have you been?" Sheri demanded anxiously. "I've been worried sick! Especially since Joe returned home before you did."

"Did you see anything, Fran?" Joe inquired, a bit more controlled than Sheri. "Did you spot anyone following me?"

"You bet I did," was Fran's firm reply. "I not only saw him follow you, but I discovered where he hides out. And better yet, I got a good enough look at him to be able to identify him."

"That's terrific!" Joe exclaimed, but his enthusiasm was dampened by Sheri's concern.

"That's not terrific," she countered. "You were not supposed to be playing James Bond, Fran. You were only supposed to observe Joe. You know what those people are capable of."

"I know it much better than you do, Sheri," Fran said. "I am a widow because of those people. We're not going to get anywhere sitting on our butts, and I'll be damned if I'm going to let them get away with what they did to me, with what they're still doing to our town. The time has come, Sheri. We either go after them, or we get the hell out of here, and I'm too old to up and move."

"You're right, Fran," Sheri said. "Of course you're right. I was just so afraid. It seems I'm always afraid lately."

"We are all afraid," Joe said calmly, lightly taking hold of Sheri's hand. "But Fran is right. The time has come to at least start taking action. Now tell us what you've been up to, Fran."

Fran related the events as they had occurred. "I never was in any real danger," she said as she finished. "But I'll tell you one thing, I was amazed at what an excellent view there was of your house from just a few yards into the woods. It's like it was made specifically for spying on you. And there were no traces of anyone having been there, except for some tire tracks going in behind some bushes. But hell, that could be from some young couple making out, for all anyone else would know." She paused for a moment, and then continued, "I was curious, Joe. Were you able to notice that you were being followed?"

"Not really," Joe said. "I did see the black car that you mentioned, but only for a few moments. He must have hung back far enough to stay out of sight most of the time. Had I not been looking for him, I wouldn't have noticed anything."

"So, Joe is being followed, and apparently by a real pro," Sheri said. Her voice showed definite signs of alarm, but she remained in control. "And we thought no one suspected anything. I guess we were wrong."

"Not necessarily," Joe tried to sound reassuring. "These people are obviously very cautious. This entire operation must have taken tremendous planning. They appear to be the kind of people who leave nothing to chance. With the questions I was bringing to the council through Andy, it makes sense that they would want to keep an eye on me, especially since I was the one that found the package they are apparently searching for. But it is possible they are only monitoring me to be safe. I agree with what Fran said before: if they wanted to harm me, or any of us, they would have done it a long time ago."

"We always seem to come back to the same inevitable question." Sheri sighed. "What do we do now?"

Joe pondered the question for a moment. "I've been thinking about that," he began. "Again, I agree with Fran. I don't think we can afford to sit and wait for things to happen. If we are going to try and help, try and do something about this mess, we are going to have to be more aggressive. I have already notified my office that I will be taking the next two weeks off for vacation. That will allow me to apply myself fully to this problem."

"That's the best idea I've heard in a while," Sheri remarked, relieved at the thought of not having to spend anymore nights alone. "But how do you propose we become 'more aggressive'?"

"I guess I don't have a good answer to that yet, but I think it's time we get the people we can trust together and start making definite plans," Joe said.

"Who do you think would be included in this exclusive little group?" Fran asked, with a hint of cynicism.

"Beth Wence is coming over Saturday morning. I have already decided to tell her everything then. I also think we should ask Andy to come. I just cannot believe he's involved in any of this. I feel a little guilty for ever having suspected him. And maybe Sherman Salinger. I don't know if he will support us or not, but we will need all the help we can get. As a group, we'll lay out a plan of action. Saturday will be the kickoff. In fact, I'll call Andy right now. He should still be at his office."

Joe quickly darted into the kitchen. Several minutes later, he returned, looking perplexed.

"Is something wrong?" Sheri asked.

"I hope not," Joe answered. "Andy's secretary said he spent all day yesterday trying to get ahold of Capsner, but she didn't know why. Today he never showed up for work. I called his home, but no one answered. He seems to have disappeared."

Chapter 19

"I'm sure he's probably just taken the day off to take care of some personal business," Sheri remarked, referring to Andy's apparent disappearance. "People do that all the time. He didn't let his secretary know where he would be because he didn't want her to know."

"I imagine you're right," Joe said, only partially convinced. "I'll try him again later on." He paused for a moment, contemplating what he was about to say. "There is something else I've been considering that I think would be very beneficial, but it could also be dangerous."

"Well, we agreed it is time for action," Sheri said. "What's on your mind?"

"Capsner is supposed to be leaving for New York tomorrow to meet with his fictitious historical society. Undoubtedly, he's really going to Miami. After my last trip, I never thought I would be suggesting this, but I'm considering following him like I did Spencer."

"Are you out of your mind?" Sheri cried. "You were nearly killed last time. Now it will be even be more difficult because Capsner is a professional. He won't be so easy to tail."

"That's true, Capsner will certainly keep a sharper lookout than Spencer did," Joe said. "But now I have an advantage because I know what's going on, at least to some degree. When I followed Spencer, I had no idea of the seriousness of the whole situation.

And more importantly, this could be a perfect opportunity to get some kind of proof for the FBI. Maybe I could even get a picture of something incriminating."

"I don't like it, Joe," Fran said. "Sheri's right. Following Capsner is far too risky. I know I just got through shooting my mouth off about taking action, but this is a little extreme. There has got to be a better way."

"Maybe there is," Joe said. "But I don't think so. Think about it for a minute. What do we really think we're going to accomplish here? We certainly aren't going to capture this group of killers and drug dealers ourselves. What we need is some evidence to turn over to the authorities. But how realistic is it that we will get any evidence here? They're watching our every move, they've torn your house apart, Fran, and we still don't even really know how to begin. But it's almost certain something will happen in Miami. It's an opportunity we cannot afford to lose. I think you both agree with me, you just don't want to admit it."

Sheri and Fran exchanged glances, and they could see in each other's eyes that they believed what Joe had said was true, but Sheri wasn't quite ready to give in totally. "You're right, Joe," she said. "We do need to be more aggressive, but there has to be limits. Following Capsner seems like suicide. Let's at least wait until the Saturday meeting and some kind of logical plan is established."

"I think that is the reasonable thing to do," Fran said. "We're finally getting organized. Let's be patient for just a few more days."

"Well, this is supposed to be a team, and if two of the three members vote that I should stay, then I'll stay," Joe said. "But we may be losing a great opportunity."

"There will be others," Sheri said. "And we'll be more ready for them next time."

The rest of the afternoon was spent taking care of the problem at Fran's house. The police had come and made a fairly brief investigation, concluding that what probably had happened was some young juveniles took advantage of the fact that Fran had moved out and ransacked her house, not really looking for anything in particular but only wishing to create a mess.

"This is really terrible," the officer in charge had said, "after what happened with Harry and all. I'm really sorry, Mrs. Rosten. I doubt we will be able to catch these punks, but if there is anything you need, just let us know. I think it would be a good idea to stay at Joe's for a while longer, if he doesn't mind."

After the police had left, Joe, Sheri, Fran, and the kids continued to sort through the remaining rubble scattered about he house. The damage was devastating but not nearly as bad as it first appeared. Most of the furniture and some of the dishes were destroyed, but mainly things were just in disarray. After several hours of tidying up, it did not look nearly as bad as when Fran first discovered it.

"It's too bad about the furniture," Joe said. "But I think that's the only thing seriously damaged."

"I'm not concerned about it," Fran responded. "It was all covered by insurance. I needed to get new furniture, anyway. This will give me the excuse to do it."

It had been a long, stressful day, and everyone agreed turning in early would be a good idea. Even the kids went to bed without much fuss, which was becoming a rarity. By nine o'clock in the evening, the McGowen house was quiet, and Joe lay on his bed, watching Sheri finish brushing her hair. Since the children had gotten old enough to occasionally wander around at night, they began keeping their bedroom door closed, although they both agreed they should never lock it. There was always the chance that one of the kids would have a bad dream or feel a need to come to them for something after they had gone to sleep. They did not want to make it look as if they were shutting the children out.

Sheri put her brush down on the nightstand and lay down next to Joe. The dim night-light from beside the bed cast a soft glow throughout the room. "Poor Fran," Sheri said. "No one should have to go through what she has."

"It is terrible," Joe agreed. "But I really don't believe the house break-in bothers her that much. She's so consumed with the idea of catching whoever we're after that everything else has become of secondary importance. But nevertheless, it has to be taking a toll on her. I think this whole business has taken more of a toll on all of us than we realize."

He rolled on his side and raised himself up on one elbow, looking affectionately at Sheri. She was wearing a simple blue satin nightshirt, which buttoned down the front and hung just below her waist. "We haven't had any time to ourselves in weeks," he said quietly.

"Oh no," Sheri moaned good-naturedly. "I know that look. How can you be thinking about sex tonight?"

"I'm not thinking about sex." Joe smiled. "I'm thinking about sharing a meaningful and intimate experience with my beloved wife. And let's face it, it's not like we've been wearing ourselves out with it lately."

"First off, it's not like our lives have been anything even approaching normal lately. Secondly, men don't know what meaningful and intimate is. You guys just need to get your rocks off once in awhile."

"Well, that too." Joe laughed. His face suddenly became serious. "Really, Sheri, I'm not looking for a quick romp. Our discussion today about the dangers of following Capsner made me realize that anything could happen in the days to come. I think Fran's remark about being a widow really hit home. I just don't want us to take each other for granted, not even for a little while. It's been a long time since I've told you how much you mean to me. It's been a while since I've even consciously thought about it myself. I love you, Sheri, very much."

"I know you do, Joe. And I hope you know that I love you too. You're my whole life, you and the kids. That's why I get so scared when you start planning to chase dangerous criminals around the country."

The Seduction of Paradise

Joe leaned over and lightly kissed her. He slid his hand over her flat stomach, and after a few moments of massaging, he pulled her body close to him. He kissed her again, this time more firmly. He eased his hand up her chest to the top of her nightshirt and began to slowly undo the buttons, first exposing her breasts then, finally, her entire body. He paused for a moment to look at her. She was beautiful, he thought. Even after three children, her body was still firm. They say beauty is in the eye of the beholder, and in his eye, no woman ever looked better.

Sheri gently ran her hands behind Joe's neck and pulled him to her, kissing him with a passion that they had not shared for some time. Joe often marveled at how exciting their love had remained throughout the years of their marriage. In many ways, it was as if each time was their first. He still felt the tingle of anticipation every time he touched her naked body, every time he felt her touch his. It was another testimony of their conviction and love for each other. No one could maintain that level of passion based solely on physical pleasure; there would always be a desire for something new and better. But for them, the physical pleasure was merely a byproduct of the intense love they shared.

Joe began to caress her breasts, very gently at first then more firmly, as his kisses moved slowly down her neck. Finally, he brought the warm moistness of his mouth to her breasts as he continued his caressing with his lips and tongue.

"Oh, Joe," Sheri whispered. "You know how to get me going." She grasped his head in both of her arms, pulling him tightly to herself. "Ohhh, I love that," she moaned. Holding her close, Joe could feel her body begin to quiver.

Joe released himself from Sheri's arms and finished stripping off her nightshirt. Then he moved himself on top of her, keeping his body slightly suspended on his elbows and knees, holding Sheri's head firmly in his hands. Their eyes became fixed on each other, communicating without words the deep desire that they both shared. Sheri reached her arms around him, lightly massaging his neck and shoulders. It was time, they were both ready. With mounting anticipation, she ran her hands down his back, sliding her fingers under his shorts and almost frantically forcing them off. Joe laid his body on hers as she eagerly wrapped her arms and legs tightly around him, and they began kissing with a passion that bordered on frenzy.

With an unexpected jolt, Sheri's body suddenly tensed as she quickly whispered, "Joe, I think I hear one of the kids."

Joe had not heard anything, and was not interested in going to check. "No, Sheri, you didn't hear anything. They're all asleep."

He continued his kissing and caressing until Sheri again whispered, "You did lock the basement door, didn't you?" She was referring to the door passing from the laundry room into the garage. They always locked all outside doors but on occasion forgot about that one because it was the least used.

"Sheri, not now. I'll check everything out later. Now, I just want you."

He kissed her again, and this time, Sheri relaxed, holding him as firmly as she could, wanting him as much as he wanted her. Joe finally entered her, letting out a deep moan of satisfaction. As their lovemaking continued, their passion intensified, causing Sheri's soft sighs to grow into mild moans, not loud enough to be heard outside of their room but sounding almost deafening in Joe's ear. The sounds of Sheri's pleasure excited Joe, resulting in the release of his own deep-throated groans. He was conscious of nothing other than Sheri as they moved together, firmly, frantically but very gently.

There was a noise, thought Joe. No, impossible! Not now. He continued to move, not wanting to think about it. Sheri's moaning increased, as did his own. But the noise persisted, almost masked by the sounds of their passion, since it seemed to be a kind of moaning itself. It was nearly masked, but it was there.

This time it was Joe who became tense.

"No, Joe," Sheri whispered. "You brought me this far. Whatever it is can wait."

Joe had completely snapped out of his mood of passion. His mind was racing; had he locked the basement door? He jumped out of bed and reached for the door, just as it burst inward and a man lunged full force into his chest.

"Oh my God!" Sheri shrieked hysterically as she cowered up to the headboard and instinctively pulled the sheets up to cover her body. "Oh my God! Oh my God! Oh my God!"

Joe grabbed hold of the man and fell a few steps backward, attempting to steady himself and prepare to fight. To his surprise, the man exerted little force against him, except for that from the weight of his slumping body. He spun the man around and let him drop onto the bed, which he did with no resistance. Joe stepped back, again preparing to fight, but the man made no move to get up from where he had fallen.

"Joe, my God, look at you!" Sheri screamed, becoming even more hysterical.

Joe looked down at himself. He was still naked, but his body was covered with blood.

"What did he do to you? Are you hurt?"

"No, not at all. This isn't my blood." Joe's mind finally began to catch up with the action, and for the first time, he realized the man was not attacking him. In fact, he lay completely motionless. Joe looked down at the man on the bed and saw that he was hurt, terribly hurt. It almost appeared as if the man's chest had been obliterated. Then in a sickening, horrifying moment, his body began to tremble as he recognized the intruder.

"Andy!" he shouted. "Andy, oh my dear God, no!"

Fran suddenly bolted into the room and took in the whole scene in an instant. She quickly sat on the bed and reached over to Sheri and embraced her, trying to calm her.

"Where did he come from?" Fran asked. She did not really expect an answer, and no one gave her one.

"Fran, go upstairs and make sure the kids don't come down," Joe commanded.

"Good idea. I'll take care of it." Fran paused in the doorway for a brief moment. "My God, what did they do to him?" Then she hurried up the stairs to see to the children.

"That c-c-can't be Andy!" Sheri stammered, slowly regaining control. "I've never seen anything like that. He barely looks human."

"I've never seen anything like it either, but it's Andy, no doubt about that." Joe leaned over and looked closely into Andy's partially opened eyes. "We need to do something for him. I think he's dying."

Andy began to stir, quietly groaning and slowly blinking his eyes. He caught sight of Joe, and for a few moments, he seemed to regain consciousness. "Joe," he murmured, barely audible, "you were right."

"Don't try to talk, Andy," Joe said. "You're safe with us now. Just relax, and we'll get you help."

Andy either did not hear Joe or ignored him. "Capsner is… drugs, here in Paradise." He was sounding almost delirious, but sensing his time was short, he pushed himself on. "Last night… Drugs…Treatment center…You were right. It's Capsner."

"I know about Capsner," Joe said. "And the drugs. I was going to tell you Saturday. Who did this to you, Andy? Was it Capsner?"

"No. Another. Rod…Rod…" His voice trailed off.

"Rodriguez? He's here?"

"You know him?" Andy was able to ask.

"Yes, I'll explain it later. Right now, we need to get you help."

"No…Too late."

Joe cradled Andy's head in his arms. "Andy, you have to hang on, please."

"I'm sorry, Joe." Andy's voice was barely a whisper. "I…should have…listened. I'm sorry."

"No, Andy. I'm sorry. I should have told you everything." Joe pulled his old friend close to him. "Andy, please, stay with us."

Andy looked at Joe, and the pain seemed to fade from Andy's eyes. With an arm that had once been powerful, he slowly reached up and grasped Joe's shoulder with the grip of a child. He had no wife, no children. This was where he wanted to be, with his longtime friend. "Joe," he barely uttered, "thank you."

The change was instantaneous. Andy's eyes went from a glowing, glistening reflection of his emotion to the blank stillness of a lifeless corpse.

Andrew Hoffman died in the arms of his best friend.

Chapter 20

"Joe, do something!" Sheri begged.

Joe held Andy tight to his breast, rocking him as if he were a baby, but he did not try to help him. Tears streamed down Joe's face as he gave Sheri the answer that she already knew to be true: "It's no use Sheri. He's dead."

For many minutes, no one made a sound. Throughout all the madness that had occurred over the past few weeks, they had experienced death several times, but never as traumatically as this. This time, it was right before their eyes, and this time, it was a lifelong friend.

Finally, Sheri asked the question that could not be ignored. "Joe, what are we going to do with him?"

Joe looked up slowly, his face showing both sadness and anger. "What are we going to do with him? We're going to call the police, then give him a decent burial. What else can we do?"

Fran had just come into the room. Luckily, the children had not wakened during the turmoil. "Joe," she said as soothingly as she could, "you know we can't do that, at least not yet. We can't tell the police, we can't tell anyone."

Joe gently laid Andy's head down and picked up his robe off the bedpost. He wrapped the robe around his blood-covered body and began pacing back and forth across the room. "I've had it," he said bitterly. "We can never talk to anybody, but one by one, our friends are being murdered. I don't know what we can do, but this must stop." He paused for a moment, pain and anger shooting out from his eyes like fire. Then, with a calmness that belied his emotions, he continued, "No, what I said was wrong. I do know what we can do. We can take the war to them. We can kill Ronald Capsner."

"Joe, you're starting to sound like the way I felt a few weeks ago when Harry first died," Fran said. "But you know that is total foolishness. Even if you were willing to do it, how could you? It's not like anybody here has any experience in killing, especially killing someone who knows much more about it than we do. And that doesn't even consider the fact that there are many others involved, most of whom we don't even know. Killing Capsner by no means resolves the situation here. Besides, you would most likely either get yourself killed or end up in prison for murder."

"Okay, okay, it wasn't a smart idea," Joe admitted. "But we must do something. We agreed earlier today to get more aggressive, then at the first sign of danger, we decided to hold back. We cannot have it both ways. There is still time to make reservations. I am following Capsner tomorrow. If there is any chance at all that I will be able to obtain any useable information, I have to take it. This is not open for discussion. The matter is closed."

He paused for a moment to collect his emotions. Then, with a bit more control, he turned to Sheri and spoke softly, "Don't you see? If we're not willing to take any risks, that just leaves the door open for them to continue. Had we done something earlier, Andy might still be alive. Initially we could reason that it wasn't our responsibility, but from here on out, no action on our part is the same as condoning what they are doing."

Sheri had gotten out of bed and put on her robe. "Okay, Joe, if that is the only way, but I want you to promise me—and I mean give me your solemn word—that if it starts looking too dangerous, you'll get out and come home."

"I promise," Joe replied firmly. "I'm certainly in no hurry to get myself killed." He stopped his pacing, and the flushness of his face brought on by his anger began to fade. It was replaced by a sad emptiness as he looked down at his friend. "First," he said quietly, "we must take care of Andy."

"I don't see why we can't just tell the police," Sheri said. "We haven't done anything wrong."

"Whether or not we have done anything wrong isn't the issue," Fran said. "The problem is that we are still assuming Capsner and his goons are not aware of how much we know. That has been our protection up until now. If word gets out that Andy died in this house, the people that killed him will naturally assume he was able to tell us everything he knew, which is probably quite a lot. We would then become prime targets."

"So what do we do if we can't tell anyone?" Sheri was puzzled. "Hiding a dead body is not an easy thing to do."

"The only feasible consideration is to burry him someplace close until all this blows over," Joe suggested. "Then we can give him a proper burial."

"Won't someone get suspicious when his body doesn't turn up anywhere?" Sheri asked.

"That's a good point," Joe responded. "Somebody out there will be expecting him to be found. For that matter, I wonder how Andy was able to get away in the first place."

"He must have come up from the river," Sheri said, as much to herself as to anyone else. "He's soaking wet, and he smells like river water."

"What on earth could have happened?" Fran asked.

"I just can't imagine," Joe said. "What was it he said? 'Last night, drugs, treatment center, you were right, it's Capsner.'"

"Last night?" Sheri questioned. "There's no way he could have survived those wounds for a whole day."

"He was an awfully strong and determined man," Joe said. "People can do amazing things with the proper motivation. He certainly lost a lot of blood. His face was so white I almost didn't recognize him."

"More than likely it has something to do with that damn mansion," Fran said. "That's on the Whiskey River, but the junction of the Whiskey and the Mississippi isn't too far from here."

"That's right," Joe said. "That must be how he escaped. He probably fell into the river and was washed out of sight of his killers. That could be an advantage for us. It's not unusual for bodies of drown victims to be lost for a long time. They get caught on some underwater debris and sometimes don't surface for months. I think it's reasonable to assume that whoever did this will believe that is exactly what happened to him."

"Where do you have in mind to bury him?" Fran asked, getting back to the real issue to be discussed.

"The only possible place would be our backyard."

"That's ridiculous!" Sheri cried. "Our children play back there with their friends. I'm sorry, that just isn't possible."

"Well, as usual, you're both partially right," Fran said. "Your backyard is just not practical, mainly, as Sheri pointed out, because of the kids. But it must be someplace very close so we can get to it easily without being obvious. To me, it would seem that the most logical place is my backyard."

There was silent consideration for a few moments. Everyone was wishing there was a better way. Finally Joe broke the silence. "I would like to say that we wouldn't think of using your place as a graveyard, but it makes too much sense. I appreciate the offer, Fran. We had better get started if we want to finish with this business while it is still dark."

"What about our friend, the shadow?" Sheri inquired. "He must have seen Andy come into the house."

"Possibly," Joe mused. "But not necessarily. Andy obviously came in the back way, since the back garage door is the only one we usually leave unlocked, and Andy was aware of that. I do not believe there is a good view of the backyard from the wooded area, at least not if a person was in position to watch the front of the house. Considering that, and the fact that it is pitch black outside, I think it may be reasonable to assume Andy was not spotted. Besides, even a spy has to sleep sometime.

"However, that does bring up a good point. With the commotion of getting Andy outside and over to Fran's yard, it is likely Mr. Shadow will realize something odd is going on and uncover what we are doing."

"How do we avoid that?" Sheri asked, afraid that she may already know the answer.

"I suppose the best way is for me to lead him on a wild-goose chase. I could go to work for a couple of hours. That's not a real common thing for me to do at night, but it's not extremely unusual either. I don't think it would make him suspicious."

"You can't be suggesting that Fran and I carry Andy over there and bury him by ourselves," Sheri protested.

"I'm afraid it may be the only way."

"We can handle it, Sheri," Fran said. "I must admit it is not something that I find very appealing, but I do agree it's the only real alternative."

It would be another hour before his relief would arrive. It seemed that this continual surveying of McGowen was pointless. It had been several weeks now, and nothing unusual had occurred. But he also knew from experience that several weeks was not necessarily a long time, especially in an operation like this. Thus far, tonight appeared to be typically quiet. Most of the lights had gone out in the house except for a soft glow in what must be the master bedroom. This certainly did not seem like a prelude to action.

It was a ways off, but the trained ear of the shadow was able to pick up a rustling noise from the back of the house. From his current position, his view of the backyard was totally blocked

The Seduction of Paradise

by the house and the trees. In order to check out the noise, he would have to move several yards off the path into the dense trees and underbrush. He quickly and silently put on his infrared head gear and peered through the small rectangular screen, which gave him a clear view of his surroundings. He easily made his way through the woods to a position offering a full view of the rear of the house and arrived just in time to see a staggering figure go through the back garage door.

Who in the hell could that be, he thought. He went back to his post and quickly dialed a number on his cellular phone.

"It's me," he whispered when he heard an answer. "Something is going on. I just saw somebody sneaking into the back of the garage. I didn't get a chance to see who it was, but he appeared to be hurt."

Suddenly, a series of shrieks came from the room with the glow in the window. Moments later, lights appeared in various other windows.

"Something is happening in there. I can't tell what it is, but I hear one of the ladies letting loose. Don't wait until your shift starts, get your ass here now!"

The shadow was joined within fifteen minutes by his accomplice. "It's been quiet since I talked to you on the phone, but there is some kind of activity going on. We should have bugged the damn house."

"Should we try to get a look through a window?" the accomplice asked.

"It would be a wasted effort," the shadow said. "All the shades and blinds are closed tight. We wouldn't see a damn thing."

They sat patiently and waited. Forty minutes later, the garage door opened, and Joe McGowen backed out in his car.

"This isn't right," the shadow said. "An hour ago, the house was closed up for the night. Then someone sneaks in, apparently scares the shit out of one of the ladies, and now McGowen is leaving. You follow him. I'm going to stay here to see if anything happens."

"Will do. I'll let you know if he goes anywhere or does anything unusual."

The accomplice left to follow Joe, leaving the original shadow to watch the house. After several minutes, he followed a hunch and moved back into the woods to where he could see the rear of the house. He sat with the patience of Job, watching through his infrared screen. He almost jumped with surprise when he finally saw the back door open and the two women emerge, obviously laboring over a heavy bundle. He flipped the screen on his headgear up and took the infrared binoculars out of the case strapped to his belt.

"Holy shit," he whispered to himself as he peered through the binoculars. "They're carrying Hoffman! How in hell did he make it here?"

Two hours later, Joe returned to his home from his decoy trip. This time, he had kept a very watchful eye out for any vehicle that may have been following him. Had he not been looking so closely, it never would have caught his attention, but it was there. The small black vehicle seemed to appear and disappear at irregular intervals, but he was able to observe it several times on his way to his office and several times again on his way back. When he entered the house, he found a very bedraggled Sheri and Fran sipping coffee in the kitchen. Sheri had small bandages on several of her fingers.

"How did it go?" he asked them.

"I don't think we feel much like discussing it right now," Fran said. "I'll say this though: we sure could have used a strong back.

Unfortunately, my old body wasn't up to the heavy work, so Sheri got stuck doing most of the digging."

"Well, it's done," Joe said. "The good news is that I could tell I was followed, which means no one saw what you two were up to. At least we can feel good about that."

Sheri said nothing. The experience had obviously taken its toll on her. Joe sat next to her and lightly squeezed her hand. He knew she needed some time to recover and was not likely in the mood for any kind of pep talk, but just being with her hopefully would provide some comfort.

"I just cannot get Andy's words out of my mind," Joe said at last. "He wasn't rambling, and I don't think he was delirious. It was almost as if he was trying to tell us something."

Everyone sat quietly, needing to rest but not wanting to go to bed. Fatigue was gripping each of them like the claws of a sinister monster, holding them, almost suffocating them, affecting what they thought and how they felt, and leaving them with no clear idea of how to combat it. Joe continued to ponder Andy's final words, his right hand absentmindedly starting to rub his chin. Time passed slowly. Finally Fran stood up, rubbing her eyes, and started for a refill on her coffee, but she stopped abruptly when she heard Joe begin to speak.

"It fits," he said quietly. He looked up at the women, his eyes shining with a new sense of excitement. "It fits!"

"I hate it when you do that," Fran said cynically. "What is it you're trying to say?"

"Remember when we were attempting to piece together the whole operation of moving drugs into this area? The one problem with tying it into the Brewster mansion was the lack of a storage facility large enough to handle any sizeable quantities."

"I remember having that conversation," Sheri said. "What brought that to mind now?"

"Something that Andy said. The 'treatment center.' I didn't know what he meant at first, but I just remembered that when we were little kids, there was a wastewater treatment center at the mouth of the Whiskey River. It shut down so many years ago everyone forgets about it. But there is probably access to it from the mansion. It would be perfect. A large storage area that is invisible to the public."

"But they couldn't just set up shop there without somebody being aware of it," Fran objected.

"No, of course not," Joe said. "That's why I said it all fits. They would need some kind of cover. The Brewster mansion restoration would be perfect. But they would also need an inside contact, someone who has control of the property who could help them with their cover-up. The treatment center is owned by the city, so they would need a city official."

"Like the council chairman," Sheri said, beginning to show signs of enthusiasm.

"Exactly," Joe said. "That's how Spencer got involved."

"But he's been gone for a while now," Fran said. "Wouldn't they need someone else?"

"I fully believe they have someone else," Joe responded. "We just don't know who."

"Mayor Carlson?" Sheri questioned.

"Maybe the whole council," Fran suggested.

"Not Beth," Joe said. "I'm sure she's on our side. Maybe Chief Winfield?"

"So we're right where we were before," Sheri said, "but now we understand a little bit more."

"And I would be willing to bet I'll find out a lot more when I follow Capsner tomorrow," Joe said. "Which reminds me, I don't know anything about his flights. I'll have to play my game with the airlines again."

Joe assumed Capsner would be on Northwest since they had the vast majority of flights in and out of Minneapolis. He called the number for reservation information and pretended to be

Capsner, just as he had done with Spencer. This time, there was no listing for Capsner at all.

It must be another airline, Joe thought. There were only a couple others to choose from, so it was not surprising that his next guess proved to be the correct one.

"Pan Am reservations," a friendly-sounding woman's voice answered.

"Yes, hello, my name is Ronald Capsner, and I'm checking on my flight schedule to New York from Minneapolis," Joe said. "My secretary made my reservations, and I forgot to get the details from her. I know I'm leaving sometime tomorrow, but I'm not sure of the time or flight number. Could you please help me out?"

"Of course, Mr. Capsner, we wouldn't want to leave you stranded. Let me see. Yes, here it is, you are confirmed on Flight 566 to JFK at twelve ten in the afternoon."

"JFK?" Joe whispered, with the definite sound of a question in his voice. He was surprised, if not thoroughly confused, that Capsner was actually going to New York instead of Miami.

"Is there a problem, Mr. Capsner?" the voice came.

"No, not at all. I usually fly into Newark, so I was a little surprised. But that is just fine. Thank you for your help."

"You're welcome, Mr. Capsner. Do you need the information on your connecting flight?"

"Connecting flight?" Joe questioned.

"Yes, sir, to Washington, DC."

Joe sat silent, stunned, even more so than when he first found out Spencer Thurman was going to Miami instead of New York.

"Mr. Capsner?"

"Uh? Oh, yes, yes, I would, thank you."

"You will be connecting on Flight 261, leaving at 4:30 p.m. and arriving at Washington National one hour later at 5:30."

"Thank you very much," Joe said. "You've been very helpful." He hung up the phone, trying to comprehend what he had just heard.

Fran and Sheri were anxious to here the news.

"Hey there," Fran said. "Are you going to let us in on whatever caused you to go catatonic, or do we have to guess?"

"I'm sorry," Joe mumbled. "It's all so confusing." He briefly related the conversation. "I cannot imagine what is going on, but this may be more important than we first thought."

"What about your friend, the shadow?" Sheri asked. "I don't think you want him to know you're taking a flight to Washington at the same time Capsner is."

"Good point. I also don't want to go on any high-speed chases through the city trying to lose him. But you're right, I must be able to get to the airport without him knowing."

The three of them sat in silence for several minutes, trying to concoct some sort of plan. Finally, Joe came up with an idea. "There is a very simple way to handle this, but it will let the shadow know that he has been spotted. But at least he won't be able to follow me."

"Maybe it's time he found out," Fran said. "Maybe it will make him back off for a while. What's your idea?"

※

At nine thirty the following morning, a taxicab pulled into the McGowen driveway. Joe had made reservations on Northwest Flight 316, a direct flight to Washington National Airport arriving at 2:59 p.m. He wanted to make sure he got to DC well ahead of Capsner, even if he ran into a few of the typical airline delays. Flight 316 would allow him two and a half hours at National to prepare for his encounter with the phony historian.

"It's time to go," Joe said with a sense of resolve. He said good-bye to his children, picking each one up and giving them a big hug. Then he turned to Fran. "Wish me luck," he said.

"Oh, you won't need any luck," Fran said. "Everything will work out just fine."

Joe took a few steps toward the door then abruptly halted when Fran called out, "Joe?"

"Yes?" Joe replied.

There was a brief moment of silence. "Take care of yourself, Joe."

"Of course. I'll see you tomorrow night."

Joe left the house and climbed into the taxi.

"Where to?" the raspy-voiced driver asked.

"I want you to head south on 169 then take Highway 12 east to 94, then go north."

"Hey, mister, I know this city like the back of my hand. Just tell me where you want to go, and I'll know the way."

"Please do exactly as I told you," Joe said shortly.

"Okay, buddy. It's your ticket. But it seems to me you're just going in a big circle."

The cabbie did as Joe directed. Thirty minutes later, they were heading north on Highway 94, in the opposite direction of the airport. A solid concrete barrier about four feet high separated the north- and south-bound lanes. Along this stretch of road, there was about two miles between the exits. Joe tried to nonchalantly check if they were being followed, but he was not able to spot the black vehicle anywhere. There was no doubt in his mind, however, that the shadow was there. Maybe he was hanging further back, or maybe he had changed cars, but Joe knew he was there.

"I want you to get in the far left lane," Joe instructed. "I'm going to ask you to stop up ahead about a mile, and it's important that you do it precisely where I ask you to. How much do I owe you so far?"

"The meter's coming up on fourteen dollars."

"Here is twenty dollars," Joe said, handing a bill to the cabbie. "In just a moment, you will see a car parked along the shoulder on the other side of the barrier facing south. Please stop alongside that car."

"Whatever you want, mister," the cabbie said, shaking his head and grabbing the twenty-dollar bill.

Eight hundred feet farther up the road, a parked car came into view over the top of the barrier.

"There it is," Joe barked. "Pull over and stop."

"Do you want me to call a tow truck or anything?" the cabbie asked as he eased to a stop.

"No thanks," Joe called. He flung the door open, jumped out of the cab, and leaped over the barrier. He ran to the far side of the waiting car and quickly climbed into the passenger side of the front seat. Immediately Sheri put the car in gear and sped off down the highway. Watching out the back window, Joe could see a small gray Sunbird in the northbound lane pull over to the shoulder and come to a full stop. After just a few moments, it moved back into the flow of traffic and drove out of sight.

"Do you think he will try and follow us?" Sheri asked.

"There is no way he would be able to find us," Joe said. "It's at least another mile to the next exit, and he would have to go through two stoplights to cross over the freeway and head back in this direction. He won't be back."

"This was a good plan." Sheri smiled. "It was just as easy as you said it would be."

"The only part that troubles me," Joe said, "is that we tipped our hand a bit. They now know that we know I'm being watched. But we can worry about that when I get back. If we're lucky, I'll get enough information on this trip to turn over to the FBI, and we won't have to worry about any of this anymore."

They drove the final twenty minutes to the airport in relative silence. Sheri parked in front of the main terminal to let Joe off. There was no point in her coming in; Joe would be leaving in a few minutes, and she wanted to get back home to the children.

Joe opened the door, then turned to look at Sheri. "I'll see you tomorrow night," he said quietly.

"You know, we never finished what we started last night," Sheri said in almost a whisper.

"We will." Joe smiled. "Tomorrow, and the next day too, and every day after that."

"I love you, Joe. You will come back to me, won't you?"

Joe reached out and pulled Sheri to him, holding her close. "I love you," he said. "I love you so much. Of course I'll be back. I will be here tomorrow night." He released her, not wanting to look into her eyes, afraid that his own strength might crumble.

Fighting the urge to change his mind and return home with his wife, he quickly stepped out of the car and darted into the airport. Sheri could only sit and watch, capturing Joe's image in her mind like a snapshot, trying to record every detail of the man she loved for later recall just in case—well, just in case. After several minutes, she wiped away her tears and drove off toward her home.

The white-haired man walked into the large office, shut the door, and slumped down into the plush leather chair. It had been a long while since he was able to relax and enjoy this office. It may turn out that in a short time he will not have access to it at all. He reached for the ever-present bottle of brandy and poured himself a drink, not really wanting it as much as taking it out of habit. So much was happening; things were slowly getting out of control again. He had thought with Spencer out of the picture, everything would progress according to plan. It did for a while, and Mr. Salvo had been pleased. But then Hoffman stuck his nose in. Why was there always someone who insisted on causing problems? Hopefully, his body would not turn up soon, but what if it did? Salvo was already indicating that he might pull the plug on this whole operation. He was very clear about no one else getting hurt to add to the already suspiciously long list of "accidental" deaths.

He was also concerned about Beth Wence. Was she going to become a problem also? Then there was McGowen and that damn Rosten woman. They seem to have been low-key the past few weeks, but his gut feeling said they were still a major threat. Somehow he must get everything back under control, and very soon. He must keep Salvo content. He had come too far to have it all end just because some old man was losing his nerve.

Luckily Rodriguez was in town. He was a man who knew how to handle people like Wence and McGowen. If he worked closely with Rodriguez, the two of them could take care of the troublemakers before Salvo was even aware of it. Yes, he would have to meet with Rodriguez soon and discuss his plan.

Chapter 21

Sharon Carlson was finishing her preparations for the meeting she had arranged with Chief Winfield. After hearing his excuses for not being able to attend on a previous occasion, she had started to worry that he was intentionally avoiding her. If that were true, was it because he suspected something, or was he involved in some way? But he finally agreed to come to her home this evening, and hopefully, after their meeting tonight, she would have answers to all her questions.

The meeting was purely for business, but since it was in her home, she felt she should provide some sort of refreshments, as any good host would do. She set a pot of coffee with the appropriate condiments on the large oak dinner table, alongside a small tray of assorted cookies. She took one last look into the wall mirror to check her makeup and hair. She had known Byron Winfield for a very long time, ever since he and her late husband began hunting together nearly thirty years ago. But she had never really become close to him personally. He was always her husband's friend. When her husband passed away ten years ago, she virtually never saw Byron socially, although they remained friends professionally. This would be an awkward meeting. She wished there was a way to avoid it altogether, but circumstances dictated what she knew she must do.

Sharon tucked a loose strand of hair behind her ear just as she heard Winfield's car pull into the driveway. She quickly walked over to the buffet next to the table for the final, and most important, step of her preparations. She opened the top drawer and stood for a brief moment, not fully believing what she was considering. Did events really warrant this? Could the circumstances in Paradise really have come so far as to turn her into this kind of person?

The soft tone of the doorbell announced Chief Winfield's arrival. Mayor Carlson reached into the drawer and removed the .38-caliber pistol, ironically the same type used by Winfield's officers. She placed the gun in her purse, put on her most pleasant smile, and went to answer the door.

The circular concourse was very familiar to Joe. He traveled frequently to Washington on business, and always on Northwest. In fact, the Northwest concourse changed very little from his days at the Naval Academy. Joe walked out through the dimly lit tunnel with the curved walls and into the main terminal of Washington National Airport, where he began to reconsider his original plan of renting a car. He traveled to Washington quite often, but he almost always went to the same office building for meetings and was not particularly familiar with most of the city. He also knew traffic in Washington was almost always congested. Following Capsner would be difficult, and nearly impossible without being spotted. This time, he decided he would wait for Capsner then pursue him in a taxi. A long line of taxis was readily available, so Joe knew he would not have any trouble getting one. He headed to the gate where Capsner's Pan Am flight was scheduled to arrive and began preparing himself mentally for whatever may be in store for him.

There were many similarities between this trip and his previous spying adventure with Spencer, but in some ways, the two experiences were dramatically different. They both involved long periods of waiting in anxious anticipation, requiring great patience and self-control. But this trip lacked any of the excitement that Joe had initially felt in Florida. This time, he was fully aware of the danger, and this time, he knew he was following a trained professional. But his motivation was much stronger now than it had been before, for now he knew the seriousness of what was happening, and now he knew he was after the men who killed Andy.

Pan Am Flight 261 arrived exactly on schedule. Joe sat in the back corner of a crowded bar offering a clear view of the gate area. After numerous people had departed, he caught sight of Capsner walking briskly but calmly out of the jet way. He looked like any one of a thousand businessmen, unlike the nervous, fidgety Spencer Thurman. Capsner walked down the concourse to the main terminal and out the door to the sidewalk. Joe knew that Capsner must be getting a taxi since he bypassed all the car-rental agencies, so he hurried out the door himself and prepared to hail a cab, easily keeping out of Capsner's view on the crowded sidewalk. As Capsner's cab pulled away from the curb, Joe jumped into the next one in line.

"Follow that cab," Joe commanded, indicating Capsner's vehicle.

"You've got to be kidding." The driver grinned. "Twenty years of driving taxi in this city, and I never once heard anybody say 'Follow that cab.'"

"Do it!" Joe shouted.

"Okay." The cabbie surrendered. "This might be fun."

The cars cruised for nearly half an hour, covering nearly every area of downtown Washington. They passed several of the famous monuments, including the White House and the large domed structure of the Capitol. At one point, when they drove along the service road in front of the Lincoln Memorial, Joe's thoughts temporarily drifted from his real mission. This was one of his favorite monuments, and even after visiting it many times, he still maintained a schoolboy's ideological sense of pride when he was here. He remembered on one occasion carrying three-year-old Brandon on his shoulders up the long flight of steps and reading aloud the Gettysburg Address carved into the side of Lincoln's chamber. He hoped his children would grow to share his love and respect of this man and this country.

"I don't think this guy knows where he's going," the driver remarked, snapping Joe out of his nostalgic daydreaming.

"I think he does," Joe said. "He's trying to give a false trail, just in case."

"So let me ask you," the driver said cautiously, "are you one of the good guys or one of the bad guys?"

"Do you think there's a difference in this city?" Joe remarked, somewhat cynically.

"You've got a point there," the driver replied.

Suddenly, he braked the car and pulled over to the curb. "Your friend is getting out about a block up ahead. I assume you would like to keep some distance between you."

"You assumed correctly." Joe flipped the driver a twenty-dollar bill and quickly hopped out the back door. Then, as an afterthought, he poked his head back in. "Thanks, buddy," he said with a smile.

"Anytime. I hope things work out."

Joe closed the door and started off after Capsner, trying as he went to get a bearing on where he was in the city. The buildings looked vaguely familiar, and he had the definite sense of being in this area before. Up ahead, he saw Capsner turn into a very large building, but from his vantage point, Joe was unable to identify what the building was. He started to run, knowing Capsner could not see him. He crossed the road at the corner and bolted up over the curb then instantly froze in horrifying confusion. The large impressive sign mounted on the sidewalk in front of the building read Federal Bureau of Investigation.

"What!" Joe said out loud. "What in hell is going on?"

He had no idea what to do at this point, but he knew he could not wander through the FBI complex looking for Capsner. The only thing he could think of was to wait where he was until Capsner returned. He crossed the street and stood among a small group of people waiting for a bus, not knowing if his vigil would be minutes or hours. As he waited, he tried to formulate some reasonable scenario that would logically explain Capsner's visit to the FBI, but he could not seem to make the pieces of the puzzle fit.

His wait turned out to be only a quarter hour. When Capsner emerged, Joe was surprised to see him accompanied by a woman. She was about forty years old and could have been attractive, had it not been for the stern, domineering expression that was etched into her face. She had the very definite appeal of being all business.

They turned left and walked briskly down the street, seeming to Joe like they were in a hurry but trying not to show it. From what he could see, it appeared as if they were talking very little. After four blocks, they turned into a small not-too-crowded bar called Capitol Tavern. Joe reached the front door and stopped before entering. He had no idea where they would be. It was possible they were just inside the door and would spot him immediately if he entered. He began pacing back and forth on the sidewalk, trying to figure out how to safely get inside. His frustration was rising to the level of near panic. Something could be going on in there that he needed to be aware of.

"Excuse me," Joe heard someone say. He looked up and saw three men and a woman trying to get to the door. Joe had absentmindedly been pacing right in front, blocking passage of the group.

"Oh, sorry," he mumbled, and stepped out of the way.

One of the men opened the door, and the four of them crowded through the entrance. Just as the door was about to close, a thought struck Joe. Without taking the time to consider the merits of his decision, he quickly stepped through the door behind the last man, using the group as a shield to protect himself from the view of anyone inside. Once in, he stepped to the side near a hallway leading to the restrooms. Here he was able to stand fairly inconspicuously and scan the room for Capsner and his female friend.

The tavern was relatively small, but the tables were, for the most part, isolated enough to provide some degree of privacy, obviously why this place was selected for Capsner and the woman's meeting. Joe immediately spotted them in the far corner having what appeared to be an intense conversation. He had no idea what they were discussing, but he felt compelled to get close enough to eavesdrop. Surveying the room, however, he did not think it would be possible. Capsner and the woman were seated in a corner where the back wall of the tavern joined a half-wall partition. On top of the partition sat numerous green leafy plants. This arrangement provided privacy for the couple, but it also allowed someone to sit on the other side of the partition without being easily observed. Unfortunately, a young couple sat at the table located there, sipping drinks and smiling affectionately at each other, occasionally giving each other a light, tender kiss.

Great, Joe thought. *I will miss getting the information that could help end this nightmare because a couple of horny kids have to play kissy-face.*

His mind raced. He considered just going up and asking the couple for the table, but that would almost certainly give himself away to Capsner.

While he struggled with other possible solutions, it was as if God decided for once to make things easy for him. The young couple clasped hands, kissed a longer, more passionate kiss, and began to get up from the table. Joe could not believe his good fortune and immediately moved toward the table before someone else had the chance to take it. The young couple had barely gotten to their feet when Joe slid into a chair facing away from the partition and with his back to Capsner. The young man gave him a startled, somewhat offended looked then walked off with his date.

Capsner and the woman were talking very quietly, but being only a few feet away, Joe was able to make out most of what they were saying.

"So you believe Salvo is going to terminate the project?" the woman asked.

"He never came out and clearly said that, but he has made it known he is very disappointed with the way it has been handled. He is a very smart and cautious man. If he believes the risks are too high, I'm sure he will shut it down."

"That would be terrible. We've invested far too much money to have it just end cold turkey. Do you think you could meet with him personally and try to persuade him to continue for a while longer?"

"I don't know," Capsner said. "Like I said, he's very cautious. He doesn't meet with many people personally. He doesn't even see Rodriguez as much as he used to."

"That's probably better. He seems to be getting out of control."

"He has always been out of control, but at least he agrees with us that we should keep the project moving."

"Maybe the two of you could meet with Salvo," the woman suggested.

"Maybe. I suppose it's worth a try. The problem is, even if he agrees, I'm not sure Paradise is a good location anymore. We have already lost all the advantages that it originally had to offer, except for its proximity to the Twin Cities, of course. It was supposed to be a sleepy little town where no one would ask questions. But look what has happened."

"The situation is not beyond repair," the woman said. "It's too late to find a new location. It's Paradise or nowhere. But Salvo is right about one thing: there can be no more killings. You are the one who is supposed to be in charge up there. It's time you start handling the situation."

"Wait just a minute, Thompson. I think I've done a pretty good job. The problem is with the damn Jamaicans. Their answer to everything is to shoot somebody. Salvo should have left them in Miami and let me handle this alone."

Every muscle in Joe's body stiffened with tension as the recognition of the name sent fear bolting down his spine like lightning. Cool droplets of perspiration formed on his entire body almost immediately. *Thompson*, he thought. Special Agent Thompson from the FBI, whom he called after seeing Spencer murdered, was a woman. The coincidence was too great. This must be that same person. But if that were true, everything took on a whole new perspective. Things were not at all as he had thought. It was not the case that the FBI did not believe him but that they were involved. And since Joe had called this Special Agent Thompson, she knew everything. That must be why he was being followed. They have known everything all along. They were just playing with Joe and his family, probably hoping to find the missing document from the package.

What else was different from what he had previously believed? Was Beth really a spy too? Maybe they convinced her to try and win Joe over. *My God*, he thought. His family was back there, totally defenseless. And then the most terrifying part of all: even if he was able to get incriminating evidence, who could he give it to? The hole he was in kept getting deeper and deeper, and now, for the first time, he truly believed there was no way out.

"What about Hoffman? Does Salvo know yet?" Thompson asked.

"He knows he was killed, but he doesn't know he turned up at McGowen's," Capsner said.

Joe's eyes grew wide in horror. He felt his body begin to tremble, and only with supreme effort could he get himself under control. *How did they know?* he thought. There must have been more than one shadow.

"Are you going to tell him?" Thompson asked.

"I think I'll have to," Capsner answered. "At least then we can put his mind at ease about him turning up someplace else. McGowen really did us a favor by burying him. I'm just concerned about Rodriguez. If he finds out, you know what he will want to do."

Special Agent Thompson pondered this. "I agree we cannot have Rodriguez starting a war up there, but the situation with McGowen concerns me. I still think we need to take him out. If it's done subtly, I don't think it will arouse suspicion."

"I disagree. We're keeping a close eye on him. If he shows any sign of being a problem, we can act then."

Just then a quiet beeping sounded from somewhere. "What the hell is that?" Capsner asked.

Thompson opened her purse and took out a small cellular phone. "I like to always be accessible," she said. She pressed a button and brought the phone to her head. "Thompson," she said quickly.

There was a pause as she listened, then, "What do you mean you lost him?"

Another pause.

"Hold on. Capsner is with me now." She cupped her hand over the mouthpiece. "McGowen just gave Mueller the slip. And it was a well-thought-out job. McGowen obviously knew he was being followed. The concern here is, where did he go? It must be somewhere important, or he wouldn't have gone to the trouble of losing Mueller."

"Shit!" Capsner exclaimed. "Not now. We have got to stop him before he does something that Salvo won't like."

"That's it," Thompson said. "No more screwing around. McGowen had better turn up soon, and when he does, I'm instructing Mueller to take him. This is too much bullshit to deal with. In the meantime, Mueller can take the rest of the family now, along with the Rosten woman." She picked up the phone again. "Execute Operation Red immediately," she barked. "That's correct, all of them."

My God, thought Joe. *I have to get out and call Sheri. She must get out now.* If he left quietly the way he came in, he should be able to get out without being noticed.

"Wait a minute," Thompson whispered. "Wait one fucking minute. Damn it! McGowen followed Thurman to Miami. Now he disappears the same day you come out here. Damn it, Capsner, I know where the son of a bitch is!"

Thompson jumped up from her chair and quickly scanned the bar. Joe put his head down, not knowing whether he should try to look inconspicuous or make a run for it.

"You think he's here?" Capsner asked.

"Of course he's here. He followed you. Maybe he's outside. You know what he looks like. See if you can spot him."

Capsner stood up and looked around. "Let's not make a scene," he said. Then, out of the corner of his eye, he noticed a body through the plants hunched over a table on the other side of the partition. "I don't believe it," he said in a low, angry voice.

Joe kept his head down, but he could hear Capsner step around the partition in his direction. Joe waited for just a moment then, with a quickness that surprised even himself, he turned and lunged at Capsner, shrieking a wild, crazed scream to further throw Capsner off guard. The much-older Capsner stumbled back and crashed over a nearby table. Thompson sprang on Joe from behind, attempting to use her FBI training to subdue him.

"Somebody help me out!" she called to no one in particular. "I'm FBI."

Initially, no one moved. Joe spun around, trying to free himself from the scrappy Thompson. She had his right arm twisted behind his back and was attempting to fasten cuffs on his wrist. Joe finally threw all his weight backward into Thompson, driving her into the wall. He took one step forward then planted his feet and drove her back again. He heard her cry out and felt her grip weaken. Frantic to get free before Capsner could recover, he spun around and ripped his arm from her grasp. With his left arm, he backhanded the already hurting Thompson across the face, splitting her lip and smashing her head into the wall behind her. Joe was reacting out of a combination of fear and rage, wanting to get free to warn his family but wanting these two to pay for what they had done to his friends and his town. But he knew he must get out before the police arrived since they would obviously side with the FBI agent.

Joe turned to flee, but for just the briefest of moments, the images of a bloody Andy lying dead on his bed and a widowed Fran trying to get on with her life alone flashed through his mind. He could not resist one last shot at the people responsible. He turned back to Thompson. "You bitch!" he screamed, and drove his fist square into her face, breaking her nose and sending blood shooting out like juice from a squashed tomato. He let her fall to the floor then made a charge for the door.

By now, the other patrons of the tavern had time to take in what was happening. Capsner, pulling himself up off the floor, repeated Thompson's earlier plea for help. "Stop that man! That woman is an FBI agent."

Two heavyset men finally moved toward Joe, but it was clear they did not have as great a motivation to capture him as he had to escape. He pushed the two men aside and burst through the door into the early evening twilight.

A police car was just rounding the corner with its siren blaring. Joe, already out of breath, bolted down the street in the opposite direction, having no idea where he was headed, only that he must get away and warn his family. He ran aimlessly for as long as his lungs and legs would allow. Finally, near total exhaustion, he collapsed on a corner bench and tried to catch his breath. He must have successfully made his escape without being spotted by the police, he thought, or he never would have gotten this far. How long had he been running? He had no idea. Probably twenty or thirty minutes. It was noticeably darker now than when he first ran out of the bar.

He needed to warn his family. He probably had already wasted too much time. He forced himself to get up and stumble over to a nearby pay phone. A small group of people near the phone quickly backed out of his way as he approached. Puzzled, he looked down at himself and became aware for the first time of what a mess he was. He was drenched in sweat, his shirt was torn up the back with the ragged edges blowing free around his waist, and his right hand and sleeve were covered with blood. No wonder people were afraid of him.

Using his calling card, he dialed the number of his home phone. *Please be there*, he thought. *Dear God, please let Sheri be home.*

"Hello," he heard Sheri's voice after the first ring.

"Sheri! Oh, thank God, you're there."

"Joe? What's the matter? Are you all right?"

"I'm fine. Sheri, listen, there is very little time. You and Fran and the kids must get out of there immediately. This is worse than we thought. The FBI is working with Capsner. They know everything—where we buried Andy, what I saw in Miami, everything. They even knew I followed Capsner here. They're sending someone to get you. Sheri, I think they intend to kill all of us."

"Joe, settle down. Who is coming?"

"We can discuss the details later. You must get out. Now!"

"Where should we go? Is there anyone here we can trust?"

"No," Joe said emphatically. "Absolutely no one." He thought for a moment. There has to be a place for them. Suddenly, an idea came to him. Of course, that would work. "Sheri, go to the airport. I'll call ahead and have tickets waiting for you. Take Fran and the kids to Los Angeles. I'll have Ryan meet you at LAX. You can stay with him for now."

"We can't just go to California without packing things. I'll need time—"

"No, you must leave now. Don't you understand? Your lives are in danger. You can get whatever you need in LA."

"What about you? What are you going to do? Will we see you at Ryan's?"

"We'll talk later. Just get out as quickly as you can."

Joe hung up the phone and immediately called Northwest Airlines to book his family and Fran on the next direct flight to LAX, which turned out to be leaving in two hours. *Two hours is perfect*, he thought. *Plenty of time for them to get to the airport.* Next he dialed the number of his brother in Riverside, California. It was three hours earlier there, but he should still be home from school.

"Hello," came a loud, cheerful voice.

"Ryan, this is Joe."

"Joe, how are you doing? We haven't talked for a while. What's up?"

"Ryan, can Sheri and the kids stay with you for a few days?"

"Whoa, hold on a minute," Ryan said. "Are you serious?"

"Yes, I'm serious. They need a place to stay. They are coming into LAX tonight at nine o'clock. Can you pick them up?"

"Tonight? Joe, I've got a date tonight, and I don't think... What the hell is going on, Joe?"

"I'm sorry I'm hitting you with this out of the blue, but something came up that Sheri can tell you about when she gets there," Joe said. "This is very important, Ryan. Just be there at nine o'clock, okay?"

"Joe, I...Yeah, sure, I can be there."

"Thanks, Ryan. One more thing, and this is very important: do not discuss this with anyone, and don't answer any questions about it if anyone asks, even if they say they're from the FBI. In fact, especially if they say they're from the FBI. Do you understand?"

"Sure I do," Ryan said. "I'll pick up your family for reasons I know nothing about, and I can't tell the FBI if they ask. Why should that confuse me?"

"Good," Joe continued, without acknowledging the obvious sarcasm. "Also, do you remember Fran Rosten? She'll be with Sheri too."

"Joe—"

"Thanks, Ryan. I'll call you later."

Joe hung up the phone, feeling at least a little relieved that his family was taken care of. Maybe he should call Sheri just to let her know he made contact with Ryan, he thought. Quickly he dialed his home number, and after four unanswered rings, he heard the sound of his own voice on the answering machine. He hung up again, relieved that Sheri, Fran, and the kids had gotten safely out.

Sheri hung up the phone, feeling bewildered and afraid.

"What was that all about?" Fran asked.

"I'm not completely sure," Sheri answered. "It was Joe, and somehow, he found out that Capsner is in cahoots with the FBI. He said our lives are in danger and that we must get out immediately. We're supposed to go to the airport and catch a flight to Los Angeles to meet his brother, Ryan. He doesn't even want us to take the time to pack."

"Is he all right?" Fran inquired.

"I believe so, but I couldn't tell for sure. I suppose we should trust that he knows what he's doing. Let's get the kids and go. If he's right, we don't have much time."

Sheri went to get Katelin while Fran helped ready Maureen and Brandon.

"Come on, you two," Fran said. "We get to go to visit Uncle Ryan. This is going to be fun. We might even get to swim in the ocean."

"Don't we have school tomorrow?" Brandon asked.

"Oh, everybody misses a day of school now and then. We'll be back soon."

"Goodie!" Brandon screamed as he dashed off to find his shoes. "No school tomorrow!"

"Mrs. Rosten?" Maureen asked quietly after Brandon had left.

"Yes, dear?"

"I'm a little scared. I heard you talking. That was Daddy on the phone. He thinks were in danger, doesn't he?"

Fran looked at the little girl. Suddenly, she did not seem as much like a child as she had before. She was getting older and becoming more aware. She could easily see through the innocent white lies told to protect her.

"Listen, honey," Fran said softly. "You're right, that was your father. He is okay, but he wants us to get away for a while. It is possible that there may be some danger if we stay, but we will be all right at your uncle's house. It is very important that you be strong for us now. Do you understand?"

"Yes, Mrs. Rosten, I understand. I will be strong, but I'm still a little scared."

Fran wrapped both arms around Maureen and squeezed her tight. "Oh, my precious sweetheart, I guess I am too a little bit. But we'll be okay. Now run along, and get your shoes on."

Just then the chime of the doorbell rang through the house. Everyone immediately froze, not wanting to know who was at the door. After a few moments, the bell rang a second time. Sheri ran into the living room where Fran was standing. She was holding Katelin tight to her breast, as if protecting her.

"What do we do?" she asked.

"I don't know," Fran answered, for the first time feeling fear begin to mount within her. "I think we have to answer the door. Whoever is out there won't just go away. Maybe it's just a salesman."

Sheri slowly walked to the door and very cautiously eased it open. "May I help you?" she said to the stranger waiting outside.

Maureen and Brandon crowded around her legs, knowing something was very wrong but not understanding what or why.

The man at the door smiled and flashed a large shiny badge contained in a leather case with a clear plastic covering. In a very pleasant voice, he said, "Good evening, Mrs. McGowen. I do not want to alarm you, but I am Special Agent Mueller from the FBI."

Sheri heard Fran gasp behind her. She looked up the short flight of steps to see Fran holding a hand over her mouth, her face very pale. "The man in the car," she whispered. "Joe's shadow."

Sheri stepped back and pushed Maureen and Brandon behind her. She stared at Mueller with a look of cold steel, her eyes flashing with determined resolve much more than with fear. "If you touch my children, I'll kill you," she seethed.

The brief tense silence was broken by the ringing of the telephone.

"Please don't answer that," Mueller said, the smile never leaving his face.

Chapter 22

Joe walked aimlessly through the streets of Washington, feeling useless and hopeless, not knowing what he should or could do, his only thoughts focusing on his family. He would feel much better when he knew that they were safe at Ryan's house in California. Then he would be able to relax, and then he could begin planning what his next move would be. At this point, it seemed like the best decision would be to go to California and join his family and stay there. He had read books and seen movies about the corruption in Washington. FBI and CIA agents were always secretly working for the other side. But he never believed it was really like that. But now, fearing the FBI as much as Capsner and his thugs, it certainly seemed to be true. Who could he turn to? Maybe it was time to admit defeat. He and his family were still alive, that was more than poor Andy could say. Maybe he should just get out while he still had the chance.

He had no idea how long he had been walking. He stopped and checked his watch: eight forty. His family and Fran should be safely in the air by now. At midnight, Washington time, they should be on the ground. Nearly two and a half more hours. He would not be able to think of anything else until then. He continued to walk, looking like a homeless vagabond, his hand and sleeve still covered with blood.

Whether it was totally coincidental or whether he was somehow subconsciously drawn, Joe found himself eventually at the foot of the Lincoln Memorial. It looked different now. All the monuments looked different. They no longer generated that deep sense of pride within him as they had before this day. He remembered back to his days at the Naval Academy and how delusional he had been when he discovered it was not the special place he had always believed it to be. But this was much worse. This whole city, the capital of his beloved country, now disgusted him. Like a little boy seeing reality for the first time, he began to believe what others had often said: there were no true heroes, no role models to follow. This was a country run by corruption and greed, and probably always had been. The Washingtons, the Jeffersons, the Lincolns were most likely no different than the power-hungry, self-serving men in office today. Joe slowly hung his head, rubbing his tired eyes with his forefinger and thumb, and with an emptiness that reached to the very heart of his being, he turned his back on the huge image of Lincoln staring down at him from his lighted throne.

He wandered the short distance to a nearby phone booth under a grove of large elm trees. The night was very warm and typically humid for Washington. Joe sat on a small patch of grass, exhausted, slowly letting the time pass. Minute by agonizing minute, he waited, hoping and praying that his family would reach California safely. Finally, after what seemed like an eternity, his watch read twelve o'clock. They should be there now. But it would be another hour or more before they reached Ryan's house.

Joe could not wait any longer. He had to know now. He went to the phone, and with the help of information, he called the number of LAX Airport. The man who answered connected him with the paging service, through which he had his brother, Ryan, summoned to the phone. After several minutes, he made his connection.

"Yes, this is Ryan McGowen."

"Ryan, this is Joe," Joe blurted with obvious urgency. "Did Sheri make it there all right?"

"Damn you, Joe! Stop jerking me around. I miss my date and fight through horrendous traffic because of some stupid whim of yours, and now no one shows up. I'm getting tired of this. What is going on?"

"What do you mean, no one showed up?"

"You know what I mean. Sheri and the kids, and whoever that other lady is. Their flight arrived fifteen minutes ago, but they weren't on it. Are you telling me you didn't know that?"

Joe said nothing. He closed his eyes and leaned against the phone, dropping the receiver to hang loosely on its cord. Finally, he could not contain himself. "No, no, no!" he screamed in anguish, beating his fist against the side of the booth. "My God, no, not my family!"

"Joe, Joe, are you all right?" Ryan's voice could be heard from the dangling receiver. "Joe, talk to me."

Finally, Joe regained some control and picked up the phone. "Ryan, be very careful. Don't answer any questions from anybody. I have to go, but I'll call you later to explain. Trust no one."

He hung up the phone and immediately called Northwest Airlines.

"Northwest Reservations, may I help you?" the robotically pleasant woman's voice answered.

"Yes. My name is Joe McGowen. My wife and three children were supposed to be on the seven thirty flight from Minneapolis to LA. My wife's name is Sheri, and she is also traveling with a woman named Fran Rosten. Can you tell me if they were on that flight?"

"Of course, Mr. McGowen, one moment."

Joe heard the endless punching of a keyboard. *Come on, come on*, he thought.

Finally, the pleasant voice returned. "I'm sorry, Mr. McGowen. It shows that they did have reservations, but they apparently never got on the flight. I'm sure there is a good reason for it. Would you like me to check anything else, Mr. McGowen? Mr. McGowen?"

The voice was speaking to an empty booth. Joe had run out, nearly destroyed by what he heard. There was nothing left. They had bled him dry. He had known the risks involved, they all had, but he never dreamed the price would be so high. It was over; the bad guys had won. It was not enough that he failed himself, but much worse, he had failed his family. Maureen, Brandon, and poor little Katelin.

Joe buried his face in his hands, trying to erase the image of his helpless children at the mercy of the wicked men. Tears streamed down his soiled cheeks as his bitter grief overwhelmed him. On the verge of total breakdown, he ran off mindlessly with no thought to his direction, wanting only to get away from his pain, from his guilt and disappear into the humid Washington night.

Book Two

Vengeance of the Just

Courage is not the absence of fear, but the mastery of it.
—Author Unknown

Chapter 23

Northwest Flight 310 made its final approach to Minneapolis–Saint Paul International Airport, passing just south of downtown Minneapolis. It was nine o'clock in the evening, and as the late August sun began to dip below the western horizon, it cast an impressive red glow on the city's skyline. Gazing out the window, Ryan McGowen attempted to identify familiar landmarks, but so much had changed in the five years since his last visit that he scarcely recognized the city he once thought of as home.

As the flight attendants prepared for landing, Ryan sat back in his seat and again found himself questioning the logic of his decision to go to Paradise. What would he do there? He did not have an answer, but he remembered vividly the anguish in Joe's voice: "Be very careful. Don't answer any questions from anybody. Trust no one!" That was just not like Joe. Something obviously very serious had happened, and for some reason, Joe chose not to confide in him. Why? Was it to protect him?

It had not been until Ryan arrived at his condo after returning from the airport the evening before that he truly felt alarmed. It was obvious something had gone wrong, but he did not believe it concerned him. If Joe and Sheri were having problems, they would have to work them out for themselves. But from Joe's remarks about the FBI and to trust no one, it had to be something much more important than that. Then, as Ryan approached his home and saw two men in dark suits at his door, he realized that now it did concern him. He did not even stop but just cruised on by, not giving the men a second look.

It was late, and he had no idea of where to go. Finally, he stopped at a roadside motel and got a room for the remainder of the night. Once inside his room, he called Joe several times, but each time, he only reached the answering machine. Next, he tried to call their mutual friend Andy Hoffman but with similar lack of success. He had been away from Paradise long enough, so he did not really have any other friends that he felt he could contact, except for maybe Beth Wence. No, he decided, it would sound foolish to call her out of the blue with a story like this.

After three restless hours of tossing and turning in the cheap motel bed, he finally gave up on sleep and turned on the television. He sat for a long while, staring at the screen but not watching the program, assessing his situation and trying to decide on his next move. He was totally confused, and more than a little frightened, but somewhere in the recesses of his mind, he knew what he must do. He had to go to Paradise. He had to find out what was going on. And most importantly, he had to help Joe and his family.

He and Joe had always been very close, and being the younger of the two, he grew up with Joe looking after him. Even as adults, he had come to count on Joe for many things, and Joe had always come through for him. Not that Ryan never reciprocated, for he was always willing to provide whatever help or support he could to Joe, but being the oldest, Joe was accustomed to handling things on his own. Now he obviously needed help, and Ryan could not just turn his back. School would not be starting for ten more days, and he had no other obligations.

Realizing any attempt at sleep would be useless, Ryan showered, checked out of the motel, and drove to LAX. The next available flight to Minneapolis was Northwest Flight 310, leaving at 3:05 p.m. He bought a ticket and used the next few hours to supply himself with extra clothes and the basic supplies he would need.

Now, as the plane touched down on the runway, he wrestled with ideas of what to do. "Trust no one," he kept hearing in his mind.

First, he would need a place to stay. Getting a hotel in or near Paradise should not be a problem. Then he would have to plan some kind of strategy for the following morning.

✦

"Hey, buddy, you can't lay here. Why don't you go home and sleep it off?"

Joe felt a nudge on his shoulder, slowly bringing him back to consciousness. He opened his eyes to the early morning sunlight and saw a uniformed police officer standing above him.

"You must have had a rough night," the officer said. "But this isn't the place to recuperate."

Joe rubbed his eyes to clear his vision then shook his head in an attempt to clear his memory. He remembered all too clearly his phone calls with Ryan and with the Northwest agent, and he remembered realizing his family must have been abducted and—and who knows what else. After that, everything seemed fuzzy. He had desperately wanted to get away but did not know where to go. He vaguely recalled running through the large courtyard between the Washington Monument and the Capitol, with the Smithsonian flanking both sides. For some reason, he had turned back, subconsciously looking for a dark hole to fall into. He apparently had found something that sufficed and must have fallen asleep in his little hideaway.

"I don't mind if you need a place to hang out," the officer went on, "but I take personal offense at this spot. It's kind of disrespectful, don't you think? It may not seem like a big deal to you, but I have some good friends whose names are on that wall."

Joe's mind had totally cleared. He glanced up to see that he was lying on the walkway that ran at the base of the shiny black wall of the Vietnam Memorial.

"Sorry," he barely muttered. "I didn't mean any harm."

"Don't worry about it, just get yourself home." Then, as an afterthought, "You know someone on the wall?"

Joe slowly stood up and made a feeble attempt at straightening himself out. "No, not personally."

"I guess I feel kind of protective of this wall," the officer said. "These guys were all heroes in my book."

Joe was not particularly interested in the officer's opinions. He just wanted to find a place where he could be left alone. His family was gone, and he felt responsible. He had given up, totally and completely, on his town, on his country, and, most despairingly, on himself.

Joe glanced down at himself and was surprised at how disgusting he looked. His shirt was dirty and torn with the dried blood still crusted on his sleeve. His trousers and shoes were splattered with mud, obviously from his late-night adventure. He did not care to even think of how his face and hair must appear. "I guess I look pretty bad," he said sheepishly.

The officer's face displayed a small, cynical smile. "You need a ride?" he asked, surprisingly sympathetic to this apparent vagrant.

"No, I'm okay," Joe replied. He glanced again at the memorial, its long shiny black wall being impressive in its simplicity. He had seen it many times before, and it always struck him as being out of place here, in a little shaded area below the Lincoln Memorial. The other monuments stood proud and strong, being visible from far off, but this one was almost completely hidden from view from anywhere but right in front of it.

The quiet stream of visitors were already beginning their stroll down the walkway, some stopping and spending a moment of private reflection, others continuing silently past, careful not to disturb anyone. Several people gave Joe a look of disgust as they passed. Joe suddenly felt very wrong, like he had committed some kind of sacrilege. Then, from somewhere deep within, a realization swept over him that was startling as much as inspiring: he had lost all faith in his government, in the people he had thought were heroes. He had felt that the ideals of this great country were a facade, a mere illusion created to convince the rest of the world that there was something special here. It was just like his experience at the Naval Academy years before. It was a fake.

But what the officer said was true. Maybe the politicians were corrupt. Maybe the FBI played both sides whenever it seemed convenient. Maybe the whole political system was dominated by greed and self-serving bureaucrats. But these people, the thousands of names who appeared on the wall, they were real heroes. They, and hundreds of thousands of others who, throughout the years and the various wars, unselfishly laid their lives on the line. It was they, the average people of this country, who made it great. Their willingness to answer the call, not for personal gain—and, in many cases, not even out of traditional patriotism—but out of a burning sense of responsibility and, most fundamentally, out of their belief that it was the right thing to do. For these people, there were no grandiose illusions of America's image or what they must do to maintain that image. It was a simple matter of not wanting to say no when called upon.

Joe thought back on the lessons he had learned while at the academy and the experiences he had since then. Several times, situations that seemed to be at their worst actually presented great opportunities. With a little hard work and sacrifice, these situations had been turned from near disaster to tremendous advantages. The situation he now faced was darker than any he had ever encountered, and even at this moment of surprising inspiration, he could not be sure he was strong enough to endure, but he knew now that he must try. He must be like those whose names were engraved in the black stone; he must answer the call. He could not allow the corruption of those in power to destroy the real heroes of this country. He might not be able to stop the madness, but it was his responsibility, his duty, to do something.

Joe tucked the remains of his shirttails into his trousers and brushed back his dirty and tangled hair with his hand. Physically there was little change, but he now projected an air of confidence and determination. "You're right, this is a disgrace," he said to the officer. "Forgive me for being such an ass."

The officer stared in openmouthed amazement as he observed the almost-instantaneous change in this man he had thought to be a street bum. "No problem," he muttered. "Take care of yourself."

Joe walked off, forcing himself to concentrate on developing some plan of action. He could not allow his thoughts to keep drifting to his family for fear of falling back into a mood of helpless despair. He must remain focused on his task of stopping the drug ring taking hold in Paradise. If there was any hope for his family, this would be the best way to help them.

Normally Joe did not carry large sums of money with him, but since this trip had involved so many unknowns, he wanted to be prepared for whatever situation presented itself. Now he was thankful for the fifteen hundred dollars cash he had brought. The first action he needed to take was to purchase a new set of clothes and get a hotel room where he could clean himself up and get some rest. Then, with a clear mind, he could more accurately assess his situation.

Two hours later, Joe stepped out of a cab at a small roadside motel called the Comfort Lodge on a quiet road just north of the city. He had asked the cabbie if he knew of any out-of-the-way hotels, and this was where he was taken. It met all of Joe's requirements: small, quiet, secluded, and from the looks of it, it was obviously cheap. The surrounding area was densely wooded, and the little motel seemed to be almost engulfed by the trees. From the three large tractor-trailers parked in front, Joe surmised that this must be a popular spot for truckers passing through.

The Seduction of Paradise

Joe thanked the cabbie and left him a generous tip then picked up his bag containing a new pair of jeans and a rugby-style jersey, and went into the small informal lobby to register. Moments later, he stood beneath the steamy spray of his shower, thinking that soap and hot water had never felt so good. It was hard to imagine that only yesterday he had been home in his own bed. Relaxing in the shower, he could feel the events of the last two days rapidly overtaking him. Exhaustion hit him like a giant wave, and after quickly drying himself off, he nearly collapsed on the creaky, sagging but heavenly bed.

Ten hours passed as if mere seconds, and when he finally blinked open his eyes, the only telltale sign that he had been out for some time was the dimness of the light. There was still some daylight left, but the falling sun was well hidden behind the tall trees surrounding the motel. Joe sat up on the edge of the bed, slowly stretching his arms and legs, feeling physically refreshed but still consumed with worry about his family and his town. He put on his new set of clothes and laid back down on the bed, trying to sort everything out in his mind.

What should I do? he asked himself. *What can I do? What is it that I know about this whole situation so far?* From his engineering discipline, he knew that the best way to approach a problem was to first make a list of all known facts, then make a separate list of all reasonable assumptions that the facts seemed to support. He had discovered that in many cases, you knew much more than you thought you did, but the lack of organization of the information made it appear more confusing and incomplete than it actually was. This situation was certainly not like the technical problems he dealt with at work, but maybe this approach would apply to any kind of problem.

He opened the drawer of the bedside desk and found a pen and a sheet of stationery. Sitting down at the desk, he began to make his lists.

FACTS

1. New York Historical Society is a fraud.

2. A group of big-time drug dealers is using the society as a front to cover up their real purpose. This group is apparently headed by a man named Salvo, from what was said on the beach near Miami. Capsner is their agent in Paradise. The maniac named Rodriguez must be some kind of hired gun to keep people in line.

3. Capsner could not pull this off alone. He needed a contact from the city council, which was Spencer. Spencer sold out his town and his friends for money.

4. Harry accidentally was given some incriminating information and was killed.

5. Andy discovered something at the wastewater treatment center and was killed.

6. FBI is involved with the drug ring. They also know about my involvement, and now apparently have abducted my family.

7. Beth Wence and Sherman Salinger are aware something is not right but have no idea how serious this situation is.

ASSUMPTIONS

1. Very important point: Spencer is only *known* accomplice from Paradise. To continue using city property for storing the drugs, there almost certainly needs to be someone else involved, maybe several others.

2. For some reason, the treatment center seems to be very important. If there was no treatment center, there would most likely be no drug ring.

Joe thought for a moment about Capsner and Special Agent Thompson. Finally he wrote the following:

The Seduction of Paradise

3. The FBI as an organization may not be involved. Thompson may be just one bad apple in the bunch. Possibly that is why she met with Capsner in a bar instead of in her office. But until more facts are known, it must be assumed that the whole FBI *is* involved.
4. Left alone, the problem will continue to get worse, possibly even spreading into other communities. To do nothing is *not* acceptable.
5. Too much has happened to go unnoticed. There must be others who would come to his aid. People like Andy and Harry. But how can they be identified?

Joe hesitated before writing his last assumption, not knowing how true it might be. But he had to trust someone:

6. Only two people can be considered allies: Beth Wence and Sherman Salinger.

Joe reviewed his two lists, not satisfied that they provided any insight as to how to proceed. The most disturbing point was his assumption that there had to be one, if not several, other Paradise residents involved, and they would have to be somewhat influential with a connection to the Brewster mansion restoration project. That limited it to only a handful of people. But one thing was very clear: he had to get back to Paradise, since it was obviously the focal point of everything. He did not know what he would do when he got there, but he could worry about that later. His immediate concern was how he would get back.

He had virtually no firsthand information about how the FBI operated, but if the books he read were even remotely accurate, they would most likely be waiting for him at the airport. Renting a car would also be risky, since he would be required to show a driver's license, which, in turn, could easily be traced. For that matter, he should not use his name at all—no credit cards, car rentals, hotels, nothing.

Suddenly, the telephone rang. Joe jumped. *Shit!* he thought, calming himself. *Damn near scared me to death.* Instinctively he reached to answer it, then froze as a terrifying thought struck him: *Who would be calling me here? Who even knows I am here?*

Then he made a connection: hotels! He had registered at this motel in his real name. How long had it been? Ten hours? Could the FBI even work that fast?

The phone continued to ring. *What an idiot I am. I need to get out, now.* Joe bolted for the door, then again hesitated. *If they know I'm here, they would probably send someone and have him waiting outside.*

The phone would not stop ringing, putting him even more on edge. He peered through the peek hole in the door and saw no one. *That doesn't matter*, he thought.

Joe raced into the bedroom, which was in the back of the motel. Carefully he peered out from behind the curtain and saw the back of the motel was deserted. The woods came up to within a few feet of the window, and with the shadows from the setting sun, he felt he would have reasonably good protection, if it should be required. The phone finally stopped ringing as Joe struggled with the window. It was obviously not intended to be taken off, at least not without proper tools. Moments later, the ringing again erupted. Joe was aware of the panic starting to build within him but was unable to control it. Finally, he raised his leg and slammed his foot into the poorly constructed frame, sending the entire window tumbling to the ground and shattering the glass in the process. He knew he would only have seconds to reach cover in the woods. If there was someone waiting for him in front of the motel, they would surely have heard the crash.

He dove headfirst through the opening and immediately rolled up to his feet. He paused for a brief moment to get his bearing as three men in suits suddenly emerged around the corner of the building, about one hundred feet to his left.

"McGowen!" one called. "Stop where you are. You can't get away."

We'll see about that, Joe thought, and began sprinting blindly into the woods.

"Freeze!" the man screamed. "We don't want to have to hurt you."

Joe looked back just long enough to see they had drawn their pistols. He pushed on even harder, weaving his way through the trees and the underbrush. Two deafening cracks filled the air as the man fired, but this motivated Joe to run all the harder. Images of Andy's mutilated chest flashed before his eyes, driving him harder still. He was vaguely aware of the branches and thorny bushes tearing at his skin.

The three men entered the woods in pursuit, waving their guns as they ran. Between the trees and the diminishing light, they were quickly losing sight of Joe. Joe continued to pound his way through the forest as distant recollections of a similar situation on a Florida beach passed through his mind. He was running out of sheer panic, but as his legs grew weary and breathing became more difficult, he knew he had to do something. Possibly he could just outrun the men, but if the stories he heard of FBI conditioning were true, they were undoubtedly in much better shape than he. But what were his choices? Looking over his shoulder, he could no longer see the men, but he could hear the cracking of branches and pounding of feet as they continued their chase.

Almost like breaking free from a tangled web, Joe burst into a clearing and was barely able to stop himself from running off the edge of a nearly vertical drop. Resting his hands on his knees to catch his breath, he crept up to the edge and peered over. Roughly fifty feet below, a small but wildly churning stream of water rushed by. There was no way he would be able to climb down the cliff, at least not fast enough to escape the gunmen. But the stream appeared far too shallow to jump into from this height.

On the other hand, maybe that was his only choice; he could hear the men rapidly approaching. He had little time to decide. Maybe he should stay and fight, he thought. Looking around, he saw a large branch about four feet long and three inches in diameter on the ground nearby. He picked it up, thinking it might be a suitable weapon. It was heavy, probably too heavy to allow him the quickness he would need. The men were now only seconds away. He had to think. What should he do?

The three men fought their way through the trees and the dense underbrush, knowing they were getting closer to their prey. Suddenly, they all held up as they heard a loud, terrifying scream, followed by a muted splash. The men exchanged bewildered glances then continued on. Only a few steps later, they discovered the same clearing that Joe had encountered moments before.

"He couldn't have jumped, could he?" one man asked.

"Maybe, but it would have been suicide," another answered. "He probably fell. Do you see any sign of him?"

"Nothing," the third said. "But that river is flowing mighty fast. It wouldn't take long to wash him away. There isn't enough light left to get a clear look, anyway."

"Damn!" the second man said. "Thompson is going to have my ass. We should have had the back of the motel covered."

"What tipped him off?" the first man asked.

"Who knows? Maybe this guy is a lot smarter than we gave him credit for."

"What do we do now?" the third man asked.

The second man, their leader, was puzzled for a moment. "Let's go back and search his room. There probably isn't anything worth looking for, but we might as well check. Then, I'm going to have to tell Thompson. Shit! She is going to have my ass!"

The men turned and slowly headed back to the motel, leaving the clearing and the rushing river behind as if nothing had occurred at all.

Chapter 24

Saturday morning on August 24 arrived with brilliant sunshine and a coolness that was a mild foreshadowing of the autumn that was just around the corner. Temperatures in Minnesota during late August could be sweltering hot or unpleasantly chilly—unpleasant, that is, for a nonresident. But Minnesotans loved the beginning of the annual cool-down, for it was this time of year that leaves showed their first signs of turning, hunters began cleaning and polishing their rifles, the famous state fair was just getting underway, and Vikings football was the main topic of conversation. Minnesota was an outdoor state, and the change of seasons is what made it so attractive to its people. True autumn was still several weeks away, but these early indications brought out a sense of excitement in everyone.

Beth Wence had other reasons to be excited this morning. Ever since her conversation with Joe in the parking lot after the last council meeting, she was eager to find out what he had to say. He seemed to know something of significance but was not willing to divulge it at that time or place. His only instruction was to come to his house on Saturday morning. She tried to call him Friday evening to set up a specific time for their meeting, but no one was home. Well, she was not going to wait. It was only seven thirty, but this was important. Joe would understand.

As she pulled into his driveway, her first reaction was that the whole family was still in bed. There were no lights on, and no one was visible in the windows. With three adults and three kids in one house, she found that to be unusual. At another time, she probably would have dismissed this thought without any concern, but in light of all that had happened, and considering no one had answered the phone the night before, she could not help but feel at least the early stages of alarm.

Beth hopped out of her car and briskly walked up to the front door, pressing the doorbell long enough to let it ring several times. If Joe was in bed, she wanted to make sure he heard it. After several moments of no response, she pressed the button again, sensing deep inside that there would be no answer.

No, she thought. *Not Joe, not his family. There must be an explanation. I cannot start jumping to conclusions.*

She stood frustrated, waiting in front of the empty house as if her presence alone would bring someone out. She was not sure of what to do next. Joe seemed to think it was very important that they talk before she confronted anyone else, but now, that did not appear to be an alternative for her. She went back to her car and started the engine but continued to sit in the driveway, not knowing where to go. She wondered if Joe had ever talked with Andy, like he said he would. Maybe Andy knew something more. He might even know where the McGowens went.

All the reporters working for the *Paradise Union* were provided with portable car phones so as to always be accessible to the editor. Picking up her phone, Beth first dialed information to get Andy's number then dialed the number she was given. After four rings, Andy's answering machine began to speak. Beth switched off the phone and flung it into the empty seat beside her.

I can't believe it, she thought. *It's not even eight o'clock on a Saturday, and nobody's at home. What am I going to do now?*

Finally, more out of desperation than out of logic, she reached a decision. She would wait no more. She would go see Chief Byron Winfield immediately. He would not be at his office this early on a Saturday, but she knew where he lived. What the hell, he was a public servant, and she was part of the public. He should expect to get rousted once in a while.

Winfield answered the door, wearing his robe and holding a cup of coffee. *Well, at least I did not get him out of bed*, Beth thought.

"Beth, what a surprise. What can I do for you?" Chief Winfield sounded genuinely chipper.

"Byron, there is something I feel we need to discuss. It's been bothering me for sometime now, and I haven't known just how to handle it. But something happened just this morning that made me feel I need to come to you. Sorry about the inconvenience."

"Oh, don't be. I've always felt that anyone in this town should feel free to contact me directly. Come on in, and tell me what's on your mind."

Beth started off cautiously, but once she started explaining all the things that she felt were suspicious, she held nothing back. She finished by describing the circumstances behind her meeting, or proposed meeting, with Joe McGowen.

Chief Winfield sat and listened very attentively, not asking any questions and not showing any sign of emotion. "You know what I think?" he said when Beth was finished. "I think you are a victim of a phenomenon that affects all people from time to time. I don't know if there is a clinical term for it, but it's a kind of hysteria. You see it everywhere there are circumstances not easily explainable. How many times have you heard about a UFO sighting, and then suddenly everyone in the area starts seeing UFOs? Or maybe you hear a rumor at work, and suddenly, everything that happens for a week seems to support that rumor. It is true, I'll grant you, that this town has seen more than its fair share of atypical events lately, but I certainly wouldn't group them all together and make it look like there is some sort of conspiracy against us. And this thing with Capsner and the New York Historical Society has nothing to do with any of it. You're trying to put two and two together to come up with five."

Beth sat silent for a moment, unsure of whether to feel embarrassed or angry. "Could you at least check out the society?" she asked.

"Oh, I suppose I could, but I would feel awfully foolish if Mr. Capsner ever found out, which I'm sure he would," Chief Winfield said. "I don't think it's in our best interest right now."

"But what about Spencer? Doesn't that strike you as odd?"

"Of course it does. But admit it, Beth, everything he does is a bit unusual. If it would have occurred six months ago, or six months from now, you wouldn't have even questioned it."

"But that's just the point, it didn't occur six months ago. Everything is happening now. And now Joe is gone. It just cannot be a coincidence."

"First off, Joe is not necessarily gone. He wasn't home one Saturday morning. So what? I'm gone a lot on Saturdays. However, that does bring up a point. As you said yourself, Joe was the one initially asking a lot of questions about the same things that are concerning you. I had planned on talking to him about that. He's getting people a bit edgy. I mean, look at you. You wouldn't happen to know how I could get ahold of him?"

Beth shook her head, feeling like she was being patronized. "Damn it, Chief, that's what I came to see you for. Of course I don't know how to get ahold of him." She looked Winfield straight in the eyes, and suddenly, she saw something that caused her to shudder with fright. Eyes are the secret to the soul, she had always been told, and she believed it to be true. Winfield outwardly appeared relaxed and, for the most part, friendly. But he was hiding something. Looking into his eyes, she could not escape the feeling that he was testing her. He knew something, something she was not supposed to discover. What was it he was really after, she wondered? She had come to ask him for help, but it was he who was questioning her. The statement Joe made at their last meeting flashed in her mind like a neon light: "There is something extremely important that I must tell you. You must not do anything about all of this until we talk."

It took every shred of her willpower to suppress the fear that was beginning to overwhelm her. As graciously as she could manage, she thanked the chief and said she must be going. "I can see myself out," she said softly, then stood and hurried to the door, trying to appear calm.

"Have a nice day, Beth," Winfield said, as jovial as when she first arrived. "Just be careful not to let people like Joe McGowen cause you to start thinking crazy things."

She barely heard the final remark. She jumped into her car and attempted to insert the key in the ignition, but her hands were trembling so severely that she was unable to do so. "Stop it!" she commanded, talking to her hands as if they would obey. She took several deep breaths, and then, only marginally more controlled, she successfully inserted the key. As the engine roared to life, she backed out of the driveway and sped off down the road, for the first time in her life knowing the feeling of true fear.

※

Special Agent Freeman of the FBI finished straightening his tie and buttoned his suit coat. He might as well present as good of an appearance as possible, even though he knew he was about to catch hell. He rapped lightly on the door of the private hospital room and waited for a response. Almost immediately a very nasal voice called out, "Get in here, Freeman."

He pushed the door open and entered the room. Special Agent Thompson sat upright in the bed, wearing a hospital smock. Most of her face was covered by bandages supporting her nose that had been shattered by Joe's blow. Her voice resembled that of a person trying to imitate the stereotyped sound of a telephone operator.

"So what happened?" she demanded curtly.

"We've got a potential problem," Freeman began. "Naturally we had the airport covered. McGowen has no experience whatsoever with this kind of thing, so we were hoping he would just fall into our hands. But he appears to be pretty sharp. When he didn't show up at the airport, we naturally assumed he would need a place to stay. We checked all the hotels in the city, and sure enough, we found him at the Comfort Lodge, basically a roadside truckers' motel just north of the city. It was a quiet, out-of-the-way spot. He was being surprisingly careful for a man with no experience. His one flaw was using his real name to check in."

"So you found him. That's great. What's the potential problem?"

"Well, you were pretty specific about not spooking him. I decided just knocking on his door would be risky. Who knows, he may have even gotten himself a gun. It seemed like a quick, overpowering assault would be more efficient, but we needed to know precisely where he was. Every curtain was pulled, but we knew there was only one phone in the room. Jacobs went next door to call him, while Drexell and I positioned ourselves on either side of the door. As soon as he answered the phone, we were going in. After he didn't answer, we decided to go in anyway, but before we could, we heard a window break in the back. We ran around the side of the motel just in time to see him take off into the woods."

"You didn't cover the back?"

"There was no reason to think he would get out that way. This guy is sharp, much sharper than anyone expected. A nonprofessional like that would always answer his damn phone."

Thompson scowled with contempt at the younger Freeman. "This guy is nearly forty years old, and he's a businessman," she said. "I hope you three young studs didn't have any trouble catching him." The sarcasm in her voice was intentionally evident.

Freeman looked down and nervously shuffled his feet. "Well, we would have. It was starting to get dark, and the woods were dense, but we were easily catching up to him. Unfortunately, there was a cliff along the edge of the woods that dropped down to a small but fairly rapid river. You couldn't even see it until you were right on top of it."

"Freeman, what the hell happened?"

"Jacobs thinks he jumped out of desperation. I think he fell. He didn't seem like the kind of guy who would take a chance on killing himself."

Thompson's eyes turned livid. The portions of her face that were exposed turned into an almost inhuman shade of red. "Are you telling me he's dead?"

"I believe that's the case."

"You dumb son of a bitch! You couldn't apprehend one lousy out-of-shape amateur. Any beginning street cop could have handled that. Damn it!" She sat back for a moment, allowing herself time to cool down. Then, "Are you sure he's dead?"

"Well, we never found his body, but I can't imagine anyone could have survived that fall," Freeman answered.

"Find the body," Thompson commanded. "We cannot have him washing up in some farmer's backyard. We need to know for a fact if he is dead, and we must find his body. It can't be that difficult, even for an incompetent like you."

Freeman held back his resentment. Now was not a time to argue. "There is one other point that I believe is important," he said. "We searched his room, and not surprisingly, there was little to see. We did find this, however, and I think it's significant." He produced the lists of facts and assumptions Joe had made.

Thompson snatched them from Freeman and quickly scanned each. "So you *think* this is significant. I think this is damn significant! He's essentially outlined the whole operation. The details are missing, but basically he's got it. From what he says here, it sounds almost like he is planning some kind of offensive action. We were aware he knew some things, but he somehow, found out a lot more than we thought, probably from my meeting with Capsner." She silently perused through each list again then finally said, "I'm very concerned about a couple of points. First, he has tied the FBI to the drug ring. He even mentions me personally, and that is not very comforting. Secondly, there are the people he mentions as allies. I don't think I need to tell you the potential problem there. It could be catastrophic for us if he has passed on what he knows. Is there any indication that he has?"

"I believe he hasn't," Freeman said. "The way he listed them as allies implies he was trying to determine what his options were. If he had already contacted them, there would be no reason to list them here."

"I agree with you, but we need to know for sure. Even if he is dead, if this information has gotten out, we have a major problem. Do you know this Wence woman?"

"No, but I know she is on the council."

"She should be checked out immediately. We don't need another crusader up there. My gut feel is we will have to take more serious action. We don't want to make the same mistake with her as we did with McGowen. How about McGowen's wife, does she know anything?"

"She claims to not know how much Joe has talked to either Wence or Salinger."

"That's great. We need to know. Mueller can check out Wence. Capsner is the only one who can check out Salinger. You need to find McGowen's body, and whatever you do, don't let his wife know what happened to him yet. She'll be much less cooperative if she knows we killed her husband. And Freeman, no more fuckups. None. Is that clear?"

"Very clear," Freeman responded.

Chapter 25

The warm tropical breeze blew over the veranda of Julio Salvo's great estate. Salvo relaxed comfortably on a padded lounge chair, sipping a drink of an ice-blue color. He looked more content than Antonio Rodriguez had seen him for months. Rodriguez sat a few feet away in a white wicker chair, sipping a similar drink to Salvo's, not knowing what it was but accepting it graciously, as was always required with whatever Mr. Salvo offered.

"So, my friend Antonio, you have done well. The storm we discussed on your last visit seems to have passed. All is ready to begin shipments of merchandise."

"Yes, Mr. Salvo," Rodriguez said. "Unfortunately, we are a few weeks behind our original schedule. I hope this does not pose a problem."

"I think we can handle a delay of only a few weeks. You know of my obsession to meet every detail of a plan, but even I am able to understand that there are certain unavoidable realities. That is the primary reason I keep you employed. You have a way of smoothing out the hills we encounter."

"I am glad you are pleased, Mr. Salvo. But the successful completion of our project was not solely my doing. I still do not completely trust Capsner, but he has done an excellent job this past month to recover from the bungling of Spencer Thurman. Removing Thurman was probably what helped the most. He was constantly slowing us down and usually created more problems than he solved. Our new contact has performed considerably more efficiently."

"Come, my friend." Salvo chuckled. "Humility does not become you. I gave you a difficult task, and you carried it out admirably."

Rodriguez allowed himself a slight, uncharacteristic smile, which quickly vanished as his more customary expressionless expression returned.

"It is nice to see that you and our friend Mr. Capsner have found a way to get along," Salvo continued.

"We will never see completely eye to eye, but he has done his job well." Rodriguez hesitated for a moment, and then, "In fact, he asked me to discuss a few issues with you."

"He did? Well, I guess I do not find that too surprising. What is on his mind?"

Rodriguez cleared his throat uneasily. "You must understand, Mr. Salvo, that these are his questions, not mine."

"Please, my friend, ask what you must. Do not pretend that I intimidate you."

"Well, first off, he would very much like to meet with you in person. Since the project is now complete, he is wondering why he cannot meet you here as I do."

"You tell Mr. Capsner that he should consider himself fortunate. He has had more contact with me than most business associates ever do. He should also understand, however, that a business associate is exactly what he is. He has done a fine job, but I told him from the start that no one comes here. No one but you, that is. And it took a very long time for me to bring you here, if you remember. Even then I felt it was a risk, but I needed at least one contact with the outside world. You are a special exception. Capsner should understand that."

"I believe he does, sir, but he has been a little frustrated lately over your refusal to take his calls. He feels he has been cut off totally."

The Seduction of Paradise

"I take calls when and from whom I wish. If there is trouble, Capsner will not find me so difficult to get ahold of. But from what I hear, all is well. Contact with the outside world is risky. He will know if I wish to speak with him. Is there anything else?"

"One last question, Mr. Salvo. Capsner is aware of your standard practice of personally reviewing each operation one time prior to opening for business. Our first shipment is due in two weeks. He is expecting a visit, and he would like to know when."

"A very legitimate question," Salvo said. "Any smart man would want to know precisely when the boss is coming. You tell him I will be there on Saturday morning in two weeks. That should be two days before you receive your first shipment. I believe that is September 7."

Rodriguez stared at Salvo, showing obvious signs of being stunned.

"You look puzzled, my friend. Is something wrong?"

"Only that I have never known you to announce one of your inspections. With all the precautions you take, it seems out of character."

"On the contrary, it is very much in character. I will explain later. Is there anything else?"

"No, sir, I do not believe so. I must say, however, that I do not recall seeing you this relaxed, especially before a major event like what is about to occur."

Salvo laid back and sipped his drink. "That is because I have peace of mind, my friend. Complete peace of mind. Now I have a few questions for you."

Outwardly Salvo continued to portray contentment, but Rodriguez saw in his eyes the icy chill of ruthless anger. Maybe things were not so well after all.

"What about the missing document that you were to locate for me?"

Rodriguez was caught off guard, believing the document was no longer a concern. "Ah...Mr. Salvo...ah...It was never found.

There is no doubt that it has been destroyed. It is not a threat to us now."

"Not a threat, Antonio? Not a threat? I thought I taught you not to think but only to act on my command. I believe it is a threat, and I believe it is a threat to me!"

"Mr. Salvo, I—"

"I am not through, Antonio. What of this Hoffman person, the man you decided it was best to kill? Has his body been located?"

"No, sir, it has not. But it must be miles away by now. If it turns up somewhere far off, it will not cast suspicion on us."

Salvo's eyes turned an unnatural shade of red. "So you believe a town like Paradise can lose another of its leading citizens, have him wash up in some neighboring community, and no one will ask questions. You actually believe that, Antonio? Even for you, that is shortsighted.

"How about the man called McGowen? There had been so much concern over him in the early stages of our project. I believe Capsner even told me he was close friends with Hoffman. What about McGowen?"

"He is not causing any trouble at all," Rodriguez said. "Actually, he never really did. He was just looking out for Rosten's widow. She finally moved in with him, and there has not been any trouble since."

Salvo's eyes turned fierce and burned directly into Rodriguez. "You are not lying to me, are you, Antonio? I do not tolerate lies from anyone, even you."

"No, sir. It is completely the truth."

"And then there is the Wence woman. Elizabeth Wence, I believe. I had a personal call from your contact, Antonio, and there is concern she is starting some kind of trouble. You have told me nothing about her."

Rodriguez's eyes widened in anger and fear. "Why were you contacted directly? That is not how the communication is supposed to work."

"It is fortunate for me that your contact has some initiative. What about Ms. Wence?"

"My contact and I did have a discussion regarding her, but it is my feeling that there is no need for alarm. She is a typical small-town American woman. What is it they are called, busybodies?"

"That is for me to decide, Antonio. Not you. Me!"

Finally, Rodriguez could not hold back. "Mr. Salvo, what is wrong? Moments ago you were so content, so relaxed. All was well. What is this all about?"

"I told you last time that I see things. I see opportunities, and I see risks. The risks are always high, and only caution and intelligence make the risks manageable. Have you ever wondered why I have been so successful, Antonio? I will tell you. I am intelligent, but even more than that, I am cautious. Why is it that no one is allowed here but you? There are others whom I would normally trust, but each time someone discovers this place, I am a little more at risk. Have you any idea how many people, how many governments would love to have me arrested? But they cannot touch me. I remain illusive to them all, but only because I will not take unnecessary chances.

"Take a look around you, Antonio. Incriminating documents missing, bodies missing, a small peaceful town disrupted. Much has been spent on this project, but no amount of money is worth this kind of risk. I tell you, Antonio, even those in Paradise who are not asking questions aloud are thinking them. It is over in Paradise, Antonio, over and done. We must count our losses and be on our way."

Rodriguez was confused. He shook his head, trying to sort out what he was hearing, but everything remained a tangled web. "I do not understand, sir. What about Capsner, and your visit in two weeks?"

"I told you I would explain. It is part of my peace of mind. I have been very concerned about this project from the beginning, and I have finally reached a decision. Now I can rest."

"And what is your decision?"

Salvo's eyes again took on the relaxed glow of a vacationing tourist. "Again, I am a cautious man. All loose ends must be tied. We must get out of Paradise, and get out clean. I want you to have our friend Capsner host a party at his restored mansion next Saturday, a week before my announced visit. Everyone with any connection to the project at all must be invited. It can be considered a kind of celebration for achieving some milestone. I realize the entire restoration effort will not be completed for some time, but I believe the ballroom is now finished. This will be a kind of thank-you party for all that have helped. The entire city council must be present, and whoever else is involved.

"There will be a terrible tragedy, Antonio. The electricians will have left some wires exposed. A fire will start, and all attending the party will perish. It will be very sad." Salvo's grin portrayed anything but sadness. Even Rodriguez was surprised at his coldness.

"Mr. Salvo, how can you expect that anyone would believe all those people were killed in an accidental fire?"

"It is over, Antonio. I no longer care what anyone believes. But I am concerned there are people who have suspicions about our project, and after we pull out, they will continue to investigate us based on their suspicions. I cannot spare the time to discover who these people are. Therefore, everyone involved must be killed. After that, what questions can be asked? You are correct in assuming people will suspect foul play, but no one remaining alive will know anything about us. The police can investigate a possible homicide forever if they chose, but we will be safely back here planning our next adventure."

"What of my contact, and of Capsner himself?"

"They have done their jobs well, and it grieves me that they cannot survive. But they are loose ends that need to be tied. As I have told you, every time someone new learns about me and how to get ahold of me, I am a little more at risk. I have built my

The Seduction of Paradise

empire by being very thorough. I never leave any loose ends to be traced."

"Why tell Capsner that you will be visiting in two weeks?"

"He is becoming anxious, and that may be a problem. This will relax him. He will concentrate on my visit and not concern himself with other matters, making your job that much easier."

Salvo saw that Rodriguez was slightly disturbed. "You should feel very thankful, Antonio. You will survive. I was angry with you, but I realized all was not your fault. And I need an outside contact. I would not be able to replace you for a long while. So you will survive, you and your Jamaican mercenaries who will help you carry out this task."

Rodriguez was truly stunned. Just when he thought he knew this man Salvo, a new and even more surprising side would surface. He did not like losing the business in Paradise, but on the other hand, he would not at all mind taking care of Capsner and the pain-in-the-ass people up there in one fatal stroke of a match. He could not resist a broad smile as he looked to his boss and mentor.

"This may be my first assignment in Paradise that I am suited for," he said. "I may actually enjoy this."

"How you feel about it is your own personal matter," Salvo said. "Just make sure you take care of it, quickly and cleanly. Have poor Mr. Capsner begin preparations for his final party. And, Antonio, this is a special occasion. Tell Capsner to spare no expense."

Salvo sipped his drink and lay back in his lounge chair, again looking totally content. "Ah, Antonio, it is good to have peace of mind."

Chapter 26

At the same time that Beth Wence was standing on Joe McGowen's doorstep waiting for someone to answer the bell, Ryan McGowen was crawling out of bed at the Holiday Inn in neighboring Brooklyn Park. He had decided not to stay right in Paradise since there may be someone who would recognize him, and until he had a better feel for what was happening, he preferred to keep his presence here a secret.

After spending several hours the night before trying to come up with some kind of strategy, he finally concluded that there was no clear-cut approach that presented itself. Since he was looking for Joe, it made sense to start at his house. Odds were against Joe being around, but maybe he could find something that would at least get him started in the right direction. Immediately after getting out of bed, he attempted to call Joe and was not at all surprised that no one answered. He thought it best not to leave any message on the answering machine; who knew who might end up listening to it?

By nine o'clock in the morning, Ryan had showered, eaten a quick breakfast, and was heading north on Highway 169 toward Paradise in his Budget rental car. It had been quite a while since he last drove these streets, but he remembered them like the back of his hand. He had never actually been to Joe's house since Joe only moved in a year or so ago, but he knew the location from previous conversations with Joe, and he knew the area well enough so that finding the house would not be a problem. He estimated it would only take about twenty minutes to cover the distance from the Holiday Inn to Joe's driveway. He would follow Highway 169 over the Mississippi River into Paradise, turn left on Bent and head west for about a mile, turn right on Port and up a hill for one block, then left onto Cottonwood, with Joe's house being about a quarter mile down on the left-hand side. It was just like he had been there yesterday. As he cruised up 169, he could not help but notice the contrast between the changes that had occurred in downtown Minneapolis and those of the northern suburban areas. He barely recognized Minneapolis, but as he approached Paradise, everything was virtually the same; there was an occasional new gas station, some expansion of housing developments, but essentially, it appeared just as it did five years ago.

As Ryan reached the top of the small hill on Port Avenue, he remembered the welcoming party he had seen at his own condo back in California. He decided the first thing he would do is just casually cruise by Joe's house to check for—well, he was not sure what he would check for but just to see if anything appeared out of the ordinary.

He drove on toward Joe's house at about twenty-five miles per hour, slow enough to get a good look around but not so slow as to attract attention. As he passed in front of the house, he was suddenly struck by an unexpected and overwhelming sense of nostalgia. It was not so much the structure of the house, since this place held no memories for him. It was the realization that this was his brother's home, the place he had often planned on coming to visit. He used to wonder what it would be like, seeing Joe at the front door and playing with his kids in the yard. But here it was—a somber, almost sinister-looking place that held an air of foreboding. The nostalgia he felt was not for this place but for what he thought this place used to be.

The house and the entire yard were quiet and deserted. Ryan drove on by and turned around several houses down in a neighbor's driveway. On his return pass, he felt confident it was safe, so he turned into the driveway and parked his car. He sat for several moments, not knowing exactly what to do. Obviously no one was home, but he knew that before he came. Walking around outside would serve no purpose. Should he attempt to break in? If he did, a neighbor would probably call the police. And what about the neighbors? Maybe he should talk to them. But his warning to trust no one kept coming back to him. It was still too premature to talk to anyone.

For lack of a clear direction, he stepped out of the car and slowly walked up to the front door. After a few moments' hesitation, he rang the bell, and again was not surprised by the lack of response. He felt uncomfortable standing there. This was his brother's house, and here he was, a stranger trying to get in. This just was not right. He wanted Sheri to come out and throw her arms around him to welcome him. He wanted Joe to show him all the special little features of his house that every homeowner thinks are unique. He wanted the kids to jump on him and ask if he brought them anything from California, which, of course, he would have.

The eerie silence bothered him. He felt cheated, and even more than that, he felt angry. He walked around to the back of the house and saw the deck and the wooden swing set with an attached playhouse that Joe had built. Finally, he decided he was kidding himself. There was really nothing he could do here. He went back to his car and drove off, not at all sure where he would go or what he would do.

Special Agent Mueller sat at his station, patiently watching the McGowen house on the chance that something, or someone, would show up that would give him a clue as to where McGowen was. His wife had been surprisingly cooperative, revealing his plan to follow Capsner to Washington, but the information did him little good since McGowen somehow eluded everyone down there. Mueller got the story from Special Agent Freeman, and chuckled to himself at the obvious satisfaction in Freeman's voice when he related the incident of Thompson getting her nose flattened.

Mueller's main concern now was the apparent savvy McGowen showed for this kind of work. Even his brother had eluded the agents in California, obviously due to being warned by Joe. He was not the typical naive civilian that Mueller so often encountered. He recalled a somewhat realistic book he had read years before, *Six Days of the Condor*, where the main character fooled all the professional agents who were after him by being unpredictable. Since the character in the book did not know what to do, the agents could not anticipate his moves and consequently were unable to apprehend him. Mueller frequently wondered what it would be like if that were a true situation. As the professional, what would he do in a similar set of circumstances? Now he had the chance to find out. This McGowen was proving to be as unpredictable as Condor, the character in the book.

Watching the house was probably a waste of time. McGowen certainly would not come back here, but Mueller had nothing else to go on at the moment. Freeman was handling things in Washington, and Capsner would be back later in the day. More or less, out of default, he continued his vigil. A woman had shown up earlier, whom he recognized as Beth Wence, the city council member McGowen had met on a couple of other occasions. At first it concerned him, but then he decided it was probably nothing more than a Saturday-morning visit. She did not do anything he found to be suspicious, so he did not attempt to pursue her.

Mueller was vaguely aware of the car that passed by, even though it was going a bit slow, but his adrenaline started pumping when the car reappeared, coming back down Cottonwood. He became even more focused when the car turned into the driveway, and let out a loud gasp when he saw who stepped out from behind the wheel. McGowen! He could not believe it. Why would he come back here?

He quickly picked up his binoculars and focused on the man walking up to the door. He had been mistaken. This was not McGowen but someone who bore an uncanny resemblance to him. The brother! What was his name? Ryan. Ryan McGowen. So this was where he escaped to. This could be serious trouble. He must know something, or he would not be here in Paradise. On the other hand, he could not know too much, or there would be no reason for him to come to this empty house.

Ryan was obviously looking for something. Could it be Joe? Maybe he was sent by Joe to find his family. Or maybe he truly did not know anything. Mrs. McGowen said he was expecting them in California. Maybe when they did not show up, he came here out of concern.

Mueller's first instinct was to apprehend the younger McGowen on the spot, but he did not want to make a scene here. He decided it would be best to follow him and wait for a more opportune moment. He may even be able to get a few questions answered in the meantime.

McGowen headed to the back of the house as the light on Mueller's portable phone began to flash. He snatched up the receiver and whispered, "Mueller."

"This is Freeman. Any news?"

"Yeah. You'll never guess who I'm watching this very minute."

"I don't know, but it's not McGowen."

"Yes and no. It's not Joe McGowen, the guy you can't seem to find. It's his brother, Ryan, from California. At least I think it is. He looks so much like Joe that it must be him."

"No shit? This is starting to get ugly. And for the record, if you hadn't lost him first, I wouldn't even be involved."

"Touché. How did you know it wasn't Joe McGowen?"

"That's why I called," Freeman said. "We were able to locate McGowen at a small motel out in the middle of nowhere. But the bastard got away from us. There was an accident. McGowen's dead."

"What?" Mueller exclaimed. "You idiot! How could you let that happen?"

"Thompson already reamed my ass, I don't need any crap from you. You know as well as I do this is a dangerous business."

"Who else knows?"

"Nobody. Capsner, of course, and the agents who were with me, but nobody else. Thompson does not want his wife to know about it. She's been helpful up until now, but I don't think we could expect much if she knew this."

Mueller thought for a moment. "I suppose that's right, although I think we have everything from her that we're going to get."

"There is another concern," Freeman continued. "We found a list that McGowen had written. He apparently was trying to understand the whole situation, maybe even plot some sort of counterattack. He knows more than we gave him credit for, including the involvement of Capsner and Thompson. I don't think he understands what is actually going on, but he definitely knows enough to be dangerous. Very dangerous."

"How can he be dangerous if he's dead?" Mueller asked.

"We're still trying to locate his body," Freeman answered. "He fell off a cliff, into a shallow rapids. Thompson won't believe he's dead until she sees his cold, clammy body. But I was there. He's dead, take my word for it.

"The problem is, in his list, he identified people he considered allies. Guess who he named? Beth Wence and Sherman Salinger. And who knows what he told his brother. And who knows who any of them talked to. This could get out of control in a hurry."

"Shit," Mueller said under his breath. "We were getting so close. Maybe this isn't as bad as it seems. From what I can tell, Ryan McGowen doesn't know anything, and I plan on following him until I get the chance to apprehend him. Wence came by this morning also but left when no one answered the door. She obviously did not know McGowen was gone, which probably means there is a lot she doesn't know. I don't think it will be a problem getting to her. Salinger is more of a concern. Capsner will have to take care of him."

"He's already been instructed to do so. But you have to check out Wence. You may be right about her not knowing anything, but we need to know for sure. We cannot afford to have any more loose ends."

"I'll get Gibbons on her right away," Mueller said. "If we're lucky, we can nip this in the bud before it spreads. I have to go now. McGowen's heading for his car."

"I'm glad you're so optimistic," Freeman said sarcastically. "Keep me posted. For your information, Thompson will be out of the hospital tomorrow with her new nose." The distinctive sound of chuckling could be heard as Freeman hung up the phone.

Ryan found himself driving down Main Street, heading east on the bridge crossing the Whiskey River. Just off to his left stood city hall atop the small grassy hill, leading down to the concrete wall that bordered the river itself. A walkway ran along the edge of the wall and continued in both directions, following the river from just south of the bridge for about a mile to the north. Just off the walkway between city hall and the river sat a large brick terrace with several sets of tables and chairs, offering a beautiful view of the river and the west side of Paradise. In the warm weather, hot dogs and ice cream could be purchased from vendors with small carts that usually lined the back edge of the terrace. With the majority of stores, banks, and restaurants in Paradise being located along Main Street, the terrace mostly served as a refuge for weary shoppers or businesspeople on lunch breaks.

Since it was pointless to continue driving aimlessly, Ryan decided to take a walk along the river and maybe have an ice cream cone on the terrace. Maybe some ideas of what to do next would come to him if he relaxed and stopped trying to force things. He parked in the city hall lot and walked over to the south side of the building bordering Main Street and descended the wide set of concrete steps to the walkway. His emotions were a mix between concern and nostalgia as he followed the walkway south under the bridge to the point where it ended—or began, depending on one's perspective. This was a beautiful little town, he thought. Standing here, seeing the slow and peaceful Whiskey River flow by, no one would ever guess that Minneapolis was only thirty minutes away.

He turned and headed back toward the terrace, no longer being as concerned about being recognized as he had previously been. In fact, maybe meeting some people he knew would help him out, give him some ideas on how to proceed. When he reached the terrace, he ordered a double-dip strawberry cone and sat at a vacant table. Between the ice cream and the breeze along the river, he began to feel a bit of a chill. There were still a few days left of August, but this was apparently going to be one of those years where fall comes early.

"My God! Ryan, Ryan McGowen! What are you doing here?"

Ryan looked up to see the pretty face of Beth Wence staring at him, looking more shocked than pleased. He was immediately filled with numerous conflicting emotions. It was good to see a familiar, friendly face. More specifically, it was good to see Beth's face. He had never really gotten over her, although he told himself that he had long ago. When he decided to come home, there was a partially subconscious feeling that he would look her up. But he had not seen her since she told him she was getting married, and he was not at all sure how he would react when they first got together. He thought it would probably be best not to see her, at least not until this mystery with Joe was resolved. He certainly did not want to be caught totally by surprise like this.

"Beth, how are you?" was all he could think of to say. As an afterthought, he quickly jumped to his feet, stumbling over the patio chair. He stood for a moment, feeling terribly awkward, looking like a lost little boy holding his large double-dip ice cream cone.

Ryan's discomfort was very apparent to Beth. Finally, she giggled in her playful way and threw both her arms around his neck and hugged him close. "It's so good to see you," she said quietly. "At least you can pretend you're glad to see me."

Ryan slowly recovered from his shock. He put his free arm around her waist and patted her back. "I am glad to see you," he said. "More than you know. I guess I was just a little surprised."

Beth released Ryan and stepped back. "You haven't changed," she said.

"You have." Ryan smiled. "You've gotten even prettier."

Beth's faced turned flush as she returned his smile, obviously a bit embarrassed by his remark.

Damn! Ryan thought to himself. Why did he say that? He was riding the emotional roller coaster. He was never sure in his own mind whether he blamed her or himself for what happened between them. He would not allow himself to feel bitterness or resentment, but he also did not want to feel any of the old fire that had once made her so special to him. Part of him felt anger, toward her and toward himself. He could sense the emptiness begin to surface from within him, bringing with it the painful memories of the lonely months he had endured when he finally realized he had lost her for good. But yet part of him felt relieved, almost peaceful. He was suddenly consumed by the desire to take her in his arms, to hold her and kiss her. This was the part that he found the most terrifying.

"I suppose you came home to see Joe and Sheri," Beth said with an odd, sort of testing look in her eye.

Ryan immediately became defensive, wondering if she may have any idea of the circumstances involving Joe's bizarre recent behavior.

"Of course," he responded. "I haven't been back for quite a while, so I thought I was about due."

"How is Joe?" Beth asked. "I haven't seen him for a while myself."

"He's fine. He's not home right now, so I thought I would take a walk through the old hometown."

"I was just taking a walk myself," Beth said, flipping her head to keep the breeze from blowing her hair in her face. "I've had a lot on my mind lately. You have seen Joe, though?"

"Does it really make a difference, Beth?"

She looked surprised, briefly taken aback. "Well, no, of course not. I was just curious." She paused for several moments then looked up at Ryan, almost apologetically. "I missed you," she said.

"Beth, I don't—"

"No, don't say anything. I understand. I just want you to know that I truly missed you."

There was another awkward pause. Ryan realized they would get nowhere standing here like this. "Why don't we go get some lunch?" he suggested. "It's been a long time, and I think we need to talk."

"I would love that, I really would, but I'm due back at my office in a few minutes. But I agree, we need to talk, about a lot of things. Could you possibly come by tonight, for dinner maybe?"

Again the emotional roller coaster. He wanted to be with her, but he did not want to take the chance of getting too close to her again. He could not trust his own feelings. But there was more at stake here than just him and Beth. He had no idea of what to do about Joe. Beth's questions seemed to contain a leading nature. Maybe she did know something.

"Sure, I can come by for a little while, but you don't have to fix dinner."

"I insist," Beth quickly said. "Seven o'clock. Here's my address." She jotted the information down on a piece of paper and handed it to Ryan. "I'll see you tonight." Then, with her playful smile returning, "How is that ice cream?"

"What? Oh shit!" Ryan exclaimed. He had totally forgotten about the cone he was holding and was oblivious to the steady trickle of ice cream now running over his hand and down his arm. "I guess it wasn't that good." He laughed.

"See you at seven," Beth called, briskly climbing the steps to the parking lot. As she approached her car, another thought struck her. *I think I should also invite Sherman tonight. We may need all the help we can get. Not to dinner—that will be time for Ryan and me to talk personal—but later on, when we discuss Joe. I think that would be a good idea.*

Chief Winfield answered the flashing cellular phone as he cruised down Main Street in the direction of his office. Mueller had not wanted to take any chances on bugged lines, so he issued these portables to Winfield and Sharon Carlson and his other key people and instructed everyone to only use them for "official" business. It was a good idea, as were most of Mueller's ideas. He was an incredibly thorough operator.

"What?" Winfield barked into the phone.

"It's Mueller," came the reply. "I've got bad news, and I don't want you going crazy on me, okay?"

"Just tell me," Winfield said.

"There's been an accident. Joe McGowen is dead. They found him in a motel outside of Washington, and he apparently fell off a cliff trying to get away."

"My God." The chief's voice was barely audible. Then, nearly shouting, "What do you mean, trying to escape! Don't your people know how to apprehend someone?"

"They were being careful. McGowen was too smart. Too smart for his own good, apparently."

"Damn it, damn it all to hell! This was not supposed to happen."

"I told you not to go crazy on me. You knew the risks involved. It just happened, okay?"

"What about his family?"

"They don't know yet, and they won't for a while. We don't need them acting up."

"You can really be a bastard sometimes, Mueller."

"That's part of my job. And like it or not, it's part of yours too. But we have another problem that needs our immediate attention: McGowen was able to find out quite a lot about the whole cocaine operation. Freeman found a list he had started, which appeared to be the beginning of some kind of plan of attack. In this list, he identified Beth Wence and Sherman Salinger as possible allies. We don't believe he told them anything yet, but we have to be sure."

Winfield fought to hold back his anger. "This is getting very messy. Beth Wence paid me a visit this morning. She was looking for Joe and was concerned about him. I obviously didn't know he was dead, but I knew where he was. Naturally, I tried to make his apparent disappearance seem ordinary, but I think she was still upset when she left."

"Does she suspect something is unusual in general?" Mueller asked. "Do you think McGowen told her anything?"

"She doesn't know anything for sure, but she senses things are wrong. She highlighted all the unusual occurrences that have taken place since Capsner came to town, and she even suspects the New York Historical Society is a front for something else. But she didn't seem very sure of any of it. She was just suspicious."

"That's too close, and it gets worse. Do you know Ryan McGowen?"

"I know who he is, but we never really met formally. He was just one of the many kids I used to see running around this town."

"He's here, in Paradise. He ran into Wence on the terrace behind City Hall. She invited him to dinner tonight, and I strongly suspect they'll be discussing more than old times."

"How did Ryan get here? I thought your people were going to pick him up in California."

"We tried, but we missed him. That's what concerns me. He must have been tipped off, or he wouldn't have given us the slip."

"It sounds to me like the FBI should take lessons from the McGowens." The chief chuckled sarcastically.

"Stuff it, Winfield. We've got work to do. After she left McGowen, she called Salinger and invited him too. I don't need to tell you what that could mean."

"Damn you and your 'foolproof' plans. Now what are we going to do? Why don't we just nuke this whole town and start from scratch?"

Mueller was growing impatient. "You're supposed to be a professional, Winfield, so start acting like one. There is some possible good that can come out of this. But we have to start getting ready for tonight."

"What about Salinger? Capsner is going to have to handle that situation."

"He is, or at least he's trying to. But I don't know what he can do by tonight. We'll just have to keep a close watch on him. I pulled Gibbons off Wence and had him look after Salinger for the rest of the day. I don't know what your plans are, but I need you here immediately. I suspect trouble is brewing, but I have a plan of how to head it off. I'll see you here in a few minutes."

Rodriguez entered the large office of the Brewster mansion and sat in a plush leather chair in front of the large desk. The white-haired man sat behind the desk, sipping brandy, his ruby ring glimmering in the sunlight streaming in from the window. He was attempting to portray an air of calm control, but it was obvious to Rodriguez that he was very anxious and on edge.

"You got my message okay, man?" Rodriguez said. "Is there something you don't understand?"

"You bet there is." The white-haired man could not contain himself. He stood and began to rapidly pace the floor in front of the window, rubbing his hands together in nervous frustration. "Don't tell me you can't see anything wrong. What about this meeting tonight at Beth Wence's house? A coincidence? That's bullshit, and you know it. What about this new McGowen? A coincidence? What about Joe McGowen? Where the hell is he? All I heard for months around here is that if we don't keep things under control, Salvo will have our ass. That point was made very clear with Spencer Thurman. Now you tell me Salvo is coming here in two weeks, and next week he wants us to have a party? I may not be the smartest man around, but that just doesn't sit right with me."

"Calm down, man. You're right, the situation is getting loose. The party is just a way of quieting things down, giving people something to focus on rather than worry about a Hoffman or a McGowen. People will be excited when they see how much has been done. Salvo's visit the next week will be perfect timing. It will go completely unnoticed.

"However, you are right about the meeting at the Wence house. But we have plans for that meeting. We do not expect anymore trouble from her or her friends."

The white-haired man sat down, not at all pacified. "Just remember, when everything is in place and shipments start coming, I'm the one who is going to be in charge here. That's what you promised me, and that's why I agreed to help."

Rodriguez smiled and casually leaned back in his chair. "Of course you will. That was the plan from the beginning. You have nothing to worry about. By the way, Mr. Salvo wanted me to extend his personal request for your presence at the party."

Chapter 27

He waited as long as his strength could hold out. He did not want to be fooled by the sound of the men leaving. They could be silently lurking above, waiting for him to move and give himself away. He held on for nearly half an hour until his muscles began to ache so severely that he felt he was in danger of falling. Finally, ever so cautiously, Joe pulled himself up on the large root he had been desperately clutching to, found a foothold on a nearby smaller root, and slowly raised himself to peek over the edge of the embankment.

Everything was clear. The FBI men, if that was who they were, were nowhere to be seen. Grabbing the trunk of a small maple tree growing near the edge, he dragged himself up into the clearing at the top of the cliff. Once on top, he rolled to his back and stretched his arms and legs, welcoming the relaxing pain caused by moving his stiff and cramped muscles. He rolled and stretched for several minutes, then finally sat up and looked over the cliff. It had been so close. It was a miracle that his plan had worked.

He had been ready to turn and fight the men. There was little chance of defeating them, but he knew jumping would be suicide. But only seconds before his attackers emerged into the clearing, he gazed down the side of the cliff and noticed a slight recess directly below him. He threw the heavy branch he had found into the stream on the chance that someone could hear the splash, possibly believing it was his body. Then, without pausing to see if it was safe, he grabbed the truck of the small maple tree and lowered himself over the edge. There was a recess about three feet down, cut back into the cliff no more than eighteen inches, apparently the result of rain and wind erosion. The only way to get his body flat enough to avoid detection was to hang on to a large root that cut through the recess area and press himself tight to the earthen wall. Since the recess was only about four feet in length, he could not let himself drop to the full extent of his arms. Wrapping his arms around the large root, he raised himself high enough to tuck his feet into the recess then froze in that position and waited. The voices of the FBI men trailed off in just a few minutes, but not wanting to take any chances, he hung on for as long as his arms would allow. It was hard to believe he escaped, but here he was, free to get up and go. But go where?

So he had been correct in assuming there were people after him who had the ability to quickly trace credit cards and, most likely, bus and airline tickets, car rentals, or any kind of documented transaction other than cash. That left him stranded. There was no way he could get back to Paradise without having some kind of traceable purchase somewhere. Or was there? An idea came to him that he felt was worth pursuing.

Joe walked back to the motel, still keeping his guard up. It had only been about forty-five minutes since the men left, and they could still be around somewhere. Reaching the back of the motel, he was amazed to see no sign of damage to the window whatsoever. The glass was in place, and there were no fragments in the grass at all. It looked as if nothing had occurred.

He went around the motel to the highway and began walking east along the quiet road. He remembered passing a restaurant some distance back when he came in the taxi. It appeared to be a quiet little place, undoubtedly a kind of greasy spoon for truckers. He needed to get there as quickly as he could. The sooner he got out of this area, the better off he would be.

The Seduction of Paradise

He set off at a brisk pace in the direction of the restaurant, but soon, he began feeling fatigued again. He was tired and dirty, and his muscles stilled ached. The refreshing sleep he had earlier seemed to be of little help to him. But he was free, and that was motivation enough to push on.

The distance to the restaurant was farther than he remembered. It continued to grow dark as he walked until finally he could barely see the road in front of him. The darkness only added to his frustration. Maybe he was confused. Maybe the restaurant was the other direction. No, he was sure this was it. His pace slowed considerably, but he continued to take one step after the other. Two hours after he started, he saw the distant glow of a red neon light. Fifteen minutes after that, he dragged his weary body into a place with the simple name of Sam's. There was only one other customer besides himself, a large burly-looking man seated at the counter. Joe sat down in a corner both, wondering if FBI agents would pounce on him any moment.

"You have a wreck?" the crude but friendly waitress questioned. "You look a little messed up."

Joe forced a smile. "No, just doing some work in the yard. Thought I needed a break for supper. Could you just bring me a couple of burgers, a glass of ice water, and a very large cup of coffee?"

"We can handle that, mister. Coming right up."

"One more thing," Joe said. "Do you sell newspapers?"

"We do, but we're sold out of today's edition, and we won't get tomorrow's until early morning. I've got my own copy under the counter. You're welcome to that."

"Thank you very much," Joe replied with genuine sincerity. "I'll only need it for a few minutes."

The waitress brought the paper, water, and coffee almost immediately. Joe quickly downed the water, instantly feeling significantly more refreshed. *It's surprising what a simple glass of water can do*, he thought. He opened the paper to the personals as he sipped his coffee. He found the section advertising car and truck sales and scanned the columns for something appropriate. He needed something reliable that was within the price range of the cash he had on hand. A cash transaction from a private party would never be traceable, at least not in any kind of time frame that mattered. Driving to Paradise from Washington would only take two days if he pushed it, but he had to be very careful not to get pulled over by the police. That would be as good as driving up to the FBI and saying, "Here I am."

As Joe relaxed and gained his strength back, his mind began to become more alert. He realized that he now had another distinct advantage that he did not have earlier that day. Apparently the FBI—and undoubtedly everyone else involved, such as Capsner—thought him to be dead. They would not be looking for him unless he gave them a reason to. If he could manage to keep a low profile and not let his name surface anywhere, he would be safe.

When the waitress brought his hamburgers, he attacked them like a starving animal. He could not believe how good simple burgers could taste. He finished them quickly and went back to studying the newspaper. There was a large selection to choose from, so he was confident he would find what he needed. After only a few minutes, he had identified ten possibilities. With his basic understanding of the Washington area, he was able to eliminate those that were too far away. He did not want to take a cab for an hour or so if he could avoid it. This left only four choices. The prices ranged from 500 to 1,300 dollars. The 1,300 would just about clean him out, but he was concerned that the five-hundred-dollar car might not be reliable enough to get him to Minnesota. The remaining two were both pickup trucks, which was fine with Joe. He chose the cheaper of the two, a 1986 Ford with 85,000 miles for 950 dollars. Providing he did not find anything obviously wrong with it, this would be his way home.

It was getting late, but Joe did not have time to delay. He called a cab from the restaurant and went to the address of the truck owner, which turned out to be only twenty minutes away. The owner was prepared for a detailed bartering session as is typical with the private sale of a used vehicle. When Joe offered the full asking price, the owner was only too willing to take the money and let Joe be on his way. Fifteen minutes later, Joe was driving north on Highway 95 in his new truck, for the first time feeling that he was regaining some control of his situation. It was Saturday, two days after he left to follow Capsner. In two more days, he would be back in Paradise. He was tired, but thoughts of what might be happening to Sheri and his children made him push on. Time was all-important. He had no idea what was in store for him, but he sensed that it would not be long before it would be too late to do anything. He briskly shook his head to help dispel the thought creeping into his mind that it might already be too late.

Ryan McGowen spent the remainder of the afternoon taking a nostalgic walk around Paradise, visiting places that he remembered from his childhood and noting how much, or how little, things had changed. In particular, he was interested in the old Brewster mansion. He was aware of the restoration project and was anxious to see how it was developing. It was only a couple of miles from city hall, and he felt the walk would do him some good, so leaving his rental in the parking lot, he set out on his short journey by foot.

As he passed through the stone gate and headed up the long horseshoe driveway, the improvements made to the mansion were immediately noticeable, and very impressive. He remembered the eerie feelings he used to get when he and Joe would play hide-

and-seek around the house when they were kids. There was a time he truly believed it was haunted. Now it looked new and clean, like the home of some millionaire.

One car was parked in front of the mansion, but no one was visible anywhere on the estate. Ryan did not want to bother whoever was inside, so he passed by the front and circled to the back of the house. Just as he rounded the corner, he caught a glimpse of a figure darting into the woods that bordered the backyard. He stopped for a moment, startled by what he thought he saw. He could not be positive, but it certainly looked like the person was a man, a black man. He cautiously walked over to where the man entered the woods, and as he approached the tree line, he was able to make out the entrance to a path.

Odd, he thought. A path running into the woods where, as far as he knew, nothing existed except more trees. Turning around, he got his first good look at the back of the mansion. He, like everyone else, was amazed at how isolated he was here, as if he had left Paradise completely. He turned back to the path, feeling an irresistible urge to follow it. It must lead somewhere, he thought. He saw someone go down it. He took a few steps in then suddenly became aware of a different feeling. He was not sure if it was this specific situation or if it had to do with this whole business of Joe disappearing, but the unmistakable feeling of fear shot through him like a bolt of electricity.

This is ridiculous, he told himself. *There is nothing to fear in Paradise.* He took a few more steps forward, the density of the woods already cutting off his view of most of the estate. He felt alone, and vulnerable. The haunting words of his last conversation with Joe began running through his mind: "Be very careful. Trust no one!" Ryan could think of no logical reason for the irrational fear that was continuing to mount in him, but he, unlike Andy, felt he should trust his instincts. He began to back out of the path.

Ahead somewhere, he heard a branch snap. Was it an animal? He could not be sure. He started moving faster as he could hear his own breathing become louder. He did not want to let his fear drive him to panic. More snapping ahead, then thumping, like the running of feet. He no longer cared if he was being rational or not. He turned and bolted out of the woods and into the backyard. It was so isolated that his fear was not relieved. He ran around the side of the house then continued down the long driveway and through the large stone gate. He did not slow down until he was completely out of view of the mansion, the place he once thought to be haunted. He went back to his car and drove to his hotel. He waited there, resting, until it was time to go Beth Wence's house.

Antonio Rodriguez glared at the frightened man running off around the corner of the mansion. He did not feel comfortable with people wandering so freely down this path. He wondered if the man had seen him. He would have to post extra guards from now on. Who was this intruder, anyway? Maybe no one, just an innocent passerby. Whoever he was, it was very fortunate for him that he left when he did. Rodriguez's breathing began to slow as he sheathed the large knife he gripped firmly in his hand.

Chapter 28

Ryan arrived at Beth Wence's house promptly at seven o'clock. He was slightly taken aback when he first saw the impressive home she lived in—far better than he ever would have been able to provide—but he quickly shook it off and went up to ring the doorbell. A smiling Beth answered the door. Ryan was pleased by her casual-but-cute style of dress. He knew her well enough to know she was not one to dress fancy, but at the same time, if there was a good enough reason, she would take extra care to achieve that just-right look. Tonight she wore a pair of tight black leggings, a white turtleneck, and a multicolored sweater that hung to the bottom of her firm derriere. Her hair hung loose around her face, with the ends having a slight inward curl. As was typical, she wore very little makeup, but she did have on a faint amount of blush with a light-colored lip gloss. To anyone else, her appearance would not seem out of the ordinary, but Ryan knew that she took a good long while to prepare herself for this evening.

"Hi, Beth," Ryan blurted clumsily, still feeling a bit awkward.

Beth seemed to be her old self, the woman he had once fallen in love with. "Well, come on in," she said with a bit of a giggle. "We certainly are not going to eat out there." She grabbed his hand and pulled him through the doorway. "What do you have there?"

Ryan looked at the package in his hand, as if he was surprised it was there. "Oh, I thought I would bring some wine since you were good enough to cook dinner. I assume that you still like red, so I got a fairly decent merlot."

"Sounds delicious," she said. "I suppose now that you live in California, you know everything about wines."

"I know what's cheap." Ryan laughed.

Beth shared the laugh, then opened the bottle and poured them each a glass. "Dinner will be ready in a few minutes. Red meat is considered taboo nowadays, but I took the chance that you still like it as much as you used to. How does T-bone steak and salad sound?"

"My favorite," Ryan replied. He found himself feeling surprisingly good. What attracted him to Beth in the first place was the ease with which he could talk to her. That apparently had not changed, even though there was definitely a little uneasiness they had to work through. But at the same time, something did not seem right. Here they were, talking about what they liked before as if nothing had really changed. But things had changed, and quite a lot. He was not sure how well he could handle this.

Beth could see he was feeling a bit disturbed. "Is everything all right, Ryan?"

Ryan sipped his wine and looked around the house. He had followed her into the kitchen, where Beth began the finishing touches of the dinner preparations.

"This is a beautiful house, Beth. You don't see many like this, at least none that belong to a high school coach."

Beth stopped and stared at the man before her, knowing full well what he was implying. Her immediate reaction was something between shock, anger, and hurt. Her playful nature quickly disappeared. "What is that supposed to mean?" she asked defiantly. "To tell you the truth, I don't know what a high school coach's house looks like. I've never had the opportunity to see one!"

Ryan realized that what he said was rude and completely uncalled for. "Beth, I'm sorry. I have no idea why I said that. I did not come expecting to dig up any old ghosts. I was just feeling so comfortable, and suddenly, it hit me that all this was yours and Stephen's. I guess I just…well…I don't know. I'm sorry. Forget I said anything."

Beth went back to her cooking. After a few moments of silence, she looked up at Ryan tenderly, understanding completely what he was feeling. "Ryan, Stephen was a very wonderful man. My life with him was special in a very personal way. But I won't pretend that I don't know what you're feeling, or that I might not be feeling a little bit of it myself. We can't go back, and I don't really want to, but having you here tonight is all I'm concerned about right now, and I don't want to lose this moment, either."

Ryan walked over to her and held her gently by her shoulders. She was beautiful, physically as well as what was within her. He knew he still loved her, but he also knew that this was not the time or place to push things. "Thank you," he whispered.

"You too," she whispered back.

Against both of their desires, they stepped away from each other. Beth went about her cooking, and Ryan sat on a counter stool and watched. Finally, after a sufficient quiet period to let the mood pass, Beth called out, "Well, I think it's eating time! I hope you're hungry."

They had a very enjoyable dinner, discussing old friends in Paradise, Ryan's team in California, and Beth's job as a sportswriter. When they had finished, Ryan insisted on doing the dishes himself—with the help of the dishwasher, of course. As he finished loading the last of the utensils, he thought he could no longer put off discussing his real purpose for coming to Paradise. His expression took on a sudden seriousness that could not escape the attention of the observant Beth.

"What is it?" she asked.

"Am I that transparent?" Ryan asked good-naturedly.

"You have always been transparent. That's one of your best qualities. You can never keep secrets from people."

"I guess I really don't know how to begin. Something strange happened the other day that has me worried." Ryan paused for a moment, trying to find the words to explain the mysterious events involving Joe and Sheri.

"Maybe I can help you," Beth said. "It concerns Joe and Andy, doesn't it? They're missing, and you can't get ahold of them, right?"

Ryan was amazed, almost stunned. "How did you know that?" he asked.

"I'll tell you my story after you tell me yours," Beth answered. "I knew it was too much of a coincidence for you to show up when you did." Much of the worry and tension she had been feeling began to slip away. She now had the ally she had been looking for.

"You're only partially right," Ryan said. "Joe and his whole family have disappeared, and apparently Fran Rosten too. But I don't know anything about Andy."

"Well, take my word for it, he's gone. But just being out of touch isn't in and of itself overly alarming. Tell me, Ryan, what exactly brought you back here?"

Ryan again recalled Joe's warning: "Trust no one!" But this was Beth; he knew he could trust her. He began cautiously at first but soon found himself rambling on about all that had happened. He told her everything—about the calls, going to the airport with no one there, the men who came to his condo, everything.

Beth listened intently, relieved to finally have someone to share her concerns with, especially since that someone was Ryan McGowen. But she was becoming even more frightened as she listened. When Ryan had finished, she took her turn and related all that she knew, finishing with her visit to Chief Winfield just that morning.

Ryan's concern for Joe quickly escalated into genuine fear for him and his family. "Beth, something terrible is going on here," he said. "Joe must have somehow stumbled across whatever it is and got himself into real trouble. No doubt he was attempting to get his family away to a safe place when he called me. My God, they must have all been captured. And he was so emphatic about trusting no one, not even the FBI. Beth, could this possibly involve them? And are they the enemy?"

Beth sat fidgeting restlessly, trying to suppress the anxiety she felt mounting. Finally, she ran to Ryan and buried her head into his chest. "Oh, Ryan, I knew something was wrong, but I had no idea it was so serious."

Ryan put his arms around her and held her tight, comforting her as well as being comforted by her. This was indeed serious, very serious. For the first time, he began considering the possibility that his brother and his family were dead. No, he could not allow himself to think that. He must do something to locate them, and he must do it soon.

Beth finally stepped back, regaining control of herself. "Ryan, there is one other person who Joe and I very briefly discussed this with. You probably know him. His name is Sherman Salinger, the old curator at the local museum. He's been spending most of his time lately with the Brewster mansion restoration, since he's the closest thing this town has to an authority on Paradise history. I knew we would be talking about this tonight, so I asked him to come over at nine o'clock. I hope you don't mind."

"Not at all," Ryan assured her. "I think we need to hash this out here and now and decide what we must do. I remember Sherman, but I never really knew him. Can we trust him?"

"I think so. We have to trust somebody."

"I suppose you're right, but no one else for now. If it's true that the FBI are the bad guys, then what about our own police? I don't think we can go to them either."

Beth's face suddenly turned white. "Ryan, I already did, when I went to Winfield's house this morning. That look he had in his eyes, he was so frightening. He knew something, I am sure of it. Now he knows about me."

"Don't worry about it, Beth," Ryan said soothingly. "You did what you thought was right. Besides, maybe Winfield's on our side. He's been chief here for a long time. I cannot believe he's gone bad."

Ryan stopped and looked at his watch. "Is Sherman normally prompt? It's five after nine."

Just then the doorbell sounded.

"Prompt enough." Beth smiled as she headed for the door. Ryan walked with her, and as they crossed the entryway, he noticed through the long narrow window on the side of the door that there was no other car in the driveway or in front of the house. Normally this would not have bothered him, but after the discussion they just had, he was suspicious of everything. As Beth reach for the knob, Ryan was suddenly gripped by a horrifying feeling that they were in grave danger. Beth had only opened the door a couple of inches when Ryan threw himself against it and locked the dead bolt.

"Ryan, what on earth—"

Her voice was cut off by the shattering of wood and glass as the center of the door was blown inward. Ryan felt the swish of bullets pass his chest, missing him by fractions of an inch.

Beth let out a loud shriek of fright as Ryan grabbed her arm and dragged her to the floor. More wood and glass erupted as the people outside released another volley of silent shots. Whoever was out there, they obviously were using silencers, for Ryan had not yet heard a single shot. The large solid oak door had several holes ripped through it, but most of it remained standing. Ryan heard the pounding of vicious kicks as an intruder tried to break through the lock. He quickly pulled Beth to her feet and pushed her toward the back of the house, in the direction of the kitchen.

"We need a weapon," he called after her. "Do you have anything we can use?"

"One of Stephen's shotguns is in my bedroom. I've kept it loaded these past few weeks. I'll get it."

In a flash, she disappeared down the hall, toward the stairway. Ryan grabbed a butcher's knife and headed back to the door, assuming the men would have broken in by now. To his surprise, no one was there. He went to the living room just off the entryway and crouched below the large bay window. He peered out at the darkness, not seeing any sign of movement. *What in hell is happening?* he thought. *Who are these people, and why are they attacking us? And why did they suddenly abandon their attack?*

He crawled on his belly to the other side of the window and peered out in the other direction. He thought he saw some movement, so he pressed closer to the window for a better look. The glass suddenly exploded just above his head, sending fragments into his forehead and scalp. He fell onto his back, temporarily dazed. He touched his fingers to his head and realized he was bleeding profusely, but he had no time to worry about this injury; he had to get up and be ready to defend himself, and Beth. He vaguely became aware of a noise from the back of the house then realized with a start someone was breaking in the back door. Agonizingly he rolled over onto his stomach, blood flowing down into his eyes, and began crawling toward the hallway.

Suddenly, a masked man appeared from around the corner with a pistol pointed directly at him. Ryan prepared to lunge at the man, not believing he would actually get the chance. His body jolted with startled alarm as he heard the deafening roar of a nearby explosion, sending the upper half of the man's body across the floor, with his legs falling limp where they stood. Ryan turned toward the noise and saw a shocked and terrified Beth Wence holding a smoking shotgun. He pulled himself to his feet and ran to her, taking the gun from her trembling hands.

"I...I thought he would kill you," Beth stammered, her eyes fixed in horror on the bloody remains of the intruder.

The Seduction of Paradise

"He would have, Beth," Ryan said. "You saved my life. But we can't let up now. There are more men out there somewhere."

More shots rang out, this time from outside. Ryan pumped the shotgun to chamber the next cartridge and ran back to the window, knowing he was no match for whoever was out there. What he saw drained what little hope he had left. Several men were running through the front yard and around into the back. Apparently, they were surrounding the house. He felt something touch his arm and turned to see Beth reaching for him, still in a state of shock. He put one arm around her and pulled her close to him.

The house again erupted with the dreadful sound of shattering glass as masked men broke through almost every possible window and door. Ryan and Beth stood helpless. Resistance would be suicide. Ryan dropped the gun to the floor and held Beth firmly with both arms as one of the men kicked the gun away. Then, for the first time in several minutes, there was silence. With the siege apparently over, two men approached them and abruptly removed their masks. Neither Ryan nor Beth recognized Special Agent Mueller, but they were sickened to see the face of Chief Byron Winfield.

Chapter 29

The sun was just a faint glow on the eastern horizon on the morning of August 27 as a 1986 Ford pickup rumbled across the Mississippi River into Paradise. Even under such tragic circumstances, Joe McGowen felt good to be home. For the past two and a half days, he had done nothing but drive and sleep. Since he felt renting a hotel room was too risky, what little sleep he managed to get was in the cramped cab of the pickup. Now, on this early Tuesday morning, he was tired and sore and hungry, and he wanted desperately to go home to his house and crawl into bed. But that was one thing he could not do, for he had to believe his house was being watched. It was important his presence here be kept a secret, especially since Capsner and his FBI cronies believed him to be dead.

The only place he thought might be safe was Beth Wence's house. He was still a little unsure about trusting anybody, but in the back of his mind, he was convinced Beth was on his side. And besides, where else could he go?

He cruised up Highway 169 to Main Street then turned right and headed east across the Whiskey River. Off to his left stood city hall, overlooking the terrace and the river. It seemed different now, not like the attractive structure he had always been impressed with. Now it had an almost sinister appeal.

Joe drove on through the small business district and finally turned right on the far eastern edge of town. A winding road took

The Seduction of Paradise

him down into the exclusive neighborhood where Beth lived, and moments later, he pulled to a stop by the curb in front of Beth's large house. He opened the door of his truck and started to step out when he suddenly froze in horror. *My God*, he thought. *What has happened here?* All the windows on the main floor were broken out, and only fragments remained of the front door.

As an impulse reaction, Joe leaped from the truck and bolted up to the front door. "Beth!" he called from the doorway. "Beth, are you in there?"

He did not really expect an answer, and was not at all surprised when he did not get one. He stepped through the opening where the door had been and quickly surveyed the damage. The wall on the far side of the entryway was full of several holes. There was no doubt in Joe's mind that these were made from gunshots. Glass lay everywhere, but by and large, everything inside seemed unaffected. It certainly did not appear as if any heavy fighting had occurred inside.

Joe walked into the living room and saw a series of small red stains under the front bay windows. He bent over and touched one of them with his fingertip, but it was completely dry. *This is blood*, he thought to himself. *I'm sure of it.* The stains seemed to form a trail in the direction of the back of the house. He turned to follow them then stopped when he saw the large grotesque red stain at the foot of the stairway. It was the same color as the others but many times larger.

Oh, poor Beth, Joe thought. *Poor, poor Beth.* He sat down on the couch and buried his face in his hands. The one person he felt he could trust was gone. Again he felt alone, like he had in Washington when he realized his family had been captured. He had to leave. He could not beat these men, not alone. And everyone he was close to either had disappeared or was killed. He had to get out of this house before someone spotted him, then he had to get out of this town forever. He got up and bolted through the doorway and ran back to his truck. In almost a panic, he turned the truck around and headed back through town.

As Joe passed the many stores and shops that lined Main Street, his anxiety began to settle, being replaced by an overwhelming sense of nostalgia. He pulled over and parked by the curb then sat for several minutes, attempting to put things into perspective. He recalled how much he had missed Minnesota when he was in the navy, and when he and Sheri were in San Diego. He remembered feeling so peaceful when he moved back to Paradise, and he remembered the pride he and his family had in this town and its people. Now here he was, on the verge of leaving it for good. True, horrible things were happening here, but he truly believed most of the residents were good people. Now he was turning his back on them. He may be the only one who knew what was going on, and by leaving, he would allow others to be endangered. His own words that he had spoken to Sheri and Fran came back to him: "Don't you see? If we're not willing to take any risks, that just leaves the door open for them to continue. Had we done something earlier, Andy might still be alive. Initially we could reason that it wasn't our responsibility, but from here on out, no action on our part is the same as condoning what they are doing."

He had decided in Washington to come back and defend his town, but at the first sign of trouble, he wanted to flee. With such a wishy-washy commitment, of course he stood no chance to succeed. It was time to see just how committed he was. It was time to stand up and be counted. He would give anything not to be in the position to have to deal with this mess, but the cards had been dealt, and now he must decide how to play his hand.

Joe took a deep breath then very slowly let it out. He looked around at the town around him, his town and his friends. This was his home; he could not turn his back and run. The odds were stacked heavily against him, but win or lose, it was here he must make his stand.

The Seduction of Paradise

The human mind has an incredible influence over how a person acts and reacts to various events. A situation considered to be hopeless generally has several potential solutions; the mind causes it to only appear hopeless. By believing there is no solution, no solution is discovered, therefore leading to the self-fulfilling notion that no solution is possible. But with a positive attitude and a determined resolve, options or choices that were previously hidden within the mind's subconscious can become apparent. The hopeless suddenly has hope; the impossible suddenly is possible.

Such a change came over Joe, and as he started his truck and pulled back out onto Main Street, various alternatives of action came into focus. He could confront Capsner in a one-on-one situation. He could confront Chief Winfield or Mayor Carlson alone to either solicit their help or determine if they had sided with Capsner. These three people were all older, and Joe felt confident he could handle them if things went sour as long as they were alone. First, however, there was one person he could contact that had already been involved, at least to a small degree. Sherman Salinger knew that Beth suspected something, and from the last discussion they had, it seemed like Sherman himself was not comfortable with what was happening. Sherman would be his first contact. Maybe it was not too late to develop an ally after all.

Joe knew where Sherman lived, but he had never been to his house. In fact, with Sherman being a rather private person, few people had been there. He was never one to socialize much, and he certainly never entertained people. His passion was his work at the museum, and now at the Brewster mansion, and his personal life was very quiet and subdued. He owned a nice but modest home about ten miles north of Paradise in a secluded area, where neighbors tended to be separated by half a mile or more.

Highway 47 headed north out of Paradise, following the winding Whiskey River to its source at the large Mille Lacs Lake about 150 miles away as the crow flies. It was a paved road but only had two lanes due to the sparse population of the area. Most of the houses along this road sat quite a distance back, some barely visible from passing cars. Sherman Salinger's house was one of these, sitting about six hundred yards from the road and surrounded by large elm and oak trees. If you did not know just where to look, you would not realize a house was even there. Another hundred yards or so behind the house ran the Whiskey River, slowly winding its way toward the Mississippi. As was typical with most of the houses out here, a narrow gravel driveway connected the house to the highway. A vehicle traveling on the driveway would stir up clouds of dirt and sand that could easily be spotted from far off. Joe considered this as he approached the turnoff. Did he really want his arrival to be announced?

He thought about what he saw at Beth's house then concluded Sherman's house may also have been attacked. Another thought struck him suddenly, something that had not occurred to him before, but now, out here in the middle of nowhere, seemed to be a real possibility. From what Andy had said, Rodriguez was here someplace, and Joe doubted that Rodriguez would be alone. Where would he and his goons stay? Possibly at the wastewater treatment center, but that place was not really set up to be a hotel. It would make sense to find a place fairly secluded, where strange men could come and go freely without worrying about being spotted. Sherman's house would be perfect, especially since it was on the Whiskey River, so the men could get all the way to the treatment center by boat without ever having to go through town.

Joe's mind began to work in overdrive as he imagined all kinds of terrible things happening to Sherman and Rodriguez taking over his house as a headquarters. The concept seemed so reasonable that by the time Joe reached the turnoff, he had convinced himself there was real danger at the other end of the long driveway. He decided driving up to the house in full view would be foolish, so he did not even slow down but cruised on by until he rounded a curve about a half mile down the road. Feeling safe, he pulled off alongside the road and parked his truck.

Clumps of trees covered the surrounding countryside, but basically, the land consisted of open flat fields. Up until a few years ago, this had been farmland, so most of the trees had long ago been cut down. Joe knew from his many boating experiences that trees were still fairly dense along the banks of the river, so he decided it would be best to follow the river to Sherman's house and approach it from the back side.

From the road, he headed in the general direction of the river, not sure precisely where it was but knowing that if he continued east, he would sooner or later come across it. He estimated that at this point it should only be about a quarter mile away. His estimation proved to be fairly accurate, and ten minutes after he left his truck, he found himself on the peaceful banks of the Whiskey River. The current here was so slow it was almost imperceptible. The trees, mainly elms and red oaks, formed a giant canopy over the water. The leaves were showing noticeable color as the air continued to maintain the coolness of early autumn.

Joe followed the meandering river southward, keeping a sharp eye out for any sign of a guard or sentry. He remembered vividly how close he came to losing his life in Florida when he was surprised by a patrolling guard. He knew he had come about a half mile past Sherman's house on the road, but the river had so many twists and turns that it could be twice that far along the bank. The traveling was relatively easy, but he was using great caution, so covering the distance to the house could take some time.

Forty-five minutes later, he came across a small dock projecting several feet out into the river. Joe knew this must belong to Sherman, since there were no other homes in the near vicinity. He crouched by a nearby tree and gazed up in the direction of the house. At first, he could only see trees and patches of dense brush, but once his eyes adjusted to the surrounding scenery, he was able to pick out a definite structure a hundred or so yards ahead. He felt his pulse quicken as he pondered over the best way to approach. Maybe he was making too much of this. Maybe Sherman was sitting inside drinking coffee and idly reading his morning paper without a care in the world. But somehow, he did not believe that to be true.

Joe checked his watch: 7:40 a.m. If Sherman was inside, he would be leaving for work any minute. Maybe it would be best to wait. Again he felt the growing impatience he experienced on his previous spy missions, but this time, he would discipline himself to better control it. Both his other trips nearly ended in disaster; this time, he could be patient forever, if need be. The minutes passed slowly with no sign of any action whatsoever. Still he waited, wanting to be very careful not to rush things. Finally, after what seemed like hours, he looked at his watch and saw that it was 8:15 p.m. If Sherman was home, he would have left for work by now.

Joe began to creep forward, conscious of every step, of each twig he stepped on, of each branch that snapped as he brushed by. The closer he got to the house, the fewer trees there were, and the heavy brush disappeared nearly completely. This took away some of his cover, but it also allowed him a much clearer view of the house. It certainly appeared as if no one was home.

Keeping about a twenty-yard distance, he circled the house to the right, continuing to use trees as much as possible for cover. Still there was no sign of anyone, but he did notice a light in the front corner room. Maybe Sherman just forgot to turn it off. But that was not characteristic of the meticulous museum curator. From his vantage point, Joe could see there were no cars in the driveway, so if someone was inside, they did not have any transportation. That could only mean someone else would be arriving later, and for all he knew, it might be only minutes later.

He finally decided to chance a closer look. He positioned into a crouch, ready to burst into a sprint, took one last look around, then darted out from behind the tree and quickly scrambled the twenty yards to the side of the house. He slid along the wall until he was just below the lit window then slowly, ever so cautiously, raised himself to a near-standing position and peered inside the room. It was the kitchen, and although no one was inside, a pot of coffee was on the counter and a plate with a half-eaten piece of toast sat on the table.

This was not from a sloppy Sherman Salinger, Joe was convinced of that. Someone else must be inside. Joe's pulse began to quicken as he crouched down below the window. What should he do now? Whoever was inside was probably a cold-blooded killer from Rodriguez's band of hoodlums. He must be very careful not to let his presence be known, for odds would be greatly against him in any head-to-head battle, and there may be more than one person inside. On the other hand, if he could somehow surprise whoever was in there, this could be a tremendous opportunity. If he had a prisoner, he may actually start getting some answers as to what this was all about. This was an opportunity he could not afford to waste, but he must act now, for others may arrive at any moment.

Joe rose back up to the window and again peered through. Nothing had changed. He had to locate where the person, or persons, were before he could make his move. His body jumped in startled reflex, and his heart simultaneously sank in despair as the presence of the unknown person was suddenly made known to him.

"Can I help you, man?" came the sharp Jamaican accent from Joe's right.

Joe looked up to see a large black man standing by the corner of the front of the house, pointing an AR15 rifle directly at his head.

Chapter 30

"What you doing here, man?" the man with the gun asked.

Joe tried to think of a believable explanation. "I'm a friend of Sherman Salinger," he began. "I was just playing a little trick on him. I had no idea he had company. I should probably just—"

"That's bullshit!" the man barked. "Inside the house. Now!"

The man took on an expression of anger and loathing. It was obvious Joe's assumption had been right; he was a cold-blooded killer. Without wanting to upset him further, Joe led the way around the corner and into the house. Once inside, the man slammed the door and locked it. He moved to the window and took a few darting glances outside, all the while trying to keep an eye on Joe.

"Is anyone with you?" the man questioned nervously.

"Of course not," Joe replied as calmly as he could.

"Don't you lie to me, man!" the man screamed, thrusting the barrel of his rifle in Joe's face.

Joe instinctively covered his head with his arms, genuinely afraid of the madman before him. "I'm telling the truth!" he screamed back. "There is no need to get crazy. Put that thing down!"

"Sit," the man commanded.

Joe sat down at the kitchen table while the man slowly circled him.

"Why are you here?" the man demanded. "And don't bullshit me."

"I told you, I was just playing a trick—ahhh, shit!" Joe screamed as the man cracked him in the head with the butt of his rifle. Joe crashed to the floor but was able to maintain consciousness. He rose to one knee, his head throbbing, then paused for a moment to let a sudden spell of dizziness pass. Blood trickled down from his head and splashed on the floor beneath him. Finally, he got up and sat back down in the chair. The man with the gun stared at him with wild, crazy eyes.

"Try it again, man, but this time, the truth."

Joe hesitated for just a moment. What should he do? This guy was just looking for an excuse to put him away, so the last thing Joe wanted to do was give him one. Things could not get worse than they already were, so maybe it would be best to just tell the truth.

The man grew impatient and raised the gun again.

"Okay, okay, I'll tell you," Joe quickly cut in. "But can I have a rag for my head first?"

"No" was the abrupt reply.

Joe leaned back and took a deep breath, trying to portray confidence and courage but thinking his charade was obvious. "All right, the reason I'm here was to see Sherman, but not to play a harmless trick on him. I wanted to find out if he knew anything about what you people are up to. You see, I know all about Rodriguez and Salvo and that son of a bitch Capsner, and of your drug trafficking in Paradise."

The man's eyes grew wide in surprise. "How do you know?" he asked.

"I've been keeping tabs on you guys," Joe said. Maybe he could make the man defensive, he thought. Maybe he could even make him a little afraid.

"Who you work for?" the man asked. "Give me your wallet."

"I don't work for anyone," Joe responded as he pulled out his wallet and tossed it to the man. "But I know you have my family somewhere, and I intend on getting them back. Do you understand that?"

"Shut up!" the man barked. He flipped through Joe's wallet, looking at various pieces of identification. "Joseph McGowen," he mused. "I have heard that name."

Joe thought he would try another tactic. "Look, I don't really care what you guys want to do in this town, I just want my family back."

"I said shut up!" the man screamed. Then, after a moment of silence, he added, "I know nothing of your family."

"Now it's my turn to say bullshit," Joe replied.

"Rodriguez will be here in an hour," the man said, ignoring Joe's comment. "We will wait for him. He will decide what to do." Then he broke into a broad, sinister smile as he added, "If I were you, I would spend the time making amends with your god."

The man sat across the table from Joe, always keeping the rifle pointing at him. Several minutes of silence passed. Joe knew if he was to have any chance at all, it would have to be before the others arrived. He must find a way to catch his captor off guard. More time passed, and even the guard started showing signs of impatience. Finally, after half an hour, Joe braved a question.

"Where is Sherman Salinger?" he asked in a casual tone.

"That is not your concern," the man replied.

Joe paused for a moment then tried again. "Where are you guys from, anyway?"

The man stared at him, as if trying to determine if this was a test or just an idle question.

"Jamaica," he finally replied.

"I thought as much," Joe said. "You know, I never understood why you guys are wasting your time in a place like Paradise, Minnesota. There can't be much money here."

The man smiled an almost-friendly smile. "You know nothing," he said. "Much money here. Much opportunity. Mr. Salvo a very smart man. He knows. You know nothing."

"I just can't believe it," Joe said. "Nobody here uses drugs, and even if they did, there aren't enough people to support an operation like you're setting up."

"You ask a lot of questions, man," the guard said. "But after Saturday, I guess it doesn't matter."

"What is happening Saturday?" Joe quickly inquired.

"Nothing, man. You asked about why we are here. Do you want to know?"

"Sure, not that it will do me any good."

"Do you know anything about cocaine, or crack?" the man asked.

"No, nothing," Joe responded.

The man laughed. "Minnesota, it is so backward. That is why this is a good location."

"I don't understand," Joe said.

"Have you heard of posses?" the man asked.

"Of course, like in the old West movies?"

"Oh, man, you are just too out of touch. I mean Jamaican posses. We are the best of all the gangs at what we do." The man said this with genuine pride. "Drug dealing in this country is not a random thing. It is very organized. You have the Crips and the Bloods out West, but they are content to stay there. We Jamaicans have always controlled the East, with our smaller groups controlling specific areas. These are posses. But we are not content to stay put. Mr. Salvo, he has found a new place to make much money."

"So Salvo is Jamaican?"

"Ha, ha, ha!" The man let out a deep laugh. "No, he is not Jamaican. He is Colombian. He does business with everyone, as long as they treat him right. We Jamaicans do most business with him, though." Again the pride showed through.

"Mr. Salvo, he realized very little drug business here. Before crack, not as profitable as other areas. But now, much money here."

"Why did crack change anything?"

"People like cocaine. They like to freebase. But freebase is difficult to sell in large quantities in short time frame. You need special place to make freebase. With crack, we can do very large quantities and sell it like retail. We can sell very much very quickly. We do not need people standing in line waiting and drawing suspicion. But we need a place to process it and store it. It must be someplace quiet and out of the way, but someplace that has access to many people."

"So you process and store crack at the treatment center, but where do you sell it?"

"Hey, man, this is Twin Cities. Over two million people here. They come to us, or we go to them. We move crack by road or by river. Mississippi connects to everything around here. If business grows, we go even further downstream. Just like early traders in this area. They were smart people." Again a long, deep laugh.

"You mean Paradise is a base to service the entire area?"

"Of course. There are no other gangs here, at least none to give us any competition. We searched for a long time to find the perfect spot, and your abandoned treatment center is it. The only access is the mansion, and your council people were good enough to let us control that. Not that it matters anymore after Saturday."

"What is happening Saturday?" Joe asked for the second time.

The man studied him, thinking about how he should reply. "Nothing," he said. "Nothing happens Saturday. You ask too many questions."

"What about my family?" Joe asked, a little more forcefully.

"Family, family, what family? I do not know what you talk about."

Unbelievable, thought Joe. So this was not just about Paradise. This was a strategic move by a large organized drug ring to establish a new market. This was big business, just like in the corporate world he was accustomed to. But what was Saturday? It was obviously something very important. He must get away, and time was running short.

"I have to take a leak," Joe said, and began to stand.

Immediately the guard raised his gun. "No!' he ordered. "Sit."

"Hey, I have to take a leak. Do you want me to piss on your toast?"

The man glared at Joe, all signs of friendliness having vanished. "Okay, man, but very slowly, and I will come with you. It is down the hall on the right."

"You're coming with me to take a leak?" Joe laughed.

The man was not amused. "Do not ridicule me, man. I can still kill you myself if I wish. Go now if you must, but go slowly. Any quick moves, and you are a very dead man."

Joe stood up and headed down the hall. His head began throbbing again as he walked. He stepped inside the bathroom and attempted to close the door. The guard immediately pushed the door back. "The door will remain open," he commanded.

Joe suddenly saw a possible opportunity, but his timing would have to be perfect. It might not be the chance he was hoping for, but it would probably be his last chance. Without any aggressive action, he feigned a scowl of irritation and pushed on the door again, saying, "What do you mean leave the door open? I'm taking a leak."

As Joe hoped he would do, the guard stepped forward to firmly push the door open. "I said leave it!" he cried.

Just as he reached for the door, Joe grabbed his arm and pulled him forward, at the same time stretching out his leg to trip the man and drive him down. The guard was bigger and much stronger than Joe, but since he was already in motion from trying to push the door open, it was easy to get him off balance. He crashed to the floor and smashed his head against the edge of the toilet.

"You bastard!" the man shrieked. "I will kill you!"

There was no doubt in Joe's mind the man meant what he said. This would be his only chance, a true fight for survival. His head pounded, but he barely noticed as he jumped on the big

The Seduction of Paradise

man's back. The rifle was trapped under the man where neither of them could get at it. The big guard began to raise himself up, easily lifting Joe with him. Joe knew if the man could even get to his knees, he would be able to pull the rifle free.

Joe reached his right arm around the man's throat and clasped it with his left hand, trying to strangle the powerful Jamaican. The man groaned and thrashed, trying to free himself from Joe's grip, but Joe would not relinquish. The man clawed at Joe's arm then reached back and attempted to grab Joe's hair, but he was starting to lose his strength and Joe was able to maintain his hold. The man's arm went behind his back, but Joe continued to concentrate on crushing the man's throat and cutting off his air supply. He was completely taken by surprise when he saw the flash of a large knife blade and felt it slice into his right arm.

Joe screamed and immediately pulled his arm back, letting the man go free. He grabbed his wound with his left hand, the blood immediately beginning to ooze through his fingers. The big man was struggling to get his breath, still dazed by Joe's choke hold. Joe knew if he allowed the man to recover, he was through. With the blood pouring from his arm, he struggled to his feet and kicked the man viciously in the kidney area. The man screamed and fell back to the floor, still clutching the bloody knife. He rolled to his side, again attempting to free his rifle. Joe kicked again, this time to the man's face. The man's head snapped back as he let out a loud, painful groan. The knife dropped from his hand, and he lay motionless.

Joe was afraid to get too close to the man for fear he was attempting to trick him, but it soon became apparent he was genuinely unconscious. Joe picked up the knife and the rifle and stepped out into the hallway to catch his breath. His arm was bleeding out of control, so his first priority had to be getting it bandaged. He found the materials he needed in the bathroom and quickly proceeded to clean and wrap his wound. To his relief, it appeared to be much less serious than the blood and the pain indicated, although he knew it would need to be stitched for it to heal properly. He would worry about that later. For now, controlling the bleeding would suffice.

The man still lay on the floor without even flinching. Joe could see his chest moving, so he knew he was still alive. Part of him wanted to leave before anyone else arrived, especially since he had already learned a good deal of information. But the man's comments about nothing mattering after Saturday kept haunting him. He felt he must find out what was going to be happening. And he also was not satisfied that the man knew nothing about his family. He wanted one more chance to get some kind of information as to where they were and if they were all right.

He grabbed the man by the feet and, with considerable effort, dragged him into the living room. Even though he now had the weapons, he did not want the man to be able to move about freely when he awoke, so he quickly searched the room for something to tie the man's hands and feet. Unable to find anything, he cut the electrical cords off two lamps. These served his needs very well.

The man still did not move, but his quiet moaning told Joe he was slowly coming back to consciousness. Joe brought a pan of water in from the kitchen and splashed it into the man's face, accelerating the reviving process. The man coughed and gasped then shook his head and opened his eyes, trying to get his bearing and trying to remember what happened. Finally it all registered, and he quickly tried to get to his feet. For the first time, he realized his limbs were bound.

"What are you doing, man?" he wailed. "You in big trouble. Big trouble, man."

Joe sat in a chair across the room, pointing the AR15 at the man's head. "It seems to me you're the one who is in trouble. I have a couple of questions for you. If you answer them satisfactorily, I'll get out of here."

"I tell you nothing. Rodriguez will be here soon. He will take care of you."

"First, I want to know about my family, and don't tell me you don't know anything."

"You crazy, man. I know nothing of your family, or anybody's family."

Joe had always been a nonviolent man, but the past few days were too much for him. Visions of Andy's mutilated body entered his mind. Memories of Spencer Thurman getting blown away on the beach came back to him. His own encounters with near death and his family being taken prisoner, with who knows what harm being done to them. He could take no more, and if this bastard knew anything, he was going to talk. In most cases, nonviolence is essential, but this kind of scum only understood one law.

Joe rushed up to the man on the floor, grabbed his hair in one hand, and roughly jerked his head back. Then, with his other hand, he brought the point of the large knife to the man's throat.

"I want the truth, you Jamaican bastard!" he screamed. "Where are they?"

"Please, I'm telling you the truth, I don't know," the man whimpered.

Joe was finally forced to concede the man probably did not really know. But he was not finished with him yet.

"What is happening Saturday?" he demanded.

"I know nothing of that either."

"I know that is bullshit!" Joe roared wildly. "You've been gloating about that for an hour. This is your last chance. Tell me!" He pulled the man's head back again even more viciously than before, and this time, he pressed the tip of the knife into the man's throat firmly enough to draw blood. The man could see the total rage in Joe's eyes and fully believed Joe would cut his throat if he did not talk. As horrifying a concept as it was, Joe was not at all convinced in his own mind that he would not.

The man was barely able to get the words out of his mouth as he began to speak. "All right, I tell you. Much has gone wrong here. Our purpose could only be served if we could avoid any kind of attention. That is why small quiet towns are sought out. But many things have happened to bring visibility and suspicion to our project. Mr. Salvo does not like taking risks. He is pulling out of here completely. But too many people may know something about who we are. There is to be a party Saturday at the mansion for everyone who has been associated with this project."

He stopped, as if the story ended there.

"What is so special about the party?" Joe demanded. "Tell me!" He jabbed the knife in a bit further, just enough to cause a little more pain and fear.

"Ahhh. Please, do not kill me. At the party, all the people will be locked in the mansion, and the building will be burned. All will die. We will be gone that night. The people of Paradise will know there was a great tragedy, but they will never know our posse was here."

My God, thought Joe. *My dear God.* How could there be people like this in the world? He never knew evil could run so deep.

"Is that bastard Capsner behind any of this?" Joe asked.

Even with the blood trickling down his neck, the man managed a smile. "No, his services are no longer required by Mr. Salvo. Mr. Capsner will witness the fire from the inside."

Through his anger and horror, Joe somehow felt an odd sense of satisfaction about Capsner's fate. He pulled the knife away from the man and released his grip on his hair. Suddenly, the outside door burst open, and two black men rushed in with AR15s ready to fire. They saw Joe and turned their guns toward him, firing several bursts of rounds in his general direction without taking specific aim. Joe was just fractions of a second ahead of them as he leaped clear of the volley in the direction of the chair where his rifle lay. Without pausing, he grasped the rifle and leaped again, this time through the window into the side yard. He knew he would have only fractions of a second, and assuming the men would fire at him from the window, he immediately wheeled about and sprayed a volley of rounds through the wall alongside the window.

No one returned his fire, and no sounds whatsoever came from inside. He slipped back up to the house and crouched below the window then abruptly stood and thrust the barrel of his rifle through the opening. The man he had bound was lying dead on the floor, riddled with the bullets from his two accomplices, bullets that had been intended for Joe. The other two were lying just off to the side of the window. Joe had assumed correctly that they would be near the opening. He was just about to relax when one of the men suddenly raised his rifle and fired. Splinters of wood sprayed across Joe's face as the bullet struck the frame of the window next to him. He immediately returned fire with several bursts, killing the man instantly.

Both of the men who attacked Joe were wearing .45-caliber pistols in their belts. Joe decided it would be wise to take one with him for any future encounters like this. He hurried around to the front door rather than climb through the window opening, which was filled with sharp, jutting fragments remaining from his escape. He took one pistol and several clips from one of the dead men, and then studied each of the men for a moment. He could not be positive, but he was reasonably sure neither of them was the infamous Rodriguez. The first man had told him Rodriguez was coming, so it was likely that more men would be showing up soon.

Joe was not sure where he was going or where he would stay that night, but he knew finding food would be difficult during the next few days. Starting to feel panic building in him again, he quickly rummaged through the house until he found a canvas duffel bag in what was apparently Sherman's bedroom. He took the bag to the kitchen and filled it with as much miscellaneous kinds of food as it could hold. Then, not wanting to chance another encounter, he raced back out the door and headed in the direction of the river. He realized for the first time that his forearms were covered with many little droplets of blood from his crashing through the window. None of the cuts were serious and they did not seem to hurt, so he ignored them for now as he hurried to find a place where he would be safe.

When he reached the river, he found a canoe tied to the dock, undoubtedly belonging to the two men who surprised him. He had no plan as of yet, but somehow, it seemed like having a canoe would be advantageous. Going downstream would be far too risky since there would be a good chance of running into Rodriguez or some of his men. He remembered a series of islands a few miles upstream, which were densely wooded and would provide a reasonable sanctuary for him until he formulated some kind of plan.

He loaded his food and ammunition into the canoe and set off upriver. He paddled for nearly an hour before he found the islands he was looking for. He maneuvered to a small inner island, surrounded by the east bank on one side and larger islands on the other, scarcely visible from the main stream of the river. He landed the canoe and pulled it up into the woods, where it could easily be concealed. Then, for the first time, he sat under a tree and attempted to relax.

Joe leaned back against the tree and tried to get his thoughts into perspective. He was fatigued, hungry, sore, and very, very frightened. *My God,* he thought, *what has just happened?* He had killed two men, and it did not even faze him, at least not until now. Another thought suddenly struck him: if Salvo is going to kill everyone involved and then pull out, he must also plan on getting rid of Sheri, Fran, and the kids. Maybe he already had. Joe pulled his knees up to his chest and wrapped his arms around his legs, holding them tight as if somehow he could protect himself from all this madness. He felt his body start to tremble, first just minor twitches then escalating into uncontrollable spasms. Finally, unable to contain himself, he let out a long, shrieking cry of anguish. He threw himself down on the muddy grass, buried his face in his arms, and wept like a baby.

※

"Sharon, this is Byron," Chief Winfield said when Mayor Carlson answered her private cellular phone.

"Yes, Chief, what can I do for you?"

"Did you hear about the party Capsner is putting on Saturday?" he questioned.

"Of course, I received my invitation yesterday."

"Mueller says this is something Salvo himself requested. Apparently, it's all on the up-and-up. But something about it doesn't seem right."

"To be honest, Chief, I was having considerable reservations about it myself, but I could not find any concrete reason to be suspicious. The way it was explained to me, it sounded like a good idea."

"I don't know," Winfield said. "I think we should be prepared for some surprises. I want to sit down and talk to Mueller and Capsner about this before Saturday. I think you should be there too."

"Count me in," the mayor said. "Just let me know when and where."

Chapter 31

Joe ran desperately along the narrow path through the dense underbrush of the woods. He had been running for a long time, although he did not know just how long, only that his chest ached for want of air and his legs barely had the strength left to support his body. He had no idea where the path was leading as it wound on and on endlessly into the woods, but he knew it would eventually take him to his family. But time was very short, and the thought of being too late terrified him to the point of pushing himself beyond his physical limits.

Branches and bushes clawed at him as he rushed by, tearing at his clothes and gouging his flesh, but he was scarcely aware of the pain. A number of times he stumbled, but he quickly sprang back to his feet and pushed on, not allowing himself to relax even for a moment. He must find his family!

Finally he rounded a curve and burst into a clearing. There stood the house he was looking for: an old three-story dilapidated structure that reminded him of a witch's lair from a fairy tale. It looked ominous and foreboding, but he knew his wife and children were in there, so he summoned all his courage and raced up the steps to the porch and pounded on the door. There was no answer; of course there was no answer! Still breathing hard, he kicked at the door—once, twice, three times. The door partially gave way, but the hinges and the lock were being stubborn. Joe stepped back, lowered his shoulder, and charged at the door,

The Seduction of Paradise

throwing all his weight violently against it. It easily broke free of the lock, and Joe crashed through the opening into the entryway of the house, falling facedown on the floor from the thrust of his momentum.

Joe quickly surveyed the layout of the old house. It was void of all furniture, all appliances, even of any type of floor coverings or rugs. It was an empty shell, existing only for the purpose of a harsh and cold prison. He looked over into the large empty room on his right, and with sharp, terrible gut-wrenching horror, he saw that his worst nightmare was a reality.

"No," he whimpered. "No, no, no!" Scattered about the room were the bodies of his family: Sheri, Maureen, Brandon, and poor little Katelin. They were dead, all of them, brutally murdered by the evilest of men.

Joe pounded his fists into the floor, feeling a retching sensation begin to build in his stomach. Suddenly he heard a noise to his left. He looked up to see the madman Rodriguez, standing above him with an Uzi pointing directly at his head. Rodriguez said nothing but smiled his broad, hateful smile, then pulled the trigger on his Uzi to release a volley of lead into Joseph McGowen.

Joe shrieked a long, terrifying primal scream that echoed throughout the woods. He shrieked again a second time, then again and again. His body was covered with cold sweat as he rolled and thrashed in the moist grass. Finally, he snapped up to a sitting position, fully awake but continuing to be haunted by the images of the all-too-real dream. He sat for several moments, sucking in deeps breaths of the fresh air. Of all the horrible experiences of the past few weeks, this dream affected him the most, possibly because in the deep recesses of his mind, he was afraid it might be true.

The sun was just beginning to peep through the trees as it slowly began its ascent in the east. Joe realized he must have slept for nearly eighteen hours. He needed the sleep, needed it terribly, but with dreams like this, he was not sure the sleep was beneficial. He stood up and stretched his cramped muscles and tried to clear the final stages of slumber from his mind. He did feel rested, more than he had in days. The dream that woke him was terrifying, but for most of the night, he must have slept soundly. He had not intended to sleep that long, but now he was glad he did. From here on, it was important he be physically as well as mentally sharp.

Looking down at himself, he realized he was a total mess. His body and clothes were covered with mud, and he was drenched in sweat. Not that he was concerned about making a fashion statement out here on this small island while he was fighting for survival, but he had always been a firm believer in the "sound mind, sound body" philosophy. If he let himself go physically, his mental faculties were sure to follow.

The morning air was cool; Joe estimated the temperature to be near 60°F, but the river water had not had time to react to the sudden coolness of the past few days. It was still warm and pleasant, so Joe stripped off his clothes and bathed himself as best as possible. The warm water was relaxing to him and helped alleviate some of the aching in his head from the blow the big Jamaican had delivered. He was careful to keep his bandaged arm out of the water, for even though the water felt clean and refreshing, it was still river water and was full of many things that would not be good to get into an open wound. When he finished with his body, he attempted to wash his clothes by sloshing them about in the water, knowing he could not possibly get them clean but hoping to at least get the heavy chunks of mud off and possibly rinse the sweat out.

He hung his clothes on some tree branches to dry in the sun and the breeze then pulled a box of Raisin Bran from his food bag for his breakfast. He knew it had been a while since he had last eaten, because the dry cereal tasted wonderful. The air temperature rapidly warmed as the sun continued to rise, but it was still cool on his wet and naked body. He enjoyed the coolness

The Seduction of Paradise

and actually felt more refreshed as a result of it. He had always preferred cooler weather, which was one of the things he loved about Minnesota. Even as a boy, his mind seemed more alert when his body was cool.

After a few handfuls of cereal, he became thirsty and realized he had made a potentially serious blunder. In his haste to escape from Sherman's house, he managed to grab some solid food but totally forgot about something to drink. Well, if worse came to worse, he had the river. Too much of that water could make a person sick, but an occasional mouthful should not be too dangerous. He lay back on a patch of grass and pondered his next move. He now had a few issues to consider. His first priority was to locate and rescue his family, but also very important was the massacre that was planned for Saturday. Today was Wednesday, so he had three days to do something about that situation.

Both issues had serious obstacles. In the case of his family, he did not have any idea of how to begin. With Beth and Sherman apparently prisoners, or possibly even killed, he did not know where else to turn. Somehow he would have to get Capsner alone and force him to talk. As far as the party on Saturday, he could probably just warn someone, but the obvious problem was that he did not know who. If he warned the wrong person, someone who was in with Rodriguez, he would be tipping his hand and losing what little advantage he may have. Again it came back to Capsner, since he apparently was on the list of those to be executed.

Joe considered this ironic twist of events, rubbing his chin with his right hand as he thought. In a strange sort of way, he may actually be able to get Capsner to help him. Even though Capsner was a murdering bastard, Joe felt Capsner may work with him on getting his family back if he knew what his friends Rodriguez and Salvo were planning for him. Yes, as always, Capsner was the key.

Getting to Capsner was going to be a problem. Joe did not know where he lived, and he really did not want to take the chance of being seen in public. It only made sense to confront Capsner at the mansion, or possibly even at the treatment center. Capsner was usually there, and Joe could get to either place by river. Of course, he would be easy prey on the river in daylight, but if he waited until dark and stayed near the shoreline, he would be virtually undetectable.

When his clothes had dried, Joe dressed himself and spent the remainder of the day trying to determine what he would do if he managed to get Capsner alone. How would he make him talk? He had to be careful to maintain his composure; it would be too easy to let his rage get the best of him and bash the miserable man's head in, but that would not be any help to him at all. He needed Capsner, at least for now. Also, he must keep in mind that he was dealing with professionals who were much more experienced at this kind of work than he was. He must be extremely cautious. Getting himself killed would certainly not help his family.

The last few glimmering rays of sun vanished behind the horizon by nine o'clock in the evening, and by nine thirty, a canopy of darkness enveloped the entire area. Joe launched his canoe and began paddling silently downstream, taking only his pistol and two extra clips of bullets. The Whiskey River was not particularly swift, but what current there was made the traveling easy and smooth. Within thirty minutes, he reached the dock owned by Sherman Salinger. Joe approached the dock very cautiously, not being sure whether or not guards would be posted. There were no signs or sounds of anyone by the shore, and as Joe passed slowly by, he looked in the direction of Sherman's house to see if he could detect lights or any indications of someone's presence. All was dark. Suddenly, Joe was overtaken by an eerie sense of death and foreboding. Were the bodies of the dead men still in there? Were they dumped someplace nearby? Had the others abandoned this place as a hideout, or were they just being more cautious and waiting to trap whoever had killed their comrades? He felt his limbs begin to tremble, but as he left the dock in the distance behind him, the sensation slowly subsided, and he continued on under control.

Joe felt fortunate that a thick layer of clouds had rolled in earlier that afternoon, for they now provided additional protection by shielding light from the moon and stars, which may allow him to be spotted. However, as he passed under the Main Street bridge and paddled nearer to the Brewster mansion, he now realized the lack of light was a curse as well as a blessing. He was able to make out the large black wall of silhouetted trees immediately to his right as the riverbank quickly rose, eventually to reach its highest peak at the point where the mansion was located, but he could not make out any specific details, and he certainly would have as much difficulty spotting a guard as a guard would have in spotting him. His advantage was that he would be expecting to see guards, and hopefully, the inverse would not be true.

He paddled on slowly and cautiously, straining his eyes for any identifying feature that would give him a bearing as to his location. Suddenly, his heart jumped as a black wall seemed to almost lunge at him from directly ahead. He was barely able to stop the canoe before running headlong into the black wall but finally managed to secure the boat to the shore just a few feet away from the dark obstacle. After a few moments of studying it, he realized it was a boathouse built out over the water. He had heard the restoration project of the Brewster mansion included the boathouse and the long seesaw stairway leading to the house. This was certainly it, he thought.

Joe stepped out of the canoe and pulled it a few feet onto the shore. He drew the pistol from his belt and crouched for several moments without moving, listening for any sound of danger. The night was still, and he could hear the faintest of sounds around him: lapping water, idle creaking of the boathouse as the water flowed by, even the quiet rustling of some animal scurrying away through the grass. If someone was out there, he would hear him.

He slowly moved forward, feeling as much as seeing his way along. He took each step with painstaking caution, staying alert for any unusual sound whatsoever. He knew the stairway could not be far away, so he stayed close to the edge of the cliff, feeling the bushes and tree branches, until finally his hand touched the wooden railing of the first tier of steps. Again he froze, making sure no one was nearby.

One by one, as Andy had done only a few days before, Joe ascended the long stairway, pausing from time to time to listen. Finally he found himself on the landing at the top; the Brewster mansion was only a few feet to his left, and the main area of the grounds extended in front of him and to his right. From what he could see of the mansion, all the lights were out, but he was close enough to the highway for the streetlights to provide some visibility, at least to the point where he felt comfortable walking about.

From this vantage point, Joe was not able to see the back of the house where he remembered the study was located. If Capsner was inside, he would probably be there. If not, he could check down at the treatment center or, better yet, find a way into the mansion and wait for Capsner to return in the morning. That would give him the advantage of surprise, although it would also add an element of risk. First and foremost, he needed to check out the study.

He knew he would not be able to get around the house to his left due to its close proximity to the cliff. He remembered from his visit earlier that spring how the porch of the mansion was built right out to the very edge. He crouched low and slowly made his way across the front of the mansion to the far side, staying alert for any signs of a guard or sentry. In the driveway, he noticed the dark shadows of two automobiles, telling him someone must be here somewhere. He reached the far corner of the house then paused again to listen. The typical sounds of the night seemed to be accentuated. The creaking of crickets, the distant croaking of bullfrogs, the breeze through the leaves—all seemed to be echoing in his ears. But that was the only sounds he could identify; there was nothing that sounded potentially threatening.

Joe moved quietly along the side of the house until he reached the back corner, then slowly and ever so carefully peered around into the back. Here the mansion blocked what little light came from the highway, and the backyard was as black and dimensionless as a bottomless coal mine, with one exception. A faint glow cast out from the mansion just a few yards away, stretching out for a short distance and disappearing into the emptiness beyond. Stepping out a few steps from the corner, Joe could see that this glow came from the window of the study. Someone was inside!

The drapes were drawn over the window, blocking out the majority of the light, but as was the case the last time Joe was here—which now seemed like a lifetime ago—there was a narrow gap down the center where the drapes did not quite meet. It was only about a half inch or so, but it was enough to get a partial look inside. He had a narrow view of the room, being able to see only about half of the large mahogany desk and a portion of the wall beyond. He could hear the muffled sound of voices but was unable to distinguish any of the words.

Suddenly Capsner appeared from behind the desk and paused for just a moment in the field of view through the gap. His face was flushed, and his eyes were glaring with obvious anger at the other person in the room. Finally he pounded his fist on the desktop and retreated off to Joe's left, presumably to his chair behind the desk. Joe could detect the movement of a shadow from his right toward the desk, but it stopped before entering the view from the window. The shadow was raising its voice, although still indistinguishable. Whoever the shadow was, it was obviously equally as upset as Capsner. Joe strained to catch a glimpse of this other person, but the gap in the drape would not permit it.

With a sudden jolt, the shadow's right hand thrust out, pointing an accusing finger at Capsner. Joe could see it was a man's hand, a white man with a large ruby ring on his pinky finger.

The light from the window suddenly vanished, leaving Joe in complete darkness. His first reaction was to stand fast until his eyes became acclimated to the darkness, but then a thought struck him which drove him to immediate action. Both men must be leaving; if he wanted Capsner, this may be his last chance tonight.

Joe quickly moved around to the side of the house and peered up at the front door. The two men had just emerged, and he could hear Capsner's voice loud and clear.

"I'm telling you," Capsner stormed. "You had better not fuck with me. This is my operation, and I'll handle it my way. If you want to go to Salvo, go ahead. But for now, you are taking orders from me. Now get out of here. I need to check on a few things down at the treatment center."

The other man said nothing but turned with disgusted resentment and headed off in the direction of the cars. Even with the faint light from the highway, the darkness was too intense for Joe to identify who he was, although there seemed to be something familiar about his walk. Capsner stood for a moment then slowly headed toward the corner of the house, the point where Joe was crouching in the shadows. Joe tensed, recognizing this as an ideal opportunity to surprise him.

The other man appeared to be fumbling with his keys and still had not gotten into his car. Joe held his breath as Capsner approached, wanting desperately to tackle him and quickly get him under control before he had an opportunity to resist. He was only a few steps away, and Joe could hear him mumbling under his breath, something about the incompetent son of a bitch. Joe quickly glanced at the other man, who had just managed to get his door open.

It is not going to work, thought Joe. *The man at the car is too close. He would be sure to hear the scuffle. Shit!* He waited so long for this, and now he was so close, but he could not take a foolish chance like this. He would have to be patient. He had come too far to risk blowing everything by being reckless.

Just as Capsner rounded the corner, only inches from Joe's grasp, Joe relaxed and watched his enemy slowly pass by. Seconds later, he heard the roar of the other man's engine as the car eased down the long drive and out onto the highway.

Chapter 32

Joe silently crept along the side of the house to the back corner and peered around, hoping to catch at least a glimpse of Capsner before he disappeared into the darkness. With the study light out, visibility was nearly as limited as down by the river. He could not have gone too far, thought Joe. It had only been thirty or forty seconds.

Suddenly, a small beam of light appeared and flashed along the row of trees lining the edge of the woods. It moved slowly one way and then the other. Capsner was obviously looking for something, most likely the entrance to a path or walkway. Joe realized an opportunity here. True, with the flashlight, Capsner had the advantage of seeing better where he was going, but on the other hand, Joe could easily spot him, while he himself would, for all practical purposes, be invisible under the cloak of darkness.

The light began bobbing and blinking intermittently, indicating to Joe that Capsner had entered the woods and was moving through the trees. As quietly as possible, Joe raced the short distance to the tree line and began searching for the opening Capsner had just entered. The darkness was playing tricks with Joe's perspective of where he was versus where Capsner had been. Joe darted a short distance to his right then back to his left. Where was it? It must be here somewhere; he just saw Capsner go in. The beam of light was moving farther away and was being interrupted more frequently. Soon it would undoubtedly disappear altogether. Where in hell was the path!

Suddenly he became aware of a narrow strip appearing even darker than the black surroundings not more than three steps to his right. It was the path! He had been in the right place all along, but it was just difficult to distinguish the opening from the dense trees. He rushed into the black void, feeling somewhat like he was stepping out into space and being swallowed up in an infinite expanse of nothingness. Almost immediately, the toe of his shoe caught a raised tree root, sending him crashing to the ground. He froze, horror-struck that he had given himself away. Up ahead, he saw the light continue to bob and blink; Capsner must not have heard him. Apparently there were no guards nearby either. Joe scrambled to his feet, not wanting to lose sight of the light but fully aware that navigating this path in the dark would be treacherous.

Slowly he moved on ahead, stumbling and feeling his way along. He quickly accepted the fact that there was no way he could keep up with Capsner, not without a light of his own. But maybe it was no longer important. He was on the path, and it was sure to take him to the treatment center. He could deal with Capsner then. For now, it was important he remain patient and make sure he got there undetected. Moments later, the blinking light vanished.

With the decision to let Capsner pass on ahead, Joe was able to settle himself down and found that following the path was not nearly so difficult. He still had to be very cautious, but he was able to make reasonably good time. He felt the path descending downward, which was not surprising since he knew the treatment center was down by the river. For a moment he even considered going back to his canoe and approaching the center by water, but he quickly dismissed the idea since he felt he would have much more cover and mobility on foot.

As Joe moved farther into the depths of the woods, images of his friend Andy flashed into his mind. The bloody, dying body lying helplessly on his bed, soaking wet with river water; Andy's desperate attempt at giving a message, "Last night...Drugs... Treatment center." Could Andy have followed this same path, followed it to his death? Joe shook away the horrible images and moved on, determined not to end up with the same fate as his friend.

Ahead through the darkness, Joe was vaguely becoming aware of new sounds. He could not tell specifically what they were, but they were clearly in contrast with the natural sounds of the woods. After another fifty yards, he was able to identify the low murmuring of human voices and the general moving about of people. Still unable to see more than a few feet, he crouched low and proceeded with even more caution. Finally, he came to the edge of a clearing, and what he saw shocked him.

Instead of an old abandoned structure, the treatment center looked like a modern loading dock. A door large enough for a small truck had been built into the side with a platform extending out nearly one hundred feet to the water's edge, obviously for bringing merchandise from a boat to the building. Sitting just in front of the door was a small forklift. Several large spotlights were positioned along the platform, illuminating it as bright as midday. A few feet off to the side was a smaller door for personnel passage. This door was open, and immediately in front of it stood Capsner and another man, apparently having a serious discussion. On both sides of the platform stood a sentry, each carrying the same AR15 riffles Joe had seen on the beach in Florida.

As Joe's eyes became acclimated to the new light, he strained to see the man standing with Capsner. Finally Capsner stepped back just slightly, giving Joe a more clear view. He felt his palms moisten as he recognized the hideous face of Rodriguez, another person he would like to deal with personally before all this was over.

The Seduction of Paradise

Joe pondered his next move. He was fairly certain there were more guards around than the two on the platform, probably several more. His best bet for now was to just sit and wait. Sooner or later, Capsner would come back.

Joe watched as Capsner finished his conversation with Rodriguez then exchanged a few words with the guards. When Capsner finished, he walked along the platform, pausing now and then to study some detail more closely. Finally he went back to the building and walked through the open door. Seconds later, light came streaming out. He apparently was inspecting the facility, probably making sure everything was ready for the drug shipments that were to be coming soon.

Joe's muscles began to cramp as he felt himself getting restless. *Calm down, Joe,* he told himself. *Be patient.* Through this whole ordeal, maintaining patience was the most difficult part.

After a fifteen-minute wait that seemed more like fifteen hours, the light from the door went out, and Capsner emerged with Rodriguez and another guard. They immediately headed toward the path, and to where Joe sat hiding. For a moment, Joe froze, not knowing if he should run or hide. With no time to ponder alternatives, he quickly rolled off the path into the brush. He was completely exposed, save for the darkness. If the flashlight beam fell on him, he would be a dead man. He pulled the pistol from his belt and held it ready. If he was spotted, he would open fire, first trying to take out the armed guard, then Capsner and his buddy Rodriguez.

The three men slowly passed by, close enough for Joe to reach out and touch them. Capsner was in the lead, and he kept the light trained directly on the path in front of him. Joe held his breath and did not dare let it out until the light was nearly out of sight.

Damn, Joe thought. This was the second time he was close to capturing Capsner. Luck was just not with him tonight. It was possible he would still have a chance to get Capsner up at the mansion, but in the back of his mind, he knew he had missed his chance this night. Capsner undoubtedly would be going home soon. But it made no sense to stay down here, so Joe carefully made his way back up the path, going even slower than when he came down. At one point, he became confused, for it seemed like the path was going in two different directions. It was at the same point where Andy had made his fatal wrong turn, where the path veered off down to the boathouse. Since Joe was not in the panicked state of mind as Andy had been, he had the time to stop and study the situation. He realized there was another path, but it was clear to him which one he should take. After an exhaustive climb, he found himself again in the backyard of the mansion. The building was dark, and a quick check around to the front revealed Capsner's car was no longer there. Capsner had gone for the night.

What should Joe do now? Go back to his island? He did not like the idea of leaving now that he was securely here. He considered himself fortunate to have gotten where he did without running into a sentry. Maybe it would be best to stay put, even if he had to wait until tomorrow night. This place was no less comfortable than the island, and even if there were guards, there were enough woods to provide cover and keep him safe if he did not move around, and if he stayed clear of the path. He had no food with him, but he would only be here one more day at most. He could easily get by one day without eating.

Quietly he crawled into the woods, far enough so he felt he was in no immediate danger. Then he stretched out in the dirt and the brush, laying the pistol by his side. *It is amazing how comfortable the ground feels when you're tired enough*, he thought. There was much on his mind, but not enough to keep him awake. Within minutes, he was sleeping like a baby.

The Seduction of Paradise

As the first rays of the morning sun found their way through the canopy of leaves, Joe McGowen opened his eyes and sat up with a start. Quickly he reminded himself of where he was and why he was here. He had made it through the night without any of the nightmares that were occurring with increased frequency lately. Unbelievably, he actually felt refreshed.

The woods provided adequate cover for the most part, but without the dark veil of night, he did not feel it was safe to do too much moving around. For nearly two hours, he lay still and listened for the sounds of voices or people walking. If a guard was patrolling anywhere nearby, he should be able to hear him. Finally, after hearing nothing, Joe felt confident enough to crawl in the direction of the mansion. When he was close enough to see it through the brush, he stopped and settled in for what he knew would be a long day. Lying there watching and thinking, he was struck with an almost humorous sense of irony of this situation. For so long he had been watched by someone from the woods near his own home, and now here he was watching the enemy from this patch of woods.

From his vantage point, Joe was only able to see the back of the mansion and several feet of one end of the drive as it curved out toward the highway. Somewhere near eight thirty, he saw a car pull in and disappear behind the mansion. He was not able to see the driver, but he was quite sure it was Capsner's car. After a few minutes, the curtains in the study were open, and although he was a fair distance away, Joe was able to identify that the person inside was indeed his prey, Ronald Capsner.

Before Capsner even sat down, a second car pulled into the drive, and moments later, a man in his late thirties joined Capsner in the study. Joe did not recognize the man, but it was clear he and Capsner knew each other well. Fifteen minutes later yet, a third car entered the stone gateway of the mansion. Joe could see there were two people inside, but again, he was not able to identify who they were. Something about the car itself looked familiar. Whoever it was, they were surely here for a meeting with Capsner. Joe could feel the anxious anticipation build within him as he eagerly waited to see who entered the study. After a few minutes, Capsner got up from his desk and left the study, presumably to greet his guests at the front door. Moments later, he returned, and Joe caught his breath in both anger and shock as he easily recognized the two people who followed Capsner through the doorway: Chief Byron Winfield and Mayor Sharon Carlson.

<hr />

"I know it's risky meeting like this," Special Agent Mueller said to Capsner, "but Winfield insisted."

"I don't think this is a problem," Capsner responded. "Why shouldn't I meet with the mayor and the chief of police? What's on your mind, Chief?"

Winfield stood up and walked nervously around the room. "Look, I don't want to make mountains out of molehills, but I just don't feel right about this party Saturday. I think Sharon agrees with me." He looked to her, and she silently nodded. "You are the only one who actually knows Salvo. Is it normal for him to do this?"

Capsner thought for a moment. "Well, as far as me knowing Salvo, no one really knows him all that well. He likes it that way. But I can tell you you're right in one regard: he does not typically throw parties like this. It calls too much attention to his operations. However, I know he has pulled some pretty flamboyant stunts in the past if he thought the situation warranted it. I'm convinced he really believes this party will focus the attention of the Paradise residents more on the restoration and less on all the tragedy that has occurred. I don't think there is anything to worry about. We're so close to opening for business, I just cannot imagine he would do anything risky now."

"I guess we'll have to trust your judgment," Sharon said. "You're the professional. Just don't be wrong, okay?"

Capsner smiled in a calming way. "I'm not often wrong. That's how I got to where I am today."

"What about Joe McGowen?" the chief asked. "Did he ever turn up?"

Mueller's face turned grave. "A very unfortunate incident. No, his body was never found."

"Might he still be alive?" Sharon asked.

"Until his body is found, I suppose anything is possible," Mueller answered. "But I must tell you, odds are pretty heavy against it. I think we should assume he's dead."

"That's a shame." Sharon sighed. "He really was a good man."

"Well, we've got a few other things to worry about for now," Capsner cut in coldly. "Have I eased your fears at all, Chief?"

Winfield was still pacing. "I suppose, a little. I guess I just have a suspicious nature. But if you think there is no trouble brewing, that's good enough for me."

"Good," Capsner responded. "Then why don't we all get back to work."

The meeting only lasted about fifteen minutes. Joe watched as they all said their good-byes and left the study. He would have given anything to hear their conversation. He was sickened at the thought of two of the leading people in Paradise, people whom he had had great respect for, working together with a man like Capsner. He thought of Harry and Andy. They had been friends with those bastards. Dealing with Capsner would not be enough.

Before this was all over, he would have to settle things with Winfield and Carlson too.

The rest of the day dragged on uneventfully. Joe did not even look for an opportunity to get Capsner during the daylight. It was just too risky. Hour after hour, Joe lay in the woods and watched the mansion, trying to keep himself together. One moment, he would feel like he could not take it any longer, like he would burst if he did not get up and do something, maybe even go back down the path to the treatment center to get a better look at in the daylight, but then he would settle down and reason would again take control. Going to the treatment center was not a sensible thing to do at all. In fact, moving anywhere would be taking a completely unnecessary risk. Surprisingly, and luckily, the lack of food for a day scarcely bothered him at all. With all that was on his mind, he did not have much of an appetite, anyway. One thing he found to be a great relief was the apparent lack of security. He had not seen or heard a single person who resembled a guard or sentry. The attendees at the brief morning meeting and a handful of construction workers were all he saw the entire day. But he was still very cautious. Maybe they patrolled more at night, or maybe they concentrated down by the treatment center. Maybe he had moved far enough into the woods so he was not able to see them, or possibly, they were just good enough so they stayed out of sight. That was what Joe feared the most, and that is what he assumed to be true.

Finally, as the sky turned the distinctive reddish-blue of twilight, the anticipation began mounting within Joe, slowly at first but then more rapidly as the eastern sky transitioned into darker shades of gray. He did not know what was in store for him this night, but he resigned himself to one firm notion: he would do what he must to end it here. He did not lose sight of the need for caution and patience, but neither could he afford to lie here forever; it was not practical for himself or his family. Who knew what kind of situation they were in? An extra day could be crucial for them, possibly even fatal.

The idea that, one way or the other, all this would be resolved tonight brought a sense of peace to Joe. He was amazed at his almost total lack of fear for what was developing. *Fear is a strange thing*, he thought to himself. It was not long ago when the idea of lying in the woods, armed with a pistol, preparing to attack a bloodthirsty madman would have been terrifying beyond comprehension. But here he was, welcoming the opportunity. He had been pushed too far; the bad men had taken too much. Fear, he surmised, is greatest when it involves only yourself. But with the safety of his wife and children at stake, with the death of his good friends still fresh in his mind, with the physical and emotional ordeals he had experienced the past few days, the consequences to himself seemed irrelevant. He imagined this was probably not too different from what soldiers feel in battle. He read once that heroes on a battlefield are not so much courageous as they just stopped caring. Maybe he had finally reached the point of not caring himself.

As the sun continued to set and the last glow of red faded from the western horizon, Joe wondered if Harry or Andy ever felt as he did now. Probably not, since it had all been so new to them. They most likely felt the horror, which could not be avoided by any decent person. Joe was thankful for the callousness he was now experiencing, for he realized it gave him a tremendous advantage his friends had not enjoyed. It allowed him to act offensively rather than be caught off guard by men who would kill without a second thought.

The light in Capsner's study flicked on, sending a jolt of tension through Joe's body. He did not want to lose sight of the need for caution, but he knew there would never be an ideal opportunity. Tonight he would be more aggressive and take some chances. Tonight he would become the hunter.

The backyard of the mansion was growing dark, but there was ample light to easily find his way across the opening. Joe had not actually formulated a plan, but it occurred to him he might have a better chance at surprising Capsner while he was inside working rather than waiting for him to come out. That way, Joe could choose his own time, and there did not seem to be a good reason to wait any longer than now. Feeling the adrenaline rushing through his body, he quickly slipped around the side of the mansion, constantly on the lookout for a guard. Carefully he peered around the front corner, seeing the porch and the large doorway standing vacant and beckoning. He braced himself for the attack, wanting to get in and get Capsner under control before he had time to react.

Suddenly the door popped open, sending a terrifying jolt through Joe's body like a lightning bolt. He instinctively fell back into the shadows by the side of the mansion, his body trembling from the unexpected shock of the opening door.

Damn! he thought to himself. He just could not seem to get a break. He forced himself to shake off the effects of the shock and again peered around the corner. Capsner stood in front of the door, apparently locking it. After a brief moment, he turned and took a few steps toward his car.

"Capsner," a voice boomed.

Joe stared to the far side of the house near the top of the stairway heading down to the river. Out of the shadows, a large black man emerged. In the fading light, Joe was not able to visually recognize the man, but his voice was clearly identifiable.

"What do you need, Rodriguez?" Capsner asked.

"One of my men found something interesting down by the river. I think we should go inside and talk about it."

"I'm on my way out. Just tell me what you found."

"Very well," Rodriguez said in his deep Jamaican accent. "It is a boat, a small boat I believe you call a canoe. It was found lying in the brush along the riverbank."

The canoe! Joe's mind began racing. He should have taken care to hide it better. It had been so dark, and at the time, he did not expect to be here for two days.

"So you found a canoe. Big deal. Kids go up and down this river in canoes all the time. Someone probably just left it there for a while."

"I don't think so," Rodriguez replied, stepping up on the porch by Capsner. He almost seemed amused that he had potentially bad information. "This is a very special canoe. It is the one from the Salinger place. Remember it was missing when we found Carlos and Juan's bodies?"

Capsner was silent for a moment, trying to understand all the possible implications. "Are you sure it is the same boat?" he finally asked.

"Positive," Rodriguez replied. "You know what that means, don't you? Whoever attacked my friends is somewhere around here, and there can be no doubt as to his purpose."

"Who the hell is this guy?" Capsner asked. "Who would know enough to be here spying? You guys aren't having trouble with any of the other gangs, are you?"

"Not here. This is not another gang. Someone has apparently taken it upon himself to take action against us."

Capsner suddenly appeared noticeably uneasy. He looked one direction then the other. "Whoever it is, he must be watching either the mansion or the treatment center."

"That's right, man. He may be watching us at this very minute. Perhaps he even has a rifle trained at your head as we speak." Rodriguez smiled his broad, arrogant smile.

"I think you should increase your guards, at least for the next few days."

"I have already doubled them," Rodriguez said. "They are also going to comb through the woods as best they can. We will find whoever is there. I just hope we find him before he does whatever he came to do."

Damn! Joe thought. *Damn, damn, damn!* Nothing was working out. He did not expect miracles, but he also did not expect things to continually work against him.

"I want you to find this mystery person," Capsner demanded, "and before Saturday. We do not need some crazy out in the woods, probably armed, when we have our party. Especially not this close to our opening. Salvo will be here in a week. Nothing can go wrong. I want to be informed as soon as you know something. Is that clear?"

Rodriguez smiled his unfriendly, contemptible smile. "Whatever you want, man. Whatever you want." He turned and headed back to the long flight of steps heading down to the river as Capsner walked toward his car.

This was it. There would not be a better chance. Joe pulled his .45 from his belt and sprinted up behind Capsner, reaching him just as he opened his car door. Joe jammed the barrel of the pistol firmly into Capsner's back, firmly enough so he would not consider resisting.

"Into the car, Capsner," Joe whispered. He kept his voice low, but there was no mistaking the seriousness in his voice. "Don't say anything. Just get behind the wheel and pull out of here nice and easy. I'll be in the backseat right behind you. If you do anything to try and warn somebody, anything unusual at all, I swear to God I'll blow your fucking head off. Now move!"

Capsner was stunned, but he very coolly obeyed. He was very experienced at this business, and he knew the voice in his ear was full of fear and panic. The best thing to do now was exactly what he was told. There would be time later to deal with this person, whoever he was. The voice sounded familiar, but he could not quite place it. He slid in behind the wheel and heard the car door behind him open and close. He started the engine and slowly eased away down the driveway. He took a darting look in the rearview mirror then let out a loud gasp. Even his cool professionalism would not let him conceal his utter shock.

The Seduction of Paradise

"McGowen!" he cried. "What in hell are you doing here?"

"I figured you would be surprised. I'll bet you thought I was dead."

"As a matter of fact, that's exactly what I thought. Put that gun down before your shaky finger has an accident that my head won't appreciate."

"Don't tell me what to do, you bastard," Joe barked. "If this gun goes off, it won't be by accident. Just get us out of here."

The car slowly followed the curved drive toward the highway. Joe saw no sign of guards anywhere, and as they approached the large stone pillars that stood alongside the entryway, he began to relax. Maybe things would work his way for once.

Suddenly, two men supporting rifles appeared directly in front of them, jumping out from behind the pillars. The car jolted to a stop, with Capsner as well as Joe being taken by surprise. Immediately, the back door flew open as a third man thrust the barrel of a pistol to within inches of Joe's head.

"It would not be smart to move," the man stated. "Put your gun down, now."

Joe was nearly at the point of collapse, frustration and disappointment culminating in a sense of deep fatigue. For a brief moment, he considered putting a bullet into Capsner's head, even though it would surely result in his own execution. He just could not bear to think of Capsner getting away without paying. His palm began to sweat as he felt the gun in his hand. As his anger grew, the urge to punish Capsner grew with it. It would be so easy. But even in his current state of mind, reason won out, and he grudgingly laid the pistol on the seat beside him.

For the next twenty minutes, it seemed like Joe was in the middle of an army camp. There were men with guns everywhere, running this way and that, mainly taking orders from the man Rodriguez.

"Are you alone?" he was repeatedly asked.

"Yes, of course."

"I don't believe you!" screamed his interrogator, the man who had held the gun to his head. *Smack!* He gave a sudden and vicious slap across Joe's face. "I'll ask again: are you alone?"

"What do you want me to say?" Joe finally bellowed out. "I keep telling you, I am alone!"

He was led hurriedly behind the mansion and back down the winding path to the treatment center. Once there, he was brought into a large empty damp-smelling room with cement block walls. A chair was brought in, and Joe was forced into it. His hands were tied behind him, and his feet were tied to the legs of the chair.

The interrogator stood in front of him with an armed guard on either side. Capsner had disappeared somewhere. Things were happening so fast it was hard to keep track, but Joe did not remember Capsner coming down the path with them. The interrogator was about to speak when a loud screeching noise echoed through the empty building as a door behind Joe was opened. Rodriguez walked through with two more armed guards.

"Did you kill our friends up the river?" he demanded.

"No," was all Joe replied.

"How did you get our canoe?"

"I believe it belongs to a friend of mine," Joe said. "I just borrowed it."

"Why were you hiding in the woods? Why did you try to kidnap Mr. Capsner?"

Joe's anger got the better of him. "Because he's a worthless, dirty son of a bitch!" he screamed.

Smack! Another blow to the face.

The interrogation continued for sometime, with Joe receiving several more blows to the head. He could feel blood oozing out his nose, but he did not feel he had been seriously hurt, at least not yet. Finally Rodriguez had enough.

The Seduction of Paradise

"I am finished with him for tonight," he said to the guards. "Untie him from the chair, but I want a guard on him at all times. Is that clear?"

The two men nodded, and Rodriguez departed the treatment center, leaving Joe to wonder what might be in store for him. One of the guards cut the rope from his wrists and ankles, and Joe fell to the cold, damp concrete floor, which actually felt comfortable to him. Almost immediately he closed his eyes, and suddenly, the world around him went completely dark.

He was not sure if he had fallen asleep or if he had passed out from the pain, but the next time Joe opened his eyes, he was looking at a new set of guards. How long had he been out, he wondered? He was sore from the beating, and his muscles still ached from being tied in the chair. What were they going to do with him? Why were they waiting?

Again he closed his eyes, and again, he went out for an unknown period of time. Periodically he would awaken, but his head ached so intensely from his beatings that he would just lie on the floor, knowing that sooner or later Capsner or Rodriguez would come for him. Once or twice, he got up and tried to walk, and he became aware of the effects of not having eaten for over two days. His energy was almost completely drained, and he became dizzy easily.

I must save my strength, he told himself. *I must be prepared to make some kind of break.*

Time seemed to stretch on for an eternity. Inside his prison, he had no sense of night or day, and he was beginning to have difficulty distinguishing hours from minutes. Again a guard change had taken place while he slept. Or had it? Yes, these were different—at least he was pretty sure they were. What were they waiting for? The emotional stress was becoming more overpowering than the physical pain and weakness.

Finally the door screeched open, and Rodriguez entered, with two more guards at his side. Joe could tell from the faint light in the doorway it must be twilight. But which day?

"Tie the prisoner," Rodriguez commanded.

The guards immediately obeyed, again sitting Joe in the chair and tying his hands and feet.

"I believe you were telling us the truth." Rodriguez sneered. "It has been two days, and no one has come for you, and we have found no one else on the grounds."

Two days! Joe thought. It must be Saturday, the day of the planned tragedy at the mansion. Now he would probably not be able to stop it.

"Since you are alone, I suppose there is no point in keeping you around." Rodriguez's face looked evil, like the devil himself.

Just then Capsner appeared through the door. He was dressed in a black suit, apparently ready for the party. "What is happening here?" he asked.

"I am questioning the prisoner," Rodriguez snarled.

"We are not going to go through this again, Rodriguez," Capsner snapped back. "I will take care of this man. I would like to talk to him alone for a while. I believe he will be more cooperative with me."

"No, man, I am not finished."

Capsner flashed a look of loathing at the bigger, younger black man. "Out of here, Rodriguez. Now."

Rodriguez hesitated for a moment then finally motioned for the two guards accompanying him to follow him out. "They stay," he said defiantly before he left, gesturing to the other two guards who had been standing behind Joe.

"Fine," Capsner said, "if it makes you feel better."

After Rodriguez and his two bodyguards departed, Capsner closed the door then calmly walked around to the front of Joe.

"Trying to capture me was a bold move, Joe. A few minutes sooner, and you might have pulled it off. Unfortunately for you,

The Seduction of Paradise

my friend Rodriguez had all his men on alert. One of them saw you pulling a gun on me."

Joe sat silent, his seething anger showing in his eyes.

"You are an amazing man, McGowen," Capsner continued. "Tell me, what exactly were you going to do with me?"

"Kill you, you son of a bitch."

Capsner smiled. "I certainly believe you would like to, but somehow, I don't think that was your plan."

"Where's my family?" Joe demanded. "What have you done with them?"

For the first time, Capsner appeared a bit uneasy. He glanced at the two guards, then back at Joe. "I don't know what you're talking about," he said.

"Bullshit!" Joe shouted. "You've got my wife and kids. I know it, and you know it. They better be okay, Capsner, or God help me, I'll kill you."

The guards began shuffling around behind Joe. He could not see them, but he could tell by their abrupt movement they were getting restless, or perhaps nervous.

"It won't do you any good to threaten me, McGowen. It appears the odds are somewhat in my favor. Just settle down, and we can talk like gentlemen. We need to know if anyone was with you, and I really do not want to have to hurt you to find out."

"I told you all I can. If you're so damn smart, do you think I would have jumped you alone and took off in your car, leaving a friend behind?"

"You know, I think I actually believe you. Besides, I think for once Rodriguez is right. If someone was with you, he would have shown himself by now."

"Tell me something, Capsner. What is it that you're really doing here? I know you guys are bringing in drugs and selling them out of this place, and I know you expect plenty of business, but Paradise? I just can't believe it would be worth everything you have gone through."

Capsner smiled, again acting almost friendly. "Well, I certainly cannot give you all the details, but I will tell you this much: if we can establish a base of operation anywhere around the Twin Cities metro area, it is staggering just how much it would be worth. Why Paradise? How many places do you know that provide so much privacy yet are so close to the Twin Cities and have access to a main highway and two different rivers? There could not possibly be a better location."

"It must be staggering to get all you feds to sell out," Joe said with obvious disgust.

Again Capsner shot a darting glance to the guards, and again, Joe heard them shuffling nervously behind him.

"You're a man with a great imagination," Capsner said. "Again, I have no idea what you are referring to."

"Capsner, give me a break. Do you think I really don't know? You and your FBI buddies are in this up to your eyeballs."

"I wouldn't know an FBI agent from a circus clown," Capsner said quickly. "I think our conversation is over. Now I must decide what to do with you. I could let my friend Rodriguez handle you. He seems to have a low tolerance for intruders."

"Is he the one who handled Andy?" Joe asked.

Capsner's expression went blank for a brief moment. "Actually, yes," he said. "That was very unfortunate."

"Unfortunate!" Joe barked, his anger rising again. "Unfortunate! Is that what you call it? Do whatever you want with me, Capsner. You'll get yours tonight."

Capsner paused for a moment, showing almost no emotion in response to Joe's lashing out. "What do you mean by that?" he asked.

Joe thought about whether he should reveal what he knew. Part of him wanted to see Capsner and his cohorts burn, but he had to remember many innocent lives were also at stake.

"For the record," Joe began, "I would just as soon see you fry. But there are other people I am concerned about. It appears your friend Salvo isn't such a good friend after all. I believe he has a surprise for you at your party tonight."

"How did you know about the party?"

Joe laughed and shook his head. "Is that really important? What is important is that if you're not careful, you and a house full of people, most of whom are my friends, will be toast in a few hours."

For the first time, Capsner showed signs of genuine concern, even hinting at panic. He glanced at the guards behind Joe then turned and began pacing the floor. Joe could hear the guards moving; it sounded like they were coming forward. Suddenly Capsner turned to Joe and produced a nine-millimeter pistol from under his coat.

"I don't believe you," he blurted out quickly. "Rodriguez is right. You should be eliminated."

He fired twice, then twice more. Joe flinched at the terrifying noise of the discharge of bullets within the concrete bunker, but like on the beach in Florida, he felt nothing. He was in such a state of shock he was barely aware of the sound of slumping bodies behind him. Capsner was on him in an instant, cutting the ropes binding his hands and feet with a knife he pulled from under his pants leg.

Joe was stunned, completely taken by surprise. What was happening? He had wanted to frighten Capsner, but he never imagined a reaction like this. A quick look over his shoulder confirmed both of the guards were dead.

"What is going on tonight, McGowen?" Capsner demanded. "I must know."

Joe had his own priority of questions to be answered. "What about my family?" he demanded in return.

"Damn it, tell me what you know. You have no idea how important this is."

Capsner was suddenly a different man. His face showed real emotion, and there was no doubt that it reflected true fear.

"I knew I couldn't trust that bastard Salvo," he cried out as he cut the last knot. "There is very little time—"

The door crashed open, and two more men burst in, rifles held ready at their sides. Capsner flung Joe to the side and opened fire on the men, who immediately returned it. For a few horrifying seconds, the treatment center was filled with the deafening roar of gunfire, bullets ricocheting off every wall. Joe lay in the corner where he had landed, huddled up like an embryo. At any moment, he expected to be struck by a stray bullet, but when the noise died down, he was unharmed.

Slowly he lifted his head and surveyed the aftermath. No one was moving. He jumped to his feet and ran to Capsner, and found his chest had been exploded by a series of direct hits. He was dead. Ronald Capsner, the man whom Joe most hated in the world, was lying dead at his feet.

Chapter 33

The sight of Capsner's lifeless body did not bring Joe the satisfaction he had imagined it would. Maybe it was because the last thing Capsner had done was to save his life. Why had he done that? Possibly it was simply a reflex action on Capsner's part, casting Joe aside to get a cleaner shot. But whatever the reason, he was now dead and Joe was alive, and however much Capsner may have deserved it, it seemed like there should have been a better way to bring him to justice than a crazy gunfight like this.

Joe quickly checked the other two men, but he already knew they were dead too. In just a few seconds, five men had been killed right before his eyes. This was madness, total and complete madness. He realized he had not become quite so callous as he previously thought. This violence—this useless, meaningless killing—sickened him in a way he could never have imagined.

What should he do now? Apparently there were no other guards nearby, or they would be here by now. They were probably up at the mansion preparing for the bonfire planned for later this evening. Nevertheless, this was not the place for him to be. He snatched up one of the dead men's AR15 rifles and pulled three clips of ammunition from his belt then bolted out into the cool evening air. From the color of the sky, Joe guessed it to be between seven and eight o'clock in the evening.

He needed a plan, some kind of idea on how to stop this tragedy in the making, but at the same time something having a reasonable chance of success. Charging the mansion with rifles blazing might be heroic, but it would only result in another casualty added to the list. Earlier, when he was on the island in the river, he had decided he could not trust anybody. Now he realized he no longer had an alternative. He had to have an ally, someone who could get help or at least warn the others. He finally decided he would try to see who was at the party and select as best as possible who he thought he could trust, then find some way to communicate with that person. He knew there would be guards everywhere, and sooner or later, someone would find out he had escaped, so they would be looking for him. Time was clearly not on his side.

Cautiously but quickly, he made his way up the path, now becoming all too familiar to him. The September air reflected the early arrival of autumn even more so than the past couple of weeks. The breeze making the tall trees sway was cool and refreshing, helping to rejuvenate Joe. There was even a hint of the aroma of changing leaves in the air. The moon was full but still low in the sky. Joe was thankful for that since he knew it would provide some light after the sun was fully set. It was nights like these that Joe used to love to take walks with Sheri, holding hands and snuggling close in the cool air. It was hard to believe he was now moving through the woods of his hometown armed and ready to kill. This was such an ugly, twisted turn of events.

Joe reached the end of the path at the edge of the backyard of the mansion and surveyed the grounds for any signs of the Jamaican guards. None were in sight, but he remembered just two nights ago when he tried to apprehend Capsner and he had not seen any guards even though he had been surrounded by them. He would not make that same mistake again. He lay along the tree line, wanting to be patient but knowing time was not a luxury item.

The Seduction of Paradise

It was now almost completely dark, but Joe still did not dare cross the clearing to the mansion. Looking off to his right, in the direction of the river, he saw that the tree line curved along the top of the bluff and came up flush with the far side of the house. He remembered several months ago on that Saturday morning when he first walked through the grounds to see how much of the restoration work had been completed. He remembered standing at the top of the bluff on the front side of the mansion, wanting to go around to the back, but the bluff and the woods came so close to the side of the house that he could not pass and was forced to go around the other side to get to the back. Now he realized this could be a tremendous benefit to him. It would be possible for him to get all the way to the side of the house under the cover of the woods, and from there, he should be able to move along the back of the mansion under the shadows of the shrubbery and of the structure itself.

Slowly, ever so cautiously, he made his way through the trees and brush, watching each and every step so as not to break a twig or crunch any leaves. He continually fought the urge to rush, realizing that at any moment the tragedy could begin. Each time he felt the desire to quicken his pace, he paused and concentrated on maintaining control. If he was detected, all would be for naught.

Finally, after an excruciating ten minutes that felt like two hours, he arrived at the corner of the mansion. The only light visible from the back of the house was in the window closest to him, which, from his earlier visit some months ago, he knew to be the kitchen. Crouching low and clutching the rifle in both hands, he took a quick darting step out from the trees and ducked behind an evergreen shrub just below the window. The full moon that had provided valuable light to aid Joe on his trek through the woods now created a potential threat to his mission. However, with the shrubbery and the shadows from the building, there was about a three-foot band of darkness along the back wall of the mansion that hopefully provided sufficient cover. More than being seen,

Joe was concerned about being heard. He was thankful for the breeze that was steadily growing in intensity, drowning out any sounds he made as he moved along.

Joe paused for a moment under the window, listening for the telltale sounds of a sentry. He realized suddenly that the wind, like the full moon, was like a double-edged sword: in the same way that it offered him protection from being heard, it presented a threat in that he was unable to hear a potential enemy. Feeling as secure as he could reasonably expect, he laid the rifle on the ground and stood up to peer into the window.

The shade was open about halfway, giving Joe a clear view of the entire room. The scene was typical of what one would expect on the night of a party: a man in a white gown was moving hurriedly from oven to stove to refrigerator, preparing several trays of hors d'oeuvres. No one else was in the room with him. This would be a golden opportunity for Joe to try and contact this person and inform him of what was in store for this evening, but the man was not from Paradise and would certainly not recognize Joe. He could be part of Rodriguez's plan, in which case confiding in him would be suicide. More probably he was an innocent caterer, hired to do this party. But even then, if he saw an armed stranger tapping on a back window, what would be the likelihood he would believe anything Joe had to say? No, it would be better to wait for an opportunity to contact someone he knew.

Just then a stream of light flashed out from the other end of the mansion, from the window of the study. Joe picked up the rifle and took a quick look around. Then, crouching low and close to the house, he moved in the direction of the new stream of light.

Special Agent Mueller shifted himself around, trying to get comfortable high in a large oak tree overhanging the bluff behind the mansion. The branch he was resting on was large and plenty firm to hold his weight, but after several hours, his muscles were beginning to cramp up. He checked his watch and saw it was eight thirty in the evening. He reached for the small electronic box strapped to his belt and pressed the button once, then paused, then pressed it once again. A second later, the small red light on the box blinked twice with a pause, then once more. Another second later, it blinked three times, paused, then one more time.

It was the silent code he and his two accomplices had agreed upon. Mueller was Code One, identified by one blink. The other two, Code Two and Code Three, used two and three blinks, respectively. After identifying themselves by the appropriate number of blinks, a single blink indicated all was well. A double blink indicated something was occurring. A rapid succession of blinking let the others know serious danger was eminent. Even if nothing was worth reporting, they would give a single blink every fifteen minutes just to acknowledge they were not in trouble. Code Two, the agent who aided Mueller in watching Joe's house, was positioned in a tree in front of the mansion, with Code Three on the ground in woods that bordered the backyard. He was not a trained agent, and Mueller did not feel comfortable having him along. After debating fruitlessly for an hour, he had finally consented but placed him where he could do the least damage.

So far, there was no sign of trouble, but Mueller was still concerned. He had not spoken with Capsner since their meeting a couple of mornings ago. Then tonight, just when the party was getting ready to start, he saw Capsner head down the path toward the treatment center, and so far, he had not returned. Something was going on, but for now, it was best to sit and watch. For a moment, he considered contacting Code Three by the portable phone that they all carried and have him investigate, but he quickly put the thought aside. If there was trouble down there, he did not want an amateur messing things up more. Besides, the phones were only to be used for emergencies; maintaining silence was crucial. In fact, the purpose of having phones at all was that if communication was needed, they provided the quietest method.

When the sun had set enough for the darkness to obscure his vision, Mueller had strapped on his headset equipped with the infrared night vision. Now, at eight thirty in the evening, the gusting wind was making it difficult to concentrate on his surveillance since even the strong oak, which served as his post, was swaying heavily. He was becoming restless and even more concerned about Capsner. He also found it curious that he had not spotted any Jamaican guards. Most likely they were gathered at the treatment center or at the boathouse, more or less on call in case they were needed.

Suddenly, movement by the corner of the mansion caught Mueller's eye. A figure darted out from the trees and hid behind a shrub. It appeared the figure was armed, but by his actions, Mueller was convinced he was not a sentry. Quickly he flipped down his telephoto attachment and focused on the shrub. After a moment, the figure rose up and reached for the window. Even with his years of undercover experience, Mueller froze in total astonishment as he recognized the figure as Joseph McGowen.

"What in the hell is he doing here!" he muttered to himself. Immediately, he signaled to Code Two and Code Three by blinking once, then twice more. "My God, he's going to get us all killed."

Mueller watched as Joe dropped from the window and headed off in the direction of the study. *I can't wait*, he thought to himself. Quickly he pulled the small phone from the long pocket on the thigh of his trousers and punched 3.

"Three," Code Three answered.

"Do you see him?" Mueller asked.

"I don't see anyone," Code Three answered. "But if he's up by the mansion, I wouldn't be able to. From here, anything past the grassy clearing looks like a giant black hole."

"Listen," Mueller said firmly, trying to keep his voice low. "I don't want you getting all excited, but guess who I just spotted spying on the mansion? It's the missing McGowen."

"What! He's alive? How did he get here? What's he—"

"Stow it! This could be catastrophic. I don't want you getting crazy, but you have to get to him before he does something really stupid. I don't see any Jamaicans around, so get going."

Mueller watched as Code Three emerged from the woods and sprinted across the clearing in the direction of the study window, staying clear of the beam of light that poured out across the yard. Code Three reached the mansion just as Joe McGowen was reaching for the sill of the window. Mueller had a clear view as Code Three pounced on Joe and pulled him to the ground behind the shrubs.

Joe felt a powerful forearm clamp around his throat and drag him to the ground. A heavy body lay on top of him, trying to hold him motionless, and he suddenly became aware of an excited voice whispering repeatedly in his ear, "Relax, Joe. Just relax. Come on, Joe, relax."

The voice sounded familiar, but Joe was sure his mind was playing tricks on him. This could not be possible. Feeling the hold on his throat ease off, he rolled over under the weight of the body and stared at the face of his assailant. He nearly fainted from the shock of what he saw.

"Ryan! My God, Ryan! What in heavens name are you doing here?"

Chapter 34

"There isn't time to explain," Ryan whispered hurriedly. "We need to get out of here. We're in serious danger."

"No shit," Joe retorted. "And I don't think you realize just how much danger. Where have you been? How did you get here? Ryan, do you know where Sheri and my kids are?"

"Not now, Joe, we've got to get back to the woods. There is much to talk about, but it will have to wait."

"Listen, Ryan, something terrible is going to happen here tonight. Everyone at this party is going to be killed." Joe's expression had taken on a new intensity, and his voice carried a tone of firmness that caused Ryan to pause and listen even though he was in a state of near panic.

"Joe," Ryan finally whispered, "that's not true. A lot of things are happening that you don't know about. I don't know why you think there will be trouble, but this is just a routine party, a celebration for the town. Capsner and Mueller have everything under control."

"You know Capsner?" Joe blurted out.

"I know what you're thinking, Joe, but you've got it all wrong. Please, let's get back to the woods. You don't understand the danger. Guards could be anywhere."

"I understand the danger!" Joe almost shouted. "I have been living with the danger for days now. And I've got news for you about your buddy Capsner: right now he's lying dead down at the treatment center. So tell me again just how well he has everything under control."

"What! Capsner's dead! I can't believe it. I've got to tell Mueller immediately."

"Who is this Mueller, anyway?" Joe questioned.

The excitement of seeing each other and the confusion from the differing information each had made the brothers completely unaware of the Jamaican guard who emerged from around the corner. The guard raised his rifle to his shoulder and aimed in the direction of the McGowens just a few yards away, then suddenly let out a cry of pain and alarm as his chest erupted into a series of blood spurts. Joe and Ryan simultaneously lurched with shocked alarm and stared as the lifeless body before them fell face-first into a small shrub. Finally, after several moments, Ryan whispered, "Mueller is the man who just saved our lives."

Just then an almost inaudible beeping could be heard, and Ryan pulled a small portable phone from his belt and lifted it to his head.

"Three," he answered.

"What are you two doing down there, having a family reunion? Get back to the woods, and I mean now!"

"Mueller, Joe said Capsner is dead. He said there is going to be an attack on the party tonight. I think we've got real trouble."

"Put him on," Mueller commanded.

"Who are you?" Joe demanded into the phone. "Are you part of Capsner's gang? And don't think I don't know what he's up to."

"I know you don't know me, McGowen, but there isn't time for any of this bullshit. You're just going to have to trust me. Why do you think Capsner's dead?"

Joe had no idea who this man was or what he should be telling him. But something very strange was happening, and this was not the time to try and sort it all out. Ryan seemed to know and trust Mueller, and Joe's gut instincts told him he should trust him too. Besides, Mueller obviously was capable of blowing them away at any time if he wanted to.

"I saw him get shot, that's how I know," Joe said. "And a few Jamaicans went with him. The important thing, if you care anything at all, is to stop the murder of all those people in the mansion tonight."

"That can't be possible. Who is behind it?"

"If you know anything, you'll know there is a guy named Salvo who's setting up this whole operation. I guess he decided to terminate it prematurely."

"How do you know that?"

"It's a long story. I guess you're just going to have to trust me too."

Mueller paused for a moment. *He knows too much for him to be faking*, he thought. *And it's not like he didn't have concerns about this very thing himself. Hell, why else would he even be here tonight except to watch out for some kind of trouble?* But Mueller never expected anything of this magnitude.

"I'm going to have to call in more agents," he said. "But it's going to take some time, possibly half an hour or more. Get yourselves back to the woods. I can see the whole backyard, and it's all clear now."

"Sorry," Joe said. "Whatever is going to happen could begin at any moment. I won't wait a half hour. I'm going to try and warn somebody in there. These people may not mean much to you, Mueller, but they are my friends."

"I have a contact inside," Mueller said. "I can warn him."

"That's great, but it's not enough. Something may be going down as we speak. They may need my help."

"Fine," Mueller sighed. "Do what you want. But you're on your own until those agents show up." Then, after a short pause, "I'll keep you covered as best I can from here."

"Thanks," Joe said. "And thanks for him too." He pointed to the dead man in the shrubbery.

Joe gave the phone back to Ryan. "I need to go in and try to warn somebody of the danger," he said. "Why don't you go back to the woods? No sense in both of us getting killed."

"Did Mueller tell you there is someone inside we can call? We don't need to go in."

"Ya, he mentioned it. But there's more to it than that. Chances are something is going to happen very soon. People inside are going to need help. I want to be there when that time comes. We'll meet up after this is all over, okay?"

Ryan's lips showed a slight sign of a smile. "I can't let you get all the glory yourself," he said. "Then you'd get all the babes."

Joe laughed and slapped Ryan on the shoulder. "Let's do it," he said.

Although not completely conscious of the transition he had just undergone, Joe suddenly felt like a man with a purpose. Suddenly he believed he had a reasonable chance for success. For the first time in days, or even weeks, he actually felt good, felt hopeful.

"First," he said, "let's find out who is in the study. It might be someone who can help us."

As on previous occasions, the telltale gap in the drawn drapes provided at least a partial view of the room. Again, all Joe could see was the corner of the large desk and a portion of the bookcase on the far wall. A hand appeared quickly, then just as quickly, it disappeared. There was someone, a man, sitting at the desk. Joe stretched his head to try and get a better view, but the crack between the curtain halves was too thin for him to see much more. Suddenly, the man walked past the crack so quickly he was almost a blur. In the fraction of a second that he was in view, Joe recognized him as Sherman Salinger.

"Perfect," Joe muttered. "It's Sherman. He can help us."

Just then the lights from the study went out. *No*, thought Joe. Quickly and firmly, he began rapping on the window. *Hear me, Sherman*, he pleaded to himself. *Hear me.*

Seconds later, the light returned, then suddenly, the curtains flew back and Sherman Salinger appeared at the window. His eyes found Joe, and his expression transitioned from surprise first to alarm and then to fear. Finally, he opened the window and bent down to Joe.

"What are you doing here?' he asked. "Why are you out there like some criminal?"

"Sherman, let me in. My brother, Ryan, is here with me. You're in danger, everyone's in danger. Let me in, please."

"Yes, yes, of course, please come in. But you must tell me what this is all about."

Joe crawled through the window, then he and Sherman helped pull his brother through.

"Sherman, there's so little time. I don't understand it all myself, but there is going to be an attack on the party tonight. Everyone is going to be killed. Help is on the way, but it will take thirty minutes or so. We need someone—we need you—to help warn the others. We need to prevent anything from happening for at least thirty minutes."

"Joe, I'm overwhelmed. I have no idea what you're talking about."

"We'll explain everything later," Ryan cut in, "but believe us, there may be very little time."

"What is it you want me to do?" Salinger asked, becoming visibly nervous.

"Go into the party and scope things out," Joe said. "See who's there. Are there any strangers? Are there any signs of danger? Then get back to us and let us know if we need to take any action."

"Joe, my goodness, I hardly feel qualified for this. But you both look so, so serious. Yes, yes, of course, I'll do it."

"Thanks, Sherm." Joe smiled and gently grasped his arm. With the appearance of nervous bewilderment, Sherman Salinger left the room.

The Seduction of Paradise

By 8:50 p.m., most of the guests had arrived. The host of the party, Ronald Capsner, had left word that he may be a few minutes late, but everyone should feel free to wander around and observe the results of the restoration. He did ask that no one go upstairs or to the study, but the rest of the mansion was open to them. After all, it was their mansion. Drinks and hors d'oeuvres were provided in the large ballroom, and most of the guests were content to mill around and visit with each other there.

Chief Byron Winfield was standing by the front window with Leonard Malekowski, commenting on how wonderful everything looked and how great it will be to have this place opened up to the general public, when he heard the light beeping of his portable phone.

"You'll have to excuse me, Leonard," Winfield said apologetically as he pulled the phone from inside his coat pocket. "A police chief is never fully off duty."

"No problem," Malekowski responded. "Boy, they sure make those things small nowadays." He walked off and joined another group nearby.

"Winfield," the chief said into the phone.

"Trouble's brewing," Mueller said crisply. "We found Joe McGowen spying on the mansion."

"Joe's alive! And he's here? That's great!"

"Ya, that's great, but nothing else is so great. Everything is happening so fast that nobody understands the full story, but if McGowen is telling the truth, Capsner was murdered tonight down at the treatment center, and Salvo, for some reason, has decided to terminate the whole project. In his typical 'no loose ends' way, he is planning on killing everyone at the party. That's obviously the only reason he had the party, just to get everyone together that he felt needed to be taken out."

"Have you called in any support?" Winfield questioned.

"As much as I could get. Local agents should be here in about twenty-five minutes, but there isn't enough to handle Rodriguez and his whole gang. More support is coming from outside, but they won't be here for a couple of hours. Maybe that will be long enough, but who knows, things could erupt at any moment."

"Sharon Carlson will be a few minutes late," Winfield said. "That may buy us some time. I'm sure they won't start anything until everyone they invited is here. And I may be able to get some help for your agents. After our meeting the other day, I had an uneasy feeling about this party too, so I had a number of men standing by."

"Great. Also, you should be aware that at this very moment, the McGowen brothers are hiding out in the study. I think they're damn fools for going in there, but I couldn't stop them. Joe is determined to get involved if trouble starts. After what he's been through, I guess I don't blame him. I think it would be a good idea for you to contact them. Let them know you're up to speed on what's happening. They apparently have already made one contact because someone let them in through the study window."

"The study!" Winfield exclaimed. "The only person here who is allowed in the study is Salinger!"

"Shit!" Mueller barked. "I should have warned them. Get in there, Winfield. Now!"

"Do you think he'll be okay?" Ryan asked, referring to Sherman Salinger.

"As okay as any of the rest of us," Joe responded. They each stood silent for a few moments, trying to take in all the recent events. "Ryan, it's great to see you. I've lost touch with so much that's happening I don't know where I am half the time. What happened after I called you about Sheri and the kids coming out? Have you seen them, or do you know where they are?"

"Joe, listen—" Ryan began. He was cut off by Chief Winfield bursting through the study door, pistol in hand. Joe immediately swung his rifle in Winfield's direction.

"No!" Ryan cried, and threw his body into Joe, both of them crashing into the bookcase. "Joe, Byron's on our side. Damn, I should have told you, I should have tried to contact him myself. I guess I'm not very good at this game."

"Are you boys all right?" Winfield barked firmly. "Mueller told me you met someone here. I was afraid it may have been Salinger."

"And so it was," came a familiar voice from behind Winfield.

All eyes turned to see Sherman Salinger enter the room, followed by Rodriguez and four other armed men. Sherman appeared to be an entirely different man as he strutted into the room with a swaggering, confident stride. No longer did he appear nervous or confused. His eyes now reflected firm conviction, appearing almost vicious as he sat down behind the desk and arrogantly combed his white hair.

"I think this calls for a drink," Sherman said smugly, and reached for the decanter of brandy on the desk. His large ruby ring glittered in the light of the desk lamp. "Now, Joe, why don't you tell us all about this attack you believe to be planned for this evening? It makes a very amusing story."

Words could not seem to find their way out of Joe's mouth. He could do nothing but stare in amazement at this man, this completely changed evil man. Finally he found his tongue.

"I can't believe it," he whispered helplessly. The more the realization set in, the more he felt his rage build. He remembered the meeting they had at Beth's house where they thought they were banding together as a team. He remembered Beth's house later, in shambles. Sherman must have been responsible for that. Joe felt his rage overtake his fear, and he found himself lunging at the traitor sitting before him.

"You bastard!" he screamed. "You sold us out! Your friends, your town. You rotten little bastard!"

Joe's hands firmly locked around Salinger's throat, but before he could do any serious harm, two of the Jamaicans pulled him away. Amid short, gasping coughs, Sherman managed to straighten his suit and brush back his hair with his hands.

"That's what I came to warn you guys about," Winfield said. "Salinger has been working for them all along."

"I'm sorry you're so upset," Sherman said, his smugness returning. "Now I want to hear about this attack. I am even more interested in this help you say is on the way."

For the first time, Rodriguez showed signs of emotion. "Help?" he questioned with a sense of nervous concern in his voice.

"I hope you don't honestly believe I'm going to tell you assholes anything," Joe said defiantly.

Rodriguez stepped forward and backhanded Joe across the face with his powerful arm, sending him sprawling to the floor. Ryan leaped forward to attack the big man but was immediately driven back and pinned to the wall by two of the guards.

"You will tell me what I want to know," Rodriguez said, "and you will tell me now." He held the muzzle of his Uzi to Ryan's head. "You have three seconds."

From what Joe had seen of this man before, there was absolutely no doubt he would pull the trigger. Besides, at this point, there was little to gain from holding back.

"All right, I'll tell you. I know the whole restoration project is actually a front for selling drugs. I know the project has failed, and this party tonight is really a means of eliminating everyone involved by burning the place down. And I know there are people on their way to help us, but I honestly don't know who they are."

Rodriguez lowered his Uzi, and the guards loosened their hold on Ryan. Slowly, and as inconspicuously as he could manage, Ryan lowered his hand by his side, found his control box, and pressed the signal button three times then rapidly in seven or eight more times.

The Seduction of Paradise

Rodriguez wore an expression of hateful anger, but the arrogance in Salinger's face was quickly fading away, being replaced by an expression of nervous alarm.

"Antonio," Salinger stammered, "this isn't true, is it? Why wasn't I told about this?"

While Joe staggered back to his feet, he couldn't resist a taunting chuckle. "So, Sherm buddy, you really didn't know about the murder of all your town friends. Why do you suppose that is? It kind of makes you wonder what they have planned for you, doesn't it?"

"Antonio," Salinger repeated, his nervousness rapidly transitioning to sheer terror. "What is this about? Antonio, please explain this!"

Rodriguez looked at one of the guards by the desk and nodded. Instantly the man pulled a pistol equipped with a silencer from his coat and fired two quick rounds into the brain of Sherman Salinger. The expression of surprise never left his face as he collapsed across the rich mahogany desk.

Rodriguez smiled his bright, evil smile. "I never did like that little son of a bitch," he said.

Special Agent Mueller was becoming impatient. Then suddenly, he saw the emergency signal. Something was wrong. He pulled out his phone and punched 2.

"Two," came the immediate response.

"There's trouble," Mueller said. "Capsner's been killed. Joe McGowen showed up. Ryan went to let him know we were here. Apparently, Joe found out there will be an attack on the party tonight and everyone will be wiped out. Joe and Ryan went in, and I just got the emergency signal from Ryan. I've phoned for backup, but it will be a good fifteen or twenty minutes before they arrive. We can't wait. We've got to go in."

Code Two was trying to absorb all the information, but it was staggering. *My God*, he thought. *How could all this have happened in such a short time?*

"How do you want to handle this?" Code Two asked.

"Have you seen any guards at all?" Mueller asked.

"Not a single one," Code Two replied. "In fact, I haven't seen much of anything, except guests arriving. The mayor just showed up a minute ago."

"The mayor!" Mueller echoed. "That means everyone is here. The attack could come at any time. I've only seen one guard myself, which seems strange. I'm beginning to think everyone is inside, probably hiding upstairs. That should give us some freedom to move around out here. Meet me in front of the mansion in five minutes. Let's see if we can do anything to help those poor bastards in there."

Joe, Ryan, and Chief Winfield were ushered into the ballroom. Several more armed Jamaicans joined them from upstairs; Joe estimated at least twenty altogether. When the group entered the ballroom, conversation ceased and random exclamations of surprise, alarm, and concern could be heard throughout. Sharon Carlson rushed up to Chief Winfield and clutched his shoulders.

"Byron, what's going on?" she pleaded, not really expecting an answer. Then she realized who it was standing with him. "Joe, you're alive! What a tremendous relief."

"Nice to see you again, Sharon," Joe said. "Unfortunately, this is not a very happy occasion."

"Everyone in the center of the room," Rodriguez ordered. "Quickly, gather together in the center of the room."

Slowly, and without fully understanding why, people began to obey. People whispered questions and concerns to one another, but no one openly objected. The Jamaicans surrounded the group and prodded those along who showed signs of resisting. After just a few moments, the group of Paradise residents was huddled together in the middle of the room, confused and intensely frightened. Rodriguez nodded to one of his men, who set to work on removing an outlet from the front wall by the window and began manipulating the wiring.

"It is a shame that your electricians were so careless." Rodriguez chuckled. "Especially in an old building like this that burns so quickly." He let out a deep, spine-chilling laugh.

"Who are you people?" Leonard Malekowski demanded. "What is it you want? Why are you doing this? Chief, can't you do something?"

"Just relax, Leonard," said the chief as calmly as he could make himself sound. "It won't do anybody any good to cause trouble. Just do what they say."

"I am ready," the man at the outlet said to Rodriguez.

"It will look like an accident?" Rodriguez asked. "No one must suspect sabotage."

"No one will," the man answered.

"Do it," Rodriguez ordered.

The people of Paradise began shifting around, some still not comprehending precisely what was taking place. Those who did understand did not know how to react. Doing nothing seemed fruitless, but clearly there was no way they could reasonably resist these men. The man by the outlet knelt down, presumably to initiate the fire. Joe and Ryan exchanged glances, each desperately hoping to see some ray of hope in the other's eyes, some possible solution to this hopeless predicament. What they saw was the same fear and helpless frustration each was feeling himself.

Suddenly, the front window exploded as the sound of gunfire echoed through the room. The man by the outlet was hurled several feet back from the impact of the bullets. Shrieking erupted from the group huddled in the center of the room. The Jamaican guards were thrown into shocked turmoil, some diving for cover, others returning fire randomly in the direction of the window.

"Everybody, down!" commanded Winfield. "Down on the floor, quickly!"

The people in the crowd had the presence of mind to listen to the chief and immediately fell to the floor as bullets whizzed everywhere overhead. More shots came in through the window, killing two of the Jamaicans. Rodriguez began barking out orders, but the shock of the surprise attack had him completely disoriented and confused. His orders were illogical and contradictory, serving only to increase his men's confusion rather than lessen it.

"We cannot allow ourselves to be trapped in here like animals!" Rodriguez shouted over the roar of the gunfire. "We must find out who is out there, and where they are." He arbitrarily selected two of his men. "You two, go out and locate them. Now!"

The two men threw open the front door but got no farther than a single step outside before being blown back through by the unseen enemy.

Suddenly, the sound of sirens could be heard above the clamor, and bright red-and-blue lights flashed through the windows. The gunfire from outside increased noticeably. The Jamaicans paid no attention to the people on the floor. They knew they were in trouble, and their chances of escape were dwindling fast. The group of black men was in a total state of uncontrolled panic, some jumping through windows, others lying low and looking for places to hide, still others taking random shots out into the darkness.

Lying close to the floor, Joe looked up to see if he could spot Rodriguez. Rodriguez was there, in the back of the ballroom, looking like a frightened little boy. The confusion and indecision in his mind was shown clearly on his face. Finally, showing his true colors as the coward he was, he deserted his men and bolted down the hallway in the direction of the study.

He must be planning on slipping out the back window, Joe thought. If Rodriguez made it to the river, he could possibly escape by boat. Joe could not let that happen. He was the one responsible for most of this. He must be stopped. He must be made to pay.

"Ryan," Joe said. "Rodriguez ran out back. I'm going after him."

"I'm with you, big brother," Ryan replied, and the two of them ran through the ballroom and down the hall, unchallenged by the panic-stricken Jamaicans. When they reached the study, the room was empty, except for the corpse of Sherman Salinger.

"Maybe he went upstairs," Ryan suggested.

"I don't think so," Joe said. He rushed to the window and looked out into the backyard. He was just able to catch a glimpse of a dark figure entering the woods.

"He's going for the river," Joe said. "He probably has a boat down there. If he gets to it, we may not be able to catch him."

"He's got a pretty big head start," Ryan said. "And he knows the woods better than we do. I don't think we will be able to catch him."

"Maybe not," Joe acknowledged. He stood gazing out the window, deep in thought. If Rodriguez had a boat, where would he keep it? Almost certainly it would be in the boathouse at the base of the long stairway. But Rodriguez went into the woods. Joe remembered the fork in the path about halfway down. It must also go to the boathouse, Joe concluded. Rodriguez could not go around the front of the mansion to the stairs, and he probably did not want to try and reach them from the back, so Joe surmised he was going the longer way through the woods, where he could keep under cover. If Joe's logic was correct, they would have time to head him off if they could manage to get to the stairs from the back of the mansion.

"It's just a guess, but I think we may have a chance," Joe muttered, more to himself than to Ryan. He leaped through the window and headed left toward the far side of the mansion. Ryan had no idea what Joe was thinking, but he trusted that he knew what he was doing and followed him through the window. When they reached the point where the woods and the bluff met up with the side of the house, Joe stepped around the corner without a moment's hesitation, clinging to branches and clumps of bushes to keep from toppling over the edge.

"What are you doing?" Ryan yelled. "Do you want to get killed?"

"Rodriguez is heading for the boathouse, I'm sure of it. Our only chance is to beat him there, and our only chance for that is to go down the stairs."

Ryan shook his head and sighed but then followed Joe along the edge of the bluff. Traversing was difficult, but the dense trees and brush provided adequate handholds, and their trek was complete in only a few minutes. When they reached the far side, they could see the commotion in the front of the mansion. Several Paradise police cars were parked in the long horseshoe drive, and men were being led out of the mansion in handcuffs. No gunshots could be heard. Apparently, the short battle was over, and the police had won.

"Maybe we should get help," Ryan suggested.

"No time," Joe countered, and he began flying down the stairs as fast as he could manage in the dark. About halfway down, he could hear a motor trying to turn over.

"He's on the boat!" Joe yelled over his shoulder. "We have to get to him."

Come on, move, Joe said to himself, talking to his legs as if they could understand. *Come on, faster.*

When he was two flights from the bottom, he heard the engine roar into life, and he spotted a large two-level boat at the end of the dock alongside the boathouse. *No*, he thought. *I'm so close.* He jumped over the entire bottom flight of steps and raced out onto the dock. Rodriguez pushed the throttle forward, and the boat began pulling away. Reaching the end of the dock at a full sprint, Joe hurled his body through the air in a desperate attempt to reach the departing craft. He landed hard on the fantail, nearly having the wind knocked completely out of him.

Rodriguez turned from his position at the helm to see what caused the crashing sound behind him. Believing he had made a clean getaway, he was startled to see Joe climbing to his feet.

"I am getting tired of you, man," Rodriguez snarled. He pulled a long, ominous-looking blade from his belt. "You will not trouble me again."

Joe felt all the horror and anger that had been building over the past few weeks swell within him at the sight of this man he hated. This was it. The final battle had begun. He sprang forward with surprising quickness, catching Rodriguez firmly in the midriff with his shoulder. The two of them crashed to the deck, each knowing they were now in a fight to the death. The bigger, stronger Rodriguez was able to break free of Joe's grasp and regained his feet. Joe rolled to the side of the boat, searching for anything he could use as a weapon. Rodriguez raised his huge knife and, with his brilliant, sinister smile, slowly approached Joe for the kill. Finally, Joe's hand touched an object he could use to defend himself. With Rodriguez only inches away, Joe pulled the fire extinguisher from the bulkhead and fired it directly into Rodriguez's face.

Rodriguez shrieked like a terrified baby, covering his face with his hands and dropping the knife to the deck. Joe leaped to his feet and thrust his foot into Rodriguez's groin. The big man shrieked again, but he did not go down. Eyes watering, he lunged at Joe, smashing him into the bulkhead.

"I will enjoy killing you," Rodriguez taunted, his powerful hands reaching for Joe's throat.

Suddenly, as if queued by some sixth sense, both men became aware that they were heading at top speed directly into a boathouse on the other side of the river. Each man's eyes reflected their thoughts; Rodriguez's widened in horror while Joe's took on a sudden glow of peace.

Back on the dock, Ryan stood breathless, unable to observe the details of the struggle in the darkness. He knew there was trouble when he saw the boat heading toward the far shore. Helplessly he watched as the boat with the two men aboard crashed headlong into the boathouse, exploding into a giant sickening ball of flame.

Chapter 35

"Joe, Joe."

He was aware only of the intense pain in his head. He had no idea where he was, or even if he was. Was he dead? His head throbbed in excruciating pain.

"Joe, Joe honey."

Voices, images. Boats, fire. Noise. The terribly loud explosion in his ears. More voices.

"Joe darling, are you okay?"

Voices. Wonderful voices. Angels' voices. Maybe he was dead. Maybe this was heaven. But in heaven, would there be the pain?

"Joe, can you hear me? It's me, Sheri."

Sheri! Sheri's voice! Could it be? Where was she? More images, clearer now. The boat, the madman Rodriguez, the crash. He had survived. Somehow he had survived. And somewhere he heard the wonderful, lovely voice of Sheri.

Joe McGowen was slowly regaining consciousness. He blinked his eyes once then a few times more. Finally, his eyes were opened. It was not a dream. It was Sheri, beautiful Sheri, leaning over him with her wonderful, soothing smile.

"Sh-Sh-Sheri," he managed to murmur.

"Oh, Joe, Joe honey," Sheri exclaimed. Tears filled her eyes as she reached out and gently touched Joe's face. The pain in his head seemed to drift away.

"Joe, look who's here with me," Sheri said softly.

Maureen and Brandon squeezed in next to her.

"Hi, Daddy," Maureen said quietly. "We missed you."

"Hey, Dad," Brandon said. "How are you feeling?"

Katelin suddenly appeared above them, held firmly in Sheri's outstretched arms so Joe could see her. Katelin, dear sweet little Katelin. She smiled and giggled and buried her face in her hands.

Joe did not have all the pieces of the puzzle yet, but hows, whys, and whats were not important to him just now. Relief flowed through him like a rushing river. Just as with Sheri, tears began to swell within his eyes. He wanted to reach out and grab them, his wonderful wife and children, and pull them close to him. But he was weak, he was tired. He just looked at them and let the tears fall.

"Get some rest, Joe," Sheri said. "We'll be here when you wake up. We're not going anywhere ever again."

"I love you, Sheri," Joe forced out. "I love you all. Is everything okay?"

"Everything is great, Joe. Everything is truly wonderful. Get some rest. We'll be here for you."

Joe closed his eyes. He could rest now. He knew it was true. He knew now, finally, everything truly was wonderful.

Chapter 36

"I'm glad you could make it," Sharon Carlson said, welcoming Joe and Sheri into her home.

"We wouldn't dream of missing this." Joe smiled. "I've got a million questions, as I'm sure everyone does."

Two weeks had passed since Joe first awoke and found himself in Mercy Hospital, recovering from a concussion and some minor burns from the boat crash, as well as having the knife wound in his arm properly stitched. He had no recollection of what had happened except for seeing the boathouse directly ahead of them and knowing they were sure to collide, then seeing the fear in Rodriguez's eyes and feeling a strange sort of comfort in realizing Rodriguez would be killed. Then all was blank until he heard Sheri's voice in the hospital. Apparently, the explosion blew him away from the fire. Unfortunately, it did the same to Rodriguez, who survived in even better shape than did Joe.

The Jamaican gang had been rounded up the night of the fateful party at the mansion. The trouble was over now. Paradise would attempt to get back to normal. But many questions were left unanswered, and the people of Paradise would not just let the matter end without understanding exactly what had taken place and why. Mayor Carlson had contacted Special Agent Thompson of the FBI, and the two of them agreed there should be an informal debriefing of the whole affair. Everyone was very anxious for the meeting, so it was planned for the day after Joe got out of the hospital at the mayor's house.

Joe and Sheri were the last to arrive. They entered the living room and acknowledged the welcome of those who were already present: Chief Winfield, Fran Rosten, Ryan McGowen, Beth Wence, special agents Mueller and Thompson, and, of course, the mayor herself.

"Well, there is much for us to discuss," the mayor began. "But I think we should begin with a little background. Special Agent Barbara Thompson is here from the FBI in Washington and has agreed to give us a detailed debriefing. A more general debrief will be provided for the entire town later, but we both felt it was important to have a detailed meeting with this group first. Go ahead, Barb, the floor is yours."

Joe looked at Thompson and could not help but chuckle to himself at the bandage on her nose. He had mentally prepared himself to be patient during the course of this meeting. It would be so easy to strike out at this Thompson woman, verbally if nothing else. He remembered his phone conversation with her and their encounter in the Washington bar. He was relieved this whole mess was now over, but he could not bring himself to be civil to people like Thompson. He came here prepared to be patient. After he heard her story, then he would make a judgment about Thompson and the rest of her FBI accomplices.

"You will all have to excuse the slight nasally sound of my voice," she began, "but I'm still recovering from a McGowen special." Everyone, including Joe, broke out into laughter. "Normally the FBI would not divulge the kind of information I will be giving you, but this town, and you people in particular, were so much a part of all this that I felt you had the right to know.

"I am sure you are all aware that there are a few drug cartels responsible for nearly all of the drug trafficking in the world. That's common information you could pick up from your local news. A man named Julio Salvo operates one of the largest, if

The Seduction of Paradise

not the largest cartel, in all of South America, which means in all of the world. We don't know exactly what his whole operation is worth, but it's estimated to be in the billions. He is an incredibly shrewd man, and even with all his success and power, he never gets sloppy or overconfident about his business. For all practical purposes, he is a recluse, but no one knows where he lives. He doesn't even meet personally with some of the highest-ranking members of his cartel. He firmly believes, and he's correct, that his lack of visibility is his ultimate protection. We believe he has an estate somewhere, most likely in Colombia, since that's where he does most of his business. We have very little information on it, but we know the staff that works at the estate is never allowed to leave, and almost no one is allowed to go there. There are only two situations in which he is vulnerable.

"First, even though he is paranoid about leaving his estate, he also believes his operations need to be run from the top with an iron fist. Therefore, if a new operation is being set up, and if it is a sizable project, he will always make one inspection of it himself before it opens for business. He will come unannounced, but he will certainly come.

"Secondly, there are, as best as we can tell, only two men he allows to visit his estate. They each represent the groups of people who do the vast majority of business with him. One of these is Antonio Rodriguez, the leader of an incredibly ruthless group of Jamaican gangs called posses. You may have heard about the posses. They're mainly located on the East Coast but recently have been expanding west. Out on the West Coast, other gangs have been in control, mainly the Crips and the Bloods. With the oncoming of crack, Salvo saw ways to double or even triple his profits, but he wanted to unite all the posses into a single organization and then expand his business into new areas."

"Excuse me, Barb," Chief Winfield cut in. "Most of us here have little knowledge about drug trafficking, or even what crack is exactly. Why has crack allowed Salvo's business to expand so much?"

"Good point, Chief. I'll explain it as best I can, but I'm not an expert myself. I'm sure you have all heard of freebasing. It's the method by which cocaine first became popular. Essentially, not to get too technical, this is a chemical process which 'frees' base cocaine from the cocaine hydrochloride powder. Crack is a form of freebase. In the early days, most freebase was made from a volatile chemical process involving ether and elaborate paraphernalia such as acetylene or butane torches. This process created cocaine more pure than crack, but it was dangerous. I think we have all heard of some celebrities being set on fire trying to freebase, and for every celebrity, there were countless unknown small-time drug users being seriously burned. Many potential users did not even know how to create freebase.

"You have to understand people like Salvo. The drug use out in the streets is not nearly as random or uncontrolled as it may appear. The big cartels operate like any other business: they are continually evaluating the market, seeing what will sell, and looking for ways to meet the needs of the users. It became apparent that cocaine had tremendous potential, but again, it was a slow and dangerous process to create it. A series of developments occurred, which you have probably heard of in bits and pieces, which helped the marketability of cocaine. 'Rock' cocaine was created and was used initially in the Caribbean, but it eventually found its way to LA. Rock is a form of crack, using a baking soda and rum recipe rather than ether. Crack was a further extension of this, only during the process, the 'paste' which is made is smeared instead of lumped together, so it dries to a powder rather than a little rocklike ball. It can be performed very quickly, very safely, and in very large quantities.

"What this really meant for the dealers was much more flexibility of their operation at a much lower risk. With the old method, users would go to a dealer's house, who would then cook up a batch of cocaine while the user waited. Aside from being slow and dangerous, it was very risky. It created a level of sustained exposure to outsiders that dealers loathed. Crack allowed dealers to create large batches of cocaine and package it so that it could be sold retail. Higher-level dealers could distribute their merchandise without interacting directly with the actual users. The existence of 'rock houses' or crack houses came into being, which were actually like small distribution centers."

"So you're saying that the wastewater treatment center was a crack house?" Mayor Carlson asked.

"Yes, only a very special kind. And that brings me to the details of this case. Salvo is a man with vision. He realized how well the crack house system was working, but there was still an element of risk. Plus, from a business standpoint, it meant there were more middlemen than was necessary. The pure cocaine would sometimes go through several hands before it ended up as crack for sale in some house. And the risk, even though reduced, was still too high for somebody as cautious as Salvo. His idea was to set up one major distribution center in an area rather than several small ones. Many times it just wasn't possible to do that, since it required several key elements."

"Such as?" Joe inquired.

"First, it required some kind of structure which could be used as a warehouse, large enough to store the merchandise as well as handle the processing. Secondly, it required easy access to lines of transportation. Thirdly, it had to be very secluded, where the work could be done relatively unnoticed. Now, when you think about these requirements, they seem to contradict each other. But there are places that satisfy all three, and Paradise happens to be one.

"No one would expect a major operation to open up in a town like this because it would not seem like the market would support it. Again, these are predominately business people we are dealing with. With the Jamaican posses trying to expand westward before the California gangs had the chance to spread eastward, the Twin

Cities became a natural target. With this kind of operation, this one center could service the entire Twin City area and all surrounding suburbs. It has two rivers and a main road passing right by it, and it's completely hidden from the public. It's perfect.

"Only one obstacle stood in their way: even though the treatment center was very well concealed, it still would not be possible to do the kinds of things they needed without somebody being aware of it. They needed support from someone in town, someone with authority. But being cautious and smart, Salvo wanted to keep as few people involved as possible. He sent people here to feel out various key residents of Paradise, predominantly the city council and the police force. They were very good at their jobs, being very subtle as to how they asked questions. Most of you here were contacted, but you probably don't even remember. It may have been a friendly stranger sitting by you at breakfast or someone you ran into at a ball game. Naturally they wouldn't come out and ask if you wanted to help sell drugs, but they asked subtle questions that would get at your sense of morals and ethics. Spencer Thurman and Sherman Salinger were identified as people they could use. We never determined how much they were offered, but it was enough to get them to side with Salvo and his people."

"They were seduced," Joe said quietly, almost to himself. He shook his head sadly, and without even looking up, he continued, "I can't believe someone from this town could be seduced into selling out everything for money."

"It happens everywhere, Mr. McGowen," Thompson responded. "Paradise is not unique in that regard.

"With the two residents in place, the operation was free to begin, but they had a tight schedule to meet since Salvo had promised deliveries to a number of potential clients in the area by September. Spencer's role became one of handling the more visible activity, mainly the actual construction and making sure the rest of the council did not grow suspicious. Salinger was more of an overall coordinator and the communication focal point with Rodriguez, who initially did not plan on spending much time here. Something about a large Jamaican walking around Paradise seemed just a bit too obvious. When Rodriguez finally decided he needed to move up here for a while, Salinger's house served as a perfect hideout. It was isolated and located on the river, so Rodriguez could get back and forth to the treatment center without ever going through town.

"Everything would have probably worked out, but Spencer could not find a way to get things done, and the project began to flounder. To his credit, Spencer may have been greedy, but he had no intention of having anyone in town get hurt. Salinger, on the other hand, fit right in with Rodriguez and his bloodthirsty gang."

"I can't believe it," Sheri said. "Even knowing what he did, I just can't believe it. I guess I never really knew him that well, but whoever would have expected he could do those terrible things?"

"I was fooled more than anyone," Beth Wence said, sitting on a couch close to Ryan. "But when you think back, no one really knew him that well. He was so quiet and polite we just assumed he was a decent person."

"Well, the fatal mistake was made when Spencer used a council envelope to disguise the details of the whole operation, then got it confused with an actual council package and sent it out. It could have gone to anyone, but it ended up at Harry Rosten's. Fran, I cannot stress to you enough what an incredibly courageous man he was."

"Thank you very much," Fran said quietly and bowed her head slightly, indicating she acknowledged the compliment but had nothing else to say.

"Harry immediately called us in. Up until that point, we knew this Western expansion activity was happening, but we were struggling to get any information at all. This information gave us the biggest break we ever had, for we not only knew what was going on ahead of time, but if we played our cards right, we could catch Rodriguez and Salvo on US soil and send them to jail forever. Opportunities like this almost never come along in our business.

"Unfortunately, when Rodriguez found out what had happened, he paid a visit to Paradise, and the terrible tragedy occurred to Harry, which is another testimony of his courage and commitment to this town. He hadn't told you, Fran, since he knew there could be trouble, and he did not want you to be in danger. He hid the package in the house, which Fran and the McGowens found by accident. When it was returned, Salvo was upset because an important document outlining the entire project was missing. There were several attempts at locating it, but no one could because we had it in Washington. We were planning on returning it before anyone became suspicious, but the Jamaicans reacted much faster than we anticipated.

"Our first step was to get one of our agents involved. There was an agent of the DEA who had dedicated the past ten years in an undercover role, trying to work his way into Salvo's organization. He had been very successful, and Salvo had taken him into his trust. His name was Roger Worthington, but you all knew him as Ronald Capsner."

"What?" Joe said. "Capsner worked for the DEA?"

"That's right. The FBI and the DEA frequently work cases together. Capsner, as I'll refer to him for your benefit, was in a very delicate position. First, he convinced Salvo that Paradise would be receptive to the restoration idea, which would allow him to be onsite and help get things moving. It also allowed construction work to go on at the treatment center completely unnoticed. It naturally did not sit well with Rodriguez, since he viewed this as his project. But Salvo is a smart man, and he knew the same methods which worked in places like Miami and New York would not necessarily work here. So Capsner was put in place, but even he was never allowed to go to the infamous Salvo estate. Our goal, therefore, was to make everything happen on schedule, and when Salvo came for his traditional inspection, we would have him. I apologize for not coordinating this with any of you, but we have found in the past that if too many people know something, leaks are inevitable. Plus, and I hope no one takes offense at this, it was important for everyone to act completely normal. Since none of you are professionals at this kind of thing, we weren't sure how you would react. On top of that, we did not know for a fact at that time who was working with Rodriguez. We just could not afford to show our hand to anyone. However, we knew you turned in the package, Mr. McGowen, and we knew you were asking a lot of questions. We assumed Rodriguez and his men knew that too. We almost pulled you and your family out at that time to protect you, but we thought that might look too suspicious."

"Even after I called you, you couldn't have told us?" Joe questioned. "After what happened on the beach to Spencer, couldn't you have told me something? Did you have to blow me off like you did?"

"First of all, when you called, I could not be sure who you were or what you knew," Thompson said. "You could have been one of Rodriguez's men trying to find out what I knew. Secondly, I'm not sure it would have been better for either of our concerns."

"All I know is I trusted the FBI to help, and they left me hanging out to dry," Joe said.

"Mr. McGowen—Joe, if I may—I regret all that has happened to you, I truly do. But you should know how much has been sacrificed on your behalf. Did you ever wonder how you got off that beach alive?"

"Of course," Joe replied. "I've thought about it a lot. I assumed a stray bullet struck the man who was about to shoot me, and I was able to get away."

Barb Thompson maintained a calm, professional appearance, but her eyes were alive with emotion. "For your information," she began, "you were saved by the FBI. Capsner coordinated with me to let me know exactly when Spencer was coming, so we had an agent in place. He was surprised to see you there, but he realized you were not part of Rodriguez's gang, so he kept an eye on you to see just what you were up to. When he realized you were about to be killed, he risked giving away his own cover to shoot the man who was about to shoot you. He ended up paying for it with his life. You see, while in pursuit of you, Rodriguez's men found our agent and killed him. In a way, he saved your life a second time. Since they had no idea there were two people watching them, they assumed he was the one they were after and gave up their chase when they caught our man, leaving you free to get away. Our agent was able to radio back before he was caught, so we knew some stranger had shown up, but until you called me, we did not have a clue as to who it was. The agent's name was John, by the way. John Alexander."

Joe was feeling embarrassed about his accusations. He suddenly realized the difficulty all players in the bizarre game were in. "Barb," he began.

"I'm not quite finished yet," she continued. "Let's not forget about Capsner, another federal agent who gave his life to save yours. And you should also know he did everything he could to keep that animal Rodriguez from hurting your friend Andy."

"All right!" Joe cut in. "If you're trying to make me feel like an ass, you've succeeded. I apologize for what I said. I guess after the past few weeks of believing the FBI was behind all this, I need some time to adjust. I'm sorry."

Special Agent Thompson realized Joe meant what he said, and she understood what he had gone through. The fire in her eyes softened considerably.

"You don't need to apologize, Joe. We certainly made our share of mistakes, and we're the ones who are supposed to know what we're doing. You saved a lot of people, and you succeeded in eluding a very serious effort by the FBI to find you. You truly are a remarkable man."

"I don't feel very remarkable," Joe responded, showing genuine humility.

"Truly remarkable people rarely do." Thompson smiled.

After a moment's pause, Thompson continued. "After your call, we again considered pulling you and your family out. By 'pulling out,' I mean take you someplace where you would be protected. In retrospect, that's what we should have done, but several things were bothering me. First, I still could not be sure you were on the up-and-up, or, in other words, that you weren't working for Salvo and Rodriguez. Secondly, we didn't know if you had contacted anyone else, such as a friend, or possibly the local authorities. We wanted to know who else knew what you knew. But mostly, we had our sights so focused on getting Salvo that we did not want to jeopardize our plan, and by having a whole family disappear right after the Thurman shooting, we thought Rodriguez would get suspicious. I guess it's my turn to apologize to you, Joe, and you too, Sheri, for not thinking more about your needs. However, we did realize that you could be in danger, so we decided to have someone follow you at all times. Gerald here was given the assignment." Thompson nodded in the direction of Special Agent Mueller. "He had help, of course, since he couldn't watch you twenty-four hours a day, but he was in charge of keeping tabs on you. Partly we wanted to know how you were handling what was happening and if you were communicating with anyone, but mainly, he was supposed to protect you and your family and let me know if you were in danger. If so, you were all to be taken out of Paradise immediately."

Joe smiled and squeezed Sheri's hand. "Imagine that," he said. "The evil man we feared was, in reality, our guardian angel."

Gerald Mueller spoke for the first time. "After the terrible tragedy of Andy Hoffman dying in your house, I knew we had to take action soon, but again, our timing was just a little off. When you eluded me on your way to the airport, I knew you had decided to take matters into your own hands, and that made you potentially dangerous both to our project and, more importantly, to yourself. We tried to locate you but finally had to admit you had beaten us. By the time I called Thompson to let her know I had lost you and we had given up the search, you were successfully eavesdropping on her conversation with Capsner."

"That would have been the golden opportunity for us to get together," Thompson said. "I guess everyone panicked a little during that encounter. Trying to calmly explain we were all on the same side seemed pointless. It seemed more reasonable to get you under control and then explain things in a civilized manner, but that idea backfired big time." With a wry smile, she reached up and rubbed her nose.

"I guess that's another apology I owe you," Joe said.

"Under the circumstances, you did a great job," Thompson replied.

"Why was it you met in a bar?" Joe asked. "Why not just stay in your office?"

"Not everyone in the FBI knows about every case," Thompson said. "With Capsner spending so much time undercover, he felt uncomfortable flashing his face around all the agents at headquarters. One never knows in this business when a cover will be needed, and he just did not want to be exposed."

"After the bar incident, I knew there would be trouble," Mueller continued, "so we decided to at least pull out your family, and Sheri here could help us locate you. Once she realized what was happening, she was very cooperative. Since we couldn't find you, Joe, and since Sheri was supposed to be going to California, we thought we should contact Ryan. By the time our men showed up at his door, he had left. Little did we know then he had driven by and saw our men at his door."

"If they would have been a few minutes later, they would have found me at home," Ryan chipped in. "But after the call from Joe, I wasn't about to trust a group of strangers at my door."

"So while I was in agony worrying about my family, they were being wined and dined in Washington," Joe said, in more of a statement than a question.

"I don't know if we were being wined and dined." Sheri laughed. "But we were treated very well."

"What I feel the worst about," Thompson went on, "is when that fool Freeman botched his attempt at contacting you at the roadside motel outside of Washington. He knew you were on the run, but I guess we were all still underestimating your abilities, Joe. We were even more alarmed when we read your fact sheets. We knew then you thought we were involved with Salvo. Believing we were the enemy made you very dangerous, but unfortunately, we were still unable to locate you."

"So then my little brother came looking for me," Joe said affectionately. "I can't tell you how much I appreciate that, Ryan."

"I didn't do anything you wouldn't have done, big brother," Ryan replied.

"That's when things started getting out of control," Thompson said, continuing with her story. "We were so close to the end of the project we did not want to abandon it, but things were starting to crumble on several fronts. First, enough was happening in Paradise so that many people were becoming suspicious, although most were willing to dismiss the events as more or less a string of bad luck. If Salvo knew how bad off things were, I'm sure he would have pulled the plug, but Capsner succeeded in keeping him pacified. Rodriguez was growing very impatient with this new, more moderate way of dealing with people, so he tended not to report as much of the details to Salvo and tried to be more aggressive without Salvo's knowledge. About that time, Beth invited Ryan and Salinger over to her house. Salinger told Rodriguez, and he decided to take matters into his own hands and planned the attack on your house, Beth."

"We were all very fortunate," Mueller cut in, picking up the story. "I had been following Ryan ever since he showed up at Joe's house. I did not want to take the chance of spooking him like we did Joe, plus I wanted to see if he might lead me to Joe. I followed Ryan to Beth's house that night, and since I was aware Salinger had also been invited, I knew there could be trouble. One of our agents, Gibbons, followed Salinger, but he never went to Beth's house, and unfortunately, we didn't have his phone bugged to eavesdrop on his call to Rodriguez. I thought I was prepared, but I had no idea anything would happen on the magnitude of what occurred. I sensed something was brewing when I saw two vans of men go by and park a couple of blocks down the street. I did not have time to call in support from other agents, so I quickly contacted Chief Winfield, who had been standing by with some of his men in case of an emergency. We did not want to tip off the Jamaicans that the authorities were on to them, so the men were not in uniform. Unfortunately, the attack started before the police arrived, so they were able to do a fair amount of damage. I'm really sorry about that, but we just were not prepared for such a blatant act.

"The fact that the police were not in uniform presented a problem: Ryan and Beth wouldn't know who was on their side, or for that matter, they wouldn't know there even was anybody on their side. If they saw us, they would have probably blown us away. We felt it would be best to first get you under control then we would explain what was happening. Therefore, even after the Jamaicans were chased off, we still burst into the house to stop you before you had time to react. It was the same philosophy Barb used with Joe in the Washington bar, but this time, it worked."

"I remember how terrified I was when you guys broke in," Beth said. "And how disappointing it was when I thought you, Chief, were behind it all."

"It just seemed like the best way to handle it," said the chief. "It was very fortunate no one got hurt."

"You really showed me something that night," Ryan said to Beth. "You really came through for us." Beth smiled and laid her head on Ryan's shoulder.

"After the failed attack," Joe spoke up, "why didn't Salvo get out then? He must have known somebody was onto him."

"The attack wasn't sanctioned by Salvo," Thompson answered. "Since it failed so miserably, Rodriguez never told him. Salvo never even knew about it."

"What about you, Chief?" Fran inquired. "Didn't you find it odd when Gerald called you about an attack in town?"

"I had already been involved with Gerald for a while," Chief Winfield replied. "I was becoming concerned about many of the same things you and Joe were. I figured it had to be related in some way with Capsner. I was developing a plan for how to confront him when Sharon said she wanted to meet with me. After a brief discussion with her, we realized we both felt the same way. We decided the best way to confront Capsner was to just go up and tell him our concern. We did, and he opened up to us totally. Once he realized we were suspicious, he knew keeping us in the dark would only make matters worse. By confiding in us, he not only avoided potential trouble, he gained two valuable allies. In fact, we began working with Gerald to try and keep things low-key until the project was over so we could get Salvo out here, but we had to promise we would keep what we knew secret. Sometimes it was difficult, like when you came to see me, Beth. I wanted so badly to be up front with you, but I had sworn not to divulge anything without talking to Gerald or Capsner first."

"Oh my." Sharon Carlson sighed. "I remember that first meeting we had, Byron. I knew something was not right, but I was like everyone else: I just didn't know who to trust. I finally decided I had to a least try and talk to you, but when the night of the meeting arrived, I became terrified. I can't believe I was actually preparing for the possibility of having to hurt you."

"We were all feeling very desperate," the chief said. "I'm just glad it all worked out."

"I think everyone knows the rest," Thompson said. "Ryan insisted on helping Gerald with his surveillance of the mansion the night of the party, never realizing what was in store. Rodriguez was cocky enough to believe he was secure, and rather than have his men guarding the grounds as usual, he had most of them hiding upstairs in the mansion. That proved to be a very costly mistake for him. Joe showed up, and through the events that occurred, a terrible tragedy was avoided. Rodriguez's gang was rounded up, and now they're all behind bars."

"How did the police arrive so quickly?" Joe asked. "One minute it looked like we were goners, then suddenly, there were cops everywhere."

"Gibbons and I held them off for a few minutes by ourselves," Mueller answered. "I think we confused them when we took out the man trying to sabotage the wiring. But the real thanks goes to your police chief."

"No more than to anyone else," Winfield said. "We were all a little suspicious of the party, even though we did not anticipate anything as tragic as what occurred. I had a group of officers on standby, the same group who fended off the attack on Beth's house. After Mueller's warning call, I immediately rushed to the study, but before I went in, I decided I had better not wait to get help, so I stopped and called my men. It was lucky I did, since I never got another chance."

"You should all be extremely proud of what you did," Thompson commended. "You are an extraordinary group of people."

"I still cannot believe how this could have happened," Fran said. "The part of Paradise I have always loved the most was the people. But now this town will be tarnished forever by this… this…this seduction. I don't know if I can stay here."

"Fran, I had been feeling the same way," Joe said with a cool sense of understanding in his voice. "I was even feeling it in a larger scale. I thought the FBI was crooked, that the whole government was corrupt, just like some of the stories that have been written. I remember when I was in Washington I felt disgusted each time I looked at a monument. But this experience has shown us that, in general, people are good. Sheri and I are like you. We love Paradise mainly for its people. What happened here did nothing to tarnish that. In fact, it reinforced it. Sure, there were two bad apples, but look at how everyone else banded together to fight for the town, and for each other. I don't know if anyone can ever be sure how sincere people are until they are truly tested. Well, Paradise was tested in a very big way, and look at the sacrifices people made to answer the call. Now, we no longer have to *think* people are special here, we *know* they are, because we have passed the test."

"You know, you're right, Joe," Fran replied, a sense of peace returning to her face. "We did pass the test, didn't we?"

"You sure as hell did," Thompson said. "And now it's all over."

"No, it will never be over," Sharon Carlson said quietly. "We responded to the call, and passed with flying colors, and I'm proud of all of us for that. But some very good people have been left behind, so this will never be truly over."

Joe thought of his neighbor Harry Rosten and the conversations they used to have in their backyards. He thought of Andy, good old Andy, and the lunches they would never again share. They did answer the call, but a dreadful price had been paid. Sharon was right: it would never be truly over. But at least they had won, the evil men were gone, and the people of the town could all be very proud. But were the evil men really gone?

"What about Salvo and Rodriguez?" Joe asked. "Such great sacrifices have been made, but the goal was to catch Salvo and put him out of business. I can't bear the thought that he will go completely free."

"Don't concern yourself with either of them," Mueller said.

"Wait a minute," Fran said, the feisty part of her personality surfacing. "I think we should know what will happen to them. Are they going to be punished or not?"

"Well, of course we have Rodriguez in custody," Mueller explained. "But we're really not at liberty to discuss either of their circumstances. Let me just assure you of one thing: as far as Salvo and Rodriguez are concerned, justice will be done."

"That doesn't sound too satisfying," Joe said. "But I guess we'll just have to trust that you're telling the truth."

"Believe me," Mueller said, "justice will be done."

"If there is nothing else, Gerald and I need to get to the airport," Thompson said. "There are a few important issues we need to wrap up."

No one had any further questions, so the group broke up, and everyone said their good-byes. As people began milling about, Joe pulled special agents Thompson and Mueller aside.

"I just want to say once more how sorry I am about my earlier comments, and how much I appreciate what you have done for me, my family, and this whole town," Joe said.

"It's our job," Thompson replied. "This is what we do. You are the one to be commended. Many people would have turned their back on this situation, but you got involved and tried to do something about it. As I said before, you're a very remarkable man, Mr. McGowen."

"I'll second that," Mueller said. "You can work with us anytime."

"I certainly appreciate the offer," Joe responded, "but I think I'll take a pass."

They all laughed and shook hands, then the FBI agents departed.

Later that afternoon, Joe and Sheri were in their front yard, playing kickball with their three children. Fran sat on the front step, watching the family of which she now felt very much a part. It was a cool October afternoon with just a slight, almost unnoticeable breeze.

"It's Uncle Ryan," Brandon called out as a car pulled into the driveway.

Ryan and Beth Wence stepped out and greeted the family.

"Do you mind some company?" Ryan asked. "We didn't want to sit inside on such a gorgeous day."

"Are you kidding? We were hoping you would come by," Sheri responded. "We really haven't had a good opportunity to talk much. When are you going back to California, anyway?"

Ryan looked slightly embarrassed, then finally responded, "Actually, I don't teach in California anymore."

"What?" Joe, Sheri, and Fran exclaimed in unison.

Ryan put his arm around Beth and held her close. "I guess I've decided to come back here and look for a job," he said. "Beth thinks there is a good chance I could get a coaching job that just opened up in this district. I decided to give it a try. I've been in California long enough."

Joe studied Ryan's face for a moment and understood Ryan's main reason for wanting to come home. He went up and clasped the shoulders of Ryan and Beth. "It's great to have both of you back," he said.

"What do we do now?" Fran asked. "It's such a beautiful day."

And a beautiful day it was. Down the street, the remaining leaves painted the trees in reds and yellows and oranges. The sky was a brilliant blue, and the air had just a bit of a crispy nip. For the first time in a good long while, they had time to appreciate the beauty around them.

"Let's all go for a walk," Joe suggested. "Let's go for a walk through our town. This is truly the greatest town anyone could hope to call home. After all, this is Paradise."

Epilogue

The helicopter stopped and began to hover over the clearing in the jungle below. The two men in the back stared at one another, the white man having a look of disgust, the black man one of smug arrogance.

"This is it!" the pilot cried to the two men. "Are you ready?"

Gerald Mueller turned to Rodriguez. "Do you think you can handle this?"

"Hey, man, I can handle anything. Let's do it and get out of here. I have business to attend to."

"Just remember," Mueller cautioned, "you only go free if you are successful. If not, this will be the last sunny day you'll ever see. Do you remember all the instructions?"

"Of course, man. Let's do it. I'm getting impatient."

"Fine, but remember the thumbs-up or thumbs-down signal when you return."

"Let's do it, man."

Mueller turned to the pilot and nodded, and the chopper slowly touched down in the clearing. Rodriguez jumped out and got into the empty car along the dirt road. He started the engine and began winding his way up the long, narrow road toward the spectacular estate at the top of the cliff. When the car was a little more than a speck in the distance, it arrived at the gate and was allowed to pass through.

"Well, my friend Antonio." Julio Salvo smiled as he stood near the edge of the veranda overhanging the cliff dropping down to the white sand beach. "I am anxious to hear how you managed to escape. I am also anxious to hear your explanation for the Paradise fiasco." His voice sounded both friendly and threatening at the same time. He turned his back on Rodriguez and looked out over the ocean. "I believe I have given you my lecture about storms, have I not, Antonio?"

"Mr. Salvo," Rodriguez began, "I do not give a damn about your storms any longer."

Salvo wheeled in anger, only to be taken aback by the sight of Rodriguez aiming a .357 Magnum directly at his chest.

"So, from this I can assume you did not escape, and that you have made some kind of deal with the American authorities. Am I correct, Antonio?"

"You have always been a very smart man, Mr. Salvo."

"Of all my associates, you are the one whom I never would have expected this," Salvo said. "You have always been like a son to me."

"Mr. Salvo, you have taught me a great deal. One thing I have learned is that no one could ever be like a son to you—not even your real son, if you had one."

"I have given you so much, Antonio. Do you really believe you can betray me?"

"Do you not remember the lesson you taught me, right here on this very spot. Everyone has a price. You said that sooner or later, if the price was high enough, everyone would sell out their own mother. I learned that from you, Mr. Salvo. And this time, the price is my freedom."

Salvo again turned his back to Rodriguez then suddenly wheeled around, pulling a small pistol from his white coat. But Rodriguez was much too quick for him, firing three rounds directly into Salvo's chest. Salvo's body lifted off the floor and tumbled over the edge of the veranda, falling the several hundred feet to the beach below.

Rodriguez followed Mueller's instructions exactly. He immediately dropped the pistol to the floor and moved quickly through the glass doors into the large estate. Walk briskly, Mueller had said, but do not run.

Guards who had heard the shots came running down the hall. "I heard shots from the veranda!" Rodriguez barked out. "Quickly, go check before the intruder can escape."

The guards were all familiar with Rodriguez and had no reason to suspect him. They dashed out to the veranda, leaving Rodriguez to escape out the front door to his parked car. He tried to maintain a calm appearance as he approached the gate, but he began to panic when he saw the guard answer the telephone. Suddenly, the guard's face took on the look of alarm as he stared at Rodriguez. He dropped the phone and reached for his holstered pistol. Rodriguez floored the gas pedal, sending up a huge cloud of dust from his tires and snapping the barrier arm as the car shot forward. Once through the gate and into his descent down the narrow, winding road, he relaxed and let out a loud arrogant laugh. He knew there was no way he could be stopped now.

Gerald Mueller saw the tiny speck of a car burst through the gate. Moments later, several cars filed out of the gate in pursuit of Rodriguez.

"Get it going," Mueller ordered the pilot. The engine kicked in, and the huge rotor began its slow acceleration as the chopper came to life. After a few moments, the pilot lifted the aircraft about ten feet into the air and stopped, hovering in place.

Two minutes later, Rodriguez's car broke into the clearing and skidded to a stop. He jumped out from behind the wheel and sprinted to the waiting chopper.

He didn't give the sign, Mueller thought. "Is it done!" he screamed over the throbbing roar of the rotor.

Rodriguez could not hear Mueller but attempted to shout something back to him. Mueller held up his thumb, more or less asking Rodriguez if his mission was successful. Rodriguez remembered the signal and frantically gave the thumbs-up with both hands. Mueller turned and nodded to the pilot, and immediately, the chopper lifted away and headed out over the ocean.

"Noooo!" Rodriguez screamed again and again. "You lying bastard. Come back for me. Please, come back!"

Mueller heard none of Rodriguez's words, but Mueller could easily imagine what Rodriguez was saying as Rodriguez jumped and waved his fists at the departing helicopter. He watched as the parade of cars poured into the clearing, and the men inside emptied out to face the screaming Jamaican.

Mueller was much too far away to hear the gunshots, but from the many small puffs of smoke, he knew there had to be several. The body of Antonio Rodriguez twitched and flipped then came to rest in the brush, never to move again.

Mueller sat back in his seat, reflecting on what he had just witnessed. In a clean courtroom in a civil country like the United States, where people wore suits and right and wrong was judged by a formal and fair set of rules, this incident would be considered criminal, barbaric, and immoral. In a civil world, justice was based on agreed-upon laws interpreted by trained judges.

But men like Salvo and Rodriguez had their own laws and played by a uniquely different set of rules. The civil systems were not always capable of handling people like that, people who could thumb their noses at the laws and the rules and hide out in their own private area of the world, being free to continue harming societies and destroying people. Sometimes it was necessary to move the game to their world, to play by their rules. Not to get around justice, not to avoid it, but to enforce justice in the only way people like that were accustomed.

As Mueller watched the sparkling water pass by below him, there was absolutely no doubt in his mind that justice had truly been done.